The image was very crudely drawn, like all the *Topoi*'s illustrations. The central focus was a tree, one side of which was in full leaf, the other blasted and dead. A skeleton sat on a heap of gold beneath the dead branches, playing with a handful of gemstones. The commentary was no more than usually terse: "Great knowledge may lead to folly, and great wealth to Death. Only by moderation is the goal achieved."

Silence murmured the cantrip that put her into the learning trance. The multiple meanings of the images exploded into her consciousness like fireworks. Patiently, she disciplined herself to exclude everything but the specific pilot's knowledge, and slowly the sense of the road came clear. *Recusante*'s course lay along the narrow path, then "up" the trunk of the tree and out through the leaves of the living left-hand branch.

Sighing, she let herself slip from trance and glanced quickly at the control boards. The musonar still showed no sign of pursuit.

MELISSA SCOTT

SILENCE IN SOLITUDE

BAEN BOOKS

SILENCE IN SOLITUDE

Copyright © 1986 by Melissa Scott

A Baen Books Original

Baen Publishing Enterprises
260 Fifth Avenue
New York, N.Y. 10001

First printing, November 1986

ISBN: 0-671-65699-7

Cover art by Neal McPheeters

Printed in the United States of America

Distributed by
SIMON & SCHUSTER
TRADE PUBLISHING GROUP
1230 Avenue of the Americas
New York, N.Y. 10020

CHAPTER 1

The apprentices' hall was dank, and smelled faintly of the cheap incense used in the workrooms on the floor above. Silence Leigh sighed, rubbing her cold fingers together in a futile attempt to warm them, then held her hands just under the tube of fixed fire that lighted her section of the table. That was a little better, but she knew from experience that the warmth would vanish as soon as she took her hands away from the lamp.

In the six months she had been on Solitudo Hermae, she had grown to hate the damp chill of the apprentices' hall. The partitions to either side, which hid her work from the other apprentices who shared the long table, gave privacy but did nothing to cut the cold drafts.

She sighed again, and let her hands fall back to the photoflashed text that lay open before her. Unfortunately, there was no avoiding the daily study sessions in the hall: half the texts she and the other apprentices had to work from were restricted—literally chained to the edge of each apprentice's section of the communal table.

There were three more books besides the open *Theater of Meditation* in her cubicle, their silvery chains glittering in the light from the fixed-fire lamp. Idly, she ran her fingers along the chain running from the *Theater of Meditation* to the massive staple embedded in the table top. She could feel the lingering resonances of the power the magi had used to forge the special metal and, after six months' intensive study, could begin to guess at the processes involved in the forging. She gave the chain a gentle tug, wondering just what it would take to break the bonds between chain, staple, and table. Then she smiled, slowly. That was a most improper thought for a magus's apprentice—they were supposed to wait until their masters deemed them ready for new knowledge, not to seek such knowledge on their own. But then, she was hardly a proper apprentice.

Her smile faded. Less than a year ago, she had been a starship pilot and nothing more. The position had been hard for a woman to win, but steering her grandfather's trading ship *Black Dolphin* from world to world had been all she had ever wanted in life.

But then her grandfather had died, and she had been plunged into an increasingly complicated and dangerous series of adventures. First, her uncle, who was her legal guardian unless she married, had cheated her out of her rightful inheritance, the *Black Dolphin*. Then he had tried to trap her into working for him in his search for the lost, semi-legendary home of mankind, Earth. She had escaped that by taking the first job that was offered—piloting for Denis Balthasar aboard the half-and-half *Sun-Treader*—and had bought her legal freedom from her uncle by joining Balthasar and his engineer, Julian Chase Mago, in a three-way marriage of convenience.

She smiled again, a little wistfully this time. They were good men, both of them, and she did not regret her choice, but the marriage had thrown her straight into even more trouble. Denis Balthasar was a courier for the pirate combine Wrath-of-God, and Wrath-of-God had been engaged in its final battle with the Asterion

Hegemony. The captains of Wrath-of-God had mustered every ship in their fleet, from the warships down to couriers like *Sun-Treader*, for a raid on the frozen world of Arganthonios—and had been ambushed and defeated. *Sun-Treader*'s crew were among the lucky ones, Silence knew: the Hegemon's navy was desperately short of men to crew its ships, and had bound some of the surviving pirates to its service. She, Balthasar, and Chase Mago had been so bound—the geas had nearly killed Balthasar—and assigned to crew a mailship carrying a special passenger to the siege of Castax.

It was then, Silence decided, that things had really begun to change. She had taken the first steps during the nightmare passage between Arganthonios and the navy depot on Sapriportus, discovering a power within that allowed her to resist the geas. But it was aboard the mailship that she had first seen how to use that strength. She had broken her own geas, then freed the others, but their escape had been blocked by their passenger, the magus Isambard. And that, Silence thought, was the real beginning. If we thought we had troubles before. . . .

That was not entirely fair, and she knew it, but there was enough truth to it. Balthasar said as much at every opportunity. The mailship had carried no weapons that would be effective against a magus. In desperation, Silence had offered a bargain. She owned an ancient starbook that gave the road to lost Earth. She would take the magus to Earth and share the fabulous secrets they were sure to find there, if he in turn would protect them from the Hegemon's people. No magus could have resisted that offer.

They had made the attempt, but the Earth road was blocked by Rose Worlder siege engines, and the badly damaged mailship had barely limped into the nearest port, on Mersaa Maia. There, with the Rose Worlder authorities looking for any excuse to arrest and imprison them all, Isambard had calmly informed the three that, contrary to all the known rules of the magi's art, Silence was herself potentially a magus, and offered to train her—if she would keep her part of the bargain and help Isambard reach Earth. She had agreed, and in a final, delightful act of revenge had stolen back the *Black Dolphin*, which had also come to Mersaa Maia in search of the Earth road.

That had been six months ago, and now, sitting shivering in the apprentices' hall on the magi's world Solitudo Hermae, it was hard to believe it had all happened. Silence shook her head slowly, not seeing the book that lay open before her. Isambard had had a hard time convincing the magi who oversaw the school that she, a woman, had the potential to become a magus, but once they had agreed to accept her as an apprentice, she had been completely absorbed into the system. Over the past months she had immersed herself in the Trivium— the Three Arts of symbology, perception, and manipulation that were the basis of a magus's knowledge. Soon she would master them, she hoped, and be able to proceed to the Quadrivium; but in the meantime there was work to be done.

She looked again at the book in front of her, forcing herself to pay attention to the elaborately symbolic drawing. It was very like the illustrations in her starbooks, and she felt a sudden surge of loneliness. Piloting she knew, had already mastered completely, not like the Trivium. But more than that, to be a pilot again meant to be in space with her husbands. At the moment, she envied them bitterly: they had already been off-world half a dozen times, first to see *Black Dolphin* refitted, and then to see if Balthasar could reestablish contact with whatever was left of Wrath-of-God. They were off-world again now, and Silence found herself torn between envious resentment and the desire for their return.

She shook herself hard and pulled the book closer to

her, trying to concentrate on the image. A woman in antique half-armor stood silhouetted against a sky that was half stormy and half clear. She held a spade in her right hand; her left rested on the ring of a huge anchor. Silence stared at it for a long moment, trying to deduce the special meaning behind the image, then sighed and reached for the hieroglyphica chained to the table in front of her. The main image, the standing, armored woman, was a common topos for metaphysical strength. The anchor, according to the hieroglyphica's table, could be anything from hope to the submaterial universe, depending on the surrounding images. She made a face: the magi's symbols were so much less precise than the pilots' voidmarks. But before she could find the final component of the drawing, something touched her foot.

She started, and in the same moment a familiar voice whispered, "Silence."

The pilot leaned back in her chair until she could see around the partitions, and glanced casually to her left. The apprentice sitting there, a thin, sharp-faced blond, gave her an urchin's grin.

"What is it, Kaare?" Silence glanced over her shoulder for the spidery homunculus that monitored the hall to keep the apprentices at work. It was nowhere in sight, and the pilot breathed a sigh of relief.

"You wanted me to keep a lookout for a ship coming in—*Recusante*?" the other apprentice whispered back. "Well, Master Fynn sent me to the port today, and I got a look at the board. *Recusante*'s due in tonight."

"Thanks," Silence said, and turned away, fighting down her sudden excitement. *Black Dolphin*, renamed *Recusante* now after her refit, was back at last. She would have to tell Isambard, as soon as the study session was over. But Isambard had forbidden her to visit the port, and she wanted very much to meet her husbands there.

She took a deep breath, forcing herself to think calmly.

Isambard's reasons for keeping her away from the port
were good ones: both the Hegemon and the Rose
Worlders were still looking for a woman pilot who had
escaped under mysterious and inexplicable circumstances.
If *Recusante* were compromised by being connected
with a woman pilot, there would have to be yet another
expensive change of name and markings before they
could make the attempt to reach Earth. Even Isambard
did not have unlimited resources; a second refit might
well be beyond his means. But . . . Silence glanced
down at herself and smiled slowly. She was wearing an
apprentice's smock and trousers—boy's clothes—as she
had been since beginning her studies on Solitudo
Hermae, and her hair was cut as short as any boy's. If
she could borrow something less conspicuous than the
apprentice's glossy white smock, she could probably
pass as a dock worker. And that, she thought triumphantly, would remove Isambard's only good reason for
keeping me away from the port.

She turned her attention back to the *Theater of Med-
i-tation*, but it was impossible to concentrate on the
elaborate drawings. Finally, she abandoned the struggle and leaned her chin on her folded hands, counting
the minutes until the study session ended. When the
three-toned chime finally sounded, she closed her book
and rose without haste, timing her steps so that she
reached the door at the same time as Kaare.

"I need your help, Kaare," she said, without preamble.

"Again?" the blond grumbled, but let himself be
drawn aside into the shadow of the refectory.

"I just want to borrow some clothes," Silence said,
running an assessing eye over the other apprentice's
body. Kaare was about her height, or maybe a little
taller; his clothes should fit, and loosely enough to
disguise her figure. "A shirt and a long coat—anything
that isn't apprentice's stuff. Will you lend them to me?"

Kaare hesitated a moment, then grinned. "You're
going in to the port, aren't you?"

Silence nodded.

"All right," Kaare said. "I've got some things that ought to fit you. I'll bring them to your room after dinner, all right?"

"That's fine," Silence said, then wished she had insisted on his bringing them immediately. Kaare was not known for his punctuality, and the longer she waited, the more likely it was that Isambard would guess her plans and prevent her.

But for once, Kaare kept his promise. He arrived almost as the clock chimed the end of the dinner hour, a bundle of clothing tucked under one arm. He opened it to reveal several shirts and a shapeless vest wrapped in a crumpled, knee-length coat, then politely turned his back. Silence hastily selected the largest of the shirts and pulled it on, then the vest. She shrugged herself into the heavy coat, and turned to face the narrow mirror.

The reflection that confronted her was not her own. Silence drew a slow, soundless breath, and lifted one hand to tug at the loose neck of the shirt. The image copied the movement. It was she, then, this lanky, black-haired youth, and Silence smiled with growing satisfaction. The reflection smiled back at her, and Silence shook her head to see even that familiar expression transformed. Experimentally, she set her feet well apart and jammed her hands into the pockets of the still unfamiliar trousers, scowling at the mirror. It was a half-trained dock worker that scowled back at her, her moderate height turned to half-grown awkwardness, her body's curves hidden beneath the layers of loose clothing.

From behind her, Kaare said, "You'll do."

Silence saw her mouth twist wryly, and looked away again, suddenly unsure of herself. She had never seriously attempted to pass as a man before. She had originally adopted the smock and trousers to try to fit in with the crowds of adolescent male apprentices, and had never made any other effort to disguise herself, though her voice was naturally low enough to fall within the adolescent range. But it was a different game altogether to attempt to pass herself off as a man in Solitudo's port and field complex.

As if he had read her thoughts, Kaare shook his head. "Trust me, Silence, no one will guess. And even if someone does, what does it matter? Solitudo isn't a Hegemonic-law planet, and even if it were, they couldn't do anything; you're Isambard's apprentice."

He was right, of course. Solitudo's laws did not actually require that women go veiled and escorted; it was merely customary for them to do so. She could not afford to be recognized for other reasons.

"I know, Kaare. But I like to do things right."

The blond nodded. "I understand. Don't worry, you won't have any trouble." He stood, stretching easily. "Are you ready?"

"As I'll ever be," Silence answered. She gave the mirror a final, measuring glance, then turned to pick up the tool bag that lay at the foot of her tidy bed. She unlatched it, checking for the worn grey binding of her *Gilded Stairs*, then relocked the bag carefully. Kaare was watching her with some amusement.

"What do you keep in there? I don't think I've ever seen you without it."

Silence hesitated, then managed what she hoped was a convincingly rueful grin. "My starbooks," she answered. "Pilots' habits die hard."

"Don't you trust the magi?" Kaare asked, laughing, and pushed open the door of the room.

Clearly he wasn't expecting an answer. Silence followed him through the maze of corridors without speaking. But he's right, she thought, more right than he knows. I don't trust the magi at all, though it's only one of my books I have to worry about. Involuntarily she tightened her grip on the bag's shoulder strap. That single starbook—an edition of the *Gilded Stairs* printed before the Millennial Wars that had destroyed the ancient, Earth-founded Union of the Human Sphere—held the key to the lost roads to Earth. Earth, and the reasons behind the broken roads and vanished records, were probably the greatest of the mysteries that still nagged at magi, star-travellers, and homeworlders alike. If the magi, or any of the thousands of others obsessed with the search for Earth, realized what she had, they would not rest until they had taken it from her.

Kaare pushed open the door that led to the main courtyard of the teaching compound, and Silence caught it automatically. The night air was cool and sweetly scented from the gardens, but there was a lingering harshness beneath the fragrance. Silence sniffed hard, frowning, and Kaare said, "The wind's from the north."

From the north and from the sea, Silence thought, and that explained the odd taint to the air. Not salt—there were no salts in the sterile waters of Solitudo's artificial seas—and not anything else, but rather the absence of the smells that made each world unique. She shook her head thoughtfully. The creation of Solitudo Hermae was a tremendous accomplishment—and the further her studies progressed, the greater it seemed—but it was still unmistakably an artificial world.

Kaare gave the door a little push, and Silence started. "Thanks, Kaare," she said. "You've been a big help."

"Good luck," the other apprentice answered. "There's usually a flat at the gate around now."

"Thanks," Silence said again, and started across the shadowed courtyard toward the compound's central gate.

As Kaare had promised, a transport flat was waiting there, its open bed empty of passengers. The servant at the gate gave her no more than a cursory glance, but woke up enough to nod when Silence asked if the flat were headed for the port. The magi, who controlled everything on this, their private world, had no reason to restrict the apprentices' movements. She nodded her thanks and pulled herself up into the flat, trying not to look at its underside. She had spent most of her life in space, where homunculi did most of the heavy work, but neither that time nor the six months she had spent on Solitudo had erased her instinctive dislike of the magi's created beings. It didn't matter whether they had the quasi-human shape of the most common homunculi, or the more exotic forms developed for specialized tasks, like the transport flat itself: she disliked them all equally.

She set her foot on the single step, and one of the eight pairs of legs that carried the flat shifted to compensate for her weight. The caricatured head, set in a low socket at the front of the flat, swiveled to face her. Silence suppressed a shudder at the sight of the dull glass eyes sunk in the folds of grey pseudo-flesh. The flat, its rudimentary intelligence satisfied, turned away again.

Silence allowed herself a soft sigh of relief, and crossed the empty bed to settle herself as far from the head as possible. She wished, not for the first time, that there were some other way of getting to the port complex. But mechanical transport, though admittedly cheaper and more efficient—at least at this particular task—interfered with the magi's Art. On their own world, if nowhere else in human-settled space, the magi could afford to ban all mechanical devices.

Silence jumped as the head swiveled through three hundred sixty degrees, checking its cargo. The flat lurched unpleasantly as the multiple legs shifted to take their first step, and she grabbed hastily for one of the handholds that studded the walls. It bounced erratically for a few moments longer, and then the sixteen legs settled into an efficient, bone-jarring trot. Twin globes of fixed fire flared briefly on the front of the flat, then coalesced and focused to throw long cones of light across the roadway.

As the flat swung southeast along the sea cliff road, its lights swept across the teaching compound, momentarily illuminating the lush gardens, then flashed along the barren ground just beyond the compound's low wall. The contrast between the elaborate greenery and the untransformed rock was dramatic enough in daylight, but at night it had the unreality of nightmare. Silence shivered, and looked up to the familiar stars. Soon, she promised herself, she would be back in space— and not merely as a pilot, but as a magus.

There was a sudden flash of light among the familiar constellations, the coruscating dissonance of a starship's keel striking atmosphere. Silence watched it cross the sky, the flickering dot growing to a delicate wedge as the ship fell toward the field complex, balancing against the harmony of the landing beam. Then the ship reached the horizon, and was hidden in the haze of light that surrounded the field itself.

Silence looked away, trying to deny the longing she felt. You wanted to be a magus, too, she reminded herself, and as badly as you ever wanted to be a pilot. But the memory of her first taste of power had faded during the months of her apprenticeship, eroded by the daily routine of advances and failures that had marked her struggle to achieve mastery. Piloting . . . She had mastered that art years ago, was comfortable with it in a way she could never imagine being with a magus's power, and right now she wanted nothing more than to return to that position of strength. If I'm not spotted, she thought, if no one recognizes me, still searching the sky for another flash of keel-light, we could get away. Denis and Julie could smuggle me aboard, and make some excuse to make a quick turnaround. We could lose ourselves among the star-travellers, and Isambard wouldn't know where to begin looking for us. . . .

She sighed then, and shook her head at her own stupidity. In the first place, Isambard was no fool. He knew the star-travellers' culture fairly well himself, and was known in ports from the Rusadir to the farthest planets of the Fringe. More than that, he had helped his fellow magi often enough, and would not hesitate to call in those debts. And even if they were clever or lucky enough to outrun Isambard's pursuit, the magus was not the only person interested in them. The Hegemony wanted her—no one else had ever broken free of the Navy's geas—and it was the most powerful political entity in space, fresh from its conquest of the Rusadir. None of the Fringe Worlds, not even powerful Delos, would dare to protect her. Only the Rose Worlds might have the strength to stand up to the Hegemon, secure in their ring of closed worlds, but the Rose Worlds were blocking the road to Earth. Her first and only attempt to fly the Earth road had proved that, and warned the Rose Worlders that she knew at least a part of their secret. She would find no refuge in their trading circle.

Silence smiled wryly to herself, glad the darkness hid her face. No, once she had made her bargain with Isambard, she had no choice but to carry it through to the end. It was not as though she gained nothing from it: Isambard had agreed to teach her to use the magus's talent she should not have had, and they would all four share in the profits from finding Earth. But she disliked being under obligation to anyone.

The flat lurched again, and Silence grunted as she was jolted painfully against the side wall. It was coming up on the field perimeter, defined by another of the low retaining walls. This one was barely knee-high, but as deeply rooted in the planet's soil as the one that surrounded the teaching compound. There was no real gate, merely a pair of simple, shoulder-high pillars on either side of the road, but the ground within the enclosure was abruptly fertile, carpeted with coarse grass.

The flat slowed to a jog, swerving slowly to pass between the lines of tuning sheds. It was heading for the row of warehouses, and Silence leaned forward reluctantly.

"Take me to the main terminal."

For a long moment, she thought the homunculus had not heard, and she nerved herself to slap the rough pseudo-flesh of its head. Then, ponderously, the flat turned back, passing between the last of the sheds and the first of the docks to stop beside the main terminal. It had chosen the back entrance, the one reserved for the magi's servants.

Sighing, she dropped from the flat. Hoisting her bag back onto her shoulder, she threaded her way around the corner of the building, into the cone of light that outlined the main entrance. For a brief moment, blinking in the sudden brilliance, she felt as though all eyes were on her. Bracing herself, she pushed through the heavy door, pausing just inside the entranceway to survey the lobby.

To her surprise, there was no one to notice her arrival. She blinked again, hard, until her vision cleared, then stood for a moment longer staring at the terminal's lobby. The main thing now was to find out where her ship was docked, but she couldn't remember where the locator board stood. She glanced around the lobby again. To either side of the door, stairways curved up to the primary level, a low mutter of coinë drifting down to mingle with the low rumble of baggage trucks. Ahead, the shallow first-floor lobby branched out into half a dozen tunnels, each leading to one of the main dock complexes. Figures were visible in the depths of most of these, men and homunculi alike indistinct shadows against the glaring lights, busy with cargo off the newly arrived starships.

Silence took a deep breath, suddenly aware of her own nervousness, and started up the stairs. The dock directory board was bound to be on the main floor, with the customs offices and all the other machinery of the port; she would go there first. She climbed the stairs deliberately, counting each step, and had to force herself to look up when she reached the top, waiting for challenge or snickering comment. The hurrying figures barely seemed to give her a second glance, and Silence shook herself, disgusted with her own timidity. Somehow, though, there was a real difference between being a woman and a pilot, and being a woman and dressing like a man. The psychic armor she had cultivated before no longer seemed to give much protection.

"Need some help, kid?"

Silence started, and turned toward the kiosk that stood just to the right of the stairway. A bored-looking man in Port Control flashes leaned across the worn counter, fixing her with an indifferent stare. "I'm looking for a ship," the pilot answered gruffly, and waited, holding her breath, for his reaction. The Port Control worker showed no sign of increased interest. Emboldened, Silence went on, "*Recusante*, she's called."

The Port Control worker shrugged. "Check the main board," he said, and looked away.

"Thanks," Silence muttered, and turned toward the dock directory board, a massive black cube suspended high above a pit of sand. Tiny multiply-armed homunculi scrambled across its faces, adjusting the bright characters that indicated where the starships were docked. On other, more normal worlds, the directory boards were mechanical; on Solitudo, where mechanics were not allowed, the magi had replaced the usual system with this more elaborate display. She could not repress a wry smile, guessing that the magi had created the cube as much to show off their Art as to provide information.

Silence pushed her way in to the rail, making herself meet the eyes of the men she displaced. A few looked annoyed, one muttering something about pretty boys, but all seemed to accept her at face value. Silence surveyed the listing with a growing sense of confidence. *Recusante*'s name was followed by a double letter and then a string of numbers, all in a vivid shade of green. Silence glanced down at the key engraved on the broad railing: JA 3381, in green, meant the main compound, third shed, dock 381, no special clearance required. And I should hope not, she thought, elbowing her way out of the crowd.

The terminal was connected to the docks and service sheds by a maze of shielded catwalks—a necessity on a world like this, where the landing window was so narrow. The starships could not begin their descent into the planet's atmosphere until the hemisphere of fixed fire that provided Solitudo with its daylight was well clear of the single field. That meant that the leading edge of the night-sky, the hemisphere of untinctured air, had to be past the zenith before the ships could land. Technically, of course, the window was a full twelve hours wide, from the moment the night-sky's edge reached the zenith over the field to the moment the edge of the day-sky swung up to the same point. But practical considerations—navigational difficulties, excess heat bleeding over into the night-sky, and a dozen other variables—narrowed it to a six-hour window except in dire emergencies. Even then, it wasn't easy to be the first ship in the landing queue. Silence was just grateful that Balthasar had landed the ship when they first came to Solitudo.

She shook herself, annoyed at the irrelevance of her thoughts, and looked down at the tiled floor. Sure enough, a dozen different-colored lines of tile led away from the directory board toward the mouths of the closed catwalks. The green line led off toward the most distant catwalk: as always, Balthasar was saving money.

The catwalk ran along the side of the terminal for a short distance, then turned abruptly left to jump across an empty roadway to the roof of a tuning shed. From that vantage point, the tinctured glass walls gave onto a spectacular view of the field, looking down the long towpath to the landing table. A cradled freighter, broad hull dwarfing the blocky shape of its tow, was halfway down the path, heading for the docks. A second tow, lighter and more maneuverable, was shoving another, much larger cradle into position on the landing table, directly over the speaker of the landing beam. Silence glanced up quickly and saw, only slightly dimmed by the lights, the flickering bronze wedge of a starship's keel riding the landing beam down onto the table.

She found herself slowing to watch as the starship dropped closer. It was big, big enough to dwarf even the massive cradle waiting for it, with the long lines of a warship. She frowned nervously, scanning its side for service markings, but the interference flickering along its keel effectively hid its insignia. It didn't look like a Hegemonic ship, but Silence hesitated at the entrance to the JA dock, worried in spite of herself.

The warship was very close now, its keelsong sounding even through the tinctured glass of the catwalk. Patches of reddish light danced along the towpath and across the landing table, reflections from the straining keel. It was time—maybe past time, Silence thought—to break with the harmony of the landing beam. She put her fingers in her ears just in time.

Light flashed from the landing table, a coruscating, rainbow brilliance that completely obscured both ship and cradle. An instant later, the basso harmony of the landing beam was drowned in a discordant shriek that rattled the glass of the catwalk. Wincing, Silence squinted through the flashing lights to see the warship check its rushing descent, slowing as keel and beam repelled each other. She was right, though, the pilot had waited a little too long to break with the landing beam. The warship settled into its cradle with a thump that must have been painful to its crew. Interference faded as the engineers stopped down the harmonium, and at last she could make out the insignia painted on the stubby bow: the stylized moon and river of Tell Sukhas. Silence sighed gently, relieved.

She knew she should move on, but instead she stayed, leaning against the tinctured glass of the wall for a moment longer, staring at the warship. Tell Sukhas was a moderately wealthy world, at least by Fringe World standards. The ship, a four and probably the biggest ship in Tell Sukhas's fleet, was of a recent design, and in reasonably good repair. But Tell Sukhas was not the sort of world whose oligarchs sent warships to Solitudo Hermae on good-will journeys. The Tell Sukhans must be in trouble, she thought, and there was really only one logical source of that trouble. The Hegemon had besieged Castax already, and the planet had capitulated after three months. The other Fringe Worlds must be worrying about who would be next. Silence shivered, remembering the massive engines she had seen ringing Castax, and turned away, abruptly disheartened. The Fringe Worlds had too many long-standing commercial rivalries even to begin to cooperate against the Hegemon's forces, and the Rusadir, united, had fallen to him anyway. All too soon, she would have no place left to run.

Silence shook herself, swearing at her own pessimism, and shoved through the door to the docking shed, slamming the push bar with unnecessary violence. The interior of the dock was dim, after the hot yellow lights of the landing field. Silence paused for a moment to let her eyes adjust to the new lighting, then studied the rows of ships laid out below her. The catwalk gave onto a narrow balcony overlooking the rows of dock spaces. Most of those were full, dura-felt baffling curtains drawn tight around the ships, protecting their delicate keels from disruptive influences. Like the main buildings, each dock had a number painted on the roofing curtain; it was the work of an instant to find *Recusante*'s cubicle. She marked her path carefully, knowing how different things would look once she was down among the ships, curtains rising to either side. Down the right-hand staircase from the balcony, left along the dock wall until she reached the first cross-corridor, then up it to the broad central towpath. Turn right, and six spaces farther was JA 3381.

Silence started down the stairs, counting spaces. She found *Recusante*'s dock without difficulty, and without drawing undue attention from the star-travellers who hurried through the wide corridors. The heavy baffles were drawn tight around the dock space, but a minuscule opening showed at the right-hand corner. Silence lifted the curtain there, shaking it gently to sound the alarm bells sewn at the upper hem, and stepped through the gap. The bells sounded softly, their sweet dissonance muffled by the dura-felt surrounding them, but even so the noise struck a whispering echo from *Recusante*'s gleaming keel, and Silence shivered with pleasure at the familiar note, staring up at the cradled ship.

No refit could change the old *Black Dolphin* into a longship. The rounded merchant hull still bulged awkwardly over the slender keel, and Silence could not suppress a sigh of regret for Balthasar's half-and-half, *Sun-Treader*, destroyed on Arganthonios. Now there, she thought, was a ship that handled like a dream. . . . But *Black Dolphin*—*Recusante*, she corrected herself automatically—would take twice the punishment a fragile half-and-half could stand, and in the search for Earth, solidity was bound to be more important than mere speed. Besides, the refit had included a complete retuning of the keel, and that was certain to improve the way she handled, Silence thought, as would the removal of some of her uncle's less intelligent additions—like the upper gun turret. Silence scanned the upper hull carefully, and was pleased to see that the raw welts where the turret had been were almost invisible beneath the fresh coat of sealant. The lower guns were the only really sensible addition her uncle, Otto Razil, had made. Their brassy muzzles showed at the open ports, their pods neatly dovetailed into the hull above the stubby atmospheric stabilizers: Balthasar was taking no chances even on this supposedly friendly planet.

The bow hatch popped noiselessly from its seating, and swung outward to settle against its stop. A massive, bearded man, so tall that he had to stoop a little to get through *Recusante*'s conventional hatchway, came forward on the cradle's walkway, staring down at her with a total lack of recognition. Silence hid her grin, and waited.

After a moment, the big man said, "Yes? Can I help you?"

A second figure appeared in the hatchway, a smaller, leaner man with greying hair. Silence saw him frown, then saw the frown change to a delighted grin. "Julie, it's Silence," he said. "Welcome home, pilot—or is it maga?"

The big man stared a moment longer. "My God, Silence, it is you," he said, and clattered down the cradle stairs in the other man's wake. Silence returned their joint embrace, but pulled away almost at once, looking at her husbands.

She had begun the three-way marriage as a convenient way of getting her freedom from her uncle's guardianship. She was still not entirely sure how or when things had changed, but she was certain they had, and equally certain the others felt the same. Still, it was a serendipitous combination. She shared something of a common culture with the big engineer, Julian Chase Mago. Like her, he was from the Rusadir, though from Kesse rather than Cap Bel, and an oligarch's son rather than of merchant stock. But Denis Balthasar, the greying second pilot and *Recusante*'s nominal captain, was a Delian and an ex-pirate, part of Wrath-of-God's combine. And yet the three of them had formed a strong and lasting bond even before their capture by the Hegemony.

"It's a good idea, Silence, dressing like a man," Chase Mago said. "I really didn't recognize you."

"It was a friend's idea," Silence said.

"That does solve one problem," Balthasar said. "If

you can pass for someone's apprentice, then we don't have to worry about explaining why we have a woman aboard." His face clouded at that, and Chase Mago shook his head slowly.

"Trouble?" Silence asked.

"Not any more," Balthasar said. He glanced away again. "Let's go aboard, have some tea, and you can fill us in on life on Solitudo."

Damn your secrecy, Silence thought, but she knew better than to make too strong a protest. That would only set Balthasar's back up, and it would take twice as long to get the information she wanted. "Good idea," she said aloud. "I thought we'd sleep in the compound."

Balthasar nodded, and Chase Mago said, turning back to the cradle stairs, "It'll be more comfortable than sleeping shipboard, that's for sure."

The curtain bells jangled softly again, and that sound was followed by the whisper of the baffle closing behind a newcomer. Balthasar's gaunt face contracted in a scowl, eyes fixed on the curtain. Silence, her back still to the opening, was nevertheless suddenly, painfully aware of the new presence. She said, not turning, "Isambard."

"Silence." The magus's voice, as always, held a certain touch of uncertainty when addressing her by her first name. His tone sharpened immediately. "Sieuri."

Balthasar growled an insincere greeting. Chase Mago said nothing, but came down from the cradle stairs to join the others.

"I expected to find you here, Silence," Isambard continued. "Despite my—request—to the contrary."

Silence took a deep breath, biting back a familiar anger. The relationship between magus and apprentice was not intended to be a comfortable one, but in their case, the usual tensions were complicated by the bargain that lay between them. When she was sure she had mastered her expression, she turned to face the magus, saying blandly, "I'm pleased not to have disappointed you, Isambard."

The magus, a small, unhealthily gaunt man with snow-white hair and beard, nodded gravely, clearly waiting for something.

"Will you come aboard?" Balthasar growled after a moment.

"Thank you." Isambard brushed past Chase Mago and began climbing the cradle stairs toward the hatch. The engineer gave him an astonished glance and followed, shaking his head.

Balthasar shrugged, waiting for Silence at the foot of the steps. As she passed, he said softly, "Stiff-necked bastard. Are all your people like him?"

Silence shook her head. "No, not really. And not *my* people, either."

Without waiting for an answer, she ran up the cradle stairs and ducked through the hatch. The refit had done more to *Recusante*'s interior volume than to her exterior. Silence paused for a moment inside the rim of the hatch before she remembered that the common room had been shifted aft, leaving room for two small cabins forward, directly opposite the ladder to the control room. The door now lay in the main, lengthwise corridor. Silence took another deep breath, controlling her anger and frustration, and pushed through the half-open door.

Isambard was already sitting at the head of the single large table, a black-robed statue with a face the color of wax but the weathered texture of aged, hewn stone. Chase Mago was busy with the galley console. As Silence entered the compartment, the engineer turned away from the heating niche, easily carrying two mugs in each huge hand. He set one on the table; Silence took another, sniffing curiously at the spicy fragrance. This was asili, a strong, thick, bittersweet brew from some Ras Gavran herb, not the smoky tea Balthasar usually preferred. She looked curiously at the engineer, and Chase Mago grimaced.

"Long flight," he said. "I need the wake-up dose."

Silence nodded, and detached one of the padded chairs from the floor cleats, swinging it around so that she could sit near, but not at, the table. It was a minor point, she knew, maybe even a petty one, but it was time she started reasserting herself. Balthasar finished fiddling with one of the wall consoles and came to sit beside her, pulling a hammock chair from its usual place. Chase Mago, with one unreadable glance at the Delian, handed him his mug and seated himself at the opposite end of the table from Isambard.

"So how'd it go?" Silence asked.

Balthasar shrugged, leaning back in his chair. "We were just testing the waters, really, so it's hard to say—"

"*We* did all right," Chase Mago interrupted firmly. "But there's trouble. The Hegemon's people are definitely looking for you, and are willing to pay a high price for information." He gave Balthasar a pointed glance. "I think you'd better tell the rest, Denis."

Balthasar made a face, but nodded. "All right. I—we went to Kilix, finally."

When the Delian showed no sign of continuing, Silence nodded encouragingly. Kilix was a Fringe World, with few resources and a bad reputation, but located at the nexus of several logical trading routes. "Kilix," she said.

"Yeah." Balthasar paused a moment longer, marshaling his thoughts, then continued. "I heard on Sisip' Catacecaumene that Wrath-of-God still had a factor there, so I figured it'd be a good idea to get back in touch with them. Well, we got lucky. The factor is Anse Valthier, and we know each other. Things are still pretty much a mess with Wrath-of-God, what with losing most of the fleet at Arganthonios, and then the Hegemon cracking down on the factors and the rest of the contact men. It's just lucky for the Council that the Hegemon hasn't tried raiding the Wrath itself. I don't know why, but he hasn't." He took a deep breath, and went on with difficulty, "What he's done—Apparently the Hegemon is willing to let the Council buy itself off. Valthier says the Council wants what's left of our people to pass on word if they're contacted by anyone who got away after Arganthonios." He squared his shoulders. "Especially a woman pilot. Valthier isn't positive, but he's pretty sure the information goes straight to the Hegemon's people."

"Charming, isn't it?" Chase Mago growled.

Silence swore softly, telling herself she should not have been surprised. Wrath-of-God, for all its fleet and its agents spread throughout Fringe, Rusadir, and Hegemony, was still nothing more than a pirate combine. You couldn't expect loyalty from people like that—but people like Balthasar gave Wrath-of God their loyalty, and were owed something in return.

Balthasar smiled bitterly. "Oh, it's not that bad, Julie, it's just the Captains'—the Captains' Council—doing this. You saw how upset Valthier was about the order, and I'm damn sure he won't report us. You have to give his Most Serene Majesty credit, though. It's a hell of a lòt cheaper for him to make Wrath-of-God tear itself apart than to try a direct attack."

Chase Mago nodded thoughtfully, and Silence found herself sighing in agreement. Of course it would be better for Wrath-of-God's controlling Council to refuse the Hegemon's "offer"—but that would bring on an attack the pirate combine was in no condition to withstand.

Isambard cleared his throat. "You're quite certain, Captain Balthasar, that Valthier won't report you to your erstwhile employers?"

Balthasar rubbed irritably at the patch of pale skin that marred one cheek, marking the spot where Wrath-of-God's identifying tattoo had been removed. Chase Mago said, "If Denis says not, then he won't."

"Then that buys us some time," Isambard said. He looked directly at Silence. "I assume you see what this means?"

Silence frowned. "I see a lot of possible implications," she said slowly. "To which are you referring?"

Isambard gave her the faint, unhappy smile he used when her answers disappointed him. "Has it occurred to you that the Hegemon—or at least his agents—are willing to go to an extraordinary amount of trouble in order to recapture you?"

Silence kept her face impassive with an effort. It had not occurred to her, and now that it had been suggested, she could not believe it. It simply didn't make sense. Anomaly or not, magus-in-potential or not, she wasn't worth that kind of effort. Still, the thought was frightening, and it was hard to keep her voice steady as she said, "Too much trouble, it seems to me. Isn't it more probable, Isambard, that acquiring information about a woman pilot was the secondary purpose, the primary one being to destroy Wrath-of-God?"

Isambard nodded, and in spite of herself Silence felt a touch of pride. "However," the magus went on, and Silence sighed, damning herself for being stupid enough to expect unqualified praise from the old man, "the fact remains that the Hegemon's agents are offering rewards for information about you, and I would be very surprised if they did not also begin making inquiries among the magi."

"There wasn't anything said about a woman magus," Balthasar interjected.

"Not yet," Isambard said. "But female pilots are rare enough, if one discounts the Misthians, and it is known here that Silence is a pilot. Even if no further inquiries were made, it would not be unreasonable for one of my colleagues to take that kind of information to the Hegemon." He paused, then said thoughtfully, "Of course, we are discounting the possibility that his Most Serene Majesty has contacts within the Rose Worlds."

Silence took another deep breath. She still could not quite believe that the Hegemon would find a woman pilot enough of an anomaly to expend so much effort in trying to seek her out—or that he would find such an elaborate revenge worth his time. But if one thing was in itself sufficient to tip the balance, it would be the possibility that this woman pilot had come very close to finding the Earth-road.

"I'm sure he does," Chase Mago said. There was an edge to his voice that made Isambard raise an eyebrow at him. "Take that as a given, Isambard. What then?"

"I should have thought that was clear," the magus said. "Solitudo will not be entirely safe for much longer."

"How safe's entirely safe?" Balthasar muttered irritably.

Silence knotted her hands together inside the wide sleeves of her borrowed coat. "How much longer will I have to stay on Solitudo?" she asked, and somehow managed to keep her tone detached, as though the question were merely academic.

Isambard looked full at her, with the impersonal appraisal she had come to expect from the magi. Silence was better armored against it now. After a moment she raised an eyebrow, waiting for her answer.

"You came to Solitudo knowing symbology better than most magi," the magus said at last. "That was to be expected in a star-traveller, especially in a pilot. Perception, too, you've mastered quickly enough, again, I expected that. Seeing the Form of a thing is much the same as seeing your voidmarks. Manipulation, even though you did nothing precisely like it as a pilot, is really nothing more than applying symbology and perception, and you've done about what I expected there. In addition, you show a certain unconventional harmonic talent. In short, you've mastered the Trivium, and I could certify that."

Silence waited, counting heartbeats, and then, when Isambard showed no sign of continuing, said, "But?"

Isambard smiled gravely. "You are really only a theoretician as yet, though you may qualify as a practitioner. I had hoped to make you at least an adept before we attempted to reach Earth."

Silence sighed. Practitioner was the third of the five ranks, but the majority of students never progressed any further, unable to master the four Arts that made up the Quadrivium and achieve the real power of an adept. A practitioner was able to do a number of simple manipulations—and, more important, was licensed to do so throughout the human-settled worlds—but no mere practitioner could expect to be of much use in breaking the Rose Worlders' barriers. "All right," she said slowly. "If I were certified as a practitioner, could you teach me the Quadrivium shipboard?"

"It would not be impossible," Isambard answered reluctantly, "but I am a specialist in the creative and destructive arts. That is close enough to harmonics to allow me to encourage you in your natural talent, but I am not really suited to teach you the other two. Beyond that, we would not have Solitudo's resources to draw on."

"But it could be done?" Silence repeated.

Isambard nodded.

"It sounds like a workable solution," Chase Mago observed.

"So," Silence said. "Isambard, if Solitudo isn't going to be safe any longer, we have to leave. Will you teach me shipboard, until I've learned enough to make our attempt to reach Earth?"

"As you say," the magus said, "there's little other choice. I would say, however, that we have at least a local month before any inquiries can reach us." He added sharply, "And you'll have to qualify as a practitioner first."

Silence nodded agreement, trying to look more confident than she actually felt. There was still no guarantee that she could pass the qualfying examination. . . . She put that thought firmly from her mind. Isambard was giving her a month, and that would have to be enough. "Denis, do you agree?"

Balthasar shrugged, but said, "Like Julie says, I don't see any other choice."

"It's agreed, then," Silence said, and yawned suddenly. It was nearly dawn by planetary reckoning, and she had been awake since just past dawn of the day before. She reached automatically for another cup of the asili, but Chase Mago touched her hand.

"Why don't you get some sleep?" the engineer asked gently. Giving Isambard a challenging glance, he added, "We could all use some sleep before we go to the compound."

"As you wish." Isambard rose, gathering his black robes about him. "However, I have work that can't wait. Good morning, sieuri."

Balthasar rose smoothly with the magus, and followed him from the common room. A few moments later, Silence heard the sound of the forward hatch opening, and then the thud as it closed.

"How'd it really go?" she asked, when Balthasar reappeared in the doorway.

Balthasar shrugged again, but to Silence's surprise, said, "A lot of work, with only me to pilot, but not so bad, otherwise. It'll be good to have you back aboard."

Chase Mago yawned hugely. "I'm dead tired," he said. "Can we talk in the morning?"

"It is morning," Balthasar said. "Sun's up—or whatever your day-sky does."

"Rises," Silence said. She stood, stretching to work out the stiffness. "You're right, Julie. Let's get some sleep."

It took another hour of desultory conversation, but at last the three were sprawled together in the simple cabin they shared planet-side. The two men were asleep almost at once, exhausted by their long flight and the difficult landing, but Silence lay awake a moment longer, sleepily enjoying the half-familiar presence to either

side. They were another reason it would be good to get
back into space. I'll have to remember to ask Kaare
about the qualifying exam for practitioner when I return his clothes, she thought. He tends to hear everything. And then her mind went blank and she, too,
slept.

CHAPTER 2

It was rising dark before Silence returned to the teaching compound, leaving Balthasar and Chase Mago to finish the paperwork for *Recusante*'s arrival. The night-sky was visible on the eastern horizon, a wedge of darkness like a distant mountain range. Silence eyed it sourly, wishing it were evening already. She had gotten barely four hours of sleep, and not even Balthasar's coffee could erase the fuzziness of mind and body. It the magi had ordered a more reasonable cargo, she thought, shifting her weight against the dull edges of the crates that filled the transport flat, I might've been able to get some sleep on the way. Great shapeless packs of Elysian grains would've been perfect—even a bale or two of cloth would've been more pleasant. But the magi's cargo came packed in metal-sheathed starcrates, each one fully protected against the contingencies of star travel, and entirely too solid to be comfortable.

The flat slowed its pace abruptly, throwing Silence against the crate behind her. She cursed the homunculus under her breath, but even that release felt halfhearted. It altered its steps again and at last jerked to a stop at the main gate. Silence hauled herself out of the open bed, dragging her tool bag with her. The flat trotted away again as soon as she had dropped clear. The pilot swore again, adjusting her crumpled coat, and glared at the servant watching her from under the arch of the main gate. To her mild surprise, however, the man did not look away to hide a smirk, but actually came forward out of his little cubbyhole.

"Are you Silence Leigh?"

Apprentices did not merit any title of respect, but the man's tone was unexpectedly polite. Silence eyed him warily. "Yes."

"Doctor Isambard left an urgent message for you," the man went on. "He wants to see you at once, in his laboratory."

What the hell is he up to? Silence thought. Aloud, she said, "Thanks. Did he say what he wanted?"

The gatekeeper shook his head. "Just that it was urgent."

"That figures," Silence said. "Thanks."

Isambard, like most of the senior magi, had been granted laboratory facilities in the Officina, which formed the far wall of the Inner Yard, a good quarter-hour's walk from the main gate. She passed through the Library's long shadow—the twenty-story tower, set at the point of the pentagonal compound, was a beacon that could be seen for miles—then followed the Masters' Walk that led between the Library and the Inner Yard, careful not to step on its polished stones. The privilege of actually touching that gleaming, moon-colored path was reserved for the magi alone, confirmed in a solemn ceremony. Once in the Inner Yard, she skirted the central close—also reserved for the magi—fumbling in her pockets for the badge that would admit her to the Officina.

She had it in her hand as she tapped on the grille beside the doorkeeper's cubicle, and displayed it as soon as the servant's ill-tempered face appeared in the opening.

"What do you want, then?" he asked, without making any move toward the levers that controlled the heavy door.

"I'm Doctor Isambard's apprentice," Silence answered. "He left word at the gate he wanted to see me at once."

The servant grunted, and reached reluctantly for the levers. "You know where you're going, then?"

Silence nodded, though she had only been inside Isambard's workroom once before. Anything, including the risk of getting lost in the Officina's labyrinthine corridors, was better than being escorted by the sullen doorkeeper or one of his messenger-homunculi. The door swung open just enough to let her in. She ducked through the narrow opening, the servant's voice floating after her.

"Mind you go straight to your master's rooms, and don't loiter."

Silence raised a hand in acknowledgement, and the door slid shut behind her. The corridors of the Officina were windowless, lit only by an occasional globe of fixed fire, and the air was heavy with the sense of the power behind the sealed doors of the magi's labs. Isambard's workroom lay on the far side of the Officina's central court. Silence found the door that gave onto the barren, cobbled yard and crossed it quickly, aware of eyes watching her from the seemingly empty lab windows. In the court, even the unchanging light of the day-sky seemed occluded, distant, and she was glad to reach the unmarked door that gave onto Isambard's stairway.

In the tiny foyer, the sense of leashed power was even stronger than before. Silence shivered, feeling it tingle on her skin, then shook herself angrily and started up the narrow stairway. In this part of the Officina, the magi's workrooms opened directly off the tiny landings. As she climbed toward the third floor, Silence could see at least two doors covered with wax seals and marked with bright hieroglyphs. Behind those protective seals, magi were working with the Four Arts, imposing the Forms of the super-material plane onto the chaotic proto-matter of the sub-material, and bringing the fused result to existence in the material world. It was no wonder the resonance of that power raised the hair at the base of her neck.

The door to Isambard's laboratory stood ajar, inviting entrance, but Silence hesitated briefly before knocking.

"Enter."

Silence did as she was told, glancing curiously around the narrow room. Her lessons were given elsewhere, in the classroom buildings and the common laboratories; her previous visit had been hurried, giving her no chance to look around. The laboratory itself was small, but every inch of space was put to efficient use. The walls nearest the door were lined with books, only a few of which bore the dangling tags that marked books from the magi's great library. A counter ran the full length of the far wall, beneath a broad window that gave onto a view of the gardens and, beyond that, the sea. A tiny, powerful furnace stood in the very center of the room. The screens that deflected the worst of its heat were folded back now that it was not in use. All along the walls stood locked cabinets. Various objects hung from hooks set in the walls above and between the cabinets. One, at least, Silence recognized as a simple monochord, used to set the pythagorean harmonies, but the rest remained unidentifiable.

"So, Silence, you're back at last." Isambard was sitting in a rather worn cushion chair, the single piece of impractical furniture in the long room. "Excellent. There's still time."

Silence jerked her attention away from the mysterious things hanging on the walls. "Time for what, Isambard?"

The magus smiled, and for the first time Silence thought she saw traces of excitement in the old man's bearded face. "I've arranged for you to be examined now, by a sympathetic committee—magi who are willing to accept a woman magus."

"Examined?" Silence repeated stupidly, and then understood. "Isambard, I had four hours of sleep last night. I can't possibly cope with a certification exam now."

"You'd better be able to," Isambard said coolly. "You won't get a better chance."

Silence took a deep breath, fighting back sudden, unreasoning panic. It was like the nightmares her fellow apprentices so often described—except that she was awake, and she really was unprepared for the examination she unexpectedly faced. . . . But I'm not unprepared, she told herself sternly. I have studied, I have worked hard, and I can be ready. Isambard wouldn't do this to me if he didn't think I could do it, if only for the sake of his own reputation. "What must I do?" she said, and was surprised at how steady her voice sounded.

"The committee will set you a simple problem from the Trivium," Isambard answered. "To create an object—a common object—from sub-material, give it Form, and fix it. That's all."

"I see," Silence said. All too well, she added to herself. A magus was certainly entitled to define such a creation as a simple problem, but it was still an application of the Great Arts. She had tried the operation only twice before, and had not yet succeeded. "How long do I have to prepare?"

Isambard glanced automatically at the window, where the night-sky was rising toward the zenith and Solitudo's arbitrary sunset, and then at the nearest of a dozen clocks. "The sooner this is done, the better," he said. "Half an hour."

"And if I fail?" Silence asked.

Isambard shrugged. "You may try again, of course, but there will be a different committee. Doctor Nagid has drawn a seat on the next one."

"I see," Silence said again. Nagid was probably the

single most vocal opponent of her presence on Solitudo.
"All right, I'll be ready."

"Good," Isambard said. "I'll inform the committee.
In the meantime, prepare yourself. You may use any
tools of mine you think you may need." He stood,
stiffly, and moved toward the door, pausing only to
add, "Good luck." Then the door closed behind him.

Silence stared after him for a moment, then slowly
shook her head. This was typical of the magi, of
Isambard. . . . She took a deep breath then, and rubbed
her forehead hard with both hands, trying to massage
some awareness back into her mind. First things first,
she told herself. Isambard offered tools, and the run of
his laboratory. I should start there.

She looked around the walls again, then tugged at
the doors of the nearest cabinet. The main doors were
locked, but the three drawers beneath opened at her
tug. The top one was filled with narrow tubes of incense, each labeled precisely in Hegemonic script with
its common name, hieroglyph, and elemental affinities.
As she sorted through the tubes, she was grateful for
the school's insistence that all apprentices learn the
High Speech, the Hegemony's official language. She
had been unilingual before coming to Solitudo, a definite handicap outside the star-travellers' culture. The
next drawer held a strange assortment of musical
instruments—drums and whistles and various sets of
strings for the hanging monochord. The third was full of
glassware that rattled dangerously as she opened and
closed it. The next cabinet held more glassware, retorts
and strange, multiply curved tubes, while its single
drawer was heaped high with papers. The third cabinet
was locked as well, but through its transparent doors
Silence could see that each of its dozen broad shelves
was lined with instruments, mostly of metal. She recognized the delicate Ficinan model, a closed cube where
colors shifted like shadows to reflect conflicting elemental harmonies, and the orrery on the shelf below that,

set up to reflect some two-planet system, but the rest
were completely foreign.

She shook herself abruptly, and turned away from
the cabinets. Most of those items, intended for very
specific operations, were useless to her. The simple
creation Isambard had described required correspond-
ingly simple instruments. She would want the monochord, to set the harmonies, and—incense? She returned
to the first cabinet, opened its upper drawer, and
stared again at the hundreds of neatly labeled tubes.
Then, decisively, she closed it again. The main thing
she would need was calm, and the incense alone would
not bring that.

She lifted the monochord from its place—the string
sighed softly as she brushed against it, a cool, pleasant
note—and walked the length of the long room to hoist
herself onto the empty counter. Below her, the gardens
seemed almost to glow in the fading light, the lush
growth vivid against the stark emptiness of the cliff
top just outside the wall. Beyond that, the shadow of the
night-sky moved westward across the waveless sea. Silence watched it for a while, hugging the monochord to
her body. Then she composed herself, reciting the cantrips she had learned as a pilot to focus the mind and
drain away fear and tension.

When the door opened at last, Silence did not turn at
once, and Isambard's voice was unexpectedly gentle.
"Are you ready, Silence?"

"Yes," she answered, closing her mind against resur-
gent panic. She slid down from the counter, still holding the monochord, and Isambard gave her an approving
nod.

"A sensible choice," he said. Before Silence could
respond to the unusual praise, the magus continued,
"Come along."

Without waiting for her reply, Isambard pushed open
the laboratory door. Silence followed him through the

Officina's labyrinthine corridors, along the length of one wing, then through a suddenly narrow hallway that made an abrupt, right-angle turn to end in a heavily padded door. Isambard set his palm to the lock plate, then pulled open the door, motioning for Silence to step through. The pilot did as she was told, but waited just inside for the magus to join her. Beyond the landing on which she stood, a wide stairway curved gently down out of sight. It was lit by oddly smoky globes of fixed fire, the tiny flames swelling even as she watched to provide a yellowish illumination. Behind her, Isambard adjusted the inner lock, which hummed deeply under his touch. Startled, Silence turned to look, and her attention was caught by a line of scribbled words on the wall just inside the door. "The shortest road to hell," they read, and to make the meaning unmistakable, there was also an arrow, pointing down the stairs.

At her shoulder, Isambard gave a grunt. "Apprentices," he said, irritably. "Come along."

Silence raised an eyebrow. It would be like an apprentice, especially a failed candidate, to add that graffito here, but even more like the examining magi to put it up as a further hazard. Isambard's attitude was nevertheless reassuring. She followed the magus around the curve of the stair, which turned twice more before it ended at another padded door. This one did not seem to be locked. Isambard pushed it open, and motioned for Silence to precede him.

The pilot hesitated, and Isambard said, "You must."

Silence took a deep breath and stepped through the door. She stood at the top of another flight of stairs, this one almost completely unlit, leading down into a brightly lit, circular area fitted out like a cleaner version of the apprentices' workshops, with a broad table set in the center of a brass isolation ring. Outside the ring, and almost outside the column of light, was a longer table that held an impressive assortment of material. Among the heap of things, Silence could pick out another mono-chord, a case of tubes that probably held incense, a mirror, and a dozen other miscellaneous pieces of equipment that she could not imagine wanting for a simple transformation.

Behind her, Isambard said, "Go on. All the way down."

Obediently, Silence started down the steep stairs. As her eyes adjusted to the strange light, she could see that the steps ran between banks of seats, empty now, and guessed that this was more usually some sort of demonstration hall. As she approached the bottom of the stairs, the pitch leveled out a little, and she could see four robed figures sitting in the row of seats to her left. Then she had reached the bottom of the stairs and stepped out into the column of light, turning to face the judges she could no longer see.

Isambard said, "Masters, I present Silence Leigh, candidate-practitioner."

There was a rustling in the darkness, and a dry, reedy voice said, "We accept the candidate."

Isambard bowed politely, and took a seat in the second row of chairs, just outside the reach of the lights. Silence waited, and after a moment, the same reedy voice said, "Candidate, are you prepared?"

"Yes," Silence answered, and when something more seemed to be expected, said, "I'm prepared." The words came out as more of a challenge than she had intended, seemed to ring on in the empty air of the chamber.

"Very well," the reedy voice said after another brief pause, and a second voice said, "Is the candidate familiar with the procedure? This is, after all, a committee formed in haste."

Silence gave a soundless sigh. The second voice was one she recognized: Fynn, Kaare's master, one of the few magi who had encouraged her training, at least as long as she continued to show promise.

"A reasonable point," a third voice murmured, and the reedy voice said, "Indeed. Candidate-practitioner, the purposes of this examination is to demonstrate that you have indeed mastered the first three Arts—symbology, perception, and manipulation—which are the basis of all further study. Rather than examine theoretical knowledge, we will set you a simple problem, which you must solve according to the Trivium. You have the free use of any of the items which you see behind you. You also have our word that nothing necessary to a solution of the problem has been omitted. There will be a time limit. Is this clear?"

Silence said again, "Yes."

"Excellent." There was a pause, as the magi of the committee whispered to each other, and then the reedy voice went on, over a rustling of paper. "Candidate-practitioner, this is the problem: You are in service at the court on Asterion, and the ladies of the court wish flowers for a banquet."

Abruptly, the reedy voice faltered, and Fynn said, "Surely we can skip over that part, sir?"

"Indeed."

Silence could hear embarrassment in the reedy voice, and was hard put to suppress her own slightly hysterical grin. The magus was reading from a common exercise book, intended to teach appropriate behavior in business situations as well as the Arts. From what little she knew of the Hegemony, she could guess that the omitted section of the exercise was intended to familiarize the budding magus with the basic rules of courtly behavior.

The senior examiner cleared his throat. "In any case, these ladies wish roses, in winter. Your task, candidate, is to create one rose, substantial and complete. You have one hour." He closed the exercise book with an audible snap. "The examination has begun."

Silence took a deep breath and let it out slowly,

turning to survey the heaped-up equipment behind her. Stripped of the ridiculous situation surrounding it, the problem was simple: seek out the Form of a rose, the ideal, essential rose, and make it real. She had free choice of procedure and materials—which was not much help, since she had not yet succeeded with any of them.

She put that thought aside, and advanced to the table. There were several ways of fixing Forms once summoned, and the materials for all were there: an alembic, its neck curving in on itself; a black mirror; crystal spheres of various sizes and shapes; prepared wax for the creation of simulacra. Silence studied them all for a long moment. A rose was a thing of nature rather than of the freed elements, which ruled out the quick, crude heat of the alembic. Best of all, perhaps, would be a simulacrum, formed from the unliving but receptive wax and then given the character of life by the summoned Form. But that method required a sculptor's talent to prepare the simulacrum itself, and Silence knew she lacked both that talent and the necessary knowledge. She had seen a living rose but once in her life, as a girl on Cap Bel. That left the mirror and the spheres, and her teachers had not yet reached the point of demonstrating the use of spheres. Carefully, she freed the black mirror and carried it to the table in the center of the isolation ring. Its surface gleamed dully, reflecting nothing.

That decision made, Silence returned to the table, glancing quickly over the profusion of material. She already had Isambard's monochord and the brass hammer to play it; now she needed only a trigger, some tangible spur to finding the Form. A glass rose lay among the litter, half hidden beneath a frayed sheet of paper. Silence lifted it thoughtfully, then set it aside again. She had no real reason for rejecting it, but it seemed too easy, too likely to be a trap. Among the

tubes of incense was one labeled "rosae." She selected
that, and the smallest of the six braziers, and returned
to the isolation ring.

The next steps were almost automatic. Murmuring
the activating word, she touched the metal of the ring
and felt the brass vibrate softly under her fingertips, a
note too deep to be heard. The ring was closed now
against the operations of the Arts, protecting her work,
and protecting the watching magi against her mistakes.
Within the ring, the air was curiously thick and dead. It
took an effort of will to convince herself that she had
not sealed out the fresh air as well, that she would not
suffocate inside a closed column. Silence reached for
the monochord, searching for the correct sequence.
The sequence would set the harmonies for any operation, the sympathetic notes being chosen according to
the process involved. This exercise would use projection, the twelfth type of manipulation; the harmony was
therefore the sequence of Saturn. For the first time
since she had come to Solitudo, Silence was grateful for
the hours she had been forced to spend memorizing the
tables of manipulations and their accompanying harmonies.

The sequence of Saturn was one of the simplest.
Silence tapped the open string, striking a note that
hung and swelled in the charged air, then slid the wand
along the treated cord to strike a second note a step
above the first. The dissonance, unpleasant to the human ear yet as perfect in its own right as the more
conventionally beautiful sequences, filled the air, then
faded to hang just at the edge of hearing. Satisfied,
Silence turned to the tiny brazier, set its disk alight,
and worked loose the stopper of the tube of incense.
Very carefully, not wanting to smother herself with the
smoke, she added a few grains to the tiny flame. The
odor was not strong enough. She added a few grains
more, then replaced the brazier's fretted cap and set it

on the table to the right of the mirror. The preliminaries completed, she turned her attention to the mirror itself, focusing all her concentration on it.

The black surface that faced her was perfectly featureless, utterly unreflective. Silence took a deep breath and murmured the first of the cantrips, letting herself slip easily into the waking trance. Gradually, the mirror clouded, then began hazily to reflect the room behind her. Silence murmured the second cantrip, and felt the world narrow around her, while at the same time the mirror began to fill with images. Some were easily recognizable, distortions of herself or the furniture; others were intrusions, symbols reflecting her own imperfect concentration. Patiently, she identified and excluded each of them—the red haze of her fear, the toiling wheel that was her exhaustion, the embarrassingly graphic images of her husbands—and the mirror cleared again.

Slowly she began to seek the Form of the rose. There were many images to sift through, tag ends of memory and learning. Her girlhood visit to the Kiollr's garden, where she had first seen a living rose, was purged of its emotions and joined to the white rose that was the symbol of purity and the blood-red rose that was a symbol of knowledge and passion. Faintly at first, and then more clearly, an image began to take shape in the mirror's depths. It wavered, colors shifting. Silence frowned at it, bent all her will toward it, and the colors steadied to a rich crimson. In that instant of stability, she spoke the final cantrip. The image seemed to take on a new solidity, as though she could reach out and pluck it from the surface of the mirror.

Cautiously, she relaxed her concentration somewhat. When the imagine did not fade, and she felt certain it would not, she reached for the flower. Her fingers touched only the glass of the mirror. Silence bit back a cry of frustration. The operation had gone well so far, it should not require anything more to free the fixed Form from the imprisoning mirror. . . .

She let her hand fall to her side, and forced herself to think calmly. This was the hardest part of the operation, bringing the fixed Form to full existence in the material world. It was this that had always defeated her before. Hastily, she thrust away that thought, and tried to concentrate on the search for a solution. The Form had been made particular, but was still trapped within the mirror. If it could only be freed, somehow, it would be real and as substantial as required. . . .

Very distantly, the reedy voice of the senior magus said, "Candidate, your time is nearly up."

Silence bit back her rising panic. There had to be a way to free the rose. If the mirror were shattered, it would probably fall free, but that was out of the question. Or was it? she thought. The magi had said only that they wanted results, not that the method had to be elegant. . . . There was also a good chance that the falling shards of glass would destroy the rose, but it was a risk she had to take. She caught up the monochord's hammer and swung it blindly at the mirror just as the senior magus said, "The examination is over."

The mirror shattered, the glass falling in a discordant shower. The rose, half-open, blood-red, perfect to its single thorn, lay on top of the glittering heap. There was a murmur of appreciation from the watching magi.

A fourth voice, one that had not spoken before, said, "I think there's no question of the result?"

The reedy voice said, "Patience."

Automatically, Silence stooped to touch the isolation ring, deactivating it, while beyond its invisible borders light faded on over the watching magi. There were four of them, besides Isambard, who sat a little apart from the others. One, the biggest of them, hauled himself to his feet, saying, "The rose has not yet been fully examined." The reedy voice was startling, coming from such a huge body.

The fourth man, younger and almost albino-fair, said fretfully, "That hardly seems necessary." Nevertheless, he followed the big man down the last few steps and out into the isolation ring.

Fynn and the other magus followed more slowly and the four gathered around the worktable. The senior magus lifted the rose from its bed of glass and examined it intently, then passed it on to the fair man, who repeated the examination, touching the petals, the thorn, and sniffing to test the perfume. Silence, swaying slightly from sheer exhaustion, found their delicate gestures almost unbearably funny, and had to bite her lips hard to keep from laughing aloud. Fynn seemed to sense her thoughts, and glanced up at her, smiling approvingly across the rose. Silence barely managed to convert her laugh into a convincing cough.

The fourth magus accepted the rose, but his examination was perfunctory. Clearing his throat, he said, "I accept the rose as substantial and complete, as required. I question the time element."

Fynn said, "The mirror was broken as time was called, if not before."

The senior magus held up his hand, forestalling further argument. "The question is legitimate," he said, and Silence drew a slow, shaky breath. If, after all she had done, they could disqualify her now. . . . At least, if they did so, she would have proved to herself that she could perform a simple creation.

The senior magus pointed to the near-albino. "Fynn, you have stated your ruling. Hanif?"

The younger man said, "The mirror broke as time was called. I would accept it."

The senior magus nodded. "As would I. Do you still protest, Zesirik?"

Slowly, the fourth magus bowed his head. "I defer to the board. I accept the time as well."

"Excellent," the senior magus murmured. He eyed

Zesirik for a moment longer, then turned ceremonially to Silence. "Candidate, I welcome you now to the company of practitioners of the Art, and will so certify you to all comers. Well done, practitioner."

The words were formulaic, devoid of warmth, but even so, Silence felt herself grinning uncontrollably. Still grinning, she accepted the formal congratulations of each member of the committee—only Fynn projected any real sense of pleasure—and then allowed Isambard to lead her out of the chamber and back up the stairs to the crooked hallways of the Officina proper. The magus paused in the arched doorway, just out of earshot of the man on duty at the entrance.

"It was well done, indeed," Isambard said judiciously, "if a trifle over-dramatic in your choice of conclusion. You will have to review—"

"It worked," Silence said. "No, it wasn't perfect, but it worked. I'm entitled to celebrate, and even you can't take that away from me."

Isambard stopped, considering. In the faint light from the wall globes, his bony face was grotesquely shadowed, almost demonic. Silence glared back at him, furious that he had taken any of her satisfaction from her. Damn it all, she thought, I know how fragile this is, I know how much I don't know. Don't spoil this success, too.

After a moment, Isambard said, almost mildly, "Very well. You have become a practitioner, after all." Without waiting for her answer, he stepped forward to the doorkeeper's cubicle, and gestured for the man to open the great door. Grudgingly, the bars slid back in their holders, and the door itself swung outward, hinges groaning. "Good night, Silence," Isambard said.

Silence stepped out into the risen night, drawing her coat tighter around her shoulders against the sudden chill. Overhead, the edge of the night sky had swung well past the zenith, and to the east, the stars had begun to come out. The glaring day-sky, now merely a wedge of white on the western horizon, cast its last feeble shadows across the courtyard. The sense of triumph had deserted her utterly. Sighing, she turned aside, skirting the edges of the central close, and left the Inner Courtyard for the barnlike dormitories where the apprentices were quartered.

Because of her unique situation, Silence had been allotted an end room, larger than the usual, and equipped with its own bathing chamber. It also opened onto the smaller side stairway, an advantage at a time like this when she wanted to see no one, strung as she was between exhaustion and triumph. The lock, in theory tuned only to the apprentices who actually lived on that stairway, was so old and jaded that it clicked open at the touch of her hand on the knob. She let the door fall closed behind her, not bothering to see if it locked again, and pulled herself painfully up the two flights of stairs that led to her room.

Her door was open slightly, spilling light into the dim hallway, and it opened further at the sound of her footsteps. Chase Mago glanced out, bearded face contracted into a scowl. His expression relaxed as he saw her, and he said, "There you are. We've been worried about you."

He held the door open for her. Silence did not have to duck to pass beneath his outstretched arm. Balthasar said, "What happened? Kaare said they were watching for you at the gate, that Isambard wanted you."

Silence nodded and murmured a greeting to Kaare, who was sitting cross-legged on the floor beside a battered portable stove. Kaare smiled nervously back at her, waiting for some further response. Clearly, Silence thought, he knew why she had been summoned, as well as by whom. Balthasar occupied the room's only chair, so the pilot dropped instead onto the bed, kicking off her shoes as she did so. "That's right," she said.

Abruptly, she found herself wishing she did not have to tell them of the examination and its results, or that it could be passed off without a fuss, without celebration.

"You're getting to be as bad as Denis," Chase Mago complained, and came to sit beside her on the narrow bed.

"I'm sorry," Silence said, and shook herself. She owed them a better explanation than this. "You know how Isambard said he wanted to see me made a practitioner before we leave Solitudo? He set up the examination for this evening, cornered me as soon as I got back."

"And?" Balthasar demanded.

"I passed."

Chase Mago pulled her into an embrace, and Kaare gave a whoop of delight.

"She passed," Balthasar said, and laughed. "Listen to her, now, as though she does this every day. Congratulations, Silence."

"I'll get Mates," Kaare said, and Silence nodded. Mates was the only other apprentice whom she could call a friend; it was only fair, she thought, that he should get to share the celebration. Kaare scrambled to his feet and disappeared. Chase Mago released Silence long enough to lean across the bed and rummage in his battered carryall until he found a carved bottle. At the sight of the ruby liquid, Balthasar raised an eyebrow.

"You're going all out, aren't you, Julie?"

"Can you think of a better reason to finish it?" Chase Mago retorted. Without waiting for an answer, he poured out three minuscule glasses of the stuff. Silence, knowing what it would do to her in her present state of exhaustion, protested feebly, but the engineer ignored her and handed one to each of the others. "To Silence," he announced, and drained his glass.

Balthasar echoed him and drank more cautiously. Silence, surrendering, sipped dutifully at the sweet gin, and felt it burn its way down her throat to explode in the pit of her stomach. She gasped—the first swallow was always the worst—and tried again. A warm glow spread slowly outward, enveloping her.

Kaare returned a few moments later, bringing with him not just Mates but half a dozen other boys, each carrying some small contribution to the party, food, a stone jug of beer. The first one hesitated in the doorway, a little uncertain about the whole situation, but Silence, emboldened by the drink she had already had, smiled and beckoned. The apprentices crowded into the room, calling their congratulations.

Silence leaned back against Chase Mago's shoulder, holding her suddenly refilled glass very carefully with both hands. The sense of triumph was abruptly with her again, filling her being like a song. She had done a thing no other woman had done—at least to the magi's knowledge—no matter how ungracefully. As she had said to Isambard, she was entitled to this brief celebration.

On waking, well past noon of the next day, Silence had only the vaguest memory of the previous night's party. What she did remember was pleasant—the shy congratulations of boy apprentices who had never seen an unveiled woman, Chase Mago's arm around her shoulder, Balthasar's fond teasing, and, most of all, the awareness of her triumph.

It was the last that did her the most good over the next few weeks. Isambard sent her a curt note by one of the provost's messengers, pointing out that her schedule had to be adjusted so that she could attend the classes in the higher arts of the Quadrivium. Almost at once, Silence was plunged into a frantic struggle to catch up with students who had begun their studies months or, in some cases, years before. Isambard pointed out caustically that every practitioner faced the same difficulties, and offered extra tutoring. Grimly, Silence set herself to master the unfamiliar disciplines. Of the four Arts that made up the Quadrivium, she found the harmonic arts—music-based manipulations, the use of proportion and numerical consonance, and so on—the easiest. With Isambard's expert help she made swift progress in his specialty, the creative and destructive arts. The magus's sparing praise for her knack with harmonics brought only extra hours of work, however. Isambard set her to learn each of the five pure instruments and the elementary scale sequences for each.

To offset those successes, she soon found she had no particular talent for the medicinal arts, at least as they were taught on Solitudo, and, to her consternation, her training as a pilot actually interfered with her ability to learn the elemental arts. Pilots were traditionally taught half-truths, which were good enough for the limited, even passive operations of piloting. Now she had to unlearn those rough expedients, and learn a new system that frequently contradicted the old one. It was not easy, and neither Isambard nor Stanek, who was in charge of the class in elemental Arts, found her excuses acceptable. Only the memory of her recent success, of the surge of triumph she had felt when the rose lay unbroken on top of the shattered mirror, kept her from losing her temper in the face of their reprimands. She had learned the Trivium, impossible as that had seemed when she began studying it; she would learn the Quadrivium as well.

The only real advantage to having achieved the rank of practitioner—aside from the gilded card that arrived two days after the examination, certifying that she could indeed practice the minor Arts on any of the known worlds—was that she had at last gained Library privileges. Apprentices were restricted to the lower floors of the twenty-story tower, and to a selection of books approved by a committee of magi. Now she could pass through the closely guarded gate to the upper floors, where the full resources of the Library were at her disposal.

No one had *unrestricted* access to these books, however. Silence paused below the gate leading from the open sections of the building to show her newly minted license to the bored servant on duty there. Then, suppressing a shudder, she walked up the three steps that led between the massive twin homunculi and stepped through the tunnel-like entrance.

The wall that separated the two parts of the Library was nearly a meter thick, and the gate was thickened even further on both sides by a heavily carved flange that held the "brain" controlling the guarding homunculi. To emerge from that narrow passage into the airy hall was like stepping into a different world. On the floors below, windows barely the width of a man's palm stretched from floor to ceiling at infrequent, irregular intervals, casting an ever-changing pattern of barred light over the rows of tables at which the apprentices worked. Here every centimeter of the two side walls was given over to multicolored glass, interrupted every three meters by one of the thick columns that supported the upper stories. The pale carpet was bathed in a tapestry of colored light, broken here and there by the slow-moving shadow of a magus, pacing along the perimeter of the room like a planet in its orbit, absorbed in thought. Even knowing what she would see, Silence was dazzled. She stood for a moment, staring, then shook herself. She might be entitled to study here, but she would never be one of the magi pacing so serenely beside the colored windows. Nor, she added to herself, would I want to be. I am still a pilot, and will remain a pilot, too, whatever else I become.

A Librarian—one of six who held that title, who neither had nor needed any other name—was waiting in his tower in the center of the room, hands folded placidly in his lap. Only his eyes moved, darting con-

stantly among the orbiting magi, the black-glass model
of the Library and the shifting pinpoints of light within
it, and the monkey-like creatures that crouched unmov-
ing at his feet. As Silence approached, his eyes fixed
briefly on her, then resumed their constant motion.

"Sir," Silence said. The Librarian's eyes flickered
downward again, acknowledging her presence. "Sir, I
request admittance. I am looking for studies in basic
elemental theory."

The Librarian grimaced, and Silence was careful to
keep her face expressionless. She knew perfectly well
that the Librarians preferred it when users requested a
single, specific text. The Librarian could then have
brought it, without the necessity of admitting a stranger
into the uppermost levels. That also gave him a chance
to rule on whether or not he would allow the user to
see a particular text—which was one of the reasons
Silence had chosen not to request the books she wanted.
None of the three were controversial, or likely to be
restricted, but she did not want to give him an opportunity for malice.

The Librarian sighed heavily. "Very well," he said,
reluctantly, and snapped his fingers at one of the creatures crouching at the base of the tower. "The guide
will take you to the section you want. Press the
button when you're ready to leave, and you'll be escorted back here."

Silence nodded, already familiar with the procedure,
and then shuddered in spite of herself as the creature
turned its noseless face to stare at her. For all that it was
lightly furred, and far more delicately made than most
of its kind, it was still a homunculus. The creature
blinked twice, then scurried away across the long room
to the row of doors that stretched across the far end of
the room. Silence followed more slowly.

The central door opened at the homunculus's approach, and the guide paused just inside until Silence

caught up. The pilot had just enough time to see that a spiral staircase led down toward the lower stacks before the homunculus darted ahead, and Silence had to hurry to catch up. The door slammed shut behind her.

There was a second staircase two meters beyond the doorway, a wider spiral than the first. The homunculus scrambled up it, using both bony paws to help it climb. Silence hurried after it, but by the time she passed the third landing, the creature was five full turns ahead of her.

"Hey, slow down," she called, panting, but the homunculus did not seem to hear. At the next landing, it scuttled off the stairway and vanished through one of the featureless doorways that ringed the spiral. Silence cursed it, and took the stairs two at a time in a vain attempt to catch up. At the landing, she paused only long enough to get her breath back, then ducked through the left-hand doorway after it.

She found herself in a narrow, shelf-lined corridor, faintly lit by globes of fixed fire. The shelves were piled high with books, papers, and thin boxes of the ancient golden disks that the earliest magi had used to record their information. Some had identifying codes scrawled directly on the tops of the boxes, or on the fraying bindings; tags hung from the rest, the faded lettering hard to read in the dim light. There was no sign of the homunculus.

Silence swore again. Wandering aimlessly in the Library was actively discouraged, it could even be grounds for expulsion, or at least for loss of library privileges. It was not her fault that the homunculus had gotten ahead of her, but that would hardly matter. She took a few steps farther down the corridor, irrationally hoping she would suddenly see the homunculus's huge eyes glowing at her from the base of a set of shelves, then took a deep breath and forced herself to walk briskly toward the nearest cross-corridor. It was empty for as far as she could see to either side.

Silence hesitated. One of the buttons used to call a guide-homunculus dangled from the ceiling here; it would be the work of an instant to press it, admitting her mistake. Instead she walked farther down the corridor, pausing now to read the labels as she went. The first few codes, a sequence of numbers followed by a complex hieroglyph that could mean either the donor or the general subject of the work, were unfamiliar. As she moved along the shelves, however, she began to recognize the sequence of numbers, and whistled softly to herself, almost forgetting where she was. She had somehow stumbled into the section of the Library that dealt with star travel. With any luck, she thought, *the subsection that deals with piloting will be nearby, and I can see what starbooks the magi keep hidden here.* She ran her finger along the nearest shelf, trying to remember how the code sequences would run. Logically, the starbooks should come at the end of the entire section, but the Library did not follow any of the usual patterns. Her best bet was to go shelf by shelf, and keep looking for the compass wheel hieroglyph that marked pilot's texts.

As she approached the next cross-corridor, something—a hint of a noise, a glimpse of motion in the cracks between the shelves—made Silence look away from the rows of books and let her hand fall to her side. She acted just in time: an instant later, the guide homunculus turned the corner ahead of her and stopped dead, regarding her with baleful yellow eyes. Silence stared back at it, striving to project an air of injured innocence mingled with relief. The homunculus hesitated a moment longer, then beckoned impatiently with one clawed paw. Silence hurried to join it. *With any luck at all,* she thought, *I can retrace my steps and come back here to look for more starbooks.*

The guide homunculus led her quickly through the maze of intersecting corridors—so quickly that it was hard to keep track of all the turnings. Silence swore under her breath, and dawdled as much as she dared. The homunculus moved more slowly this time, but still too fast for her to fix on any definite landmarks. Then, abruptly, it reached the first row of shelves that contained the textbooks on basic elemental theory and stopped. They had not come very far from the section on star travel. Silence nodded dismissal, wishing the creature would leave as quickly as it had come. It waited a moment longer while the lights, triggered by its continued presence, slowly brightened overhead. Silence bit her lip and lifted a book at random from the shelf in front of her to hide her impatience. It was one she had been looking for for the past two weeks, but she no longer cared. She turned its pages one by one, hardly seeing the words, until at last the homunculus scurried away. Silence forced herself to count slowly to a thousand before she moved.

The lights had dimmed almost to darkness in the corridors outside the elementals section. Silence moved cautiously, trying to picture the route exactly, feeling her way by the glow of the emergency lamps. Despite her caution, she took a wrong turn almost at once, and realized her mistake only when the *INTL* markings gave way to the crossed arrow that indicated ceration. The Library's quiet was affecting her. She did not even swear as she retraced her steps, until she found the place where she had chosen wrong. From there, knowing how she had gone wrong, it was easy to find her way back to the star-travel section, and from there to trace her way along the shelves, squinting in the dim light, to the starbooks.

There were nearly two dozen volumes, their unlettered bindings marked only with the compass-wheel hieroglyph, but as Silence pulled them one after the other from the shelf, flipping them open to the title pages, she felt a growing sense of disappointment. These books were nothing special, she thought. They were the sorts of manuals available in any reputable charthouse anywhere in the known worlds. Even the Hegemony's pilots had access to them. Then, very slowly, she began to smile. It was still nice to think that the pilots had managed to keep a good part of their art secret from the supposedly all-knowing magi. *Unless, of course, the Librarians have filed the more interesting texts in some other part of the Library,* she added to herself, and her smile faded a little. Since the starbooks had proved to be nothing new and exciting, she knew she should go back and look at the books she had come to study. But she could not bring herself to leave without some reward for her daring.

Frowning, she glanced at the shelf of texts beyond the starbooks. It was a mixed lot—a stack of crudely bound notebooks piled next to a box of disks whose gold coating was badly chipped, which in turn stood next to a series of photoflashed texts bound in fraying cardboard. Curiously, Silence lifted down the first of the notebooks. To her disappointment, it was written in a script she could not identify. Even when she carried it out to the stronger light of the main corridor, she could not read the crabbed and drastically abbreviated handwriting, though she was able to figure out that the writer had used one of the Hegemonic alphabets. Sighing, she put the notebook back where she had found it, and moved slowly along the shelves.

A tag hanging from one of the photoflashed volumes caught her eye. She could not decipher the numbered code—only the Librarians were allowed fully to understand how the system worked—but a second, once-red label caught her eye. It read, "*/*," the code for information that was both incomplete and invalid. Silence frowned again, more deeply this time. Pilots' texts did not change much over time; the basic principles, in fact, had remained unchanged since the first years of exploration, when mankind had still been confined to Earth, before the Millennial Wars. *I could understand* labeling it incomplete, she thought, but not invalid. Carefully, she pulled the book from its place on the upper shelf and lifted the fragile cover.

The name at the bottom of the title page seemed to leap out at her: *The Masters of the Leading-star*. The Leading-star Guild was the first of the great pilots' guilds that had flourished before the Millennial Wars; it had first codified the system of voidmarks. That system had been superseded in the years since the Wars by the less complicated Cor Tauri system, but Leading-star's accomplishment was still respected. Certainly where pre-War texts like her own *Gilded Stairs* were involved, the Leading-star system was still unmatched.

The rest of the title read, "A Discussion of the Mediate Symbols on the Road of the Perilous Pit." Silence flipped through the text, barely recognizing the voidmarks it described. The article ended abruptly. It was little more than a pamphlet, Silence realized, bound in with a miscellaneous collection of other pamphlets. There was some justification, then, for the magis describing it as both incomplete and invalid.

Idly, she flipped through the next pamphlet—"The Descent of the Moon and the Black Sphinx of Mornag" —and then through two more without seeing anything of particular interest. The final pamphlet was of a different style from the others, with an oddly patterned border. Silence paused to examine it more closely.

The first thing she noticed was the date—206 N.A. She whistled soundlessly at that. Her own *Guilded Stairs*, old as it was, dated only from the year 781 of the New Age reckoning, which counted from the first years of star travel. She glanced quickly at the title. "Maledictions Returned Unto the Maledictor," she read, and, in smaller letters below that flamboyant heading, "A Criticism of Portolan Use, with a Brief Compendium of the New Voidmarks, according to the Masters of the Leading-star." This, then, was a pilot's manual from the very earliest days of star travel. Even though this was only a photoflashed copy, Silence eased her hold on the greying pages.

The printing in the body of the pamphlet was unclear, the lines of type on the underside of the page showing through the thin paper to make the copy almost illegible. Heedless now of the danger of meeting another guide-homunculus, Silence returned to the main corridor, holding the book directly under the central light globe. Now, with an eye-straining effort, she could make out the text. It was a dialogue between two pilots, one of whom was urging the merits of the Leading-star system against the other's "portolan." The teachers at the pilots' school on Cap Bel had never mentioned such a system. Hastily, Silence ran down the list of accepted hieroglyphicas and symbolic systems, then recited the list of the unacceptable systems. None of the names could ever have been a corruption of "portolan."

Frowning thoughtfully, Silence read on. It was hard to follow the debate, founded as it was in an active controversy: the writer rarely bothered to explain any of his terms, or to mention why certain seemingly trivial points were important. But, very slowly, Silence began to make sense of the argument, and felt herself tremble with excitement. As best she could tell from the convoluted debate, the "portolan" was not a system but a thing, or at least a thing as well as a system. It was a book like her own starbooks in that it guided pilots from star system to star system, but completely different in the way in which it worked. Under the Cor Tauri system, and under the Leading-star system, and every other system of voidmarks, the passage through purgatory involved an actual manipulation of the voidmarks. Once the harmonium, its music magnified by the starships' sounding keel, had brought the ship to the twelfth of heaven that marked the beginning of purgatory, the pilot found the appropriate voidmarks for the planets involved, and then took the ship through them. There was an interaction between pilot, ship, and symbol. But using a portolan. . . .

Silence frowned even more deeply, and turned back a few pages to reread the clearest description she had found. If she understood the writer correctly—and infuriatingly, the three charts at the end of the pamplet showed only the Leading-star's standard tables, without the portolan system's drawings for comparison—was little more than a collection of roadmaps. The pilot used the voidmarks as just that, marks by which to steer through the void, rather than allowing the ship to use the power of the symbol. It was no wonder the system had been abandoned, she thought. From the descriptions here, and the first speaker's criticisms, it was clear that this system of star travel was very slow, requiring the pilot to drop out of purgatory at regular intervals to check his position in the mundane universe. But it was the final argument that had really caught her attention.

She turned to those pages and read them again with great attention, fixing the essential details in her memory. The first speaker, an adherent of the Leading-star system, reminded the second pilot that the portolans were almost useless outside the worlds of the Ring, while the Leading-star's voidmarks worked equally well inside or out. The six worlds of the Ring, Silence knew, were the Rose Worlds; the seventh world of the Ring was Earth.

The portolan system worked inside the Rose Worlds, at least, and probably on the Earth road as well. The Rose Worlders' siege engines worked by disrupting the harmonies necessary to the interaction of pilot, ship, and symbol: Silence had learned that much from Isambard even before she came to Solitudo. But the siege engines could not disrupt a ship that used a portolan to steer through purgatory, since no manipulation of the symbols was involved. Silence smiled slowly. If all their other plans failed—if Isambard was unable to break the power of the engines—they might still be able to use this new system to find Earth. If she could obtain a portolan.

Silence's smile faded slightly at the thought. That might not be at all easy, especially since she doubted that any other pilots would recognize the term. She would have to go to the magi, and to the hordes of other scholars who populated the known worlds. More precisely, Isambard would have to approach them— unless, of course, the Library itself possessed one. She turned back to the corridor where she had found the starbooks, hastily sliding the collection of pamphlets back into its place. As she had thought, there was nothing among the row of starbooks but the most ordinary texts. On the other hand, given the Library's unique organization, a portolan might well be kept in some other section, unrecognized for what it was. But it would be better to let Isambard look for that.

Quickly, she set the last starbook back into its place, and retraced her steps to the elemental arts section. There she took a deep breath, shifted a few books in their places, then glanced quickly at her reflection in the dull metal of the shelving to make sure she bore no signs of her unauthorized explorations. Only then did she press the button that summoned the guide-homunculus.

The creature seemed to take hours to answer that call, and when at last it did appear, it traveled so quickly through the maze of corridors that once again Silence was hard put to keep up with it. This time, however, she managed to keep it in sight, and emerged breathless in the lobby. The Librarian gave her a rather sour look from under his thin eyebrows, but Silence ignored him, opening her bag for the homunculus who guarded the tunnel door. The creature gave the starbooks only a cursory inspection, and did not hinder her passage.

Silence made her way through the upper reading room and down the long staircase to the main doors, trying not to hurry. In the main lobby, she paused at one of the long counters to scribble a brief note to Isambard, asking him in veiled terms to meet her at her rooms as soon as possible. She sealed it tightly, fixing the thin tape securely all around the edges. Then, too excited to feel her usual disgust, she stopped at the alcove by the door where a bored apprentice monitored the homunculi the school used to carry messages among the magi, and paid the half-mark fee to send one of the long-legged creatures in search of Isambard. Only then did she allow herself to head back toward her own rooms.

CHAPTER 3

Balthasar and Chase Mago were both in her rooms, Balthasar frowning intently at a dice-board, while Chase Mago stared vaguely out the single window, watching the turning sphere of the day-sky. Both men looked up as the door opened, clearly glad of any break in the monotony of their day, and Balthasar said, "Good news?"

Silence grimaced. "I didn't think I was so transparent."

Chase Mago smiled, saying nothing, and Balthasar said, "Come on, out with it."

Silence nodded, setting her tool bag on the floor at the foot of the bed. The two did need to be told what she had found before Isambard arrived. Quickly, she ran through the important parts of her discovery, unable to resist dwelling on her adventures in the Library itself, and was rewarded by an approving nod from the engineer and a thoughtful whistle from Balthasar.

"A neat trick, if we can manage it," he said, "but it sounds as though you have to spend a lot of time in normal space."

Silence nodded again. "That's the one problem I can see. But if we can't break through the siege engines'

60

interference. . . ." She let her voice trail off as the others nodded.

"If you can get hold of a portolan," Chase Mago murmured.

Silence made a face. She had almost forgotten, in her excitement, that she still had to find one of the ancient mapbooks. More soberly, she said, "The Library may well have one, even though I didn't find it. Isambard can look—he has full access to the catalogues. If nothing else, maybe he can find out something about the principles involved, so maybe we could reconstruct the maps. Anyway, I've asked him to come here as soon as he can."

Balthasar nodded, and swept the dice and counters together off the board. "You know, if we get to Earth, we can ask for whatever we want from the Hegemon. I bet he'd be only too glad to forget about that mailship, and one minor midshipman, as long as we told him how we did it."

Chase Mago laughed softly, but before he could say anything, there was a knock at the door. Silence called, "Who's there?"

"Isambard." Before Silence could move to undo the latch, the door flew open and the magus stepped into the room.

Out of the corner of her eye, Silence saw Balthasar sigh deeply and slip his heylin back into the pocket of his coat. Her own heart was racing painfully. "What is this, Isambard?" she demanded. "My message wasn't that urgent."

Isambard glanced at her with a brief, puzzled frown. "I didn't get any message from you," he said. "I came to tell you that we have to leave Solitudo at once. The Hegemon is circulating an inquiry, and the description is—accurate."

Balthasar cursed softly, and Chase Mago said, "How long do we have?"

"No time at all," Isambard said grimly. "Get your things together now. We'll leave at once—"

"Wait a minute," Silence said. Isambard glanced at her again, then looked away. "Listen to me," Silence said, more sharply this time, and the magus stopped, turning to consider her with a visible effort.

"I've found something very important in the Library," Silence said, looking for words that would catch the magus's attention at once. "A new way of reaching Earth."

"Ah?" Isambard's sudden interest would have been comic, Silence thought sourly, in other circumstances. "Yes. Do you know anything about a thing called a portolan?"

The magus shook his head.

Hastily, Silence explained again about the pamphlet she had found, adding, "If we can't break the siege engines—and you said there'd be trouble, since I'm only a practitioner—a portolan should give us a way around the blockage."

Isambard hesitated an instant longer, then nodded once, decisively. "Very well," he said, and allowed the deceptively battered carryall to slip from his shoulders. "Take this with you, then. I will check the Library catalogues, and join you at the starport as soon as I'm finished with that."

"It's another four hours before we can lift," Balthasar said. "And that's assuming we can get a place at the head of the liftoff queue."

"Do your best, captain," Isambard said. He looked at Silence. "They will think twice before questioning me—at least on Solitudo!—but you are another matter entirely. You must leave the compound at once."

"All right," Silence said. Across the room, Chase Mago was already throwing her belongings into the nearest carryall. "But where—?"

Before she could finish the question, the magus had vanished. Silence swore softly to herself and turned to help the engineer, saying, "And where do we go once we get off-world?"

Balthasar shrugged, staring again out the narrow window that overlooked the courtyard. "Anywhere. Leave that to me, Silence. I've had plenty of practice——" He broke off abruptly, still staring out the window. Silence frowned, and moved to look over his shoulder. In the court below, a tallish man in magus's robes was talking with one of the apprentices, who frowned, then pointed to the window where the two stood. Silence swore again.

"I can't disobey a direct summons, not without convicting myself or losing my license. We've got to get out of here."

Balthasar nodded grimly. "Your books?"

"I have them." Silence ran her gaze rapidly around the room. There was nothing else here that she could not do without, though she would be sorry to leave some of it. . . . There was no time for regrets. She caught up her own carryall, and then, with an effort, lifted Isambard's heavy bag. Chase Mago stuffed a final shirt into the half-empty carryall, and latched it.

"Come on," Balthasar said, and opened the door.

Silence darted past him, already aware of the presence moving slowly up the main stairs, and beckoned for the others to follow her down the back stairway. She had never been so glad of its existence. The others followed more cautiously, Chase Mago pausing briefly to lock the door behind him. At the bottom of the staircase, Silence started to push open that door, but Balthasar pulled her back.

"Wait," he said. "Take off that damn smock." He was shrugging off his own coat as he spoke. Silence, not fully understanding, pulled the loose shirt over her head, and took the coat from Balthasar.

"Put it on," Balthasar hissed. "And the cap. You want to look like a star-traveller again."

Silence did as she was told, stuffing the discarded

apprentice's uniform into her bag on top of the starbooks. Balthasar's coat was too big, the sleeves falling almost to her knuckles, but there was no time to adjust that now. Already, she could hear movement at the top of the stairs. The others heard it, too. Chase Mago cursed softly and snatched up Isambard's bag, motioning for the others to hurry. Silence abandoned her attempt to turn back the cuffs and pushed open the door, blinking as she stepped out into the fading light. The night-sky was rising rapidly but, as Balthasar had said, it was another four hours before any starships could begin leaving Solitudo, and six hours before most of them would be willing to try it. She glanced quickly around—there was no one in sight, not even a wandering apprentice to notice their hurried departure—and started quickly for the main gate, Chase Mago at her heels. Almost at once, she stopped: Balthasar was still standing in the open door, bending over the lock. Silence hesitated, not wanting to shout. The Delian straightened, slamming the door behind him, and loped after them, waving for them to keep moving.

"What the hell?" Silence demanded as he joined them.

"I jammed the lock mechanism," Balthasar answered, grinning. "Should slow down even a magus. With luck, he'll think it's been jammed for a while."

Silence gave the captain a dubious look—the magi were better than Balthasar was inclined to admit—but when there was no sign of pursuit, she slowed her steps a little, adjusting the sleeves of the borrowed coat.

"And now, Denis?" Chase Mago asked.

Silence grinned at the engineer's tone. Chase Mago sounded as wary as she felt about Balthasar's improvised plans. Of course, Balthasar was rather good at improvisation—it was just unfortunate that he had to do it so often.

Balthasar shrugged. "Get back to the ship, see how early we can get in the queue. We can probably have

the leading place, if we're willing to go as soon as the
window opens. Then we wait for the magus. What else
can we do?" He gave Silence an appraising glance, and
added, "Put on that cap you were wearing before.
You'll have to pass for an apprentice—one of ours, I
mean, not one of theirs. And rub some dirt on your
hands—your face, too."

Silence grimaced at the arbitrary orders, but Chase
Mago rummaged in the bags he carried until he found
the cap, and handed it to her. Silence jammed it tightly
on her head, then, reluctantly, stooped and caught up a
handful of dirt, rubbing it on her hands and then smear-
ing dirty fingers across her forehead. Balthasar nodded
approvingly. "We'll leave by the servants' gate," he
said. "No sense attracting undue attention."

"Do we have a story?" Chase Mago asked mildly.

Balthasar grimaced, and Silence said, "You've made
a delivery here, haven't picked up work, and are trying
to make another contract back in the Fringe."

"Sounds good to me," Balthasar said, and Chase Mago
nodded.

They were approaching the busier parts of the teaching compound, and Silence fought the urge to hide her
face. It would only look furtive, she told herself. No
one has seen you in anything but an apprentice's robes;
no one will recognize you. She forced herself to look
around boldly, staring up at the twenty-story height of
the Library, then gaping like any stranger at the school
buildings and at the black-robed passersby. A few she
recognized—magi that she knew by sight—but none
gave her a second glance. Still, it was a relief to leave
the well-travelled walkways for the dreary paths that
ran behind the servants' barracks.

The servants' gate was always locked, and there was
no attendant on duty. Silence glanced warily at the
others, wondering if the servants had already been
warned to stop her. Balthasar made a disgusted face,

and Chase Mago muttered, "It's always the same. When you want them, they aren't here."

Balthasar grunted agreement, and reached for the bell that hung beside the locked gate. He shook it vigorously, and then, when nothing happened, shook it again. After what seemed a very long time, a door opened in the nearest barracks, and a man came out, half a sandwich held in his teeth as he shrugged awkwardly into his coat.

"Caught me at lunch," he explained, taking the sandwich out of his mouth just in time. Shrewd eyes flicked from Balthasar to Chase Mago to Silence, then back, with veiled approval, to Balthasar. "Transport to the port, sieuri?"

"That's right," Balthasar said.

The servant nodded again, and passed his hand across a square of cloudy glass set into the wall beside the gateposts. After a while, a square of brighter turf between two of the barracks lifted almost noiselessly, and a four-legged transport flat—a smaller version, with seats, of the cargo flats Silence had ridden before—plodded slowly into sight. The servant touched another square of glass, opening the gate itself, and said to the flat, "These gentlemen are going to the port."

"Main terminal," Balthasar added, and the servant said, "Take them to the main terminal."

The controlling head, set low between the first pair of legs, gave no sign of having understood, but Balthasar swung himself into the padded seat without hesitation. Chase Mago tossed his bags into the space between the seats, while Silence scrambled up beside Balthasar. She braced herself against the footrail and held out a hand to Chase Mago. Nodding his thanks, the engineer pulled himself up behind them, just as the flat began to move.

The ride to the port complex was something of an anticlimax. They passed only a couple of other flats on the road, both heavy transports, their beds piled high with cargo. Inside the port itself the workers were too busy preparing for the liftoff window to spare them more than a cursory glance. Nevertheless, Balthasar insisted on going alone to the astrologers' offices in the main complex, and Silence was just as happy to let him. She and Chase Mago made their way through the maze of enclosed walkways to the shed where *Recusante* was docked. The walks, only partly protected from the day-sky's heat, were uncomfortably warm, and Silence did not dare take off the disguising coat. It was a relief to climb down into the cool dimness of the docking shed, but she did not remove the coat until she was inside the ship itself.

Chase Mago vanished immediately into the engine room, leaving Silence alone in the common area. Sighing, Silence switched on the tea machine, and settled herself to wait, leafing slowly through her starbooks. She could do nothing to plot a course until someone told her where they were going. Still, there were some obvious destinations—Delos or the Madakh in the Fringe, Naryx or Astapa in the Hegemony—where they could lose themselves among the hordes of other star-travellers, and still be in a good position to make the attempt on Earth. Idly, she turned to the tables in the *Speculum Astronomi*, looking for the roads leading from Solitudo to the various planets, but set the book aside as soon as Chase Mago's huge form appeared in the hatchway.

"Is everything all right?"

"Fine," the engineer answered. "All my boards show orange. We'll be ready whenever Denis—or Isam-bard—is." He drew himself a cup of tea from the machine on the bulkhead and seated himself at the table, staring into the depths of the mug.

"There's something wrong," Silence said.

Chase Mago grimaced. "I don't like this bargain. I never have. And we should've settled on a destination before Denis split off, so you and I could be doing something useful."

Silence nodded her agreement. The engineer was

right, on all counts. Before she could say anything,
however, the faint noise of the curtain bells sounded
through the open hatch. Though it could only be
Balthasar, Silence felt a knot of fear in her stomach.
Chase Mago rose quickly and headed for the main
hatch. Silence followed him, reaching into the pocket of
Balthasar's coat for the heylin he had left there. The
touchplate was comfortingly warm under her thumb: a
full charge, then, she thought. Balthasar never carried
anything smaller than a ten-shot, which should be more
than sufficient to deal with any intruders. . . .

It was Balthasar, of course. He grinned cheerfully up
at them from the bottom of the cradle stairs. Silence
sighed deeply, and stood aside to let the captain into
the corridor, letting the heylin drop to her side. Balthasar
raised an eyebrow, seeing the weapon.

"You were expecting trouble?" he asked.

In the same moment, Chase Mago said, "So where
are we going, Denis?"

Balthasar glanced over his shoulder as he headed for
the common room. "The Madakh, I thought—at least
officially."

Silence said sharply, "What do you mean, officially?"

Balthasar grinned, but said nothing. In the common
room, he headed for the tea machine and drew himself
a mug, then seated himself comfortably at the table. At
last, he said, "We have to go into the dead roads
anyway to get to Earth, right?"

Silence nodded. The dead roads were relics of the
Millennial Wars, roads which had been abandoned and
then forgotten because the planets to which they had
once led had been destroyed. Wrath-of-God had used
those roads for their own purposes, and Balthasar, who
had been a pilot for the pirate combine, knew them
well enough. "And the departure course for the Madakh
coincides with one for the dead roads?"

"You got it." Balthasar reached into his trouser pocket,
and brought out a much-folded sheet of paper. Silence

took it, unfolding it carefully to study the neatly jotted formulae. After a moment, she reached for her *Gilded Stairs*, turning to the supplement to find the matching formulae, then back to the main tables to find the voidmarks for Decelea. The table listed an unfamiliar road, the Salamander's Path. Silence frowned, flipping through the pages to find the half-page miniature and three-line commentary that described the voidmarks. Decelea had been destroyed, and the destruction of the planet had irrevocably distorted the voidmarks of all the roads leading to that planet. It would be nearly impossible to learn the road from the elaborate image of the *Gilded Stairs*.

"Denis, have you flown the Salamander's Path?" she asked.

"Not by that name," Balthasar answered. Silence held out the starbook, and the Delian's expression changed. "But I've flown that one, yes. The Fire-Lizard, we called it. It hasn't changed that much, compared to some of the others. The flames look higher—you have to fly through them to reach the dragon's head—and the tail's twisted, kinked up, almost. But that's all."

Silence gave him a sour look—that was a fairly substantial change—but closed the book again and tucked it under her arm. "I'll be in my cabin, then," she said. Balthasar nodded, his attention already returning to the departure course.

Silence closed the cabin door behind her, and then, after a moment's thought, latched it. It had been months since she had calculated a course or learned a set of voidmarks; she would need both time and absolute privacy to do her work properly. The narrow cabin, unused since the first flight to Solitudo Hermae, was chill and oddly musty. Frowning, Silence flipped on the monitor console that dominated one bulkhead, adjusting the ventilators, then seated herself cross-legged on the bunk, the starbook open in her lap.

The image seemed to leap out at her. A clawed

lizard, its spine patterned with stars, lay comfortably in the heart of a roaring fire, looking up with sleepy, golden eyes. The multiple symbolism flooded her mind. The salamander was rebirth and control in passion. It was another symbol for elemental fire, and for the suit of wands. It was also mastery, and could even be the symbol of ecstatic saints. . . . Silence swore softly and looked away.

All of those meanings were present in the salamander, and were necessary for a magus, but they were less than useless for a pilot. She set the book aside for a moment, rubbed her eyes hard, then forced herself to concentrate on a pilot's discipline. It was the problem of the gate that was not a gate, and that was all it could be. The voidmarks were merely voidmarks, not greater symbols. She took a deep breath, and looked back at the picture.

Slowly, the pilots' meaning came clear. The Salamander's Path was a simple enough road, at least in its original form, the course plain along the back of the lizard, following the star-shaped markings. The flames symbolized dangerous dissonance to either side of the road, to be avoided at all cost, but the salamander was a promise that the central path was perfectly safe. She studied it for a few minutes longer, until she was certain she had a clear picture of her course, then closed the book again.

That was still only the original form of the road, and Balthasar's verbal description was no real substitute for a good set of drawings. She stilled that negative thought and shut her eyes, trying to remember exactly what Balthasar had said about the changed road. The flames were higher—only to be expected, she thought, with the destruction of Decelea still echoing through the star system—and the ship had to fly through them to reach the salamander's head and the first voidmark. That would be the trickiest part, and she would need Chase Mago's help if the ship's keel were not to be damaged by the howling dissonances. Then, Balthasar had said, the tail was kinked. . . . Probably another sign of the increased dissonance, Silence decided, but less dangerous than the higher flames. It was simply a further indication that she would have to be precise. She kept her eyes closed a moment longer, picturing the route in detail, then opened them and stretched slowly. The chronometer on the monitor showed that nearly three hours had passed.

Silence grimaced, and set the *Gilded Stairs* on the shelf above the bunk. She hesitated a moment, then lifted the other starbooks from the carryall and set them beside the *Gilded Stairs*, closing the guardrail across them. Her shipsuits, the specially treated bodysuits worn to hide some of the more disturbing effects of purgatory, were still folded neatly in the storage cell. She pulled one on, fighting the clinging fabric, and shoved the others back into the cell, throwing the bag on top of them. Then she unlocked the cabin door and stepped out into the companionway. The main hatch was still propped open a few centimeters, the entry bell hanging from the inner face. Apparently Isambard had not yet come aboard. Silence shrugged to herself and went on into the common area.

Balthasar and Chase Mago were sitting at the table, both also wearing their shipsuits. They looked up as she came in, and Balthasar said, "Where the hell is he? I should've known better than to get a spot at the head of the queue—"

"Relax, Denis," Chase Mago said, and Silence said, in the same moment, "He'll be here, worse luck."

"You said it, not me," Balthasar muttered, but subsided again, staring into his tea.

"We're at the head of the queue?" Silence asked after a moment, and looked at Chase Mago.

The engineer nodded. "But there's another hour before the tow boss shows up to drag the cradle. And we can cancel, if we have to."

Silence nodded, though she knew Chase Mago was really talking to Balthasar. Balthasar made a face, but before he could say anything, there was a noise from outside. Silence jumped in spite of herself, and Balthasar jerked around in his seat. "Curtain bells," Chase Mago said succinctly, and headed for the main hatch.

Silence started to follow, but Balthasar caught her arm. "Wait, put on your coat."

"Damn," Silence said, and took the heavy garment. As she shrugged it on, she thought, I'll have to be more careful. It was harder than she had expected to remember that she was passing as a man now, and that everything depended on passing successfully. She fastened the last clip, and hurried out into the corridor.

Isambard was already aboard, half hidden behind Chase Mago's height as the three men came back toward the common area. Balthasar brought up the rear, scowling irritably at the release of tension. That was a predictable reaction, Silence thought, but she was careful to hide her grin as she asked, "Any luck with portolan, Isambard?"

The magus shook his head. The lines that marked his face seemed starkly apparent, and Silence gave him a worried look. "Is something wrong?" she asked.

The magus sighed, and seated himself carefully at the table. Really alarmed now, Silence gestured for Chase Mago to get him a cup of tea, ignoring Balthasar's gesture of annoyance. Isambard took the huge mug gratefully, inhaling the steam with an expression of contentment. Silence waited, and after a moment, the magus said, "As I told you, the Hegemon is circulating an inquiry regarding a non-Misthian woman pilot who may be showing anomalous abilities." He looked up, and even managed a rather weary smile. "His Most Serene Majesty alleges piracy and murder against this person."

Balthasar said, "Will we be able to get off-planet, magus, or will your people be searching the ships?"

"My people?" the magus asked.

Balthasar made a face. "Your security, whatever you call them."

Isambard shook his head. "Not yet. I was able to avoid any direct inquiry, as you were, Silence. They will wait until they are certain we're not somewhere in the compound before they take so drastic a step. Indeed, I do not believe they have decided on any official course of action as yet. The majority are simply curious about the affair."

Silence sighed softly. For once things were working out the way they had planned. Aloud, she said, "But you weren't able to find a portolan?"

"I do not believe—no, I am certain the Library does not contain one," Isambard answered. "There are other possibilities—Inarime, for example." He paused, looking expectantly at Silence.

The pilot frowned, then remembered. Inarime's satrap owned a collection of ancient texts that rivaled many a magus's. "The satrap's supposed to be particularly interested in old documents."

Isambard nodded. "I suggest, however, that we postpone any visit to Inarime—or any other attempt to find a portolan—until after we've tried conventional methods. I need not stress how important it's become that we find Earth."

Silence nodded, almost to herself. The Hegemon was after blood: they had escaped his geas, stolen a ship, killed one of his nobles—though admittedly a minor one—and in general proved that it was possible to defy the Hegemon and live. They would need something of very great value indeed if they were to obtain his pardon—but, as Balthasar had said, the secret of the Earth road should be enough.

Chase Mago said, "I hope his Serene Majesty will be willing to bargain."

Isambard cocked his head to one side, and smiled

very slightly. "I think he will be. Indeed, I am quite certain of it. He would not dare to do otherwise."

"You hope," Balthasar growled. He stood abruptly. "Be that as it may, Silence, you and I had better get up to control and make the final checks." He gave the magus a final baleful glance, and added, "Especially since we're at the head of the departure queue."

"Relax, Denis," Chase Mago said. There was a note in his voice that suggested he had said the same thing a hundred times already, and Silence didn't bother to hide an affectionate grin.

"Plenty of time, Denis," she said. Nevertheless, she followed the captain forward to the lower bridge, settling herself in the second pilot's couch.

Recusante's lower bridge was even less comfortable than it had been before the massive refit. The newer, more sensitive musonar complex was shoehorned in between the triple display screens and the keyboard that gave the pilots minimal control of the harmonium's pitch. Still, it was good to be back on a starship's bridge again, especially *Black Dolphin*'s. Silence felt her eyes fill with tears, and she looked away. Balthasar said nothing, concentrating on his own boards as he flipped the switches that powered up the various instruments. After a moment, Silence got herself back under control, and reached to activate the secondary controls. "I'm all right now," she said softly. "Thanks, Denis."

Balthasar shrugged, then gave her a quirky smile. "Good to have you back," he said.

"Thanks," Silence said again, then forced herself to be professional. "You'll handle the liftoff?"

Balthasar nodded. "It's a short run-up to the twelfth," he said. "There's nothing much out here to interfere with the celestial harmonies."

"I'll be ready," Silence said, a little grimly. Privately, she could not help being a little nervous. It had been months since she had last taken a ship through purgatory, and she could not help wondering if the rudiments of a magus's learning would help or hinder her. But then she put that thought firmly aside. She was a pilot; she could—she would—fly the ship.

A light flashed on the communications panel above Balthasar's head, and the Delian reached quickly to flip the switch that lit the viewscreens. "*Recusante.*"

"*Recusante*, this is your tow boss," an unfamiliar voice said. The triple screen showed only the folds of the baffle curtains. The tow had to be sitting outside, Silence thought.

"Are you ready for us?" the tow boss went on.

"One moment," Balthasar said, and flipped a second set of switches, cutting the outside transmitter and opening the inships channel. "Julie, the tow's here. Are you set?"

Chase Mago answered, "Everything's amber. I can give you systems power any time, and I'll go to green on your word."

"Go ahead with both," Balthasar answered. "Isambard, we're beginning liftoff procedures. I suggest you go to your cabin—the one you had before—and strap down. This is likely to be rough." He cut the internal channel without waiting for an answer from the magus, and waited until a new line of lights flared first amber, then green across his boards, before opening the outside line again. "We're ready here, tow. Come on in."

"Confirmed." In the right-hand screen, Silence saw the baffle curtain move slowly back, drawn by a homunculus the size of a small monkey. The tug, sitting squat and powerful atop its treads, looked like an ordinary machine from any of the human-settled worlds, though a little larger, but Silence knew perfectly well that its power came from homunculi walking an endless internal treadmill. She shook her head, and turned her attention to the lights winking along her boards.

"I show full systems power, Denis," she said.

"Right," Balthasar said, and flipped the switch for the inships transmitter. "All set, Julie?"

"All set below," Chase Mago answered over the rising note of the harmonium. Silence shivered at the familiar sound.

"I'm releasing the cradle lock," Balthasar announced, and threw five switches in quick succession, leaving a trail of orange lights across one section of his board. He touched another switch, and said, "Tow, I've released the cradle lock. You can link when ready."

"Thank you, *Recusante*," the tow boss answered, and cut his transmission.

In the screen, Silence watched as more homunculi, spindly, delicate-looking things, with oversized hands to manipulate the tow hooks, swarmed from the tow itself, and began to attach the hooks. Balthasar, watching, shook his head.

"Damned expensive equipment."

Homunculi were expensive to grow, and even more expensive to teach. Even these specialized creatures, capable of only a single act, would cost tens of thousands of Delian pounds apiece on the Fringe Worlds. But then, this was Solitudo Hermae, and the magi looked after their own. Silence said, "The magi don't want anybody using mechanics here and polluting the harmonies. The adepts have to grow them as part of their training."

Balthasar grunted, then winced as the larger of the two homunculi jostled the cradle. Silence barely noticed. There was one advantage to leaving Solitudo now, she realized, and that realization made her smile rather ruefully. She would not have to grow a homunculus herself. That could be either good or bad—after all, having to tend one of the creatures through the long stages of its growth might cure her dislike of them once and for all— but she was just as glad to have avoided it.

The ship jerked, and Silence shot a quick look at the screens. The hookup was complete, and the tow was moving slowly out of the berth, dragging the cradle with it. The cradle jerked again, and Balthasar muttered a curse. Then it settled to a gentle swaying, and the captain relaxed. Cradle and tow moved toward the massive doors of the docking shed, which opened slowly at their approach. The cradle bounced once, and then they had left the dock and turned ponderously down the long taxiway leading to the launch table.

It was still very light outside, though the shadows were lengthening. Silence touched the keys that would adjust the exterior cameras, switching from one to another until she could get a picture of the sky. The image dimmed hastily, blocking out most of the light, but Silence could still see that the night-sky had only just reached the zenith above the port complex.

"Cutting it a little close, aren't we?" she asked.

"Just a little," Balthasar agreed. His smile was utterly without humor. "But we should be all right."

Silence settled back in her couch, trying to loosen the growing tension in her arms and neck. *I wonder if I secured everything in my cabin?* she wondered suddenly. All they would need, after a difficult lift and a short run-up to purgatory, was to have all the unsecured items in the ship start wandering about, looking for their functionally proper place as the harmonium stimulated the minute amounts of celestial material present in all things. But it was too late to worry about that now.

The tow reached the launch table at last, and turned slowly in its tracks, dragging the cradle around until *Recusante*'s bow was pointing toward the rising night-sky. Balthasar watched his own directional readouts, and signaled the tow boss as soon as the ship was lined up along the path laid out by the astrologers in the tower. The tow boss gave a signal, and the homunculi detached the tow from the cradle, then climbed onto the tow for the short ride to the bunkers. Balthasar ignored them, switching on the Ficinan display that stood between the two consoles. The projection globes dimmed, then brightened, showing the harmonic envelope, the *musica mundana*, surrounding the planet. Balthasar fiddled with the controls, refining the area displayed, and Silence shook her head at the swirling, multicolored dissonances. Most of it was caused by heat leakage from the day-sky: there were no other planets, or even a natural sun, to interfere with Solitudo's own harmony. The edge of the day-sky was sharply delineated, but even as she watched, that brilliant wedge of color slid from the globe, leaving only lighter streaks and whorls in its wake.

Those smaller streaks were dangerous enough, representing dissonances and pockets of interference that could easily tear a ship apart, or so distort her tuning that she could never reach purgatory, and would wander lost in the immense distances between the stars. Silence glanced nervously at Balthasar, and saw her own fears reflected in his face. Then the speaker chimed twice, and the Delian visibly shook away his worries, reaching for the switches that controlled the communications console.

"*Recusante.*"

Silence reached for her headset and eased it into place, feeling singularly useless. Under normal circumstances, communication with the planetary authority was her responsibility, but to speak now would be to betray the presence of a woman pilot aboard *Recusante*, and alert the very people she was trying to avoid. Still, it was a strange and frustrating experience to listen to Port Control's brief checkup without responding.

In the Ficinan model, the flaring dissonance was fading a little, easing to tolerable levels through the lower forty-five degrees of sky. Balthasar took a deep breath, just as Port Control announced, "*Recusante*, interference levels have dropped to acceptable levels for a low-line lift."

Balthasar touched the button for the in-ships speaker. "All secure below, Julie?"

"All secure," Chase Mago answered.

Silence glanced quickly at her own boards. The lights
all showed green, except for the double row of lights
that showed the harmonium's status. Those lights glowed
orange. Chase Mago had already tuned the harmonium
to its highest settings, ready to override as much of the
interference as possible. Automatically, Silence adjusted
the pilots' keyboard to match the changed settings.
Balthasar nodded, and flipped a last series of switches
on the communications console. "Solitudo Control, this
is *Recusante*." His voice sounded very calm, almost
bored. Silence glanced at his hands, and saw that they
were trembling. Balthasar stilled them with an effort,
and continued, "We're ready to lift."

"You may lift when ready, *Recusante*. Good voyage."

Despite the friendly words, Solitudo Control sounded
distinctly uninterested in their welfare. Balthasar grimaced, and said, "First sequence, Julie."

"Coming up," Chase Mago answered. The harmonium's music rose steadily as he spoke, sending a sympathetic shudder through the hull. Then the engineer
opened the last stops, and with a second, greater shudder, the ship lifted from its cradle. It rose very slowly,
Balthasar's hands busy on his keyboard, shaping the
enveloping sound to steer a flattened course toward
that section of the night-sky low on the horizon where
the interference appeared lightest. The harmonium
wailed, the music of the planet and the celestial harmonies that lifted the ship in painful conflict. Silence,
slammed against the back of her couch by a crushing
weight, fought to reach her own keyboard to correct the
rising dissonance, but Chase Mago was there before
her. The pitch shifted subtly, easing to a different note,
and the worst of the interference faded, leaving only a
nagging whine just at the edge of hearing. Silence
turned her head painfully, saw that the interference
indicator was showing, the column of light flickering
just below the danger line. She said, raising her voice
to be heard over the harmonium's noise, "Denis—"

Balthasar said, "I hear. Numbers?"

"Five-nine," Silence answered, struggling for breath. "Six now."

Balthasar swore softly, eyes darting from his viewscreens to the Ficinan model and the musonar display, and back to the viewscreens. Silence followed his glance, recognizing his dilemma. Balthasar had chosen a shallow course, one that closely followed the curve of the planet before finally rising through the shell of air at a point of lesser interference. On any other planet, it would have been the best choice, with solar and related systemic harmonies to counteract the pervasive music of the planet itself. But Solitudo Hermae, with neither sun nor sister worlds to modulate the music of its core, was setting up a greater interference than he had expected. Though the harmonium had been able to lift the ship, it had been unable fully to establish its protective field.

Chase Mago's voice sounded in the headphones. "Pull out now, Denis?" Despite his size and strength, the engineer sounded faintly breathless.

Balthasar hesitated a moment longer, eyes roving across his board. "We go. Silence, help me."

Silence cast a last glance at the Ficinan model—the globe was filled with reddish swirls like frozen whirlpools, heat leaking from the fixed fire of the day-sky—then fastened her attention on the multiple interference gauges. Raising her voice to carry over the noise of the harmonium, she began to recite the shifting numbers. Balthasar listened a moment longer, choosing his time, then said, "Now, Julie!"

The harmonium roared as Chase Mago opened all the stops, cutting in the upper register for a brief instant. *Recusante* trembled, then rose under Balthasar's sure handling. The crushing weight vanished abruptly, the harmonium at last overriding the planetary music. Light flared once around the ship as it burst through the layer of interference, and then they were free of Solitudo.

Hastily, Chase Mago stopped down the harmonium, closing off the upper register. The ship steadied to the normal music of interstellar flight, which faded rapidly as the celestial harmonies asserted themselves.

Solitudo Control said placidly, "*Recusante*, we confirm a successful liftoff."

"Acknowledged," Balthasar said, busy with his own readouts, and then the contact was lost.

"Nice work," Silence said, and meant it. Even if it had been an avoidable crisis—and she was not convinced that it had been—it had still been a pretty piece of flying. There was a noticeable lack of response from the engine room.

After a moment, Balthasar looked up from his controls. He gave Silence a wry smile, and flicked the switch for the in-ships channel. "All right, Julie, I blew it. But we're still in one piece, aren't we?"

"No thanks to you," Chase Mago said, but he sounded mollified by the apology. "I could've overloaded the entire system, blown out every pipe we have, cutting in the upper register so far below purgatory."

There wasn't any answer to that, Silence thought, except a further apology. She looked curiously at Balthasar, but the captain showed no inclination to respond. There was nothing she could say, either. Sighing, she settled back in her couch to wait for the ship to reach the twelfth of heaven.

As Balthasar had warned, it was not long before the distant stars began to show the faint coronae that marked the transition to purgatory. Silence unstrapped herself from her couch, and pulled herself up the ladder to the upper bridge. Her feet and hands clung slightly to the rungs, so that she had to make an effort to pull herself loose. It was a common effect of purgatory, usually too familiar to notice. After so long planetside, Silence savored it.

Already, the dome of the upper bridge was fading to translucence, the ringed stars showing faintly through the specially treated material. Hastily, Silence took her place before the control wheel, working her feet into the depressions on the platform in front of it. The status lights glowed amber along the main spoke.

Despite the change of name, the massive refit done with Isambard's money, the upper bridge remained *Black Dolphin's*. Silence stood very still, momentarily overwhelmed by a sense of time askew. Nothing had changed. The pilot's bridge remained exactly as it had been a year ago, when she had been a mere pilot working for her grandfather and uncle. It was almost startling when Balthasar's voice sounded in her ears.

"Silence? We're ready to switch to the upper register— properly, this time."

Silence shook herself and reached quickly for the lock. "Ready on the bridge," she said.

"Ready below," Chase Mago said.

"Go ahead, all," Balthasar said.

"Switching now," the engineer announced.

The keelsong changed, broadening, adding whole octaves and less-human scales. The last shadow of the pilot's dome vanished, and in the same instant Silence flipped off the lock, the wheel moving freely under her hand. It moved too freely, and the void was suddenly full of signs and images, a hundred different symbols obscuring the central, necessary salamander. Silence gasped and looked away, only to see still more symbols wreathing the blood-laced bones of her hands, moving in the shadowy depths of her own flesh. She cried out, startled and yet enthralled, her hands jerking on the wheel. The symbols darted through and along the blood vessels, coiled around bones and nestled in muscle and cartilage. . . .

The keelsong rose, shifted further to a note of strain and then active protest. Silence forced herself to look out again, to confront the shifting images and close them out, seeking only the voidmarks, her voidmarks, and nothing more. Slowly, the chaos faded, resolving itself into the expected image. The salamander lay in the heart of flame, no longer the sleepy-eyed, benign creature of the starbook, but a demi-dragon, its mouth half open to engulf *Recusante*. Silence swore, suddenly aware of Balthasar's voice in her earphones. Cautiously, she shifted the wheel—it moved more stiffly now, its symbolic linkages fully engaged at last—pulling the ship up and back, away from the open mouth. The keelsong eased a little, but there was still a raggedness, a note that pulsed with the movement of the flames that swept past the salamander's head. *Recusante* was moving very fast. There was no time to choose a safe course through that illusory fire. Silence braced herself and eased the wheel farther over, bringing the ship up to skim the salamander's nose. There was a great shriek of song, the keel crying its protest in curious harmony. Then they were through the flames, sliding with sudden leisure down the salamander's star-dappled spine.

Cautiously, Silence loosened her hold on the wheel, only too aware of the lack of comment from the others. Her piloting had been appalling, and she could only begin to guess why. Her half-finished training was the main cause, no doubt; the magi had taught her to see, but not how to be willfully blind. Even as she thought that, the ghostly symbols reappeared—cup and sword, rose and lily, horned moon and ringed planet—dancing just out of her line of vision, threatening to seduce her from her work. With an effort that was almost painful, Silence ignored them, concentrating instead on her proper voidmarks. The salamander's back stretched smooth before her. She forced herself to see every scale, to examine each tongue of flame as it curled up from beneath the lizard's belly. Slowly, the intrusive symbols faded again.

Silence took a deep breath. If she could not control her own perceptions, she would be useless as a pilot. . . . She suppressed that thought, reciting the pilots cantrips under her breath, until not even the shadow of an extraneous mark remained to distract her. Then, with exquisite care, she looked around again.

The Salamander's Path was a short road. Already, the lizard's spine sloped sharply down to the tail, the safe course almost obliterated by leaping flames. They arched over the tail, met and merged to form a tunnel of fire through which *Recusante* must pass. Silence could feel the illusory heat on her face, was dazzled by its light. Balthasar had warned her that the tail was kinked, somewhere here, but she could not see farther than a ship-length into the fiery tunnel. Muttering a curse, she shifted the wheel to its left, easing the ship onto the line of stars that marked the salamander's spine and the center of the safe path. The heat was growing stronger, but Silence did not dare lift a hand to wipe her sweating face. The opening in the wall of flame seemed impossibly small.

Then *Recusante* entered the tunnel of fire. Silence's world narrowed to the flames above and to either side, and the scaled tail that was her only link with safety. The flames seemed to be closing in, and the tail itself was glowing as though made of metal. Silence cursed softly, unable for a moment to decide between risking the dissonances of the fire or the unknown dangers of the glowing tail, then brought the ship lower, so that the keel was almost touching the salamander's scales. The heat grew worse, as though the lizard were hotter than the flames, but the keelsong stayed true and clear.

As abruptly as Balthasar had said, the tail dipped and swerved to the right, the flames closing to an impossibly tiny opening. Silence had been watching for that kink in the path, but it was only a pilot's instinctive reaction that saved her. She brought the ship up a hair, then put the wheel hard over to thread the needle's eye. The harmonium wailed a protest, and a surge of distant music shook the starship from bow to stern. Then at last they were free of the fire, sailing down the fading tip of the salamander's tail toward the twelfth of heaven and the mundane universe. The pitch changed as Chase Mago closed the stops of the upper register, and the dome of the upper bridge clouded, solidity returning.

Balthasar said, sounding faintly breathless, "I have the con."

"You have it," Silence acknowledged, and snapped on the locks. After her erratic piloting, she had no desire to return to the lower bridge, to face Balthasar's questions and criticism—or worse, his pity, but to navigate Decelea's broken system successfully, the Delian would need her help. Reluctantly, she slid down the ladder, glancing from the Ficinan model to the musonar's display even before she landed. Balthasar, absorbed in the effort of controlling the ship against the dissonances of the system, did not even look up as Silence took her place in the left-hand couch.

From the musonar, it looked as though Balthasar was aiming for the nearest clear area, well outside the slowly pulsing rings of interference that marked the spot where Decelea had been destroyed. Something—the passage through purgatory or the music of Decelea's system— had untuned one of the captain's preset harmonies, setting one note sharp and sour. Automatically, Silence adjusted that, and felt the harmonium ease a little. Balthasar nodded his thanks.

Silence smiled, too busy monitoring the various readouts to manage a better answer. At last, *Recusante* slid into the dead spot, shielded from the last echoes of long-vanished siege engines by the music of Decelea's sister planets. Balthasar adjusted his own controls, locking the harmonium to a note that would hold *Recusante* to this position, and leaned back in his couch.

"What a ride," he said.

Silence flushed and looked away. After a moment, Balthasar went on, "Are you all right?" There were worlds of meaning in his tone.

Silence frowned irritably. "Of course I am. . . ." Her

voice trailed off as she saw the look of concern on Balthasar's face. It was not unreasonable of him to ask, since he was nominally captain, and the back-up pilot, and risking his life, but there was more than merely professional worry in his eyes. She managed a wry smile. "It's been a while since last I took anything through purgatory, that's all. It's harder just to see the voidmarks, without pulling in other symbols—the magi do all their work through purgatory, after all. But I think I've got the hang of it now."

Balthasar's expression eased a little. "I certainly hope so," he said, and unfastened the webbing that held him in his couch.

That was more like Balthasar, Silence thought. Sighing, she reached to do the same.

Isambard and Chase Mago were already waiting in the common room. The magus had a dozen or more battered books open on the table in front of him, and the engineer was looking discreetly over his shoulder. Both men looked up as Silence entered, and Chase Mago's expression grew worried. Soundlessly, he shaped the words, *are you all right?*

Silence nodded, focusing her attention on Isambard. "You need to teach me how not to see, as well."

The magus tilted his head, an oddly birdlike gesture. "It was different, then?" Silence nodded again, and Isambard said, "How?"

Balthasar, at Silence's shoulder, cleared his throat. "Can that be discussed later? We can't hold position here forever."

If Isambard showed any indication of knowing anything that might help, Silence thought, I'd insist. But he didn't even know for certain that there would be differences. "Let's get on with it, then," she said aloud.

They had made their preliminary plans in their first weeks on Solitudo, and now the four spread the fruits of those planning sessions on the table before them. It had been agreed from the beginning that Isambard would do most of the actual work involved in breaking the Rose Worlders' barriers. Siege engines were the magus's specialty, and he, at least, was certain that the Rose Worlders' engines were merely a variation of that basic instrument. But the breaking of that control was only a part of the work that would have to be done to reach Earth.

Silence scanned the spreading pile of papers until she found the rough notes she had made weeks ago. After *Bruja* had nearly been destroyed, the first time they had attempted the Earth road, they were all agreed on the need for an escape route. The trick was to choose the right one. She had known the voidmarks and the bearings involved—they had been seared into her brain on the crazy flight from Castax to Decelea. It had been a relatively simple exercise to pick out a parallel course, one that used an identical harmonic bearing and a set of voidmarks that reflected a set of objects in the mundane universe similar to the linked suns reflected in the Earth road. The deeper theory she had learned on Solitudo assured her that, since all places were the same in purgatory—which was itself both all places and no particular place—she could switch from one star road to the other, within certain limits, if their attempt failed. Still, she had never heard of such a thing being tried before, much less tried successfully. She sighed and turned her attention to the scribbled figures before her. She was limited to similar bearings and voidmarks by the power of *Recusante*'s harmonium: if she had the power of a Navy six or seven behind her, she could choose almost any road she wanted.

But there was no point in such thoughts. Sighing again, she shuffled the more recent notes until she found a sheet covered with Balthasar's scrawl. It was only part of what she wanted. "Julie, do you have the most recent bearing?"

"Here," Chase Mago said, and slid a slip of paper

across the table. "I took these as soon as we reached the null zone."

"Thanks," Silence said. Space was unstable along the dead roads. How could it be otherwise, she thought, with all the dead planets and poisoned suns to distort the harmonies? The normally static harmonic bearings had a tendency to drift. Under normal circumstances, there was enough leeway in the listed bearings that this hardly mattered—unless, of course, the shift was a major one. Balthasar had a cruelly funny story of the horrific results when a Wrath-of-God ship took another of the dead roads from the wrong bearing. But if the escape route were to function as it should, she had to match the bearing precisely. She glanced quickly at the set of numbers and the noted pitch for each, then turned to her original set of notes, with the bearings for the Earth road and a half-dozen different roads with similar voidmarks. She found a three-way match almost at once, correct to the third place, and gave a soft exclamation of pleasure.

"So where are we going?" Balthasar asked, without lifting his head from his own work.

"Just a minute," Silence answered, irrationally irritated. She took her time, ostentatiously rustling pages, though the answer was clearly noted. "Sisip' Catacecaumene," she said at last.

Balthasar gave a pleased grunt, and continued studying a single sheet of paper. Silence suppressed her anger, belatedly recognizing it as displaced fear. Chase Mago and the magus were still deep in discussion of some arcane principle, but even as the pilot looked curiously in their direction the engineer straightened with a sigh.

"That means retuning, you know."

Balthasar looked up, shocked, and Chase Mago said hurriedly, "Not a major retuning, Denis, but some. Nothing to worry about, though."

"That's what they all say," Balthasar muttered, darkly.

"Can you do it?" The question slipped out before Silence thought about it. The answer was clear even before Chase Mago began to speak. Of course he could—all engineers were trained to do it, if the emergency were great enough. And Chase Mago, having worked for Wrath-of-God and escaped the Hegemonic net around Kesse before that, had probably done an emergency retuning more than once. Mercifully, however, Chase Mago did not seem inclined to take offense.

"I've done it before. I've got everything I need," he said, smiling rather tightly. "I can do it."

"I'll want to spend some time getting the feel of her," Balthasar said.

Silence nodded. "So will I." A change in the tuning would change the feel of the ship, the way it responded to the most ordinary things—which was all she needed, when she was uncertain enough about her ability to take the ship through purgatory. . . . She cut off that thought with an effort, telling herself unconvincingly that she had already passed that hurdle.

"As long as you need," Chase Mago said soothingly. He stood, huge, competent, and reassuring. "I'll get on it right away."

"You do that," Balthasar muttered, clearly not appeased. The engineer grinned, ruffling the other man's greying hair before ducking through the hatch to return to his engines. Balthasar grimaced, more because it was expected of him than because the engineer had failed to reassure him.

Silence said hastily, "I'll be in my cabin. I want to go over the voidmarks again."

Balthasar nodded, but Isambard said, "Could you spare me a moment, Silence? I want to review our part in this."

Silence sighed, biting back the anger that was really fear, and said, "All right, but I do need some time for the marks."

"I'll leave you to it," Balthasar said. There was an

odd note in his voice, almost of jealousy, but before Silence could be certain of what she had heard, the Delian was gone. She shrugged to herself, putting the whole thing down to an overstrained imagination, and turned to the magus.

"The key to this operation," Isambard began thoughtfully, "lies in the manipulation of the final four symbols, does it not?"

Silence ran a hand through her short hair as if that would help her concentrate. The Earth road was a peculiar road, one that possessed two distinct sets of voidmarks. And, yes, it was the manipulation of the final four—the elemental symbols—that allowed a starship to break free from the maze of the road. "That's where the Rose Worlders have blocked it, yes."

"And the first part of the road," Isambard pursued as though she had not spoken, "is preparation, as alchemical marriage is preparation for the creation of the philosopher's tincture, is it not?"

Silence nodded, remembering the twining king and queen that lay at the heart of the illusory maze. But of course Isambard had seen that image as well, on their first attempt to open the Earth road, and would have recognized the symbolism from the beginning.

"So I will not be needed until we have reached the final stages of the road," the magus finished.

"That's right," Silence answered, rousing herself from contemplation of the Earth road and its gorgeous, seductive voidmarks. "Stay below until then." She hadn't meant to sound so abrupt, or to give such an uncompromising order, and felt her face grow hot with embarrassment. But before she could offer an apology, the magus nodded.

"Very well, I see the sense of that."

Not only that, Silence thought, he doesn't even sound offended. She ducked her head over the sheets of paper to hide the fading color in her cheeks. Was that the best way to deal with magi? She kept her head down, unable to suppress a sudden, mischievous smile. Not likely! "When we make the turn," she said aloud.

Isambard frowned. "The turn?"

"The—" Silence checked herself instantly. She had gotten away with one sharp comment already; there was no point in pushing her luck. And besides, there was no reason to think that the Earth road's voidmarks would have burned themselves into the magus's memory: their lure was for pilots alone. "It's part of the road. You have to bring the ship as close as possible to the twinned suns—the royal couple—and then turn very sharply away. You don't see the four elements until after you've made that turn. You'll see when we get there. Better still, ride the run-up on the lower bridge. That way, Denis can warn you as we get close, but I don't think you could miss it."

Isambard nodded again. "And the elements are my business," he said. "I will want your help, as we discussed before." He paused, looking at her as though to assess her abilities for the hundredth time. Silence stared back, meeting his gaze with all the impassivity she could manage, and for the first time she realized the magus was as nervous as the rest of them. No, she thought, not precisely nervous, but certainly cautious, excited, wary. . . . Isambard spoke before she could find the word she was looking for.

"It's your strength I want," he said, "and then your pilot's knowledge. Nothing more."

In spite of her resolution to remain impassive, Silence lifted an eyebrow at the other's tone, even more peremptory than usual. Isambard was right, though, she thought. I still don't know enough, for all I've passed one exam, to be of any active help. "Very well," she said, unconsciously mimicking the magus's acquiescence. "But now I want to study my voidmarks."

Isambard waved dismissal, already engrossed in his own notes. Most of those, Silence knew, had been compiled after their first attempt to reach Earth, on the way from Mersaa Maia to Solitudo, and then during the time on Solitudo. But the magus would have cause to remember the details of the force that had nearly destroyed them, she told herself firmly, for the same reasons that she remembered the voidmarks with such clarity.

Silence shut the door of her cabin and latched it behind her, then settled herself comfortably on the narrow bunk. There was no real need to review the voidmarks of the Earth road, but even so she lifted her copy of the *Gilded Stairs*, opening it to the familiar page. The uncolored design seemed to shout its various meanings. The man in the long coat, who used a giant compass to inscribe the final circle of the ancient symbol for the completed Work on a crumbling wall, was the pilot and the specialist and a warning against the seductive pull of the voidmarks. . . .

Silence closed the starbook with a snap, forcing herself to ignore the multiple meanings. That attraction was even more dangerous to her now that she knew a little of the magi's art, and she would have to be fully on her guard against it. To the best of her knowledge there had never been a pilot who was also a magus—or at least no one had ever reported on that magus's piloting—but she did know, from horrific legend and even more dreadful example, what could happen if a pilot lost control of the voidmarks. At best, the ship might survive the tearing distortions, to emerge from purgatory far from any sun. If the keel were not too badly damaged, the ship might be able to regain purgatory, but without a known beginning, the starbooks could not indicate the proper road. The ship could easily wander until air and supplies gave out, until, even the elemental water that powered the harmonium was exhausted, and the ship plummeted from purgatory to be destroyed in the nearest star.

Silence shook herself abruptly. It had been a long time since she had thought of those possibilities, a long

time since she had last had cause to doubt her own
skills as a pilot. But she had managed the dead road
that brought *Recusante* to Decelea, and the Earth road
was no worse. I'm warned, she told herself firmly. I will
be prepared.

There was little point in attempting to review the
images in the *Gilded Stairs,* she decided. She remembered, with an almost painful clarity, her first attempt.
The power-laden symbols of the starbook would only
add to the confusion. She reached instead for the fussy,
reliable *Star-Followers' Handbook*, flipping through the
index until she found the road she wanted, from Decelea
to Sisip' Catacecaumene. The overcrowded drawing for
the Road of the Drowning King was mercifully free of
the sort of powerful symbols that filled the illustration
of the Earth road. A turbulent stream ran between
overgrown banks, twisting down toward a whirlpool
where a crowned figure struggled, arms in the air,
mouth open in a futile cry for help. The meaning was
easy enough to extract. The stream was the correct
path, dangerous because of interference—the rocks that
studded the channel made that only too clear—but less
dangerous than the ugly, twisted vegetation that reached
down almost to the water. The ship would have to
follow the stream to the whirlpool itself, then through
the whirlpool and out into the mundane universe. Silence glanced at the single line of commentary to confirm her certainty. It read: "The way runs clear, but
only the intervention of the king can save the virtuous."
Silence nodded to herself. She had been right, but it
was good to have that pilot's insight corroborated, especially after the hard passage from Solitudo. She set the
starbook aside, reaching for the intercom key.

Before she could press the switch, however, there
was a knock at the door. She frowned, a little annoyed
by the interruption, but hit the lock switch. Balthasar
stood in the doorway.

"Julie's finished the retuning," he announced without preliminaries. "Do you want to come up now and get the feel of it, or do you need more time with the books?"

Silence sighed, bracing herself. "I'm ready."

To Silence's surprise, however, the shift in the tuning did not seem significantly to affect how the ship handled. The sound was different, of course, with new, more lavish harmonies, but Chase Mago had done an excellent job. *Recusante* responded easily to the changed notes. Silence and Balthasar spent three hours flying the ship in lazy circles, from the edge of the null zone to the first and then the second lines of interference, and back again. At the end of it, Balthasar pronounced himself satisfied, and the two returned to the common area to snatch a hurried meal before facing the Earth road.

It was not a long flight out of Decelea's system. Silence relinquished her place on the lower bridge to Isambard, not without unspoken objections from Balthasar, and climbed to the upper bridge to take her place before the control wheel. There were no instruments by which she could monitor *Recusante*'s progress toward the twelfth of heaven. Instead, she listened to the note of the harmonium, first pure, then strained and dissonant, and finally shifting again toward the familiar celestial harmonies as *Recusante* fought free of the broken system. Silence took a deep breath, reaching for the wheel lock, then, with an effort, let her hands drop to her side. *Recusante* was not nearly at the twelfth of heaven. She took refuge in her memories of the Earth road instead.

Almost before she was ready, Balthasar's voice sounded again in her earphones, oddly formal. "Two minutes to upper register. All secure, Silence?"

Silence frowned, wondering at the Delian's sudden change of tone, then remembered that Isambard was on the bridge beside him. It was something of a relief to realize that the magus's presence could be inhibiting

even to Balthaser. "All green here," she announced,
and flipped the last switch to make it true. The row of
lights glimmered through her fading flesh, striking strange
greenish glints from her bones. She looked away quickly.

"Julie?" Balthasar went on. .

"Ready below," the engineer answered promptly.

"Stand by," Balthasar said. Silence could almost hear
him counting off the final seconds. "Now."

Even as the captain spoke, Chase Mago opened all
the stops, and the harmonium's note swelled gloriously.
Silence flicked off the wheel lock, and sought her
voidmarks through the now-transparent dome. She stood
suspended for a moment among a wilderness of symbols, and then the pilot's discipline reasserted itself.
The voidmarks, hauntingly familiar even after a single
passage, sprang into existence before her. But there
were differences. Instead of the solid walls of greenery
framing the path that led to the heart of the maze,
there were gaps—almost, she thought, as though a sort
of autumn had fallen in this illusory garden. That alone
would be no great problem—the path was still clear—
except for the scenes she glimpsed through the gaps.
To her left, two monstrous animals, a dragon and something the likes of which she had never seen even in a
hieroglyphica, were locked in deadly combat; to her
right, a man with bleeding stumps where hands and
feet should have been struggled toward the hedge.

She swore softly and looked away, forcing herself to
concentrate on the approaching turn. The central core
of the maze loomed before her, and this time there was
no screening hedge to mask what lay within. The king
and queen lay locked together, her absolute dark feed-
ing on his absolute light, both featureless, yet of a
perfection that could only be felt, not seen. . . .

Then it was time to make the turn. Silence swung the
wheel hard over, heard the sudden change in pitch as
the harmonium's various notes began to cancel each
other out. Her eyes were wet. She wiped at them

impatiently, not sure if she was weeping for knowledge lost, or for the sheer beauty of it, or simply because the blinding light had nearly been too much for her. She sniffed hard, and said, "Isambard—"

"Here," the magus answered calmly.

Silence started in spite of herself, but did not turn her head. "The marks will be coming up," she said, and damned herself for the betraying huskiness of her voice.

To her surprise, Isambard said nothing, and she risked a glance over her shoulder. The magus was standing motionless, eyes closed, lips moving in calculation. All around them, the harmonium's note was fading, merging into a sound that was almost, but not quite, a single note.

"Six-twelfths of heaven," Chase Mago announced, as though that were the most ordinary thing in human space. "Seven, eight-twelfths."

Was there a hint of surprise in his voice that time? Silence thought. The music touched a chord deep within her, set something singing, as the sounding keel answers the harmonium, and she laughed aloud for the sheer beauty of it all.

"Steady, girl," Isambard said, but he did not sound entirely disapproving. Did he feel it too, Silence wondered, this joy too intense for anything but music?

"Steady," the magus said again, and this time Silence realized he was speaking to himself.

Then the first of the voidmarks appeared, a rusted, pitted world that should have showed the oily gleam of elemental earth. Silence took a deep breath, bracing herself to answer Isambard's demands. The magus remained still, and it was all Silence could do to keep from making the necessary course correction. She waited, holding herself motionless with an effort, and then at last Isambard shouted aloud. It was no word Silence knew, nor even any language that she recognized, but it struck echoes from the keel and from the very fabric of purgatory. It *was* elemental earth—solid, cold, dry, the very Form given tongue. The voidmark wavered, shifted, and in that instant Silence swung the wheel, bringing the ship around to face the next mark. It gleamed balefully, the bands of gas that whirled across its surface an even uglier green than she remembered.

Again, Isambard waited until the last minute, then spoke the word that was the Form of elemental air. The colors cleared, then blued, and Silence eased the wheel again, aligning the ship to face the final pair of signs. So far, she thought cautiously, Isambard's plan seemed to be working, and the magus had not yet had to call on her strength.

They approached the sullen, reddened sun that was the sign of Fire, and Isambard spoke again, the word this time crackling dry and hot. The voidmark did not change. The magus frowned and shouted again, adding a second, reinforcing word. Reluctantly, as though someone had blown on dying embers, the sun brightened. The final voidmark, a frozen world, its snows tinted yellow, loomed before them. Isambard spoke again, and the ice cracked, dissolving momentarily into water. Silence adjusted the wheel a final time.

"Now," Isambard said, and in the same moment reached for Silence's shoulder. She glanced at him, startled. The magus wore no shipsuit, and she could see the power glowing behind the fence of his bones.

"Now," he said again, and Silence felt something like a touch deep within her being. It shaped, gave direction to the singing she had felt as they reached eight-twelfths of heaven. She submitted willingly to that knowledgeable control.

Without need of further orders, she pulled back hard on the control wheel, bringing *Recusante* up and around in a great loop that would bring the ship into a new position relative to the four elemental symbols. The harmonium surged—Chase Mago had been waiting for that moment—its note momentarily overriding the Rose Worlders' engines, then wavered painfully into dissonance. The ship shuddered, the wheel bucking in Silence's hands.

Isambard spoke again, a chain of words that merged and melded into a single note that cut through the dissonance, binding *Recusante* to its sound, then swelling as if it would change the very stuff of purgatory. The voidmarks remained obstinately the same. The magus shouted a second phrase, and Silence felt him drawing on her own strength to reinforce its harsh command. Still nothing happened, and now Silence could sense, with the part of herself that was still purely a pilot, that they were cutting things very fine. If Isambard did not break through the interference soon, the ship would leave the outlined path and enter unknown territory. She opened her mouth to speak, but realized that Isambard had already read her thought. The magus shouted again, a string of words even more commanding than the last, packed with even more compelling music, but nothing happened. Silence knew the magus's decision even before he spoke.

"I can do no more."

Instantly, Silence wrenched the wheel over, turning back into the path that would swing them back around the central linked figures. That bought them time to make the transition from one star road to another. She took a deep breath and turned her will to the voidmarks. She fought to see the path that stretched before her as the surface of a stream, not the indeterminate cloudy gravel that it now seemed. The leafless hedges must become trees, gnarled and dangerous, overspreading the path. Slowly, so slowly, the gravel rippled and became sullen water; the stems of the hedge twined and grew together to a single trunk. . . . With terrifying abruptness, the entire scene shifted. *Recusante*, bobbing and twisting like a cork caught in a maelstrom, swept at impossible speed toward the central whirlpool. Swearing aloud, Silence struggled with the wheel as the drowning king's mouth gaped to swallow them.

And then they were through, the harmonium sliding down the scale, while Balthasar's voice echoed in their earphones, demanding damage reports.

Chase Mago answered instantly and incredulously. "Stressed, but nothing major."

Silence clung to the wheel a moment longer, then summoned the strength to snap on the lock, turning control back to Balthasar. She was suddenly, intensely exhausted, barely able to keep her feet. She was remotely aware that Isambard had vanished from the upper bridge. Balthasar's voice seemed very distant in her ears.

"What the hell? Julie, put everything on automatic for now, and come and help me with the damn magus."

"What's wrong?" Chase Mago responded sharply, and Silence could hear the music change as he adjusted the harmonium to hold the ship in place.

'He's passed out on me." Balthasar paused, and then, almost in spite of himself, sounded relieved. "Hell, he's asleep—snoring."

Silence giggled.

Chase Mago said, "I'll be right there. See to Silence, Denis."

That sounded very pleasant, Silence thought. She let herself slide slowly to the decking, leaning back against the column of the wheel. She was only dimly aware of footsteps on the ladder, and then of being lifted and lowered carefully down to the main bridge. She was fully asleep long before the two men got her to her cabin.

CHAPTER 4

Silence slept through the landing on Sisip' Catace-caumene, and through the customs inspection that followed. She did not stir even when Customs, represented by a team of three nearly identical blondish men, insisted on entering her cabin and verifying her living presence. By the time she woke, Chase Mago had completed the minor repairs and he and Balthasar had already made a quick circuit of the port. Sisip' Catacecaumene was a major transfer point within the Hegemony, living off other peoples' trade rather than its own resources, and like most such worlds, it had an extensive star-travellers' Pale where everything could be bought and sold. Balthasar, with his Wrath-of-God connections, already knew most of the information brokers in the Pale, and had spent a few of Isambard's marks on inquiries. His discreet questions had brought mixed results. As usual, there was no real word out of the Rose Worlds, not even enough to let them know if their attempt to break the barrier had been noticed.

"It must have been," Silence said, and Balthasar shrugged.

"Who knows? In any case, there's no hint of a hunt out for us."

"Except the Hegemon's question," Chase Mago murmured, staring into his second mug of coffee. "That's still circulating."

"Which means you should probably stay out of sight, Silence," Balthasar agreed. "They saw you were a woman, so we had to tell Customs you were the stewardess— that we were chartered by Isambard."

"What?" Silence gave the Delian an indignant look. Balthasar shrugged again, a little uncomfortably this time.

"It was the best I could do, on the spur of the moment."

"The hell it was," Silence said, "you've been planning that story for months, I bet."

Chase Mago laughed softly. "The first time he admits he hasn't had everything worked out ahead of time, you don't believe him. Serves you right, Denis."

Silence relaxed slowly. It was true that Balthasar rarely planned things in advance, trusting to luck and inspiration to see him through, and equally true that that was the best explanation for a woman's presence on board a starship. *I don't want to know how they knew I was female,* she thought—*what I don't know won't embarrass me.* Aloud, she said, "I suppose. Anyway, it's the Rose Worlders' response that worries me more. They must know someone tried to break the barrier. I just wonder if they could have identified the ship."

"Possibly." Isambard stood in the hatchway, one hand resting on the frame. He still looked miserably tired, his face drawn, its lines more prominent than ever above the uncombed beard. Even the color of his skin had greyed. For the first time, Silence was fully aware of the fact that he was an old man.

Chase Mago said hastily, "Tea, sir?" Even Balthasar looked a little alarmed, and shoved a chair in the magus's direction. Isambard seated himself with a hu-

manly grateful sigh, but when he spoke again, his voice
held all its old austerity.

"In any case, no good can come of delay. I think it is
time we tried your suggestion, Silence. We must go to
Inarime." Absently, the magus accepted the cup of tea
Chase Mago handed to him.

"Inarime?" Balthasar asked.

"Inarime," Isambard repeated, and glanced at Silence. It was as if he had gestured for her to speak,
reducing her in an instant to his apprentice.

The pilot bit back an angry retort, and said, rather
shortly, "The satrap of Inarime has a reputation as a
great collector of curiosities—especially old documents.
If the Library on Solitudo doesn't have a portolan,
Inarime's the next logical place to look." She fixed
Isambard with a challenging stare. "May I ask why you
think the satrap will let you have the run of his
collection?"

The magus did not seem to notice her tone. "Adeben
Kibbe is an old—" He hesitated over the word. "Yes,
an old friend of mine. And in my debt. I think he will
help us."

"Tsa, that's it," Chase Mago said abruptly. The Rusadir
accent was suddenly very strong. "Inarime—I knew
there was something I'd heard about that world, about
the satrap. Do you remember, Denis, on Wrath-of-God?"

"The satrap of Inarime?" Balthasar shook his head.

"And it was your story, too," Chase Mago murmured.
"The satrap of Inarime had trouble with his customs
people—the Hegemon had him flogged for not keeping
a better eye on them."

Balthasar snapped his fingers in sudden recollection.
"So, of course. Which also means he has no reason to
love the Hegemon."

"Just so." Isambard nodded gravely. "He is a very
proud man."

"How soon can we lift?" Silence asked.

Chase Mago gave her a proud smile. "Any time you're ready. We're back in perfect tune again."

"As soon as we can get clearance?" Balthasar asked, and looked at Silence.

"Give me six hours to find and learn the road, and I'll be ready," the pilot answered. And I will be, too, she thought with some surprise. She was learning not to see too much; already she had learned enough to anticipate the worst parts.

The easiest road from Sisip' Catacecaumene to Inarime was one Silence had flown a hundred times. It did not take her long to review the voidmarks, and by the time Balthasar was able to top off *Recusante*'s supply bunkers and get a place in the lifting queue, Silence had completely submerged herself in her piloting. The flight itself was uneventful, the familiar voidmarks only somewhat changed by Silence's new perception. On a different road, Silence knew, that would be different, and the crowding, complicating symbols would return. Even so, it was reassuring to be able to slip back into her old place, if only for a single flight.

Inarime Approach Control was very friendly—almost too friendly. Silence and Balthasar exchanged wary glances as Approach greeted them not only with guidance into the roads, but stayed on the frequency to offer advice about docking and port fees, and to insert a few casual questions into the stream of talk. Balthasar was careful to switch off his own communications console before saying, "There's something up down there."

Silence nodded, staring at the multiple viewscreens. Two showed the picture from the long-range cameras mounted in *Recusante*'s stubby wings. The third gave the musonar's view of the space surrounding the planet. To the camera's eye, Inarime was a pretty, undistinguished world, blue-oceaned and banded with clouds, much like any other world in human-settled space. But the musonar view was strangely empty, showing none of the glittering dots that marked the usual heavy traffic surrounding a Hegemonic world. And Inarime was a satrapy, too—a sector governor's world. . . . "There should be more traffic than this," she said aloud.

Balthasar nodded, and reached to open the communications channels again. "Inarime Approach, this is *Recusante*. Will you reserve us a class-two berth in Tycha Mainport? We're on a charter, so we won't be needing heavy-cargo facilities."

"So sorry, *Recusante*," Approach answered promptly. "There aren't any class-twos available at Tycha—no berths at all, in fact. You'll have to divert to Port Mosata. There's plenty of room there."

"Impossible," Silence whispered, and Balthasar frowned deeply.

"My charter's business is in Tycha—" He broke off abruptly, staring at the Ficinan model. Silence followed the direction of his gaze, and swore softly. A brilliant orange light had blossomed in the display globe, trailing *Recusante* at a respectable but still deadly distance. A warship, certainly—the orange light meant that the ship's sensors had picked up the characteristic note of cannons and armor. The question now was whom it belonged to.

"Sorry," Approach said again, not sounding particularly regretful. "But don't worry, captain, Mosata's not far at all from Tycha city."

Silence ignored Balthasar's grumbling response, and reached for the board that controlled the cameras. At the very end of its track, the port camera could just pick up the shape of the trailing warship. Silence slowly increased the magnification and enhancement, and at last the slender shape came clear. It was a navy six, the second-largest of the Hegemonic warships, guns bristling along its narrow, keel-heavy length, but its insignia was the red hart of Inarime. Silence let out a long breath—at least it was not directly part of the Hegemonic Navy—and glanced at Balthasar's board to make sure the pickup was turned off. The telltale glowed red, and she said, "It's not Hegemonic, Denis."

Balthasar grunted. "Inarime's private navy still looks Hegemonic to me," he muttered. "And I've got three more on musonar. What the hell is going on down there?"

"Isambard might know," Silence began, but a crackling from the speakers cut her off.

"*Recusante*, this is Inarime Approach. You will enter atmosphere in thirty-three minutes. Please switch to Port Mosata control frequency. Good landing!"

"Thank you, Approach, for your good wishes," Balthasar said, keying the transmitter again. He adjusted the frequency as directed, and said, "Port Mosata Control, this is DRV *Recusante*. We're standing by for landing instructions."

Mosata Control was slightly less cheerful than Inarime Approach, but just as polite. It answered instantly, which also was unusual on a busy world. Silence and Balthasar exchanged another look. "*Recusante*, this is Mosata Control. Are you ready to receive your landing beam?"

"I wish to hell we could just cut out of here," Balthasar muttered, almost inaudibly, and flipped an intercom switch. "Julie, you hear?"

"I heard," Chase Mago answered grimly. "I'm ready to tape it—if you want me to."

"No choice," Balthasar said, with a rapid glance to make sure the main transmitter was off. "There's a navy six sitting on our tail, and a couple more swanning around in the outer planets."

Chase Mago sighed heavily. "Let's get it over with."

Balthasar opened the main channel. "We're ready to take your beam, Control."

"Transmitting," Control answered promptly.

A moment later, Chase Mago said, "Received and recorded."

"Thanks, Julie," Silence said, and heard Balthasar

repeat the engineer's words to Mosata Control. It was all Silence could do to lean back in her couch and monitor the various readouts when every nerve screamed that the Hegemon or his agents were waiting for them on Inarime. *Balthasar is right,* she told herself, *there's nothing we can do to get away from at least three heavy warships. If there were, Wrath-of-God would have taught it to him, and he'd already have done it.*

Balthasar gave her a quick, nervous smile, as though he'd read her thoughts. "Cheer up, Silence," he said softly. "I figure if it was the Hegemon, it'd be his people down there, not planetary troops. He wouldn't risk letting you fall into a satrap's hands."

Silence grimaced and did not answer. *It's all very well for Denis to say that,* she thought, *but I know I'm not all that important. Why shouldn't he let a satrap handle our capture—unless the Hegemon knows we almost reached Earth?* There was no point in such speculation. With an effort, she closed off that line of thought, forcing herself to concentrate on the landing.

Balthasar brought *Recusante* to a textbook landing on the waiting cradle, signaling Chase Mago to break the sympathetic harmony at just the right moment. The starship settled almost without a jolt, and the cradle's padded clamps closed gently around the hull.

"Nice landing, *Recusante,*" Mosata Control said. "Stand by for a tow."

Balthasar glanced quickly at Silence, then said into the open microphone, "Not much traffic, Control?"

There was a fractional hesitation before Control answered, "It's been slow today." That hesitation was more than enough. Silence gave a soundless whistle, and saw Balthasar's face tighten. If there were no places left in the bays at Tycha Mainport, and all of the planet's traffic was being funneled through Port Mosata, there should be more than enough arrivals to keep Mosata Control busy. If nothing else, Silence thought, Control should be screaming for us to clear the table, so that he could bring down some more ships. But there had been no merchant ships visible on musonar, only the patrolling warships. Balthasar nodded, as though he'd read her thoughts, and fumbled in the pocket of his trousers until he found a flat, glittering key. He flipped it across, and Silence caught it almost by instinct. It was the key to the arms locker.

"Get out the little heylins we bought on Kilix, the ones that're supposed to be undetectable," Balthasar said. "One for each of us."

"Isambard, too?" Silence asked, already loosening the straps that held her in her couch.

The Delian hesitated, then nodded. "Isambard, too. And a couple of extra clips for each of us. The damn things're only five-shots. Let's hope we don't need them."

Silence nodded, and worked her way free of the final bank of controls. The arms locker was no longer in the captain's cabin, as it had been when this had been her grandfather's ship. Instead, Chase Mago had installed an inconspicuous, and larger, cabinet in the common room, just to the right of the intercom panel. The lock worked smoothly, and Silence slid back the panel to reveal the rack of weaponry. Balthasar—who after all had the most experience, from his long service with Wrath-of-God—had bought mostly heylins, relatively cheap and unrestricted handguns that threw a bolt of fixed fire. He had also purchased a pair of sonic rifles, which now hung at the bottom of the rack, their bell-shaped muzzles gleaming dully in the lights. Silence hesitated, looking at them—they were far more effective weapons than the heylins—but put the thought aside. Instead, she reached for the heylins Balthasar had requested, flat, ungainly-looking things only a little larger than the palm of her hand. The smooth grey-green metal felt oddly grainy to the touch, as though it mimicked wood. Frowning, she tucked the four weapons into the pocket of her smock, filled the other pocket with the spare charges, and headed aft to the engine room.

Chase Mago was waiting in the hatchway, the orange warning lights that ringed the opening throwing strange shadows across his face and untidy beard.

"All secure?" Silence asked automatically.

The engineer gave a grunt of agreement, then raised an eyebrow as the pilot pulled out one of the heylins. "Serious trouble?"

Silence shrugged. "You heard yourself."

Chase Mago nodded and accepted the heylin, running a knowledgeable thumb across the touchplate to confirm a full charge.

"They're supposed to be invisible to most sensors," Silence said, and managed a smile. "I hope they're right."

"Only five-shots?" Chase Mago said.

Silence nodded, her feeble attempt at humor dying. "I have to get back to control. And I want to warn Isambard."

"Right," the engineer answered. He was still staring very thoughtfully at the little heylin, turning it over and over in his huge hands. Silence shivered, and hurried back up the central corridor to the magus's cabin.

Isambard opened the door almost before she had finished knocking. "Is there trouble?"

Quickly, Silence explained what was happening, and as she finished, felt the decking jerk and sway underfoot. The tow had arrived, and was hauling the ship toward the docking sheds. Isambard frowned deeply, a new, worried look in his eyes.

"I do not think Adeben would give me up without a struggle," he murmured, almost to himself. "I have done too much work here for that. . . ."

Silence said, "Isambard, do you want a heylin?" She held out the little weapon. The magus stared at it as though he were not sure what it was. Then, quite slowly, his expression changed to one of vast amusement, and he laughed aloud. Silence flushed angrily.

"No," Isambard said, his laughter vanishing almost as soon as it had begun. "I have no need of it—and neither have you, girl." His tone sharpened. "Or did you learn nothing on Solitudo?"

"Nothing useful for self-defense," Silence snapped, but even as she said it, she realized that it was not true. A number of things she had learned—minor tricks of perception and illusion, certain types of manipulation, even the greater Art of transformation—could be turned from peaceful uses to something far more deadly. Isambard nodded as though he had read her thought.

"Go, quickly, put those toys away." He dismissed the heylins with a contemptuous wave of his hand. "They will only get you into trouble."

Still blushing, though now less from anger than from embarrassment, Silence did as she was told, restoring two of the three heylins and their ammunition to the arms locker. Then she hurried forward to the control room to give Balthasar his weapon. The Delian accepted it absently, his attention on the screens, which showed the cradle approaching the huge docking shed. Silence leaned over his shoulder to monitor the balance while Balthasar stowed the heylin and its extra clips deep in the inner pockets of his coat.

"Thanks," Balthasar said. "You better get back to commons—and get Isambard there with you."

"Right," Silence said, suppressing a stab of resentment. The Delian was right. She could not be found on the bridge, could not afford to start the Inarimans thinking about women pilots—if indeed any of them spotted her sex beneath the concealing smock. It had all been planned in advance, down to their carefully forged papers and Isambard's simple, believable story of the charter, but it was still very difficult for her to sit quietly in the common room, without even a screen to monitor, while someone else brought her ship into an unfamiliar shed.

Isambard was already there, seated patiently at the

table. Silence paced the length of the room. She stumbled when the cradle lurched across the threshold of the shed, but was too nervous to sit down. You have your papers in your pocket, she told herself repeatedly, and they're good forgeries, the best that money and Wrath-of-God connections can buy. And you're Isambard's apprentice. He'll protect you.

At last the cradle shuddered to a stop. The intercom panel whistled, and Silence jumped to answer that signal.

"Commons."

In the same instant, Chase Mago said, "Engineering."

Balthasar's voice was fractionally distorted by the cheap speakers. "We're in the bay, and—shit." There was a pause, during which Silence could hear scuffling noises as Balthasar fumbled with various controls. It was only with a great effort that the pilot kept from demanding information. After what seemed an eternity, the Delian spoke again, breathlessly. "Customs team's here, army backed, with a heavy sensor suite—"

He broke off as a new voice sounded over the external channel, tinnily repeated by the intercom. "*Recusante*, open to inspection."

Balthasar answered promptly and politely, and Silence gave a soft sigh of relief. "Opening the main hatch." There was a pause, and then Silence heard, quite distinctly, the soft popping as the four-point seal was broken. "Main hatch is open." Balthasar hesitated, then asked, "Is there some problem, Customs?" His voice held just the right mix of innocence and wariness, Silence thought, and jammed her hands into her pockets to hide their shaking. Any star-traveller would be nervous, seeing planetary troops in with Customs.

"Assemble in your common area," the Inariman voice said flatly. "Anyone found outside the ship's common area will be shot on sight. You have sixty seconds to comply."

For a heart-stopping moment, Silence thought Balthasar would try something foolish. Then the Delian said, just as flatly, "Acknowledged."

Both Balthasar and Chase Mago reached the common room just in time, only seconds before the main hatch sighed open. The sound of heavy boots carried clearly, a rush of feet moving suddenly fore and aft, and then the common room hatch was flung open. A tall, hard-bitten man in a faded, practical uniform with a colonel's crescents on his high collar stood in the hatchway. He was flanked by two troopers with lowered sonic rifles.

"This is everyone?" the colonel snapped.

Balthasar spread his empty hands very carefully. "This is all, crew and passengers, sir. May I ask—"

"You may not," the colonel snapped. "Remain here. You, Hedeon, stand guard. At the first sign of trouble, shoot them."

"Sir!" The trooper snapped briefly to attention, then took the colonel's place in the hatchway, his sonic rifle already lowered for action. The colonel nodded abruptly and vanished back into the corridor, taking the second trooper with him.

Silence shivered, and fought to hide her despair. Everything they had been through, everything they had done, was useless; they were caught again like rats. . . . Isambard cleared his throat, and the trooper shifted the rifle to cover him. The magus ignored the threat and said, almost conversationally, "I see these are his Highness's men. We should have nothing to fear."

Balthasar made a choked sound of disbelief. Chase Mago lifted an eyebrow, but then, after a moment, nodded thoughtfully. Silence hunched her shoulders inside the anonymous coat, working her hands deep into the pockets. Isambard was right. These soldiers wore the badge of Inarime on their drab uniforms, and it was—fractionally—better to face Inarime's men than to face Hegemonic troops. That is, she thought, if Isambard's credit with this satrap is still good.

They waited for what seemed an eternity, listening to the sounds of soldiers moving through the ship, until at last the colonel reappeared in the hatchway. Silence saw Balthasar's shoulders stiffen, his left arm, the weapon arm, almost painfully motionless at his side. She frowned at him as unobtrusively as she could, thinking, *don't do it, not yet,* but the Delian did not relax. Chase Mago, closer to the captain than Silence was, laid a warning hand on the smaller man's shoulder. Then the colonel gestured brusquely for the waiting trooper to put up his weapon, and himself stepped into the common room.

"Your pardon, captain, but this is a matter of internal security." The Inariman's voice was indifferent: clearly, Silence thought, he didn't care whether or not Balthasar accepted the perfunctory apology. "Your papers?"

One by one, they handed over the thin folders. The colonel looked hard at them, then passed them on to a smaller, weedy man in Customs blues, who subjected the papers to further scrutiny before finally photoflashing them and returning them to their owners.

"Doctor Isambard," the colonel said abruptly. "Your business here, Doctor?"

The magus lifted an eyebrow at the Inariman's tone, but answered with great tranquility, "I have worked for his Highness before. I have a new proposition I thought might interest him."

"I see." Before the colonel could continue, a younger man with a major's star and a massive decoration at his throat appeared in the hatchway. The colonel turned, scowling, but the major said something in an undertone that eased the other's expression. The colonel listened a moment longer, then gave a startlingly human sigh, almost of relief, and turned back to face the star-travellers. "Thank you, major, that will be all. Captain, doctor, once again, I ask your pardon, but all foreigners are being restricted to the Pale until further notice. Internal security."

Balthasar murmured his agreement. By the look on

his face, Silence thought, he would agree to anything out of sheer relief. Isambard said, still mildly, "My business is to his Highness. What pass or privilege will I need, and how may I obtain it?"

"If his Highness is able to see you," the colonel said, with deliberate emphasis, "he will send an escort and the necessary documents. You should apply through the usual channels."

"Thank you, colonel," the magus said. His lined face was very thoughtful.

"Sieuri." The colonel gave them a stiff nod, almost a salute. "I remind you, you are restricted to the Pale of Port Mosata. I cannot answer for your safety if you venture outside." With that, he turned on his heel and was gone, drawing the troopers after him. After perhaps a dozen heartbeats there came the faint sound of the main hatch closing again behind them.

"Internal security," Chase Mago said, very thoughtfully.

It was plausible enough, Silence thought, watching idly as Balthasar crossed to the intercom panel and began running a quick status check, looking for hidden listeners or any other devices, organic or mechanical, that the colonel might have left behind. "Internal security" was the usual euphemism for popular rebellion, and that sort of upheaval was common enough in the repressive Hegemony. Though surely that was more likely in the newly conquered worlds of the Rusadir, not in the long-settled worlds of the Hegemony proper?

"All clear," Balthasar announced, turning off the last set of switches. "There's nothing aboard that doesn't belong here."

"Internal security," Chase Mago said again. "I can well believe it, knowing the Hegemony, but. . . ." He looked up, frowning. "It just doesn't ring true, somehow."

Balthasar shrugged. "But with luck, it's not our business." Seeing the others' expressions, he sighed. "Look, we may be restricted to the Pale, but that doesn't mean we can't find out what's going on. We'll do just what the colonel said, keep our noses clean, but it's perfectly reasonable for us to ask a lot of questions." He grinned suddenly. "Hell, it'd look strange if we didn't, after that welcome."

Isambard nodded. "Yes, I think that would be the best. And while you make your inquiries, I will attempt to make an appointment with Adeben."

Silence said, a trifle grimly, "Denis, I'm going with you."

To Silence's surprise, neither of the two made more than a token protest, Balthasar insisting only that she discard the apprentice's smock for an equally concealing tunic of his own. It was a concession she was prepared to make. If the satrap's men were watching the ship— and even Balthasar was not willing to hazard a guess either way—they saw only two men and a gawky boy leave the ship, and head through the working port to the less public pleasures of the Pale.

The Mosata Pale was small, compared to most such places, and lay entirely within the confines of the port. Like all the star-travellers' Pales throughout human-settled space, though, that small area contained a be-wildering variety of shops, bars, and cheap hostels, staffed by men and women from a dozen different worlds. *Recusante*'s crew made the rounds, first to the chart house, where Balthasar submitted Silence's starbooks for updating. Silence prowled nervously along the walls of the waiting room until they were returned, and snatched back the carryall as soon as they were outside again. Then they went to the engineers' quarter near the tuning sheds, where Balthasar and Silence waited in the growing dusk while Chase Mago exchanged the gossip of his profession, and at last to the bars. Silence hovered in the background, close enough to listen but not to talk, while the two men tossed back thimbleful after thimbleful of harsh quiyan, and asked their questions. By midnight, they had visited most of the larger bars along the three main streets, and had found out very little for their pains. Neither Balthasar nor Chase Mago was very drunk—Silence would have been more surprised by that, if she hadn't seen Balthasar empty several of his drinks down his wide sleeve, while Chase Mago swallowed sobrei-pills between bars—but even so, Balthasar stopped beside one of the brightly lit fountains to splash cold water on his face. It was a warm night, the breeze only just edged with chill. Suddenly very tired, Silence sat down on the edge of the fountain and, after only a second's pause, Chase Mago sat down beside her. Balthasar looked quizzically down at them, but made no move to join them.

"So," he said, after a moment, "shall we try—oh, I don't know which one—next?"

"I think we should go back to the ship, Denis," Chase Mago said. He glanced around the square, empty except for a few shadowy figures weaving their way from one bar to the next and the red eyes of the Watchers crouching under the eaves. He lowered his voice almost to a whisper. "The off-worlders don't know any more than we do, and the locals—they've been told not to talk."

Silence nodded. The engineer's words crystallized her own impression of the evening's questions. Something out of the ordinary—something that smelled of politics—was happening on Inarime. The Inarimans knew it, but, most untypically, they held their tongues.

"All the more reason to keep on," Balthasar began, then smiled rather ruefully. "No, you're right, Julie, there's no point to it. But if this is an internal security matter—" His tone gave the words vicious quotation marks. "—I'm the emperor of Earth." He held out his hands and pulled the other two to their feet. "Let's go."

"Maybe Isambard's heard something," Silence said, without much hope.

By the time they returned to the ship, however, the magus's cabin door was closed. The next morning, Isambard made it clear that he had learned no more than they had, and then stalked away to closet himself with a fellow magus, who handled most of the port business. Over the next six days, Isambard divided his time between the port magus and the ship's communications panel, speaking with various minor officials of the satrap's household. It was not until the seventh day that he reached someone with enough authority to remember him and carry his request to the satrap, but once he did, things moved with startling rapidity.

Silence was dozing through the noon heat, her head pillowed on her copy of the *Topoi*, when Balthasar kicked at the door, waking her. "What the hell do you want?" she called, embarrassed at being caught sleeping, but the Delian didn't seem to notice.

"Isambard got through to the satrap. He's sending a car for you now, and Isambard says to wear your good robes."

"How long?" Silence asked, and swung herself upright, bad temper forgotten.

"They're on their way now," Balthasar said. "Better hurry."

"Right," Silence answered, and pushed herself up off the bunk. She had only one good robe, and it was still the glossy, unadorned white satin of an apprentice, not yet topped with the black hood and stole of a licensed practitioner. She had never bothered, on Solitudo Hermae, to order the formal hood—and in any case, it was Isambard who held the purse strings. Well, Silence thought as she unfolded the heavy fabric, wincing at the travel wrinkles, it's his fault as much as mine if I'm not properly dressed. And it's the license that matters, not the clothes.

She hesitated for a moment, wondering if she should continue to wear trousers and shirt beneath the gown, or if she should appear in her own proper person. Then, shrugging, she pulled on her one good shirt and the cleanest pair of trousers, then adjusted the heavy gown over them. If Isambard wanted me to be a woman, he'd 've said so, she told herself, and glanced quickly at the mirror on the back of the cabin door. She looked very young, more like a boy of fifteen than a woman nearly twice that age. Silence made a face at that deceptive reflection, and left the cabin for the common room.

Isambard was waiting there already, dressed in his own formal robes, the jet black cloth relieved only by the gold-edged scarlet of his hood. The hood's lining showed brilliantly blue at his throat, the color echoed in the massive enameled shield that clasped his gown. Surprisingly, the heavy folds did not dwarf the magus; rather, he seemed to draw strength and confidence from the impressive draperies. Silence sighed, wishing she felt one-tenth as confident as he looked, and said, "I'm ready, Isambard."

The magus looked her over critically, appraising the fall of the shorter white gown, and said, "You've forgotten your hood."

"I don't have one," Silence retorted, and broke off abruptly as the magus pointed to the flat box lying on the table.

"Quickly, girl. Adeben's men will be here any minute."

Silence opened the box as she was told, and saw almost without surprise that it contained a practitioner's black hood. She donned it awkwardly, settling the hood at the nape of her neck and allowing the two narrow bands of the stole to fall over her shoulders to her waist. It was better balanced than she expected—the stole's ends were weighted to counterbalance the slipperiness of the material—but she was glad to see that Isambard had also included the guard chain that would hold it more securely in place. She fastened the first pin, a golden circle no larger than her thumbnail, careful to catch the fabric of both stole and gown in its clasp. She straightened the short length of chain that connected the two pins, but before she could adjust the second pin, Isambard clucked impatiently and twitched the material out of her hands. Silence stood meekly, feeling like a child again, while the magus gave the hood a slight twist, exposing its grey lining, and then fastened the remaining pin. Isambard stepped back, cocking his head to one side, then gave her an approving nod. Silence made a face, but before she could think of a suitable retort, Chase Mago appeared in the doorway.

"The satrap's people are here," he said.

"Excellent," Isambard answered, and gave Silence a final searching glance, like a general inspecting his troops. "Come along, Silence."

The pilot followed him, too annoyed and too nervous to make any comment, and Chase Mago trailed behind her, laying one hand on her shoulder in cautious consolation. Balthasar was waiting just inside the main hatch, peering warily around the frame, but at Silence's approach he, too, gave her shoulder a quick squeeze, whispering, "Good luck."

Silence managed a rather nervous smile for them both, and followed Isambard out of the ship. A double-domed transport was waiting at the bottom of the cradle stairs, flanked on either side by unsmiling men in the uniform of Inarime's planetary army. Their commander, a youngish lieutenant with a delicate, overbred face, saluted as Isambard reached the bottom of the stairs, and then, with his own hands, tripped the latch that opened the rear dome. That was unprecedented courtesy, from a Hegemonic officer to a magus. Silence could not suppress her lifted eyebrow, but Isambard accepted it as no more than his due. Gathering his heavy robes about him, he eased himself into the transport, beckoning imperiously for Silence to follow. Silence scrambled, less gracefully, into the seat beside him. The lieutenant closed the dome over them, and then, to Silence's surprise, hit the switch that opaqued the glass.

"What the hell?" Silence began in a cautious whisper, but Isambard raised a hand in warning, then shook his head. Silence subsided into her seat, watching unhappily as the dome clouded over. Through the thickening milky color, she caught a last glimpse of the soldiers taking their places on the broad running boards, one hand reaching for the grab bars that studded the twin domes, the other on the straps of their slung sonic rifles. Then the dome was fully opaqued, and she was jostled back against the seat cushions as the transport jerked awkwardly into motion. Slung rifles. . . .

It took a moment for the significance of that final detail to penetrate, but when it did, Silence sat up straight, hardly aware of the sluggish swaying of the transport. Not a protection squad, then, to guard the satrap's magus against local rebels—a protection squad wouldn't dare to travel without heylins and sonics and cannon all lowered and ready—but a guard of honor. And that meant, as if she needed further confirmation, that the whole tale of "internal security matters" was indeed a lie. She longed to tell Isambard her thoughts, but the magus wore his most forbidding face. Probably he was right, she thought. The lieutenant is bound to have ways to listen in on this compartment. But I want to talk to him—I wish he would tell me what he makes of all this, if nothing else.

The transport made very slow progress, often stopping for inexplicably long times. The first time it paused, Silence could hear the low growling hum of some large engine. Isambard heard it, too, and tilted his head to one side, listening with an abstracted expression on his bearded face. Seeing his expression, Silence strained to listen, but could not make out the source. Neither could the magus: after a moment, Isambard gave a tiny shrug and relaxed into his place again. Silence tried to copy his calm, folding her hands placidly inside the wide white sleeves of her gown, but she could not still the rapid beating of her heart.

The blind journey ended so suddenly that it seemed to be merely another of the inexplicable pauses until the lieutenant swung back the transport's dome. There was a rush of heady fragrance, as though the transport had stopped in the middle of some fabulous garden. Silence sniffed at it, entranced, trying to identify the various scents. Then Isambard prodded her with a bony finger, and she shook herself out of her reverie. The lieutenant had mistaken her preoccupation for uncertainty, and extended a hand to help her out, saying, "Better get a move on, boy."

That reminder of her disguise steadied Silence. She let the lieutenant pull her from the transport, then turned respectfully to help the magus. The perfect apprentice, she took her place at the magus's left hand, trying not to stare at the magnificence around her. The transport had come to rest in the center of a giant circle of some dark blue-grey stone some five times the length of the transport in diameter. Its surface was etched with delicate hieroglyphs. It was ringed on three sides by a stand of trees that had been carved and trained into fantastic twisted shapes—or perhaps, Silence thought, a thousand years of careful breeding had made that branching spiral the tree's natural shape. A few leaves had fallen into the circle, shining like copper coins against the dark stone. They were the source of the wonderful scent, and it was all Silence could do not to pick one up and sniff at it.

The lieutenant said, "If you'd follow me, Doctor?"

Silence started, and had to hurry to catch up with the magus. The escorting troopers, falling into step at her

back, laughed softly, and Silence felt herself blush
fiercely. The lieutenant led the way through the fra-
grant trees and onto a broad path that led up a gentle
slope to the satrap's palace.

It was a handsome building, very plain in its design,
but magnificent in its severity. Nothing but the most
expensive stone had been used in its construction, the
pale, blue-grey Lebidi marble of the facade a glowing
backdrop to the jet-veined charcoal of the cloud-agate
columns and the cinnabar-red choorl keystones of the
arched windows. The richness of the materials gave a
strange splendor to the sober geometry of the rows of
windows, each one precisely the same distance from
each of its neighbors, each one perfectly aligned with
the windows above and below. Even the gabled windows in the roof were proportionately placed, one jut-
ting above every other window on the main floors. The
main door. . . . Silence gasped in spite of herself. The
main door seemed to be made of a single, solid sheet of
beaten gold.

One of the soldiers laughed again, and another said,
"Better than the magi's world, eh, boy?"

Silence said nothing, hunching her shoulders in a
deliberate imitation of Kaare's sullen embarrassment.

As they came up to the door, the lieutenant said,
pitching his voice to carry to a pickup hidden somewhere in the carvings that almost hid the doorframe,
"Doctor Isambard, to see his Highness. He's expected."
Almost as an afterthought, the lieutenant added, "And
his apprentice."

There was a long pause, and then the door swung
open, very slowly. A wrinkled older man, well-dressed
but wearing the flat cap of a house-servant, appeared in
the opening. He bowed respectfully to Isambard, and
said, "Thank you, Eli." It was clearly a dismissal. The
lieutenant saluted sharply and backed away. The servant ignored him, saying, "If you would be so good as
to follow me, Doctor, his Highness will see you now."

"Of course," Isambard murmured, gathering his robes around him. Silence hurried after him, unwilling to be left behind with the soldiers.

The interior of the palace was as magnificent as the exterior, and in much the same somber way. The house-servant led them through hallways paneled in carved Oeud Tessaan blackwood, easily the most expensive wood in human-settled space, over carpets that had been laid over a bed of softly scented herbs. Through half-open doors, Silence caught tantalizing glimpses of still more magnificence—tapestries that glittered as though they were woven of spun jewels; books bound with bands of silvered metal, sealing them against any reader but the satrap; everyday objects, a bowl, a vase, a pencase, made from precious metals; flowering plants so rare that even Silence recognized their value—but the servant moved so quickly that the pilot barely had time to realize what she was seeing.

Then the house-servant pushed back a door and bowed them through into another long hallway. It, too, was paneled in carved blackwood, but the outer wall was one long window, supported at regular intervals by cloud-agate pillars. The red hart of Inarime had been cast in the center of each panel, throwing ruby shadows across the blackwood paneling.

At the far end of the corridor stood another door, quite unadorned. A boy of sixteen or seventeen in the brocaded court-livery of a noble's page stood outside, thin features impassive. As Isambard approached, the boy bowed very deeply. "His Highness greets you, Doctor. Please enter," he said. With a flourish, he touched the lockplate with a red-tipped wand, and the doors swung open before him. Silence hid a sudden grin. It was not much of a trick to have the doors of a house set to respond to such a control rod; any halfway competent practitioner could do it. Hell, she thought, half startled by the idea, I could probably do it.

Isambard nodded his thanks and stepped through the open door, but when Silence started to follow him, the page barred her way. "His Highness wishes to speak to the magus alone," the boy informed her haughtily, and closed the doors in her face.

Left to herself, Silence turned away from the door, and paced the full length of the corridor before she got a grip on her temper. How dare they shut me out like that? she thought. How dare they, when I'm their key to Earth? But they don't know that, she told herself, and it's better that they don't know, at least for now. Besides, the farther away you stay from this satrap, the better off you'll be.

Unbidden, a Cap Bel proverb rose in her mind: "To sup with nobles, you need a long spoon indeed." And Cap Bel, like most of the Rusadir worlds now groaning beneath the Hegemony's yoke, was hardly a world that lacked a privileged class. But the Cap Bel oligarchs, trade-rich and trade-powerful though they were, distrusted the Hegemonic nobility, and she would do well to follow their example. After all, the satrap of Inarime was the Hegemon's vassal, and might well consider it his duty to hand her over to the Hegemon.

Sighing, she walked back along the corridor, under the blackwood carvings that showed their copper highlights to the setting sun, and seated herself on the single long bench that stood against the wall at the precise midpoint of the corridor. It was not very comfortable. The cushions were not padded at all but trompe-l'oeil carvings made of the same wood as the rest of the bench. She settled herself on the least uncomfortable part of the carvings and composed herself to wait.

The shadows had lengthened perceptibly, the blobs of red light cast by the window decorations sliding slowly across the floor and up the paneled wall, before the door opened again. By then, Silence had regained her self-control. She gave the page a polite, incurious glance, and did not rise until he said, "His Highness will see you now, boy—I mean, sieura."

Silence rose gracefully, copying Isambard's stately carriage as best she could. So he's told the satrap who—and probably what—I am, she thought. Now we'll see. Somehow that thought robbed her of any pleasure in the page's discomfiture. She kept her face impassive as she stepped through the double doors into the satrap's inner sanctum. The page closed those doors gently behind her, announcing, "Sieura Leigh."

The room was very dark, despite the clusters of fixed-fire globes in each corner of the room. It took a long moment for Silence's eyes to adjust to the sudden gloom. As she hesitated, blinking, an unfamiliar voice said, "So. You can see it, when you're told, but . . ." The voice trailed off doubtfully, and Isambard said, "With more light, Highness, you would see better."

The satrap, little more than a stooped shadow in the center of the room, sighed noisily. "Light the lamps, boy," he said. Resignation and hope warred in his voice.

The page touched some hidden control, and there was a sudden scurrying in the shadows near the almost invisible ceiling. Silence bit back a startled exclamation as a pinpoint of light flared up, revealing a mass of tiny, monkey-like creatures scrambling frantically around an inverted pyramid of wire. Each held what seemed to be a candle, though Silence was quite certain it was some more lasting creation of the magi's Art. Two of those quasi-candles were already lit; as Silence watched, each monkey shape thrust its candle into the first flame, and scrambled back to its place on the wire pyramid, to freeze into some fantastically twisted attitude. The shadows retreated.

"A pretty toy, Highness," Isambard said, in the tone of one giving praise where praise was due. "Lel Rida's work?"

"Yes," the satrap said, his eyes still on Silence. The

pilot returned his scrutiny. Adeben Kibbe was not a particularly tall man, but he carried himself with the assurance of someone twice his size. Like most of the members of the Thousand—the highest ranking nobility, from whom the Hegemon drew his elite guard—he had a high-boned, hawkish face, shaped by generations of privilege. Unlike many of the Thousand, he carried that authority lightly, without undue conceit.

"So," the satrap said again. "You are the cause of all this trouble."

He had used the High Speech instinctively—or, more likely, as a test. Silence said nothing—there was nothing she could say to that—and after a moment the satrap nodded to himself. "Very well, sieura, be seated." He gestured vaguely at the cluster of tabourets drawn up in the center of the room.

Silence seated herself cautiously, careful to choose a seat that was both to Isambard's left and lower than the magus's tabouret. By the furnishings—a massive, paper-strewn desk, heavily curtained windows, locked book-press filled with account books, locked and shielded computer cabinet—this was the satrap's private office, and she took comfort in that realization. It implied that the satrap was willing to do business with Isambard, rather than hand them over to the Hegemon.

"Sieura Leigh." The satrap was leaning now against his desk, hands braced behind him on its massive surface. "Silence Leigh. Pilot, perhaps a magus, and a woman."

In the pause that followed, Isambard started to say something, but the satrap lifted a thin hand in rebuke. "Let me go about this my own way, Isambard. Your master has explained to me what it is you want, sieura, and he has offered me no small share of the inevitable profits." The satrap smiled thinly, allowing a faint hint of irony to color his tone. "As it happens, I have the volume—the portolan—you seek. Oh, yes," he added, forestalling some comment from the magus, "grant I

know my own collection that well, Isambard. But—"
His gaze returned to Silence. "—my price is somewhat
higher."

She waited, a dozen different questions chasing each
other through her brain. None of them was proper, or
safe, not yet, but the satrap was obviously waiting for
her to say something. "Indeed, Highness?" she asked,
and managed just the right note of polite indifference. She
used the High Speech herself, and out of the corner of
her eye, saw Isambard's fractional, approving nod.

"Indeed." The satrap's face hardened suddenly. "You
will have noticed the security precautions when you
landed, and I don't doubt you wondered about the
cause. Sieura, the Hegemon has offered me and mine
an unforgivable insult, one that can only be wiped out
in his blood. I intend to make him pay that debt, with
his blood and with his crown."

Involuntarily, Silence gave a soundless whistle.
Balthasar's story. . . . Yes, a public flogging was more
than enough to turn a member of the Thousand into the
Hegemon's deadly enemy, but. . . . "Why—what is my
part in all this?" she asked, still in the same polite
voice. "If you wish to hire a magus, Isambard is my
teacher and my superior, yet you speak to me."

The satrap nodded, and for the first time seemed to
falter. "It's my daughter," he said, and straightened his
shoulders abruptly. "My eldest daughter, the only child
of my first wife. After my—disgrace—the Hegemon
commanded Aili to return to Asterion, ostensibly as a
companion to his sister, the Princess Royal, but actually
as a hostage for my good behavior. I thought that I
would be able to win her release, and went ahead with
my plans, but I have not been able to free her."

Silence frowned. Giving the Hegemony's laws, an
imprisoned daughter should make little difference to
the satrap's plans. After all, women could neither in-
herit nor hold power, or even minor property, without
some man to act as her guardian.

Isambard said softly, "Aili is the only surviving child of his Highness's First Wife, thus the most legitimate of his children."

"More than that," the satrap interrupted, with a bitter smile, "if I were to sacrifice her—and I would do it, don't mistake me—that would give the Hegemon an excellent propaganda weapon to turn against me." His voice rose in savage mimicry. " 'If he was willing to lose his own daughter's life, why should he respect yours?' Bah."

Silence nodded. "But why me?" she asked again.

The satrap raised one thin eyebrow in surprise. "My daughter is in the Women's Palace."

That, at least, Silence understood. The Women's Palace on Asterion was the secluded residence of the Hegemon's female relatives, whose chastity had to be protected at all costs, and of any other single women attached to the court. No men were ever allowed to enter the confines of the Palace, which stood on an island in the center of a lake, which in turn was at the center of a heavily guarded forest preserve. She said slowly, "You must have agents of your own on Asterion, but they'd be men, of course. Which means they probably couldn't even contact your daughter, much less rescue her. And you want me to do that for you."

The satrap was watching her with new respect. "That is so."

"The security must be very heavy," Silence said. "Doubly heavy where your daughter's concerned."

"My agents have investigated," the satrap answered, with a wry smile. "They tell me it would be easier to break out from the inside than to break in from the outside, but in either case, a magus's skills are needed. An impossibility, I thought, but now I've found a woman magus—a maga?" He glanced at Isambard, who shrugged.

Silence ignored the byplay. "And if I refuse?"

"That is better not thought of," the satrap answered silkily.

"If," Silence said, ignoring Isambard's warning frown.

The satrap shrugged. "I would have to confine you here until the fighting was over. After that. . . ."

Silence nodded. The consequences were obvious. If the satrap won, they would be at his mercy, and would have displeased him by refusing. If the Hegemon won, they would be part of the spoils of war, and the Hegemon was already making efforts to find them.

"But let us consider the more likely alternative," the satrap said, after a moment. "My plan is simple. Your looks are—adequate, sieura, and I believe that with teaching you could pass for a woman of the Ten Thousand. As such, I can place you as my daughter's waiting-woman, in the Women's Palace itself. I have agents on the planet, as I've said, and they would be able to contact you. And as you have a ship of your own—"

He glanced at the page, waiting motionless in a corner, and the boy said softly, "*Recusante*, Highness. Merchant craft, of Delian registry."

The satrap nodded. "*Recusante* has no known connection with me or mine," he went on. "Your companions should have no difficulty landing on Asterion, and will be ideally placed to retrieve you and the shazadi once you've broken free of the Palace."

"You're—" Silence bit off the rest of the sentence, and searched for a more diplomatic phrase. "Your Highness, this plan relies on any number of uncertainties. And I'm merely a practitioner, not a magus."

The satrap held up his hand, cutting off any further protest. "Obviously, sieura, this is only the bare bones of a plan. But even so, I would like you to consider it."

It was not a request. Silence sighed. "Your Highness," she said abruptly, "I can't—I don't have the right to make this decision alone. As Isambard has probably mentioned, I have two husbands, and their rights must be considered. Will you give me time to talk this over with them?"

The satrap nodded graciously. "I will send for them at once," he said. "You will spend the night here, in the guest wing, and can give me your decision in the morning."

A nice try, Silence thought, but not good enough. She had hoped to get back to the ship. She bowed politely. "Thank you, your Highness. You're most kind."

CHAPTER 5

The guest wing was as luxurious as the rest of the
palace, and showed the same curious mix of magnificence and sobriety. Silence was escorted to a bedroom
not much smaller than one of *Recusante*'s holds by a
second, even more supercilious page, who made certain
she had seen all the amenities the room offered before
he bowed himself out.

Left to herself, Silence pushed back the curtains—
rich blue-and-gold brocade over pale blue silk so fine as
to be almost transparent—and stared out into the garden that filled the central courtyard of the palace. The
sun had almost set, and the garden was a bowl of
shadows lit only by pale sprays of lantern-flowers, but
she barely saw the beauty of the scene. Isambard had
managed to put them into an impossible situation, and
now it was up to her to get them out.

Almost as if her thought had conjured him, there was
a knock at the door, and the magus called, "May I come
in, Silence?"

Silence made a face. "Why not?" she demanded, and
then had to hurry to touch the proper keys on the cube
that controlled the room's various functions. It was a

mechanical toy, Delian work. She glared at it, wishing she were back on Delos herself.

The magus coughed politely, and Silence wheeled to confront him. "How much of this did you know about?" she demanded.

"None of it," Isambard answered. He looked old and tired, and Silence felt her anger ease slightly. He could not have known what would happen, and it was not entirely his fault that the satrap had seized on her as the obvious answer to his problems.

"And what about the search for Earth?"

Isambard sighed. "I regret the delay—you can't know how much I regret it—but Adeben has left us with very little choice."

"There are other options," Silence began, and stopped abruptly, less out of fear of being overheard than out of the realization that their options were pitifully limited. She had been thinking of somehow making her way back to *Recusante* and escaping into space, but the mere articulation of the thought was enough to show her how poor the chances were. Even if she and the magus could make it back to the ship—she herself had no idea where the Palace stood in relation to the port— they would still have to raise ship illegally and then escape the cordon of warships that ringed the planet. And that would be almost impossible, even drawing on Balthasar's Wrath-of-God training.

"Do you think I haven't thought of all of them?" Isambard demanded. "And a few others you couldn't know of?" His expression softened suddenly, became almost pleading. "Yes, there will be a delay, but at the end of it, the certainty—the *certainty*, Silence—of reaching Earth. Adeben will keep his word, and we'll have the portolan you need."

Silence regarded him sourly. "What if I fail, or die succeeding?"

Isambard hesitated, then said, "I don't know. But you should not fail."

Silence made a face. She had been on Solitudo long

enough to learn to read something of a person's thoughts in the involuntary movements of his body, and Isambard's real answer was almost painfully clear. If she died and the magus survived, Isambard believed he could still persuade the satrap to let him have the portolan. With it, any pilot could reach Earth. "I wouldn't bet on it," she muttered, and added, more loudly, "I do understand the situation, believe me. But I still want to talk to Denis and Julie first."

Isambard nodded, almost the gesture of equal to equal. "Very well. I will see you in the morning, then."

Before Silence could think of an appropriate answer, the magus had gone, closing the doors gently behind him. Silence cursed him in a whisper, then settled herself in the narrow window seat to try to work out some better plan. The satrap had not spared any expense in the decoration of the guest rooms, but Silence barely noticed the rosilk cushions or the subtle fragrance of the Sareptan orchids that floated in shallow bowls beneath the long windows. Over the next two hours, she formulated, tested, and regretfully discarded half a dozen plans for escaping from Inarime. By the time the control cube chimed and announced the arrival of Balthasar and Chase Mago, she was almost ready to admit defeat.

The two men had been given rooms directly opposite her own. She found them both in Balthasar's room, staring at the decorations—a motif of goats and grape clusters—with expressions somewhere between outrage and amusement.

"They've got your number, Denis," Chase Mago was saying. He stood, hands on hips, surveying the goats.

Balthasar gave him a rather sour look. "Was this your idea, Silence?" he demanded.

Silence shook her head, uncertain quite how to begin.

"Trouble?" Chase Mago asked.

"We have to talk," Silence said, grateful that the engineer, at least, had recognized her worry, and glanced around the room. The carved paneling, the grape-cluster chandelier, the ornate bedstead, and the tasseled cushions provided many possible hiding places for listening devices. Like all apprentices, she had been taught the technique of creating an aphonic ring, but she had never had reason to practice the procedure outside the workshops.

"Not much chance of that, at least not privately," Balthasar said.

Silence did not answer, glancing again around the opulent room. She closed her eyes, letting herself slip into the awareness that was the first stage of perception. She could feel the elemental harmonies of Inarime's core rising through her feet, until her whole body quivered in response. She opened her eyes, and saw the same currents trembling in the air, just at the edge of vision. As she had expected, the palace had been built to take full advantage of the planetary harmonies, and with that to draw on, she should have no trouble setting the ring. She let herself slip out of that unnatural stillness, and saw the others looking expectantly at her. She smiled, and in the same moment, Chase Mago said, "What can we do?"

Silence did not answer for a moment, studying the furniture, then dragged three tabourets together into the center of the room. "Sit there," she said, and managed a smile of apology for the brusque orders. "And don't do anything."

The two men did as they were told, but kept their eyes fixed on Silence. She was only too aware of their regard. You'll just have to ignore them, she told herself firmly. Begin.

The carpeting in this room was a deep monochromatic pile, the sort that showed every footstep. With finicky care, Silence sketched a broad ring in the pile, encircling the three tabourets. She dragged her foot two and three times over the same spot to make sure the ring would keep its shape. When the circle was

complete, she stepped inside it, turning her back on
the others. Closing her eyes, she let herself slip back
into the hyperawareness of the first stage, feeling again
for the elemental harmonies. When she was sure she
had fixed them in her mind, she murmured the First
Cantation, the words that bent the solid reality of the
material world and allowed her to shape that substance
to a new Form. This was not the sort of major creation
that had formed her examination, but rather a reshap-
ing of something already present in the air around her,
and she was grateful for that. She took a deep breath
and whispered the words that were the Form of the
aphonic ring. The harmonic lines quivered and thickened, resisting the new and unnatural shaping. Silence
could feel the floor tremble, very faintly, and spoke
again, repeating the Form of the ring. This time, the
Form compelled obedience. The subtle tension eased
abruptly, the harmonic lines flowing and shifting to
encircle the tabourets, the harmonies of earth and air
mingling to shut out all sound. Silence relaxed slowly
and turned to face the others, a proud smile on her lips.
This was the first time she had used her newfound
talents outside the classroom and without Isambard's
supervision, and it was both a relief and a triumph to
find that the ring had actually worked.

Balthasar was staring at her, and Silence felt her
smile widen into a grin. Chase Mago nodded slowly and
said, "Most impressive, maga."

Balthasar closed his mouth with a snap, as though
he'd just realized he was staring. "Yes, very nice, but
what's the occasion?"

Silence grimaced, annoyed that the Delian had broken her moment of triumph. But he was right, she told
herself, there was no time to waste on self-congratulation.
Still, her voice was a little more acerbic than she had
intended when she answered, "The satrap's got a
portolan, but he wants a pretty stiff price for it."

"We might have expected that," Chase Mago said calmly, after a moment. "What does he want?"

"He wants us to get his daughter back," Silence said. The others were looking at her, Balthasar with deep suspicion, Chase Mago with a resigned, world-weary smile on his bearded face. The pilot took a deep breath and explained. The two men were quiet for a long time after she had finished. Finally, Balthasar said, matter-of-factly, "The son of a bitch can't really expect us to do that—it's impossible. What do you think he really wants?"

"This is what he really wants," Silence said, and Chase Mago nodded.

"His daughter—she'd be a shazadi, I suppose—is too important politically for him to risk. He can't afford to lose her."

"Wonderful," Balthasar muttered, then added, more loudly, "It's too risky. You pass yourself off as a lady of the court, Silence, while we fly into Anshar' Asteriona, pick you up, and then fly out again, with the whole Hegemonic Navy on our tail—assuming, of course, they don't spot us the minute we land?" He glanced over his shoulder at the window. "How far do you think we are from the port?"

"I have no idea," Silence said. "They brought us in a closed transport."

Chase Mago said, "If we get to the port, Denis, can you get *Recusante* through that cordon we passed on the way down?"

There was a long pause, and Silence felt her heart sink. Until then, she had not realized quite how much she had expected Balthasar to come up with a way out. But for once the Delian was facing a problem that could not be solved by one of his wild schemes. And if Balthasar had no plan, Silence thought, there simply wasn't an answer. The same realization was clear on Chase Mago's bearded face, and Balthasar wore an expression almost of guilt. He met her eyes only reluctantly, shaking his head. "I'm sorry," he murmured, so softly Silence almost didn't hear him.

The pilot shook herself angrily. Since there was no alternative, they would have to go through with this plan and somehow make it work. She forced a smile. "You better hope I can look like a high-born lady," she said, and reached to touch the invisible barrier, destroying it.

Chase Mago laughed softly and after a moment, Balthasar managed a smile. Silence nodded to them, trying to project a confidence she did not truly feel, and slowly the mood lightened. Still, she was very glad to spend that night in Balthasar's bed, the warm bodies to either side giving her the illusion of security.

In the morning, Isambard was waiting, sitting stiffly on a tabouret outside the door of her room. He seemed mildly surprised to see Silence emerge from Balthasar's room, but before he could say anything, the pilot scowled at him and said, "Well?"

"Your decision?" Isambard answered placidly.

"What do you think?" Silence retorted, with some bitterness. "We'll do it, all right—but the satrap owes us most of the profits."

Isambard nodded and stood up, gathering his robes around him. "I will inform him."

Silence muttered a curse at his departing back, and pushed the latchplate to open the room door. Discreet servo-mechanisms had already been at work: the curtains were drawn back to admit the daylight, and a breakfast table was drawn up in front of the windows. A clothes horse had emerged from a wall niche, bearing a floor-length, long-sleeved gown and a heavier, sleeveless overdress. Silence recognized the style as some sort of court dress, and her eyes narrowed.

Before she could investigate further, however, a light flashed on top of the room's control cube and a chime sounded softly. Silence touched the receive button, and a disembodied voice—a woman's, this time—spoke.

"His Highness requires that you admit the visit of the Domna Kalere, who will begin your lessons. The domna requests that you receive her wearing the clothes which have been provided for you."

Silence's mouth tightened. Either Isambard had moved more quickly than she had expected, or the satrap had simply assumed her cooperation. She controlled her voice, and answered mildly, "Very well. When will the domna arrive?"

To her annoyance, the woman did not answer, and the light went out on the top of the cube, signaling the end of the conversation. In that case, Silence thought, I'll eat first. The satrap, or his housekeepers, had been generous: she ate with real pleasure, and then made herself sit at ease until she had finished the last of the carafe of sweetwater. There was still no sign of the domna, and Silence toyed with the idea of waiting until the woman arrived to do the satrap's bidding. Then she shook her head, angry with herself this time. There was no point in putting off the inevitable, and no sense whatsoever in provoking this Domna Kalere—yet. Reluctantly, Silence turned her attention to the clothes horse.

The gown and overdress were of finer material than she had realized at first, and Silence fingered the heavy folds with new respect. There were more things folded on the platform beneath the dresses. Silence pulled them out one by one. A pair of embroidered slippers, a thin undershift, a grey silk fan, plain and unpainted . . . The last item was a loosely folded pile of thin black material, and Silence unfolded it suspiciously. As she had expected, it expanded into the enveloping, uncomfortable formal veil worn by noblewomen. Experimentally, she threw it over herself, letting it settle around her until she was completely hidden in its floor-length folds. She could see dimly through the thin cloth, but a glance in the mirror confirmed that it concealed any details of her features.

With sudden revulsion, she scrambled free of the veil, almost tearing the delicate fabric in her haste. She hated the thing, hated it with a passion as the badge of slavery. She would never wear it. . . . She calmed herself with an effort that left her spent and trembling. She would wear it, because she would have to, if she was to rescue the shazadi. It was just a part of the job, nothing more—and she would wear it by her own choice, not because she was ordered to do so. The thoughts were hollow, and even when she had regained enough control to begin the laborious process of changing clothes, she left the veil lying where it had fallen.

The doorchime sounded almost as soon as she had finished dressing. Silence gave the control cube a suspicious glance—the domna's timing was almost too good to be true—but opened the door without comment. A greying older woman, not tall, with a lined, thoughtful face, stood there, a maidservant hovering behind her.

"I am the Domna Kalere," the older woman announced.

"Silence Leigh." Silence stepped back to allow the other woman to enter.

Kalere came into the room, and motioned for the maid to set her bundle on the nearest table. "That will be all, Daru. You may go."

The maid bobbed a quick curtsy and vanished. Silence touched a button to close the door behind her and waited, watching the other woman. Kalere returned the stare quite steadily and, after a moment, nodded to herself.

"Well, your hair's a bit short, but it'll do. I am told you are a pilot and a magus?" Kalere's voice was frankly skeptical.

"That's right," Silence answered.

"Where were you trained?"

"As a pilot, on Cap Bel in the Rusadir, under the Cor Tauri guild-system," Silence answered. "Then on Solitudo

Hermae, apprenticed to Doctor Isambard. Do you want
to see my practitioner's license, sieura?"

"Domna," Kalere corrected automatically. "The Cor
Tauri guild? Then you're trained to the Chanfro exercises?"

"Yes," Silence said, a little warily. Those were the
teaching rituals the pilots used when a great deal of
information had to be imparted in a very short time.
The method was effective, but exhausting. She had
been subjected to it twice, once during training and
again just after the Hegemony conquered the Rusadir
worlds, when the guild-seniors had passed along as
much information as they could before the Hegemon's
troops burned their library. It was not an experience
she would care to repeat.

Kalere was nodding again. "Then we may be able to
do this after all," she said. "Sieura Leigh, his Highness
has explained what it is you are to do for him, and I
assure you I will do everything in my power to help
you. Aili—her Highness the shazadi—was my nursling,
and my charge after that. But even with the Chanfro
techniques, it will take time to learn everything you
need to know." She turned briskly to the bundle waiting on the table and unwrapped it, exposing an odd
miscellany of objects—books, a flat gilt box, a collection
of tubes and jars. "You will go to Asterion as Jamilla
Sahen, whose father is commander of his Highness's
fleets. She is of appropriate birth to act as companion to
her Highness, and that will give you the rank of domna
as well. The papers are already being processed." She
stopped abruptly. "You do understand the duties
involved?"

Silence nodded. "I think so. To be a companion—a
sort of glorified maid, isn't it?"

"In a manner of speaking," Kalere answered, rather
dryly. "You will act as the shazadi's representative to
the outside world. If she requires something from outside the Palace, for example, you will inform the guards,

and you will accept it when it's brought to you. If there are visitors, you will act as chaperone. If they are of lower rank, you will meet them on the shazadi's behalf."

She looked expectantly at Silence, and the pilot nodded. "I see. No, wait, I have a question."

"Very well." Kalere seated herself at the table and began to sort the objects into rough piles.

"This Jamilla Sahen, whose papers I'll be taking. Won't her pictures be on file somewhere in the royal archives or something?" Kalere was regarding her with an expression of amused incredulity. Silence flushed, but continued doggedly, "It seems pretty likely that I'll be spotted before I even get to the Palace."

"My dear girl, Jamilla is a lady of the Ten Thousand. Not even the image of her face may be seen by outsiders." Kalere smiled. "The admiral will swear you are his daughter—his Highness has taken the perjury on himself—and no one would presume to disbelieve."

Silence raised an eyebrow at that. If the Women's Palace was as closely guarded as everyone said it was, then the guards would be suspicious of everyone and everything just as a matter of routine. At least there would be no photorecord to betray her. For once, the Hegemony's laws would work for her, not against her. It was a new experience, and Silence allowed herself to feel a cautious optimism.

"Now." Kalere studied the piled miscellany for a moment longer, then handed the stack of books to Silence. "We have much to do—thank God you know Chanfro!—we'll begin with these."

Silence turned over the books to study the titles emblazoned on the spine. Thanks to the accelerated study on Solitudo Hermae, the Hegemonic script no longer looked peculiar to her, but the titles were old-fashioned enough to make her hesitate, mentally shifting from one alphabet to the more familiar coinë characters, before she was certain she understood them: *The Art of Courtly Behavior, Recollections of a Long*

Life, Regulations of the Royal House, The Register of the Thousand, and the even larger *Register of the Ten Thousand*.

"Most of it will simply be memorization," Kalere went on, "but there are things—the proper gestures, and some rituals—that will have to be rehearsed. You can begin by memorizing those."

Silence glanced dubiously at the books. "You expect me to memorize the entire Hegemonic nobility—at least eleven thousand families?"

"The important ones are marked," Kalere answered. "The *Regulations* and the *Courtly Art* will tell you the basics of proper behavior; you must concentrate on those. In the meantime, you must move into the women's quarter—"

"No," Silence said, flatly.

The older woman frowned. "It is not appropriate for you to remain here with the men."

Silence took a deep breath. "Domna Kalere, I accept that I must learn to behave like a woman of your kind and class. Fine. I'll study my lessons and all that. But if I'm going to rescue your precious shazadi, I will need to have access to my husbands—" Kalere flinched almost imperceptibly, and Silence repeated the word with relish. "—yes, my husbands, both of them. To Isambard, too, to figure out how to get out of the Women's Palace once I'm in it."

Kalere's lips tightened to a thin line, but after a moment, she nodded. "Very well, you have sufficient reason. But a word of warning. Don't expect to get your way so easily on Asterion."

"I don't," Silence answered.

"Good." Kalere rose to her feet, leaving the litter of objects on the table. She studied Silence for a moment longer, as if trying to assess the pilot's worth, and then her stern face softened. "It's to help Aili," she said, almost to herself, then added, "I will return this afternoon. Begin with the *Courtly Art*. If you finish, go on

to the *Regulations*. Both are compatible with Chanfro—
well, you'll see the structure once you begin."

"All right." Silence settled herself comfortably on the
nearest tabouret, drawing her legs up beneath her.

"No."

Silence looked up in genuine surprise, then realized
what she was doing. Her own mother had once cher-
ished ambitions of seeing her married to a Cap Bel
oligarch, and had tried for years to teach her daughter
more ladylike behavior. The pilot laughed softly. It was
to be hoped she could learn it now, when so much
depended on it.

Kalere gave an exasperated sigh. "No," she said again.
"If you are to learn in time, you must begin now. When
you wear those clothes, you must *be* Jamilla. Put your
feet on the floor, straighten your dress. . . ."

Dutifully, Silence suppressed her laughter and sat up
straight, tugging at the material of the overdress so that
it fell in heavy, graceful folds. She opened the first book
at random, one hand under the spine, the other touching the pages, and glanced up at the domna.

"Well, someone's made a start," Kalere said tartly.
"Remember, you are an admiral's daughter, a woman
of the Ten Thousand, and behave as such. I will return
at the sixteenth hour, and we'll go over afternoon informals." Without waiting for a reply, she stalked from the
room.

Silence rose to lock the door behind her, then returned to the tabouret and picked up the copy of the
Courtly Arts. She had no idea what the domna had
meant by "afternoon informals," but she intended to
find out.

Even after she had read through the section on informals, however, she was not entirely certain. The term
referred to some sort of light meal, that much was
clear. An "informal" could take place in the morning or
afternoon, and was further categorized as "sweet" or
"salt," depending on the food served. No intoxicant of

any kind could be served—to do so changed the meal
from an "informal" to a "gathering." All this information
was arrived at by inference, sifted out of the endless
discussion of the proper topics of conversation, the
proper number and status of guests, suitable clothing,
accessories, tableware, and decorations—no more than
four small pieces.

Silence shook her head and closed the book. This was
the most extreme case of the sort of life most women
led. She had almost forgotten—had done her best to
forget, in the eight years she had been a pilot, acting as
a man in the men's world—how much time could be
spent on the obsessive interpretation of every gesture,
every action, until boredom and constraint created an
unspoken language and a society in which the bitterest
feuds were fought with nuance and the lifted eyebrow,
and the slightest error of ceremony could doom one to
perpetual exile. The merchant classes of Cap Bel, to
which Silence's family had belonged, had been relatively free of such concerns—Rusadir women were only
bound by the Hegemony's laws since the conquest, and
traditionally had helped in the family businesses as best
they could—but Silence's mother had been ambitious
above her station, and had done her best to interest her
daughter in the ways of the oligarchy. The pilot shook
her head again, remembering adolescent awkwardness
and rebellion. Her mother was revenged, it seemed;
she would have to learn the rules after all.

Silence shook herself then. It was not at all the same
thing, she told herself angrily. Thinking that way will
only hurt you. You're learning this for your own purposes, to rescue this shazadi and to get the damned
portolan so that you can reach Earth—and you're doing
it on your own terms. She made herself savor her small
victory to the fullest: she was not confined to the wom-
en's quarters, and wouldn't be until she arrived on
Asterion. She had demanded to be allowed to stay with
the others, and had won. Not much of a triumph,

perhaps . . . No, she corrected herself, here it's a very real victory. But now there's work to be done.

She spent the next three weeks in a whirl of activity. The first week was spent committing the contents of half a dozen texts—the essentials, according to Kalere, of courtly behavior—to memory. The Chanfro techniques, with their tricks for speeding the absorption of information, helped the process considerably. At the end, Silence, exhausted though she was, was still able to survey the complicated interrelated mnemonic chains with a sense of grim pride. Through those linked images, she could recall in seconds the proper behavior for any situation and act on it. Admittedly, her knowledge was purely theoretical, and that gave her responses a rather stiff, mechanical quality. Kalere did her best to drill away that stiffness, but agreed with Silence that it suited an admiral's daughter. As the pilot's education progressed, she was allowed to join the other women of the satrap's household for various meals and gatherings, passing herself off as one of Kalere's poor relations, until at last the domna professed herself satisfied.

Silence was not given much time to dwell on that success, however. As soon as she had learned the basic rules, Kalere began drilling her in the more subtle, unwritten rules of courtly life. Isambard, too, reclaimed a portion of her attention, arriving every afternoon precisely at fifteen hours to cram in as much advanced training as he could before she left for Asterion. He concentrated on the parts of the Four Arts that he guessed would be of most use in the Women's Palace, and Silence wished she could go back and fill in the gaps that she knew existed in her knowledge. In the evenings, when Silence could stay awake, she and Balthasar and Chase Mago pored over the maps and holocubes of Asterion and her sister planets. Balthasar grumbled loudly at the information in the navy holocubes provided by the satrap's servants. The three sister worlds, Falathar, Mim Seras, and Niminx, all boasted heavily fortified moons, each the base for a double-strength pursuit squadron, and Asterion had a defensive patrol in permanent close orbit. Still, the captain allowed himself to be somewhat appeased by the satrap's promise that the patrolling ships would be "distracted."

"Though precisely what he means by that, I don't know," Balthasar grumbled.

"Are you sure you want to know details?" Chase Mago asked.

Silence laughed, and Balthasar smiled reluctantly. "I wouldn't want to be the pilot, I grant you." He glanced sideways, reaching for the jug of wine that stood half buried under the piled charts. "More your speed, Silence."

The pilot made a face. They had not been told the precise details of the satrap's planned "distraction," and would not be, for obvious reasons: if they were captured, they couldn't betray what they didn't know. It was not something Silence liked to contemplate. She reached quickly for the nearest map of Asterion, swinging it until she found the large blank spot that marked the Women's Palace.

"What's the probable error in this again?" she asked.

Balthasar refilled his own glass and held out the jug in mute question. Chase Mago nodded, saying, "Here's the one the satrap's agents produced. It's supposed to be accurate to within a hundred meters along the shoreline."

He slid the smaller sheet of paper across the table, and Silence took it, nodding for Balthasar to refill her glass as well. She sipped thoughtfully at the wine, studying the map. All the maps of Asterion produced by the official Hegemonic cartographers left a blank where the Women's Palace should stand; the best traced the outline of the Palace park and left the interior empty. This one, a highly unofficial production, concentrated on the park and Palace. The park itself was an irregularly shaped area of woodland covering nearly one hundred and thirty square kilometers. The lake that contained the Palace itself stood not in the center of that wood, but in the southwestern quadrant, only forty kilometers from the border. She ran her finger slowly along the green line that marked that edge, wondering if it would be safer to try and rendezvous with the others outside the Palace park. Balthasar shook his head.

"That side's the cliff—most of the park is on a natural plateau—and it's heavily guarded anyway. Look at the patrol lines. I figured we'd lift from Anshar' Asteriona and land somewhere in here." The Delian traced a short arc along the northern border of the lake.

"The guardpost's there," Chase Mago objected.

"I know," Balthasar answered, "but the ground's rougher, and it doesn't seem to be patrolled as well."

"We hope," Chase Mago muttered.

Silence stared at the network of fine lines running through the park. Each one represented an established patrol run—or so the satrap's agents had thought. There were bound to be other patrol routes, both established ones and occasional spot checks. "It seems to me," she said slowly, "that we shouldn't set a rendezvous point now. The satrap's people ought to have more information by the time you land—and they must change the patrol schedules on a regular basis anyway."

Balthasar nodded. "That makes sense, especially since they promise I'll be able to contact you." He studied the map again, then reached for his glass. "But almost certainly somewhere in there."

Silence nodded, yawning. They had spent over two hours tonight on the maps, and she had lost count of the other evenings they had spent planning the landing and rendezvous. "I think—" she began, but she was interrupted by a knock at the door.

Chase Mago frowned, glancing at the chronometer, but said, "Yes?" Silence saw without surprise that Balthasar's left hand was deep in the pocket of his coat.

"Your pardon, sieuri, for the late hour." The voice was familiar from other late-night visits: the satrap's most trusted page, the one who had been in attendance when Silence first encountered Adeben. "But his Highness wishes to speak with you."

"Again?" Silence whispered, and reached for the man's coat hanging on the back of her chair. Here in the privacy of Balthasar's room, she wore coat and trousers, in defiance of Kalere's orders.

Balthasar slid the heavy heylin out of his pocket, setting it on top of the pile of maps. "I wonder what he wants this time?"

Chase Mago shrugged and opened the door. "At once?" he asked.

The page nodded, his eyes sweeping across all three of them. "Yes, Sieur Chase Mago—oh, good, his Highness asked specially that Sieura Leigh wear man's clothes."

Silence raised her eyebrows at that, but there was no time to ask questions. She swung the disguising coat across her shoulders and jammed the cap Balthasar handed her onto her untidy hair.

"What's all this about?" the Delian asked.

"I'm sorry, Sieur Balthasar, but I may not tell you." The page gave them an inquiring glance. "Are you ready, sieuri?"

"We're ready," Silence said, biting back an annoyed comment—the boy had emphasized the word "may"—and gestured for the page to precede them from the room.

He led them by a roundabout route, through darkened corridors and past rooms filled with shrouded furniture. At last they emerged into a familiar, glass-walled corridor, and Silence realized they had been brought once again to the satrap's private chamber. Chase Mago and Balthasar exchanged a glance, but said nothing as the page touched the doorplate with his control wand.

"Highness, I bring Sieur—the sieuri, as you ordered," the page announced, and gestured for the three to enter.

Silence did as she was told, grateful for the others' presence at her back, and heard the snap as the lock closed behind them. Only a few points of flame showed at the very top of the great candelabra, casting bizarre shadows across the carpeted floor. Most of the light in the long room came from globes of fixed fire smaller than a woman's fist, each encased in a fretted sphere that cast even more strange shadows. The satrap sat in his thronelike chair just inside the circle of light thrown by one of the globes; there were other figures in the shadows.

Silence heard Balthasar whisper a curse, and kept herself still with an effort. There were at least half a dozen strangers, each sitting with their faces in shadow. More than that, she realized, each one of them was masked. . . . Startling herself with her own presumption, she said, "Your Highness requires?"

There was a stirring in the shadows to her left, just out of her line of sight, but she did not move. The satrap nodded once, his face impassive. "Please be seated, sieuri."

Three tabourets had been drawn up at the edge of the light thrown by the candelabra. Silence seated herself carefully on the central one, realizing as she did so that their presence would complete the circle, and waited. Balthasar and Chase Mago took their places to either side.

"These are the agents?" It was a dry, papery voice, filtered through an expensive distortion-mask. Silence disliked it instantly.

"They are." The satrap's tone precluded further questions. "Sieuri, I have asked you here tonight for two reasons. First, to prove to my associates that in truth I am not indifferent to the fate of my eldest daughter."

Was it just my imagination, Silence thought, or did he look at the papery voice when he said that?

"Second," the satrap continued, "I wished you to know something of my larger plans, so that you might face your own part in them with more confidence."

"Damn decent of you," Balthasar breathed. Silence ignored him, watching the satrap.

"As you have surely guessed," the satrap said, "I am not without allies among the great ones of the Hegemony. Many others, both of the Thousand and the Ten Thousand, have felt the Hegemon's unjust anger and are ready for a new regime." He gave a thin smile. "Some are even willing to lend their own troops to the cause. When my fleet attacks Asterion, it will be supported by attacks on a dozen other key worlds, and—" He glanced to his left, still smiling. "—By persons within the Hegemon's own armies."

There was a movement in the shadows, and a new voice said, in a crisply military tone, "We of the True Thousand have been blamed unreasonably for trifling errors. We will not allow this to continue."

The True Thousand. Silence kept herself still with an effort. Then that man, he of the soldier's voice, was one of the Hegemon's elite guard, the people who had captured and bound herself and her husbands back on Arganthonios. She felt numbly certain that her escape was one of the "trifling errors" for which the soldiers of the Thousand were being blamed, and was very glad of her man's dress. And the satrap wanted me to wear it, too, she thought. That was considerate of him.

"Adeben, you are a fool." That was the papery voice again. "Why do you tell them these things, when they will certainly betray you if they're caught—will probably betray you anyway?"

Silence held her breath, hearing Chase Mago's angry hiss. The satrap said sharply, "You're the fool, if you don't see it. These people will be risking their lives to save my daughter. I owe them some promise that I, and mine, will be doing our part."

Silence let her breath out slowly, remembering Isambard's way of dealing with the satrap. "And your Highness has told us nothing that would not be immediately obvious to the Hegemon if we were caught," she said boldly.

There was a momentary pause, and then the satrap said, "That is also true."

"Nevertheless, I'm glad to hear my assumptions confirmed," Silence went on, and heard someone in the shadows whisper, "A magus . . . ?"

The satrap turned his head to look directly at the source of the papery voice. "Are you satisfied with my arrangements?"

There was a movement as though the figure bowed his head. "I am satisfied."

"And the rest of you?" the satrap demanded. There was a murmur of agreement, and the satrap's voice softened slightly. "And you, sieuri, have you any questions?"

Not that I'd ask here, Silence thought, but she made a production of glancing at Balthasar and then at Chase Mago before she answered. "No, your Highness, we are satisfied."

"Thank you. Then you may go." The satrap beckoned to the waiting page, who moved quickly to unlock the door. Silence rose with all the dignity she could muster, and bowed to the satrap before she stalked from the room.

None of the three said anything until they were back in Balthasar's room and Chase Mago had carefully locked the door behind them. Then Balthasar gave an explosive sigh and reached for the jug of wine. "I'm not happy," he said.

"I'm happier than I was," Chase Mago answered. "Rebellions and raids on twelve other worlds besides Asterion, plus a mutiny, or at least a sympathetic party within the True Thousand—that should keep the Hegemon busy. And it should mean our 'distraction' will be on a similarly large scale."

"It should be, yeah," Balthasar said, "but that's not what I meant. I don't trust that guy with the raspy voice. I wish he weren't on our side."

"They have to be careful," Chase Mago said, mildly enough. "A rebellion on this scale is dangerous, Denis."

Balthasar opened his mouth to continue the argument, but Silence said, "It's the satrap's problem, not ours. He'd better know his people by now." She yawned ostentatiously. "Right now, I'm for bed." Grumbling a little, the others agreed, but unaccountably Silence found herself unable to sleep. She lay in the darkness, listening to the men's breathing, and wondered if she had been right to dismiss Balthasar's worries so calmly. She didn't trust that man either. . . . But you have to assume the satrap knows which of his friends he can trust, she told herself again. Obviously, he thinks he can trust this one. And *you* have to trust *him*. She paused, staring up into the darkness at the invisible goats. There was always the possibility of selling the satrap to the Hegemon—the plans for the rebellion in exchange for her pardon—but aside from the fact that she found the idea distasteful, she was quite certain the Hegemon would not agree. She smiled wryly. Which leaves us where we always were: we have to do this. There simply isn't any other choice.

Suddenly, all too soon, it was time to go. Silence woke to the sound of Balthasar's clock chiming nine. She had slept a full twelve hours; the others were up and dressed long ago. And, she remembered abruptly, she was supposed to be aboard the transport at noon. She flung back the covers and made a hasty toilet, hardly noticing the chill of the water in the bathing pool. She dressed quickly, the long gown and overdress no longer completely unfamiliar. Then, more reluctantly, she set in place the headpiece that would support the full-length veil. Once she was accepted on Asterion, she had learned, she would only have to wear the more comfortable face veil, but until then she would have to observe the strictest regulations. Sighing, she pinned the veil to the headpiece, but did not draw it down into place: there was still her baggage, the three starcrates full of clothes and jewelry that were considered appropriate for an admiral's daughter, to be sealed and sent ahead to the transport.

The crates were already gone from her room. Startled, Silence looked around for a moment before she found the slip of paper tucked under the corner of the control cube. It took her a moment to decipher Balthasar's handwriting and the drastically abbreviated coinë —one of the more irritating results of the Delian's obsessive secrecy—but at last she figured it out. "Gone to *Ballisarda* with trunks," it read. "Back soon." Naturally, Balthasar had not noted the time of writing, but he could not have been gone long. Silence settled herself on a tabouret beneath the window and composed herself to wait.

It was very sunny in the garden, and for the first time since her arrival on Inarime, Silence had the leisure to study the exotic flowers in the daylight. She recognized very few; the rest were merely vividly beautiful, or, in the case of one gnarled, woody ovoid that grew on a twisting, two-meter-tall stalk, spectacularly grotesque. She soon turned away from the window. She was afraid, she decided dispassionately, but that fear was for the moment overridden by sheer physical relief: this was the first time in weeks that she was not on the edge of utter exhaustion. She found herself wishing that she had not been too tired the night before for anything but sleep, and resolutely turned her mind away from such an unprofitable speculation.

Despite all their work, the plan remained in essence

exactly the one that the satrap had outlined to Isambard
when the magus first arrived on the planet. She would
travel to Asterion aboard one of the satrap's small personal liners, its actual size and crew complement
precisely calculated to match her supposed rank. Once
there, she would be taken to the Women's Palace as the
shazadi's new domna. And there, Silence thought, was
the first of many uncertainties. There had been no safe
way of alerting the shazadi to her arrival. The satrap's
best agent was not able to contact the shazadi except
through the well-monitored ghost-lines. The satrap had
added private alert-codes to the formal announcement
of "Jamilla's" appointment, and the agent had passed on
a similarly cautious coded warning that something was
about to happen, but there was no way for Aili to reply
to either message. There was no guarantee that the
shazadi would accept Silence as Jamilla Sahen, and if
she didn't, the mission would be over before it had
properly begun.

Silence shook her head angrily. The satrap swore his
daughter would cooperate—that she was clever enough
to be expecting almost anything after receiving the two
coded messages, and a good enough actress to respond
accordingly. The pilot would just have to hope he was
right. At least Balthasar and Chase Mago had been
provided with new papers—genuine papers, for once
made out by the satrap's own Port Authority—in the
names. They also had a new registration file for *Recusante*
and even a semi-legitimate cargo for a cover. They
should have no trouble landing safely, or in contacting
the satrap's agent. Isambard, too, had new papers, but
in any case, no one would dare question a magus too
closely.

Silence made a wry face. She had not been told the
name or the station of the satrap's agent, and that told
her just how slim her chances were thought to be. If
she survived the security checks and her first meeting
with the shazadi Aili, she still had to figure out some

way to get past the elaborate security system of the Women's Palace, and bring both herself and the shazadi to a rendezvous with *Recusante*. For all the satrap's praise of his daughter's intelligence and levelheadedness, Silence doubted the girl would be much use when it came to real action, and she was not looking forward to having to act as nursemaid. On top of everything else, Kalere had made it clear that Aili had to continue to observe all the customary strictures, or forfeit her status as one of the Thousand. Unfortunately, Silence thought, no one's told me how I'm going to do all this. The satrap's data on Palace security had been pitifully meager, little more than what was available to the general public.

Suddenly unable to keep still, Silence rose quickly and paced the length of the room, automatically adjusting her stride to the weight of her robes. This was certainly the most difficult thing she had ever contemplated doing, and there was a small, not-quite-suppressed part of her that kept repeating that it was impossible. Not even aboard the Hegemony's transport, locked under their geas, had she wanted so much to be back in space, preferably millions of parsecs from Inarime.

She was well on her way to blind panic, and knew it. She took a deep breath and fought back grimly. She was at least free this time, and doing the job under the semblance of her own choice. And she was a magus—half-trained, perhaps, but more powerful than anything she would encounter in the Women's Palace. She would manage.

The light on top of the control cube flashed, and an unfamiliar voice said, "Domna Jamilla, your escort attends you." Before Silence could answer, or demand to wait for her husbands, the light flashed again and Kalere's voice cut in. "Sieura, I was asked to tell you that your husbands have gone ahead to the field, and will meet you there. His Highness requests you accompany the escort."

"Very well," Silence answered, and reluctantly drew the veil down over her, hiding face and body. She took a final deep breath, and touched the key that unlocked the room door.

The door slid back to reveal a heavyset, middle-aged man in the uniform of the satrap's personal fleet. Four more men, two in fleet livery, two in house uniforms, waited at his back, gleaming sonic rifles slung at their shoulders. The first man—a deck-officer/third by the twists of his shoulder braid—bowed punctiliously. "Domna Jamilla, your car is waiting."

"Thank you, officer," Silence answered, and was surprised to find her voice steady.

The officer bowed again and offered his arm. The pilot gathered the folds of the veil around her with her left hand—she had discovered early on how easy it was to trip over the billowing material—and laid her right hand, still discreetly veiled, on the officer's forearm. He led her down the long corridor and out into the courtyard, the escort following a discreet three paces to the rear.

The waiting transport was exactly like the one that had first brought Silence to the satrap's palace, a double-domed, six-wheeled vehicle chosen for the comforts that would fit into the passenger dome rather than for speed or efficiency. Punctiliously polite, the officer handed Silence into the passenger compartment—the pilot managed to take her place without too ungraceful a display of foot and hand—then seated himself on the pull-down shelf opposite her, and gestured for the nearest escort to close the dome. The soldier did as he was told, and took his place on the running board just before the transport shuddered into motion.

This time the driver did not cloud the dome, and Silence was able to get her first real look at Port Mosata. It looked like a pleasant city, most of the houses moderately wealthy, the streets clean and in good repair—as of course they would be, Silence thought. Port Mosata contained the satrap's favorite residence, and his private ships used its starport almost exclusively. Of course the city government would do its best to present an appealing facade, even if it had to remove the poor to do it. But then the transport turned onto a broader, more heavily travelled avenue, and Silence could see, behind the rows of storefronts, lanes of cheap stackhouses. They looked old, but reasonably well cared for, and the pilot grudgingly adjusted her opinion of both city and satrap. There was some difference between hiding poverty and controlling it—though of course it was always possible that the poor had merely been expelled from the city, as rumor said had happened in the capital on Aja. But remembering her meetings with the satrap, Silence did not think that had happened here.

The wide avenue led directly into the walled port. The transport did not pause at the massive, jade-green gate, but drove straight through, the officer touching his forehead to return the guards' precise salutes. They did not pause at any of the usual buildings, either, but continued straight through the tangle of buildings toward the satrap's private hangar. To reach it, the driver had either to cut directly across the field itself or turn aside and follow the usual service roads. Silence winced as the soldier chose to keep to his inflexible course, and looked up quickly, squinting through the veil for the interference light of a landing starship. At this range, any keelsong would be at least painful, and probably actively dangerous. . . .

She saw the officer looking curiously at her and looked away again, fighting to keep her expression neutral. Of course no other ships would be landing, she berated herself. Not only is one of the Ten Thousand about to embark, but Inarime's closed off, all the traffic being rerouted anyway. It was not a bad mistake, but a mistake nonetheless, and it chilled her. It was so easy to

arouse suspicion, and so hard to answer it once roused.
She would have to be much more careful in the future.

Then the transport pulled up to one of the private
docking sheds, set well apart from the rest of the port
buildings. This special area was like a port within a port,
with its own docks and tuning sheds and tug bunkers,
even its own miniature control tower set a little apart
from the rest. One of the escorts pulled back the dome,
and the officer scrambled from his seat, turning quickly
to assist Silence. The pilot accepted his help automatically, her attention on the half-open door of the shed.
She could just see the satrap's liner *Ballisarda*, a slim,
streamlined ship twice the size of *Recusante*, waiting on
her cradle a few meters from the door. The unshrouded
keel gleamed coolly in the dim light, running with
colors like oil-film on water. Silence gave a sigh of sheer
desire. *Ballisarda* was a beautiful ship; it would be an
act of pure joy to pilot her.

Another man in the full-dress uniform of the satrap's
fleet was waiting for her at the door of the shed. He
bowed sharply as Silence and her escort approached,
and as he straightened, Silence saw the twin crescents
at collar and shoulderboards: *Ballisarda*'s captain.

"Thank you, Brishen. I relieve you," the captain said
formally.

The deck officer saluted with equal formality, and
turned away, accepting the dismissal.

"Domna," the captain said, and offered his arm. Silence accepted numbly and let herself be drawn inside.
There was still no sign of either Chase Mago or Balthasar,
and she was hit by sudden panic at the thought of
leaving Inarime without a chance to make some sort of
farewell.

"Or should I say, sieura?" the captain continued,
lowering his voice.

Silence glanced sharply at him, and saw that he was
smiling. Beyond him, hidden from anyone outside the
shed, were Balthasar and Chase Mago. Silence allowed

herself a long sigh of relief, and then realized that both Isambard and the satrap were waiting with them.

"His Highness has explained something of the circumstances, sieura," the captain went on, "and I am under orders to help you in any way I can. My name is Mali-Mehtar Varid. I am captain of *Ballisarda*."

"Yes, thank you," Silence said, her attention on her husbands, and Varid bowed again.

"If you will excuse me, domna, your Highness," he said, raising his voice so that his words carried to the satrap, "I will make ready for liftoff."

The satrap nodded and then came forward to greet Silence, as the captain hurried up the cradle ladder. "You understand the plan?" he asked, without preliminaries. "Do you have any questions?"

Silence shook her head, a little annoyed by the questions. "You didn't have the only other information I needed; I understand the rest fine, thank you."

The satrap frowned, his face darkening with anger, then, quite abruptly, bent his head a fraction. "I accept your stricture. I speak out of concern for my daughter." He took a deep breath. "Your baggage is already aboard, and your cabin prepared. You must go aboard momentarily."

"Wait a minute," Silence said. "I want to say goodbye."

The satrap's thin eyebrows rose, his expression half scandalized, half amused. "I was given to understand this was a marriage of convenience."

"Wrong," Silence said shortly, and stalked past him.

Neither Balthasar nor Chase Mago came forward to meet her, and Silence was momentarily hurt, until she realized that the men were standing in the shadow of a large pile of starcrates which effectively blocked the sightlines of anyone on *Ballisarda*'s bridge. The pilot smiled rather wolfishly as she approached, and saw her own expression mirrored on Balthasar's lean face. Then she, too, was out of *Ballisarda*'s sight, and both men stepped forward to catch her in an awkward joint embrace. Silence returned the clumsy hug eagerly, and realized to her horror that she was on the verge of tears. She sniffed angrily, fighting them, and Chase Mago gently stroked her hair through the heavy veil.

Balthasar said, the tone belying his words, "That thing's damned clumsy. Can't you take it off?"

Silence laughed through her tears, and fought free enough to fold the cloth back over her headdress, exposing her face. "I suppose you count as family."

"I should hope so," Balthasar said, but his heart wasn't in it. "Ah, Silence . . ."

"Be very careful," Chase Mago said, and put out a hand to touch the pilot's cheek.

Silence nodded. There was suddenly nothing to say—or rather, she realized, there was entirely too much to be said, and none of them were articulate in such things. With a choked cry she reached for both men, pulling them into a tight, wordless embrace. They stood so for a long moment, until a chime sounded high in the roof of the docking shed, and a disembodied voice announced, "The boarding period is ending. All passengers aboard, please. All passengers aboard."

Silence sniffled hard and pulled herself away. "You be careful, too, both of you." She tried to think of something light and clever, but nothing came to mind. "Just be careful."

"Wait," Chase Mago said, rummaging in the pocket of his coat. "Take these. They shouldn't be noticed." He pressed something small and hard into the pilot's hand.

Startled, Silence accepted the objects, turning her hand to reveal three rings, solid bands of what looked to be cloud agate. She looked up, meeting Chase Mago's eyes, and the engineer nodded.

"Never had the time to get them before," he said, and held up his own left hand. Three matching stone bands circled his ring finger. Silence felt the tears rising in her eyes again. Then Balthasar grabbed her left hand, and almost roughly slid the rings onto her third finger. There were three more matching rings on the Delian's hand.

"You'd better get going," Balthasar said, and for a wonder his voice was thick with tears.

Silence nodded, unable to speak. With a shaking hand, she lowered her veil into place just as the boarding chime sounded again.

"Go," Balthasar managed, and Chase Mago said, strongly, "We'll see you on Asterion, Silence."

The pilot nodded again, and echoed, "On Asterion, Julie, Denis." Then she turned and almost ran for the cradle steps, grateful for the veil that hid her tears from the midshipman waiting at the hatch. The boy offered her his arm with stiffly military courtesy, saying, "May I show you to your cabin suite, domna?"

Silence inclined her head under the veil, unable to trust herself to speak, and set her own hand on the boy's elbow. He clicked his heels, and said, "You're on the main level, domna, in the quarters." Silence barely heard him, listening for the sound of the hatch closing behind her. It came—a dull, almost soundless thud— and she was truly alone.

CHAPTER 6

The cabin to which the midshipman led her was actually two connecting compartments, set apart from the rest of the ship by a sturdy metal grate that closed the corridor leading to the compartment's door. Both Varid and the satrap were waiting by that grating. The captain bowed low at Silence's approach, saying, "Welcome aboard, domna. I hope you will find these quarters to your liking."

Silence got a grip on herself with an effort. "I'm sure I will, captain, thank you." Her voice was shaky, but no one seemed to notice.

"Domna Jamilla." The satrap made a brisk demi-bow, and turned his attention to the captain. "Captain Lord Varid, I commend to you the domna Lady Jamilla Sahen, and place her under your hand. Domna Jamilla, I entrust you to Lord Varid; he speaks with my voice."

As she had been taught, Silence extended a veiled hand and the satrap took it, placing her fingers on Varid's proffered wrist. Silence murmured the proper response: *"Imn' zhayan."* I shall obey.

The satrap gave her a final, dubious glance, then straightened briskly. "Captain, I will not delay you further. Domna, if you please?" He gestured to the half-open grating.

Silence stiffened unhappily, but this, too, was part of the procedure she had so hastily memorized. She—or, rather, Jamilla—was not of high enough rank to be granted a human servant, but at the same time some formal precautions had to be taken if she was to travel unescorted on a ship crewed only by men. Therefore, she would be locked into the two-room suite, and would be released by the satrap's vizier on Asterion. Mustering all her dignity, Silence stepped through the gate and watched while the captain drew it closed. The satrap himself locked it and then placed his own seal-strip across the lock mechanism. In an emergency, of course, the captain could easily open the grating, but it was unlikely he would do so for less than utter disaster.

"Domna Jamilla," the satrap said quietly. "I send you with my own good wishes, and with my warmest greetings to my daughter. May your service on Asterion be pleasant, its burdens light."

Silence bowed deeply. "It shall be so," she answered, and in spite of herself her tone was all too fervent.

Varid stepped in hastily to cover the mistake. "Domna, you will find a welcome tray set out, and also the elixir for the transitions through purgatory. Also, should you require anything, please inform your guard-of-honor, or please use the call-crystal to tell me, and it will be done."

"Thank you, captain," Silence said, her voice under complete control again.

The satrap nodded. Silence curtsied deeply, and the satrap turned to leave, Varid following. As soon as they were out of sight, and the midshipman had taken up his blank-eyed watch outside the grating, Silence turned back to the cabin and went inside, closing the door firmly behind her.

As Varid had promised, a welcome tray was waiting on the thickly carpeted dais that served as a table in the suite's main area. Silence wrenched off her veil and tossed the supporting headdress after it into the nearest corner, then dropped to her knees beside the dais to examine the tray. As was traditional, the bidi-silver tray held a small flask and a miniature goblet of iridescent glass, a shallow silver bowl full of salty-sweet pombe nuts, and an inlaid plate with three perfect chocolates. Silence ate one, hoping the sweet would improve her mood, then reached for the flask to pour herself a glass of whatever liqueur Varid had thought appropriate for an admiral's daughter. If nothing else, she thought, I can get myself happy, or at least well out, before we even leave the planet.

Instead of pura, or one of the other sticky, syrup-sweet liqueurs that were commonly offered to women of rank, the drink was almost clear, and had the faint pungency of Auxuran gin. Silence sipped cautiously: it was Anxuran gin, cut with maratha, and both were of the best quality, too. I bet I have Denis to thank for this, she thought, and her eyes filled again with tears. She shook herself angrily and took another, larger swallow of the liquor. Then she pushed herself to her feet and, glass in hand, began to investigate the cabin area.

She had never travelled in such luxury before. Even in her present state, the elegance-in-miniature of the cabin-suite was enough to distract her, reducing the knot of fear and loneliness. The outer room, furnished with floor-bolsters rather than more conventional furniture, was paneled in oil-wood as light and glowing as fine marble. A carved screen hid an elaborate mechanical galley—an extremely expensive toy, considering the cost of shielding that large a machine to keep it from interfering with the harmonium—but to Silence's disappointment, there was only a single, inadequate repeater screen linked to the ship's main monitor system. Of course, she reminded herself, very few of the women who travelled in this ship would be interested in—or trained to follow—the starship's progress. And I'll be asleep anyway, once we hit purgatory.

With that thought in mind, she went on into the second of the two cabins. It was considerably smaller than the main room, but so beautifully designed that it did not feel crowded. The recessed bunk, lace-curtained and discreetly lit, took up most of the space; a mobile table stood beside it, the black lacquer oval of a medicine case prominently displayed. Silence checked the dosage: enough and more to put her into a sound sleep, proof against even the most seductive music of purgatory. She had made the journey through purgatory without either drugs or her own work to distract her only once. That had been as a prisoner aboard a Hegemonic transport and it was not an experience she would willingly repeat.

Frowning, she shook away the memory, and checked the tiny storage alcove and the bath nook. The single starcrate that held the few things she would need for the journey was in place in the alcove, her formal robes already stretched across a clothes horse to keep them from wrinkling. The bath nook was something of a disappointment: the fixtures were exactly the same as those on *Recusante*, except that they were trimmed with precious metals.

Sighing, Silence returned to the main room, and settled herself cross-legged beside the welcome tray. She missed her starbooks, not just their comforting weight against her hip, but the knowledge of where and by what road she would be travelling. By the time *Ballisarda* was positioned on the launching table, Silence had finished the two glasses of gin and most of the pombe nuts. The pilot made her way into the bedroom, and reached for the oval box with its three tiny, glittering bottles. She uncorked the first bottle and swallowed its contents, then stretched out on the bunk to wait for the elixir to take hold.

The flight to Asterion was a little over fifty hours long, entering purgatory twice. Silence slept through the first passage, and spent the waking hours refining her plans for Asterion. Most of that involved reviewing the persona she had invented for "Jamilla." Knowing she could not learn enough to take full part in the life of the Women's Palace, Silence and Kalere had decided to emphasize the fact that Jamilla was an admiral's daughter, and had travelled with him during his tours of duty. That, they hoped, would explain any oddities in her behavior. She reviewed the material she had memorized under the Chanfro techniques, until the mnemonic chains and convoluted images seemed to shine as though polished. Still, the preparations and review could not last forever, and she was very glad to swallow the last dose of elixir and sink at last into a dreamless sleep.

She had timed the dose so that she was stirring just as the ship reached the edge of Asterion's system. The monitor in the outer room was talking quietly to itself as she came slowly back to full awareness. She had left the machine on so that she would know what was happening, but it was the harmonium's note that first told her *Ballisarda* was approaching planetary harmonies. She pulled herself upright, still fuzzy from the drug, and listened to the flow of data from the monitor. *Ballisarda* was still well out from the planet, and on a leisurely course. She had a little time.

Silence lay back against the pillow, tasting the bitter aftereffects of the elixir, but still too dizzy to do anything about it. After a few minutes her head cleared a little, and she reached for the last of the bottles in the medicine box. She drank off the counterdrug, and sat massaging her temples until the drink began to work. Then she staggered into the bath nook and turned the shower on full power, letting the pulsing stream of water beat the last cobwebs from her mind.

When she was sure she was fully alert again, she

turned the power down, and adjusted a secondary control to add a hint of amberwood to the water. She scrubbed herself, then, reluctantly, toed the switch that cut off the water and triggered the warm-air blowers. She felt almost normal as she stepped from the bath nook, except for the growing knot of fear in her belly. *This will never do,* she thought, and closed her eyes, forcing herself into the mindless relaxation of the first-stage exercises. The tension eased to a manageable level.

The monitor in the outer room was showing only an hour before *Ballisarda* landed at Asterion's main port, the imperial capital Anshar' Asteriona itself. Silence's mouth set into a grim line, and she returned to the bedroom to dress. Formal wear seemed to involve an almost infinite number of layers. Even in the perfectly controlled climate of the starship, Silence was sweating lightly by the time she had donned the final overgown. There were two layers beneath that, a thin silk shift and a heavier brocade dress cut tight in the bodice and full in sleeves with a lightly stiffened bell-shaped skirt. The overgown, of a sober wine-black satin that fell in heavy pleats straight from the shoulders, flared slightly over the skirt, opening a few centimeters at the hem to reveal flashes of the brighter brocade beneath.

Silence surveyed herself in the mirror, and had to admit that the colors, at least, had been chosen to flatter her black hair and pale skin. As for the rest . . . the style had dignity, and Silence was still unwillingly impressed by the row of carved gemstones that buttoned the overgown to the waist, but other than that, the pilot could find little to recommend in it. It was uncomfortable, and almost impossible to move in, and the full court-veil only made things worse.

Silence sighed and glanced at the monitor. *I'll wait till we land before I start on the veils,* she decided.

There's no point in being miserable until I have to be. Instead, she settled herself against the bolsters to watch the landing on the monitor. *Ballisarda*'s pilot was good. The big liner settled easily through the planet's atmosphere, the details of the field swelling slowly, only slightly reddened by the interference as *Ballisarda*'s harmonium overrode the ethereal notes of the upper atmosphere. The Inariman pilot cut the harmony at just the right moment, dropping the starship into its cradle with barely a jolt. Silence sighed her envy, wishing that that was all she had to worry about, and went back into the bedroom to finish dressing.

There was no point wasting time on jewelry or makeup: either would be hidden beneath the enveloping veils. Silence took a deep breath, knowing she couldn't put it off any longer, and fitted the supporting headdress into place. This was a more elaborate structure than the usual light coronet, a complicated structure of gold wires that rose to a slight peak above the wearer's forehead, and formed a close cap across the back of the skull. Two gemmed clips, like the cheek-pieces of an archaic helmet, framed the pilot's face. Silence grimaced at them—they were uncomfortable, and the headdress as a whole was heavy—and then, reluctantly, fitted the ends of the underveil into the clips. The solid rectangle of cloth covered her face from cheek to chin, falling below the collar of her overgown at its longest point. Silence twitched at the cloth, adjusting the folds, and made a face at her image in the mirror. Only the tightening of the skin at the corners of her eyes betrayed the grimace. That was one advantage to the system, Silence thought—maybe the only advantage. Sighing, she picked up the filmy main veil and fitted the gold eyelets in its center onto the tiny hooks of the headdress. The almost transparent grey-black silk fell heavily around her ankles, weighted by the meter-wide band of metallic embroidery at the hem. The complete ensemble weighed over twelve kilograms, and Silence was grateful that custom decreed that women of the Thousand did not travel afoot.

She had cut things rather fine after all. Almost as soon as she had finished adjusting the fall of the outer veiling, the monitor buzzed discreetly, and an unfamiliar voice said, "Domna Jamilla, the vizier Halian n'Halian has come aboard to escort you to the Women's Palace."

"Thank you," Silence said, feeling a sudden tightness in her throat. She could feel herself beginning to shake as she took up her position in front of the cabin door, and took deep, calming breaths. The trembling eased, but the tight knot of fear was back at the pit of her stomach. Then the tiny green light set into the bulkhead above the doorway winked out: Varid and n'Halian were at the grating. Silence hit the switch that opened the cabin door.

The vizier was a tall, gaunt man who wore his court dress—silk trousers, brocade coat, and gorgeously embroidered sash-shawl—with an air. As the door opened, he bowed slightly from the waist, and touched fingers to his lips. As he took his hand away, Silence saw that his forked beard was gilded at the tips, as though he had leaned forward into a pot of liquid gold. The effect was so startling that she almost missed his formal greeting.

"—Anshar' Asteriona. In our common masters' names, I greet you." N'Halian took a quick breath, and continued sonorously, "You have been commended to my care for the brief time until you reach the Palace of Women. I trust, Domna Jamilla, this is acceptable to you."

"*Imn' zhayan*," Silence answered, with a brief inclination of her head. N'Halian smiled glintingly—his teeth, too, were set with gold, Silence realized. She was hard put not to laugh aloud at the sight.

The vizier seemed not to notice. "If you will bear witness, my lord captain?"

"As my lord wishes," Varid murmured.

N'Halian nodded, and with a flourish, stripped the sealtape from the lock. He folded the piece of tape carefully and tucked it into the folds of his waist sash. With another flourish, he produced a glittering lock-box and unlocked the grating. A junior officer—a lieutenant this time, Silence noted—hastened to pull back the grating, and n'Halian extended a long hand to the pilot. Silence came forward slowly, putting out her own hand, decently covered by the outer veil, to touch the other's wrist.

"If you will come with me, domna?" n'Halian went on.

"*Imn' zhayan*," Silence answered automatically, then contradicted herself. "Oh, but a moment, my lord. Captain Varid, I thank you for your courtesy in the preparation of my quarters. My journey was most pleasant."

"Our pleasure to serve," Varid answered.

N'Halian nodded. Silence wondered exactly what in her he was approving—her courtesy, or her bravery in speaking to the captain without the vizier's consent— and started down the starship's corridors. All the crewmen had, of course, been told to stay clear. Silence found the empty spaces disconcerting, and she was glad when they reached the main hatchway.

The cradle stairs were covered by a crimson carpet, and servants—beautifully formed homunculi—waited at the base of the stairs. They held a gold-fringed canopy blazoned with Inarime's red hart. As the two human beings approached, the homunculi lifted the canopy in salute. The vizier did not appear to notice as he took his place beneath it, Silence still modestly half a step to the rear.

The homunculi escorted them through Inarime's private docking shed, and out into the blazing sunlight of Asterion. *Ballisarda* was docked in the secluded sector reserved for the ships of planetary overlords; even so, Silence was amazed by the elaborate facilities. There were whole planets, in the Rusadir and on the Fringe, that lacked a single starport as elaborate as this private park. She counted nearly a dozen docking sheds, each one reserved for a single noble, and three or four support buildings before n'Halian cleared his throat softly, drawing her attention.

A temporary barrier had been set up about twenty meters from the Inariman shed, and half a dozen uniformed men waited beside it. There were more men, in the brighter uniforms of Inarime's private forces, waiting on the far side of the barrier, but Silence had eyes only for the first group. She recognized the sober blazoning only too well: these were men of the true Thousand, the elite aristocratic soldiers who were the real base of the Hegemon's power. Silence controlled her shudder with an effort, reminding herself of the officer who had been on Inarime, the one who had been present at the satrap's secret conference. Not all the men of the true Thousand were her enemies. Still, her hand trembled on the vizier's wrist. N'Halian gave her a sidelong glance and a quick, private smile.

"Courage domna," he said softly. "You have nothing to fear."

Silence kept her face expressionless behind her veils. She did not know if n'Halian knew about the satrap's plan, and could not tell from his words. In either case, she thought, I know better than you just how much there is to fear. I was on Arganthonios when the Thousand retook it from Wrath-of-God; I've been their prisoner. I know.

As they approached the barrier, the officer in command of the troop stepped forward, touching a hand to his heart in greeting. He wore a captain's crescent pinned to his collar. Seeing that, Silence allowed herself a soundless sigh of relief. If her real mission had been betrayed, surely the Hegemon would have sent a higher-ranking officer and a larger squad to arrest her.

"M'lord vizier, domna," the captain said. "May I see the lady's papers, my lord?"

"Of course, captain," n'Halian answered, and produced a slim gilt case from the folds of his sash. The women of the Hegemony did not carry their own papers, either: Silence had never even seen the documents on which her safety rested.

The captain accepted the case with a slight inclination of his head that might have been intended as a bow, and flipped back the lid. He carried a jeweled scanner on a waist chain, and brought it up smartly to record the information set out on the engraved plaque. In spite of the satrap's promises, Silence tensed beneath her veils. She still found it hard to believe that the Hegemony did not keep better track of the women of the Ten Thousand. Even if photos were prohibited, there were half a dozen other, equally accurate ways of ensuring identity. *I suppose*, Silence thought, *they think one woman more or less couldn't make any difference. And who would believe a satrap would lie?* Still, she was hard put to hide her sigh of relief as the captain snapped the case closed over the plate's micro-graved oaths and seals, and handed it back to n'Halian.

"In his Majesty's name, I welcome you to Anshar' Asteriona, Domna Jamilla," the captain said, and saluted gravely.

Silence bent her head in response, but could not quite bring herself to thank him for his courtesy. N'Halian shot her another quick look, and then the soldiers of the Thousand were trundling the barrier aside. The Inariman troops moved forward, bowing and touching hands to lips in Silence's direction.

A gaudy ground-effect vehicle was waiting, balanced

on its cushion of air, flanked by grounded escort pods.
N'Halian gestured to the gever's pilot, who lowered the
bulky vehicle, fans whining in protest, until Silence was
able to step easily into its carpeted interior. N'Halian
followed her, and the gever bobbed back to its normal
cruising level. The soldiers took their place in the escort pods and lifted rapidly, closing in around the gever.
N'Halian touched a hidden control, and a clear dome
slid into place over the passenger compartment. To
Silence's pleased surprise, however, the vizier did not
darken the glass but signaled the driver to proceed.

Anshar' Asteriona was a magnificent city. Silence had
always known this, from star-travellers' stories and the
tapes she had studied on Inarime, but the reality was
enough to take her breath away. The main administrative complex, with its high spires and lacy, glittering
walkways connecting each of the lesser buildings into a
spectacular whole, was larger and more beautiful than
most oligarchs' palaces in the Rusadir.

The pilot turned the gever onto a rampway that led
into and then through the glass-roofed central arcade of
the complex. Silence was dizzied by the sheer variety of
figures flashing past, Hegemonic nobles in brilliant silks
mingling with star-travellers in the dress of half a hundred worlds. Then the gever flashed under a meter-
wide security band—it turned briefly white, then green,
registering both the escort's weaponry and its right to
carry the heavy heylins—and swept down a second
ramp, to turn onto a wide, park-lined avenue. This was
the famous Street of the Triumphs. Silence gave up her
pretense of indifference, and stared open-mouthed as
the gever slid beneath the first of the massive arches
that spanned the roadway. The arch, of the semipre-
cious bluemarble found only on Elysium, was carved on
every available surface with inscriptions in the flowing Hegemonic script and complicated, gem-studded
reliefs.

"That's Fadil III's Triumph," n'Halian said, smiling. "To commemorate the Treaty of Elysium and the establishment of the Hegemony."

Silence nodded, still staring. They passed beneath a second arch, this one ten meters thick, carved from what seemed to be a single solid block of crystal. Within its depths, ghostly images formed and shifted. Most were starships locked in mortal combat, but the keystone, the most vivid image, showed a panoramic battle, a planet under attack.

"Adeben II's Triumph," n'Halian said, "celebrating the victory over Wrath-of-God. It's said—" The vizier gave a rather malicious smile. "—that his Most Serene Majesty wants to build his own Wrath-of-God triumph, after the fighting on Arganthonios."

Silence snorted angrily, but managed to bite back the rest of her instant, bitter response. Arganthonios had been an ambush, not a battle; it hardly merited a commemorative medal, much less a Triumph to match the others. N'Halian gave her another unreadable glance, and Silence wondered again just how much the vizier knew about her mission.

The gever flashed beneath a third Triumph, this one black stone inlaid with line after line of silver Hegemonic script, and traffic began to pick up appreciably. The pilot slowed, muttering to himself, and n'Halian tapped one hand against the hidden control box. Silence, caught up in the spectacle outside the gever, barely noticed their impatience.

A dozen other gevers, each badged with the symbols of a noble house, made their way up the broad avenue, their escorts jostling for position. Other, slower ground transport hastily made way for them, while air scooters, their modified harmoniums humming like swarms of angry insects, darted in and out of the ponderous processions, the gaudily dressed young nobles who rode them exchanging cheerful obscenities with the soldiers of the escorts. One scooter darted perilously close to

her own gever, and Silence caught a good look at the
riders. The driver was a noble, of course, black-haired
and with a neatly trimmed black beard, coat and sashes
flapping in the wind, but his passenger was a woman.
She was veiled, as law and custom required, but both
her billowing drapery and the coat and trousers beneath it were sheer, almost transparent, revealing jeweled breast and crotch pieces. Silence raised an eyebrow,
and n'Halian chuckled softly.

"A—dancer," he said.

"A dancer," Silence repeated, and did her best to
sound as though she believed him. N'Halian laughed
again, but before he could say anything else, the pilot's
attention was distracted by a heavily guarded palanquin, permanently joined to the shoulders of four heavy-
service homunculi. The palanquin's curtains were laced
tightly closed beneath the metal mesh shell, and the
heavily armed escorts stayed very close to its sides,
heylins at the ready. Even the most reckless of the
young nobles were careful to give it a wide berth.
Silence glanced curiously at n'Halian, but the vizier was
looking elsewhere, and the pilot did not want to betray
her lack of knowledge by asking outright. It was probably someone's wife, she decided, or maybe an unmarried girl—certainly a woman of desirable age and good
family.

The Street of Triumphs led directly to the Grand
Palace itself. The gever slowed still further as it passed
the perimeter markers, two slender white wands set
into the immaculate turf to either side of the roadway.
Silence eyed them curiously, feeling the tingle of leashed
power, but the gever was still traveling too quickly for
her to figure out exactly what defense screen they controlled. Then they were coming up on the deceptive
outer wall of the compound, and Silence concentrated
on the part she had to play.

There were more of the Thousand's troopers waiting

beside the gate, led by another crescent-badged captain. N'Halian exchanged sonorous greetings with him, and handed over the case containing Silence's papers. The captain examined it with excruciating care, then motioned for the gever to proceed into the Palace. He did not return the case. The escort remained outside, grounding their pods to wait for n'Halian's return.

The captain led them not to the main buildings but to an auxiliary complex, then through a series of winding passages to an unroofed courtyard. A slim flyer was waiting there, its modified harmonium throbbing gently. At n'Halian's signal, the pilot lowered the gever almost to the ground, and the vizier stepped out, turning at once to help Silence disembark. Silence was grateful for his steadying hand as she turned to face the captain. He bowed sharply then, and returned the case to n'Halian. The vizier nodded thanks, and gestured sharply at the waiting flyer. A hatch slid back stiffly along its gleaming hull, and stairs unfolded with a gentle clicking.

"This will take you to the Women's Palace, my lord, lady domna," the captain announced.

"Thank you, captain," n'Halian answered, and motioned for Silence to precede him up the steps and into the flyer.

The interior of the flyer was very dark, and Silence reached instinctively for the control that would lighten the window glass. N'Halian shook his head, pointing to a pinpoint light on the forward bulkhead. "You can clear the windows when that light goes off," he said. "Security."

I should've guessed that they'd require that, Silence thought, and settled herself for a blind flight. When the cartographers went to great lengths to conceal even the general position of the Women's Palace on their maps, it stood to reason that the security troops would not advertise either the exact location or the particular routes used to get there. Then the liftoff slammed her back against the seat, and it took all her self-restraint to suppress a very unladylike curse.

The light stayed on for a little over an hour, straining Silence's nerves almost to the breaking point. When it winked out at last, Silence twisted the control so hard that the knob nearly came off in her hand. The windows lightened, and she peered out eagerly.

The flyer was just crossing over the shoreline of a large lake, heading out over open water. Silence had just enough time to register that the surrounding area was heavily wooded, without visible clearings or roads, when the flyer banked sharply, cutting off her view. This time she did swear, and apologized stiffly, too aware of the amusement in n'Halian's eyes. Then the flyer banked again, less steeply this time, and Silence caught her first glimpse of the Women's Palace.

It was set in the very center of the lake, on an island with banks so regular that they had to be artificial. The Palace itself, an odd, four-lobed building topped with extravagant towers and dotted with hidden court-yards, filled most of the available land, leaving only four thin triangles of grass in between the lobes of the building. Then the flyer straightened, cutting off Silence's view again, and began to descend toward the shoreline.

Silence frowned, and n'Halian said, "We land at the guardpost, and take a boat across to the Palace."

"Oh."

The flyer landed gently, but n'Halian did not move from his seat. After a moment, the hatch folded upward, and a helmeted face peered into the compartment. Silence tensed, but relaxed a little at n'Halian's discreet hand signal. A moment later, the head was withdrawn, and the steps unfolded themselves, clatter-ing down to the pavement. N'Halian rose, stretching a little, and offered Silence his arm. The pilot took it, and

together they descended the little stairway into the
sunlight.

Another squad of the Thousand's soldiers were waiting on the smoothed landing field, drawn up in the
double lines of an honor guard. Their commander, a
full colonel this time, brought up his decorative sword
in punctilious salute, but Silence's attention was caught
by the heavily armored vehicle that stood to one side,
its double cannons trained on the flyer. At least they
don't suspect us, she thought, a little numbly, or they'd 've
blasted us already. With an inward shiver, she let
n'Halian draw her toward the lake, following the colonel between the rows of soldiers.

An elaborate, flag-bedecked barge was drawn up
against the end of the field that projected into the lake,
and still more of the Thousand waited beneath the
fluttering streamers. They saluted at their colonel's approach, and one—a thin, graceful boy in a common
soldier's coat—hurried forward to help Silence into the
barge. The pilot accepted his help, and let herself be
led to a seat in the very center. N'Halian took his place
at her left shoulder, one hand resting casually on the
back of the chair.

"Cast off," the colonel ordered, and one of the troopers released his hold on a heavy line. Its engine throbbing throatily, the barge swung slowly away from the
field.

The lake was very calm, kept so, Silence guessed, by
elaborate counterharmonics and damping fields. The
snow-white buildings of the Palace seemed to float like
an icy sculpture just above the surface of the water.
Viewed abstractly, it was very beautiful, but Silence
was in no mood to appreciate its charms. All too soon
now, she would be inside those walls, trapped by the
rules of the Palace itself even if she was not inadver-
tently betrayed by Aili. She closed her eyes, mentally
repeating relaxation exercises. The panic ebbed, but
the cold knot of fear stayed solidly in her stomach.

Then the barge slid neatly against the Palace dock, and two of the troopers leaped out to secure the lines. N'Halian cleared his throat nervously. Silence gave a convulsive start and forced to move. Her fingers were icy: in a distant, irrelevant way, she felt sorry for the young officer who extended a hand to help her from the barge. Like a sleepwalker trapped in a nightmare, she followed the colonel and N'Halian down an interminable, blue-ceilinged corridor, until, quite suddenly, they emerged into a tiny courtyard. The walls surrounding it were completely windowless, the apparently solid stone pierced only by a door directly opposite the one from which they had just emerged. Silence could not resist a quick glance over her shoulder: the two were identical.

A broad band of black stone ran across the courtyard, dividing it into two equal sections. The colonel stopped well back of the line, and gestured to one of the troopers, who produced a small, curling trumpet. He sounded it, producing an ugly honking like a nahr-cat in heat, then sounded it again. Moving with an almost visible reluctance, the far door swung open.

Five women moved slowly into the courtyard. Three were clearly high-ranking servants like "Jamilla," the outline of the domna's robes plainly visible beneath their veils. Silence had eyes only for the other two. One, the smaller of the pair, wore a dress so full that her veil was stretched almost taut over the stiff skirts, displaying its bejeweled hem to great advantage. Silence guessed she was the shazadi Aili. The other, taller woman wore an outer veil that seemed to have been woven from solid gold. It was she who spoke first.

"Well, colonel?" The harsh voice seemed to come from nowhere. Silence shivered again, recognizing a will to match her own behind that concealing golden curtain.

The colonel bowed very low. "Your Serenity, I present the lord n'Halian, who speaks for the satrap of Inarime."

So the woman in the golden veil was the Hegemon's sister Radiah, Silence thought, the person who held at least nominal authority in the Women's Palace. And from the sound of her voice, her power is much more than merely nominal.

"Speak, Inarime's vizier," Radiah said. Her tone was not encouraging, and Silence saw that n'Halian bowed very low indeed.

"Your Serenity, I bring to the Palace and present for your approval the domna Jamilla Sahen, to be a companion to my master's daughter."

Radiah was silent for a long moment, then said, in the same discouraging tone, "Come here, girl."

That was not part of the ritual Silence had so carefully memorized. She did her best to hide her fear, however, and walked forward to the very edge of the black line. She could not step over it until she was officially accepted into the shazadi's household, but she would obey the Princess Royal's order as closely as she could. The golden veil shifted slightly, and Silence knew Radiah was examining her from behind its heavy folds. Even behind her own veil Silence braced herself, and was grateful when at last the Princess turned away.

"Inform your master, Inarime's vizier, that we accept this Jamilla Sahen into our household—provisionally." Radiah turned, the metallic veil moving stiffly with her. "You, Jamilla, will come with me. Colonel, you are dismissed."

The colonel and n'Halian bowed again and backed toward the door by which they had entered the courtyard. Silence stepped unwillingly across the line and followed the other domnas through the second door. It slid closed behind them, leaving them in sudden darkness for a moment before the corridor lights clicked on. Silence heard Radiah mutter a startling curse and, quite suddenly, her own fear faded, eased by that evidence of human frailty. The Hegemon's sister was only a woman, after all, and an ill-tempered one, at that. I can deal with her, Silence told herself. Somehow, I can.

This corridor was much shorter than the one through which Silence had entered the Palace. It ended quite abruptly, a lighter door rolling back to reveal a pleasant, tree-lined walk. The domna to Silence's left gave a quite human sigh of relief, and hurried to help Radiah divest herself of her outer veil. Other women were waiting to help Aili and the domnas. Silence allowed one of them, a plump, pleasant-looking girl a few years younger than herself, to help her fold the heavy cloth back over her headdress. Aili, small and dark and slender, had already removed both veils, and advanced on Silence with outstretched arms. The pilot took a deep breath, knowing she couldn't delay any longer, and pulled off her underveil.

Aili checked, but only fractionally, and said, "Lord, Jamilla, you've changed." Without waiting for an answer, she embraced Silence warmly.

"It's been a long time, Aili," the pilot answered, cautiously. Over the shazadi's shoulder, she could see the Princess Royal watching them closely, and was suddenly glad Aili had explained her surprise.

"So," Radiah said. She had not removed her underveil, and did not seem inclined to do so; instead, she watched the younger women over its muffling folds. "You are Jamilla Sahen—Admiral Sahen's daughter?"

Silence bobbed a curtsy, as she had been taught. "Yes, your Serenity."

"Then you must play nago," the Princess Royal continued. "Good."

Nago was the most popular gambling game in the Hegemonic Navy. Silence had been taught the rules, but she had no particular knack for gambling. Kalere had quickly decided that it would be better if she did not play at all, and had created half a dozen excuses for almost any social situation. However, Silence had not expected to have to produce them so soon. "I beg your Serenity's pardon," she stammered, "but I'm afraid I don't play." She saw Aili's eyes widen slightly, as if in dismay, and Radiah's thin eyebrows drew together into a frown.

"The Jamilla Sahen of whom I am aware once defeated a full complement of ship's officers at nago." There was more than a hint of frost in Radiah's voice.

And why didn't someone tell me that? Silence wondered remotely. "My noble father was not pleased by the exploit, your Serenity," she improvised. "Thus, I do not play."

Aili relaxed slightly, but the Princess Royal continued to frown. "And if I command it?"

"Your Serenity," Aili interposed. She had a pleasant voice, low and sweet. "I beg your indulgence for Jamilla. If the lord admiral has forbidden her to play, surely she shouldn't go against his wishes? And in any case, she's just arrived, practically this instant. She must be exhausted from the trip, and I've so much to talk to her about."

The artless prattle seemed to soften Radiah's temper—or was it all so artless, Silence wondered, watching the ways Aili's movements contradicted her words. The shazadi at least thought she had found a weak spot in the Princess Royal's armor, and was exploiting it to the fullest.

"Very well," Radiah said, "I will hold you excused for now, Jamilla. You may show her to your quarters, Aili."

"Thank you, your Serenity," Aili said, curtsying, and Silence copied her. The shazadi tugged at Silence's arm, drawing her off down the tree-lined walk, talking as she went.

"The homunculi will bring your luggage as soon as the colonel is satisfied it's safe." Aili's laugh was beautifully unforced. "I have most of this wing," she added, as they passed through a series of arches into a semi-enclosed arcade that looked out onto a small, unpretentious garden. At irregular intervals, the keystones were set with tiny carved faces. Watching closely, Silence saw one face open its eyes, following their passage, and looked away hastily. The garden looked pleasant. A fountain played gently in the center of the concentric circles that were the paths, and Silence could not help smiling at the sight.

"I'm glad you like it," Aili exclaimed. "This is one of my favorite places, too. Come on." Without waiting for a response, she pulled Silence through the nearest archway, and out into the garden. She led the unresisting pilot to the fountain, and seated herself on its edge, gesturing for Silence to sit beside her. "Now," Aili said, still with a smile that belied her sudden fierce whisper, "who the hell are you?"

Silence glanced quickly around, and saw no human eavesdroppers or any more of the carved faces. Even so, she lowered her own voice to an almost soundless whisper before she answered, "Your father sent me. By token of the nargal."

Aili relaxed slightly but visibly. "Thank God."

She sounded very different from the dutiful daughter Silence had been led to expect, and from the giddy child she had played for the Princess Royal. The pilot eyed her with new respect, saying, "Is it safe to talk?"

Aili gave a sudden, elfin grin. "As safe as anywhere, which is not very."

Silence nodded, as much to herself as to the other. She had expected internal security to be fairly tight, and had made her plans accordingly. Besides, she thought as she closed her eyes and felt for the harmonic lines running beneath the Palace, *a direct demonstration is the best way I can think of to convince her I'm a magus.* The Palace was laid out roughly in tune with the planetary harmonies—it would have to be, Silence thought, if they were using large numbers of homunculi as servants. She would not have to draw a ring, either: the nearest encircling path would do very nicely. She felt for the elemental harmonies, held them, and subvocalized the cantation that bent them to her will. She whispered the words that called up the Form of the aphonic ring, shaping air and earth with them, and felt the ring leap into place around them. She opened her eyes to see Aili staring at her.

"You're a magus," the shazadi stated flatly. "How in God's name did you get past the Seer?" Her eyes searched Silence's body in startled, appalled speculation, but then she shook her head, murmuring, "But even neutering couldn't change the chromosomes . . . ?"

"I'm a woman," Silence said impatiently, and then, as the other's words registered, added, "What Seer?"

"The black band in the entrance court," Aili said. "If a male crosses it—and it defines 'male' by the genetic typing, not by bodily equipment—alarms go off, the homunculi attack, and so on." She shook her head and returned to her primary question. "You can't be a magus. It's impossible."

I'm glad I didn't know about the Seer when I crossed it, Silence thought. Aloud, she said, "I am a magus— and a star pilot, too, for that matter. I'm an anomaly, nobody's quite been able to explain me. It doesn't really matter, anyway. What does matter is that I have a magus's power, and I know how to use it." *Mostly*, she added, to herself.

Aili still looked skeptical, but the aphonic ring surrounding them, perceptible even to non-magi, was convincing evidence. "And my father sent you to—what?"

"Get you out of here," Silence said. Even inside the aphonic ring, she lowered her voice as she added, "He's planning to attack the Hegemon and take the throne for himself, but he has to get you out of the way first, so you can't be used as a hostage."

Aili sighed. "That, Jamilla—or whoever you are—is

likely to take some doing." Her voice changed suddenly, eyes focusing on someone behind Silence. "Quick, dissolve the ring!"

Silence made the necessary pass, and the ring vanished.

"Household homunculus," Aili hissed, "coming our way."

Silence turned at the creature's approach, successfully killing a shudder. Aili said, "Yes?"

"The mistress's pardon," the homunculus said in a flat, uninflected voice. "The new domna's baggage has arrived. Where shall it be put?"

Aili pulled herself to her feet. "We'd better see to that," she said. Silence sighed, agreeing, and followed the other woman into the depths of the Palace.

CHAPTER 7

It took only a few days for Silence to accustom herself to the routine of life in the Women's Palace. She was given a suite of rooms in the wing reserved for the shazadi and her household. The suite—main room, study, bedroom, and lavish bath—was small by Palace standards, but luxurious in comparison to the life Silence was used to, and even more elaborate than the room she had occupied on Inarime. In the mornings, she accompanied Aili to the Observances, the quasi-religious recitation of the Hegemon's names and titles, accompanied by formal protestations of loyalty. The Princess Royal was strict in meeting her own obligations, and would tolerate nothing less in the women who shared her palace. Then she waited on the shazadi through the interminable late-morning meal.

In the afternoon, she and Aili roamed through the Palace compounds and explored its facilities, ostensibly catching up on the years they had spent apart, but actually examining the security arrangements. Evenings were spent in the Princess Royal's quarters talking, playing dominoes or nago or any of a dozen different card games, performing or listening to music. The Princess Royal did not ask Jamilla to play nago again, but

185

Silence was often aware of Radiah's thoughtful gaze, and was very grateful she did not have to spend any more time in the older woman's company. She did not know exactly what, if anything, she had done to rouse the Princess Royal's suspicions—the nago incident seemed absurdly small—but she did her best to stay out of Radiah's way. The Princess Royal was not at all the spoiled, ornamental female Silence had been led to expect. She was a strong-willed, intelligent woman, who missed very little of what was going on in her kingdom. At the evening gatherings, Silence caught enough glimpses of books and study tapes to guess that the Princess Royal still dabbled in Hegemonic politics, and redoubled her efforts to avoid notice.

At least none of the other Palace inmates seemed to pose the same dangers as the Princess Royal. There weren't many of them, either: Silence, counting carefully, could find only six. There was the Princess Royal, of course, and the Queen-sister, the unmarried sister of the Hegemon's chief wife; Aili and four other shazadis, daughters and sisters of planetary satraps held unofficially as hostages; and one of the Hegemon's natural daughters, kept at the Palace until an appropriate alliance could be sealed with her marriage. She was a sweet, stupid girl of fourteen who took an unaccountable liking to Silence. Each of them had some kind of household, of course, ranging from a single domna to the six women who waited on the Princess Royal, but all told, Silence thought, there were fewer than forty women rattling about in a Palace clearly built to house several hundred.

"Where is everyone?" she asked abruptly.

Aili looked up curiously. The two women were sitting in a narrow, glass-enclosed gallery that overlooked the lake on one side, and the shazadi's favorite garden on the other. Silence had sealed it against prying her second day on Asterion. A piece of crystal, tossed casu-

ally into a flower arrangement, would glow red if anyone tampered with her work. Even so, old habits were
hard to break: both women still spoke elliptically, their
voices lowered.

"What do you mean?" the shazadi asked.

"The Palace. . . ." Silence shrugged, annoyed with
herself for being unnecessarily curious. "It just seems
as though there ought to be more people here, that's
all."

Aili grinned. It was her private smile, a fierce, boyish
grin that she was careful to hide from the other inmates. Seeing it, Silence was again reminded of how
wrong she had been in her expectations. "Most of the
Thousand would rather keep their women at home
these days," the shazadi said. "His Most Serene Majesty's temper is a little—uncertain, of late. No one wants to
leave him a hostage if they can help it. The only women
here who aren't part of his family are hostages, like
me." Aili lowered her voice, glancing automatically over
her shoulder. "And then, of course, there's Radiah."

"Radiah?" Silence asked. "What about her?"

"Don't you know the story?" Aili returned. "Where
have you been?"

Silence was strongly tempted to answer, but bit back
the words just in time. She was not angry at the shazadi
at all, but at the entire situation, at the necessity for
caution and methodical planning, when every nerve in
her body still screamed for her to run. "No, I don't,"
she said aloud, and the shazadi looked properly contrite.

"I'm sorry, Jamilla, I wasn't thinking. They say that
Radiah was exiled here because she meddled too much
in politics. I hear it's true, all right, but her real crime
was that she was smarter about it than his Most Serene
Majesty. It's certain the Hegemon's policy has been a
lot less clever since she took up residence here."

"That's not very reassuring," Silence muttered.

"No, I suppose not," Aili admitted, her smile fading.

She set aside her needlework and leaned forward. "What do you think our chances are?"

Silence sighed, and did not answer at once, staring out over the calm waters of the lake. The afternoon sunlight, pouring in through the thick glass, was an almost physical weight pressing against her skin; it sparkled gaily from the tiny wavelets. The lake itself was the greatest obstacle. The Palace's defenses were intended to keep people out rather than to keep people in. Silence had already spotted two unused water-gates she thought she could open.

"I don't know," she said at last. "There's the old boathouse gate, and the spot over the intake—you were there when I found them, so you know. I'm pretty sure I can get us out." She stared morosely across the glittering water. "The trouble is, first, I don't know if I can keep the alarms from sounding. Hell, I don't even know what the alarms are, or how they work. And then, I don't know how to get us across the lake before we're missed. The guards would have no trouble at all spotting us on the water."

Aili nodded thoughtfully. "Some sort of diversion?" she began doubtfully, and Silence shrugged.

"I really need to know more about the alarm system."

"Of course." Aili looked up, her eyes sparkling. "If I were to get you access to the Palace library, do you think it might hold information on the alarms?"

"It might," Silence said. More probably it wouldn't, she added to herself, and even if it does, it will be well hidden and well protected from prying eyes like mine. Seeing the excitement in the shazadi's face, however, Silence didn't have the heart to voice her thoughts. "It's worth a try. I didn't know this place had a library."

"One of her Serenity's better-kept secrets," Aili answered.

Silence nodded. That actually might improve the chances of the information she wanted being in the library, and accessible. She said aloud, "In the meantime, I think it's time we made contact with your father's agent here. There are some things I need to make a start on breaking out, and the sooner I get to work, the better."

Aili nodded, consulting the chronograph pinned to her skirt. "I can do that within the hour." She gave a sudden, almost shy smile. "I play chess with him every afternoon."

Silence's eyebrows rose. Aili had a regular game of chess—by ghost-link, of course—with one of the officers of the Thousand attached to the lakeside guardpost. The pilot had spent a number of dull afternoons draped in her uncomfortable veiling, watching a similarly veiled Aili move sensitized pieces across a gemstone board. A magus's link-spell carried her move to the man waiting on the lake shore, and moved the ghostly reflection of his pieces along her board. "Coded moves?" she asked.

"Not exactly," Aili answered. "I wouldn't spoil my game for anything. You'll see." She stood, glancing over her shoulder into the garden, and stiffened abruptly. "Oh, lord, Jamilla, it's your shadow."

Silence stood, too, and swore softly. Ceiki, the Hegemon's illegitimate daughter, was moving purposefully along the paths, heading for Aili's quarters. The shazadi said, between amusement and annoyance, "She's got quite a crush on you."

"If only she weren't so damned stupid," Silence said.

Aili frowned, this time at Silence. "She's not so much stupid as uneducated. I doubt she can do much more than write her name—his Most Serene Majesty doesn't believe in wasting money on tutors for his bastards, especially the girls."

"With all the tutors in the world," Silence said, unwarily, "she'd still be stupid."

There was a moment's dangerous quiet, and then Aili said, very slowly, "You don't like women very much, do you, 'Jamilla'?"

Silence turned on her, stung, but there was enough

truth in the shazadi's words to cut off the instant response. After a moment, she said, "I haven't known many. But I'm learning."

Aili relaxed a little, muttering an apology, and Silence managed some embarrassed response. It was a deserved reproof, the pilot admitted. She had been trying so hard to fit in as a pilot, on Solitudo, and even before, that she had started to believe the things men said about women. There was absolutely no reason to feel that way, either, there was always Misthia, an entire planet ruled by women, to disprove the slanders. The Misthians she had known—too few of them—were good people. Tasarla, the best of them, had died on Arganthonios, saving another Misthian's ship; two more Misthians had been instrumental in helping her get back *Recusante*. Silence's eyes filled with unexpected tears. She sniffed angrily, trying to decide what to say, how to defend herself, but before she could think of anything, there was a knock at the door.

"Get the field, quick," Aili hissed.

Silence made the gesture that dissolved her security rings, and the shazadi opened the door to admit Ceiki. The Hegemon's daughter was a stocky, round-faced child who reminded Silence of nothing so much as an importunate puppy. Mindful of Aili's criticism, the pilot did her best to be gracious to the girl, and to her surprise Ceiki expanded under the attention. By the time Aili reminded them of the time, and her upcoming chess game, Silence was almost willing to admit that the shazadi might be right. Certainly Ceiki was deplorably ignorant; equally certainly she was interested in at least a few things other than the approved talk of clothes and marriages and babies. Still, it was hard to tell the difference between ignorance and stupidity, and Silence could not quite decide which Ceiki was. One thing's for sure, though, Silence thought as Aili sent the girl on her way and prepared to settle down to her chess game. If I'd met Ceiki in the Fringe—on Delos,

say—she's just the sort of kid I'd want to tell star-
travellers' stories to.

Aili had had the homunculi screen off an alcove for
her chess set. There was barely enough room in the
tiny enclosure for two chairs and the specially built
table. Usually, the shazadi negotiated the confined space
with unconscious grace. Today, however, she managed
to bump against the table, sending some of her own
pieces crashing to the floor. She and the guardsman had
been in the middle of a game. Behind the light, informal veil, Aili made a self-disgusted face, and reached to
pick up the pieces. They had been late in arriving, too;
already, the link had been established, and the translucent shadow-shapes of the guardsman's pieces were
already in place.

Aili hesitated theatrically, then set her knight back
on the board. She had put it in the wrong place, Silence realized abruptly, and her interest sharpened. An
instant later, the guardsman's shadowy red knight rose
from its place, tapped a different square, and returned
to the place where it had started. But that wasn't the
white knight's position, either, Silence thought. Aili
smiled behind her veil, and put the knight where it
belonged.

The shazadi repeated the performance with the fallen
bishop, putting it on the wrong square, allowing herself
to be "corrected", and finally returning the piece to its
proper place, then settled down to play out the rest of
the game. Silence watched with half an eye, her mind
on the coded messages. It was an extremely clever
code, she thought admiringly—it was reasonably flexi-
ble, it fit perfectly into Aili's established routine, and it
was impossible to decipher without the key. She was
barely able to control her impatience, but at last, the
hour-and-a-half allotted for chess dragged to an end, and
the guard's pieces faded gently away. Aili gave a reluc-
tant sigh and stood, stretching.

Silence moved to help her with her veil, saying softly, "Well? Did you get through?"

"Oh, yes," Aili said absently. Her mind was clearly still on the game. "He's very good, that one. I hear he was a planetary junior master, when he was a cadet."

Silence paused, the coded message driven momentarily from her mind. "You don't just hold him even, either. I've seen you win, oh, at least twice. How good are you, Aili?"

The shazadi faced her. "Women of the Thousand may not compete in the tourneys," she said. "But. . .Four years ago, there was an open competition on Inarime, and I entered anonymously—I played from a covered palanquin. They computed my rank then at the system-tourney level."

Silence whistled softly. There were only a couple of hundred men in human-settled space who could regularly compete in the systemwide tournaments. For Aili to equal them, without their opportunities to practice and compete. . . . Silence did not finish the thought.

"Anyway," Aili said, shaking away her mood, "I passed along the message. He'll be here the day after tomorrow."

As the shazadi had promised, two days later Silence was summoned from her lunch to stand in for Aili in receiving a message from the satrap. The pilot had been well briefed in the appropriate procedures on Inarime— the satrap's agent was not of sufficient rank to allow him to meet Aili face to face, and so had to convey all messages through the shazadi's domna—but her briefing had not prepared her for the Princess Royal's disapproving presence at the ritual veiling. It took all Silence's concentration to remember everything, unnerved as she was by Radiah's unwavering stare, and she was already exhausted by the time the homunculi led her down the chill corridor to the entrance court.

The door slid back, disclosing the slim figure of a young man in the full formal uniform of the Thousand standing just across the black line of the Seer. Silence took a tighter grip on the innocent-looking worry-stone she carried beneath her veil—it was actually one of Isambard's warning devices, and would grow warm if they were being monitored. She stepped into the court-yard just as the homunculus announced flatly, "Domna Jamilla Sahen, I present Captain-Lieutenant Marcinik."

Somehow, Silence kept from crying out, but she stopped in her tracks, unable for a moment to go on. *Marcinik.* . . . That figure had looked vaguely familiar, but she hadn't been able to place it from the one brief glance. Marcinik had been an officer on the Hegemonic transport where she had first discovered her anomalous powers. He had shown them all a sort of distant kind-ness when they thought Balthasar was going to die, and he would certainly, unquestionably, remember Chase Mago and the Delian, even if he didn't recognize Si-lence beneath the concealing veil.

The pilot forced herself to move forward again, aware she was drawing the wrong kind of attention from the captain-lieutenant. The Marcinik she remembered had been a mere lieutenant, she thought without much hope. Maybe this is a different man. Then they faced each other across the Seer, and that hope died. The captain-lieutenant had not changed much over the months since Silence's capture and escape. He was still very handsome, in the almond-eyed, aristocratic way of the Thousand, but there were two faint, fresh lines bracket-ing the corners of a surprisingly firm mouth. He was eyeing Silence curiously, as though trying to place her while he waited for her to speak.

Etiquette demanded that she speak first. Trying to disguise her voice as much as possible, the pilot said, "Captain-Lieutenant Marcinik?"

Marcinik's eyes widened sharply, and he said, "Si-lence Leigh." His voice was the merest thread of sound. Nevertheless, Silence winced, tightening her grip on the sensor egg. It remained reassuringly cold to the touch.

"I fear you're mistaken," she began, and Marcinik shook his head.

"I couldn't forget you, sieura. Not after all this." Her confusion must have shown through the veil, Silence realized, because Marcinik managed a humorless grin. "My dear Sieura Leigh, service at the Women's Palace is no great honor, not even when it comes with a promotion. The Hegemon was very angry at your escape; I'm one of the many who got blamed for it."

Silence felt her blood run cold. If Marcinik blamed her for his demotion—as well he might, she thought dizzily, it did seem to be her fault—not only could he refuse to help her, but it would be easy to turn her over to the Hegemon. He would certainly earn back his place in the fighting ranks—even win a real promotion for it. Desperately, Silence sought for something to say to persuade him not to turn her in, but to help them all.

The captain-lieutenant's smile abruptly disappeared. "And you're serving her Highness?"

There weren't many occasions for complete honesty, Silence thought, but this was one of them. "We—my husbands and I—are working for his Highness of Inarime. We've come to rescue Aili before the attack."

"Them, too?" Marcinik's jaw dropped, then set into a mulish scowl. "Does his Highness know what he's dealing with?"

"Yes," Silence snapped, "and I'm the only person who can help Aili now. But I can't do it without an outside contact."

She watched the play of emotions on Marcinik's handsome face—anger at her, at his demotion, at the Hegemon—and chagrin warring with his loyalty to the satrap of Inarime and his daughter. Abruptly, the captain-lieutenant shook his head. "I've sworn an oath," he said, "to serve him and to protect her." He jerked his head almost imperceptibly at the Palace beyond the courtyard walls. "And to have vengeance. What do you want me to do?"

Silence let out a soundless sigh of relief. "First, I need you to establish contact with my husbands. They'll be arriving on Asterion within the next day or so. It's just possible they're already here, but I doubt it. Their ship is a small freighter, about a hundred-twenty mass units, called *Recusante*. They're officially under charter to a magus called Jeks." Isambard had felt an alias was necessary, after he had vanished rather precipitously from Hegemonic service. "He'll probably have some things for me. Can you smuggle them into the Palace?"

"Would this Jeks be the Doctor Isambard who deserted during the siege of Castax and was subsequently condemned in absentia by the Hegemon himself?" Marcinik asked wearily.

"Condemned?" Silence shot back.

The captain-lieutenant nodded. "To death."

"I didn't know that," Silence said. "I don't think he did, either."

"The proceedings were kept semi-secret," Marcinik answered. "Only the people already involved with you know about it. But the port authorities will be looking for him."

"Damn," Silence said. "Oh, damn." Without Isambard's advice and his ability to procure the things she would need to escape from the Palace, she was not at all sure she could manage.

"However," Marcinik went on, still in that same, tired voice, "you are here, so I think it's safe to assume that he made it, too. What do you need from this Doctor Jeks?"

Silence shook herself. The captain-lieutenant was right, there was no point in worrying yet. "He'll have a packet made up—a basic magus's kit. Can you get that in?"

"And you're a magus, too." Marcinik gave her a rather bitter look. "There's nothing in it that would show up on sensors as overtly harmful?"

Silence shook her head.

"Then I can probably pass it in as a medical supplement," Marcinik said. "The message I've brought's a medical one."

The sensor egg grew suddenly hot in Silence's hand. She hissed at Marcinik to be quiet, saying quickly, "Her Highness will be relieved at that." As she spoke, she glanced overhead. A brilliantly hued creature, like a Ras Gavran jewelfly but twice that insect's size, hovered overhead, watching and listening.

Marcinik, obedient to the pilot's hint, was droning on about the results of Aili's latest scan-check. After a moment, the giant jewelfly darted away. The egg slowly cooled, and Silence remembered to breathe. "It's gone," she said softly.

Marcinik nodded. "I'll take your messages," he said, "but for now, I must be going." He brought out a message-wafer sealed in a gaudy envelope, and set it down just on his side of the Seer. He managed a sort of apologetic smile as he added, "I'm afraid you'll have to take that from there."

Silence smiled back and stooped as gracefully as she could manage for the envelope. As she came upright again, Marcinik bowed sharply. "My best compliments to your mistress, domna," he said. "Until we meet again."

"Until we meet again," Silence echoed.

To Silence's unspoken relief, the Princess Royal was otherwise occupied when she returned, and it was the placid, easygoing queen-sister who superintended the veil-raising. Her questions—intended to make sure that the domnas were not corrupted or unduly influenced by their work—were perfunctory, and rather wistful. Silence guessed she missed the world outside.

As soon as the brief ceremony was over, she was free to do as she liked. Trying not to seem in too much of a hurry—she did not want to rouse any gossip or speculation as to the contents of the message—she made her way back to the shazadi's rooms. Aili was waiting on the protected gallery, staring out over the lake. She turned quickly as Silence entered.

"Well?"

Silence did not answer at once, hastily making the gestures and whispering the cantrips that activated her security seals. When she was satisfied everything was in place, she said, "He'll act as our liaison. He'll be bringing in a magus's kit for me soon. I don't know when, exactly, but it'll be coming in as a medical kit. He said it'd tie in with this message." She took the bright envelope from the pocket of her overdress, and handed it to the shazadi. Aili took it absently, snapping the seal, but did not open it at once.

"Tell me," she said, and there was a new note in her voice that made Silence look up sharply. "How is Marcinik?"

"You didn't tell me his name—I didn't know you knew it."

"You know him?" Aili's hands closed tight on the message-wafer.

"In a way," Silence answered grimly. She did not think this was the time to go into her life's story. "I wish you'd told me."

Aili took a deep breath, her eyelids fluttering in uncharacteristic embarrassment. "I beg your pardon, Jamilla. I didn't mean to be so abrupt."

With a start, Silence realized that the shazadi was not apologizing for withholding the captain-lieutenant's name. Before she could figure out quite what it was that Aili was sorry for, the shazadi went on, "But tell me, is he well?"

"He seems to be," Silence said. "He looks about the same as when I saw him—a little less harried, maybe. Why do you ask?"

"He plays a good game of chess," Aili answered, her eyes still lowered. Then she looked up again and said, defiantly, "Because I'm interested in him. Because if my father wins, I will be his first heir, and I can marry whom I like. And I like him."

All this from a few games of chess? Silence thought, feeling suddenly very old. Then again, why not? Hell, I decided to marry Denis and Julie because we made a good starship's crew. And from all I saw on that damned transport, Marcinik's better than most of his kind. Aili was still watching her, waiting for some response. Silence said, "What does he want?" It was not quite what she had intended to say, but somewhat to her surprise, the shazadi did not seem offended.

"I know my worth. If my father wins, there's no man in human-settled space who'd refuse me." Aili's face softened slightly, shyly. "But I think he might want me anyway."

"Then good luck to you." Silence glanced at the still-unopened envelope, but Aili forestalled her.

"Are you married?"

Silence hesitated, but answered truthfully. "Yes."

"I know so little about you," Aili mused, almost as though she had forgotten there was someone else in the room. "I didn't think you would be. I mean, why would you, a magus, bother?"

Silence laughed aloud. "You wouldn't believe me if I told you." Aili was still staring expectantly at her, and the pilot sighed, sobering. "I married my husbands—yes, two of them—because it was convenient, for a lot of reasons too complicated to go into. And I stayed with them because we suit each other. We work well together and, I suppose, we love each other." Quite suddenly, she was afraid for them, landing on Asterion without knowing there was a price on Isambard, and closed her eyes to hide the fear.

"I'm sorry," Aili said again. "I shouldn't pry."

"It's all right," Silence said, indistinctly, and pointed to the letter. "What about it?"

Aili pulled out the message wafer, scanned its cryptic symbols and, unexpectedly, laughed. "I've been diagnosed as suffering from *tristitia*, compounded by home-sickness. The doctors prescribe various herbs, elixirs, and such, compounded from Inariman ingredients, plus extra attention from home—and, most of all, familiar company. That means you, Jamilla."

Silence nodded, smiling. *Tristitia* was one of those nebulous complaints that often afflicted women of the Thousand. Its presence was hard to disprove, and its cure provided an excellent excuse for receiving visits and packages. The satrap's plan was proceeding on schedule.

Aili snapped her fingers. "I've got more good news, too," she exclaimed. "I spoke to the Princess Royal today. I told her you were interested in naval history because of your father, and she said you could use the Palace library if you wanted. You're to report to her after the Observances tomorrow, and she'll show you what you can and can't touch."

"Wonderful," Silence said, without much enthusiasm.

The next morning she dressed with special care, choosing her plainest dress to wear beneath the sober overgown. After a moment's hesitation, she tucked a small informal veil into the gown's pockets. She should not need it, but the Princess Royal was enough of a martinet to invoke one of the minor rules and require her to wear it while reading books written by men. There's no point in borrowing trouble, Silence told herself sternly, and headed for the hall where the Observances were held.

At the end of the tedious ceremonial—after the first day, Silence had resolved never to allow anyone to trace her family tree—the pilot presented herself before the Princess Royal. She bobbed a curtsy, well aware of Radiah's disdainful stare, murmuring, "Her Highness informed me that you've condescended to allow me to use the Palace library, your Serenity?"

The hovering domna sniffed, but Radiah answered

mildly enough, "That's correct. She told me you were interested in history?"

"Naval history, your Serenity," Silence said. It was dangerous to correct the Princess Royal, but the pilot guessed Radiah had made that slip quite deliberately. "My honored father encourages it."

The Princess Royal made a noncommittal noise, and said, "Come with me."

She turned and stalked away without waiting to see if Silence would follow. The pilot had to scramble to catch up. The Princess Royal led them rapidly through a maze of corridors, across a narrow strip of gardens, and back into the Palace corridors. Silence, who had gotten a fairly clear picture of the Palace's layout during her explorations with Aili, realized that Radiah was deliberately leading them astray, doubling back on her trail at least once. For an instant she wondered why the Princess Royal would bother, but then, looking at the domnas, the pilot thought she understood. If she could not find her own way to the library, Radiah would have an even better excuse to send her own domnas as escorts—and to keep track of Silence's movements. The pilot hid a smile. She was perfectly willing to let a domna escort her back and forth, as long as that domna let her alone to work. At last Radiah brought them up a spiral staircase into a dim, wood-paneled corridor.

This was the old administrative part of the Palace, Silence realized, built over the corridor that led from the main gate to the Seer's courtyard, and she felt a sudden surge of hope. If the library was part of that complex, there was a better chance that she could find information on the security arrangements. After all, the original administrators would have had to have access to that material.

The Princess Royal stopped abruptly in front of a door banded with strips of what appeared to be raw gold. She produced a slim, jewel-headed control wand from somewhere in her voluminous robes, and passed it twice across a concealed receptor. A moment later the door swung back, and a strange object creaked into view.

It was a homunculus, Silence realized at once, but of a totally unfamiliar kind. It had a standard, humanoid head and torso, shaped so as to be completely sexless, but that torso was set into a wheeled pedestal that glittered with lights and strange, inset characters. It was very old: the grey pseudo-flesh had a blurred, worn look, as though the details of its formation had been rubbed away over the years. With more creaking, it managed a sort of jerky bow, bending from the neck and bobbing its shoulders a little, and said, in a voice as dusty as the top of its pedestal, "The Princess Royal requires?"

"I wish to admit a new user to the Library," Radiah answered. Without looking back, she snapped her fingers at her own domna, who hastily put something into the Princess Royal's hand. "Her name is Jamilla Sahen, domna to the shazadi Aili of Inarime. This is her card." She held up a thin metal plaque, letting it dangle by its silver chain. The plaque itself seemed mostly blue, but changed colors as it moved, waves of gold and green and red washing across its surface.

The homunculus made its peculiar bow again. "I accept the Princess Royal's wishes."

Radiah eyed it without favor and turned to Silence. "Domna Jamilla, this is your user's card. You must wear it while you are inside the library. If you remove it, or if you should—accidentally, of course—attempt to use books outside the area in which you've declared an interest, the Librarian will be summoned, and you will lose your privilege. This card only grants access to the historical materials." She seemed to be smiling grimly behind her veil. "I would regret to hear that you had been careless."

Silence curtsied again, and allowed the Princess Royal to place the chain around her neck. "I'll be very careful, your Serenity, I promise." *And I will, too,* the pilot added, *but not quite the way you mean.*

"I'm sure you will," Radiah said, disconcertingly. She gestured to her domna. "Pilisi will return for you at noon."

Silence curtsied once again, murmuring her thanks, and the two women vanished down the corridor. The homunculus made a throat-clearing noise. "If the lady domna will follow me?"

"Lead on," Silence said, and followed the strange construction into the library.

The room was much taller than she had expected. She paused, disoriented, then realized she must be at the base of one of the towers that sprouted from the main buildings. It was like being at the bottom of a well, except that the walls were lined with shelf after shelf of books, rising to a ceiling five stories away. What Silence had at first taken for sunlight was the light of a faceted lamp set at the very point of the tower roof. For a moment, she could not figure out how one could reach the upper levels of books, then realized that a narrow ramp spiraled up the tower wall, giving access to all the shelves.

The homunculus was waiting patiently beside a high carrel. Silence shook herself and moved to join it, still trying to take in everything at once. There were only two study tables, each with a heavily padded chair and a separately lighted noteboard, but there were a few other, less comfortable-looking chairs set at intervals along the walls and on the ramp itself.

"This is the catalogue," the homunculus announced sonorously, and Silence dragged her attention back to it. One twig-fingered, grey-fleshed hand was pointing to the set of six heavy volumes chained to the shelf above the carrel. The pilot suppressed a shudder, and nodded.

"As you can see, the volumes may not be moved from this place," the homunculus continued. "You may obtain the shelf location from the Catalogue, and then either I will fetch them for you, or you may get them yourself, if you wish to do so. You may move freely along the ramp, but do not touch the books except in the areas for which you have been granted privileges. Do you have any questions, Domna Jamilla?"

"Yes." Silence had been studying the room as the creature spoke; now she pointed at a glass case that stood at the opposite end of the room from the Catalogue. It held what seemed to be a crystal sculpture, but it was impossible to make out the details at a distance. "What's that?"

The homunculus's eyes flashed red. "Restricted!" it rasped, in a voice entirely unlike its previous, polite drone. Silence whispered a curse, furious that she had already managed to get her privileges revoked, and then the homunculus's primary imprinting reasserted itself, overriding the security print. "I beg your pardon, lady domna, but that is restricted, part of the security system. The case should not even be uncovered. I will have to ask you to excuse me." It rolled away without waiting for Silence to reply.

"Of course I'll excuse you," Silence said. "I'll be sure to keep well away, too." At least, she added, until I can find a way to override this card, and get a good look at it. Whatever the thing is, if it's part of the security system, I want a look at it.

The homunculus drew a heavy grey-blue cover up over the case, and Silence's interest sharpened even further. The cover looked as though it were made of dura-felt, the specially treated material used to protect a starship's keel against interference. If the case's contents had to be protected by dura-felt. . . . Then the homunculus was rolling back toward the Catalogue, and the pilot hastily smoothed her expression.

"The Catalogue is organized on the Solitudo system," the homunculus went on, as if there had been no interruption. "Do you need further instruction, lady domna?"

Silence suppressed a laugh, and shook her head. "No, thank you, that will be all." She reached for the first of the Catalogue volumes and the homunculus rolled away again, to return a moment later pushing a high, wheeled stool. It carried a noteboard and stylus in its free hand. Silence took them, muttering her thanks, and settled herself to work, flipping through the first volume. She was almost painfully familiar with Solitudo's system, after the time she had spent in the magi's great Library. She found the first set of entries on her ostensible subject without trouble, and began automatically to copy out the shelf notes, letting her mind range freely.

Her job here was twofold, she decided. First, to find out if the information she wanted was here. Involuntarily, her eyes strayed to the covered case at the far end of the room. And, second, to figure out a way to get at that information. Thoughtfully, she caressed the user's card on its chain around her neck, rubbing its lightly incised surface between her thumb and forefinger. It had the slick, coated feel of a magus's work. She rubbed harder, and felt it vibrate gently in response, more a tingling in her brain than a real sensation. It was a simple harmonic receptor, then, she thought, tuned to a particular harmony, and set to broadcast the dissonance if someone picks up the wrong book. The question now is how the book's harmonies are set—probably a sounding disk somewhere in the book itself, since the homunculus said the alarm was set off by touching the wrong books. That was easily enough checked, later, but for now it was more important that she find out about the security systems.

Glancing over her shoulder, she saw that the homunculus had retreated to a corner and seemed almost to doze, its thin arms folded across its chest. Silence took a deep breath, and trying not to look too furtive, lifted down the Catalogue's fourth volume. She was braced for alarms, but nothing happened. Of course not, she told

herself almost angrily, flipping hastily through the pages.
The Solitudo system is so strange that you can't ever
predict exactly where you'll find a reference. They can't
sensitize the Catalogue. She found the section she was
looking for quickly enough, and skimmed through it,
pausing only to memorize a pair of shelf listings. There
was, of course, no entry reading "Palace security blue-
prints," but she was familiar enough with the peculiari-
ties of Solitudo's codes to guess that "Custodiae,
aleph/second-trial, blue and green" was probably what
she wanted. She set the volume back in its place and
rose stiffly, stretching. The homunculus, alerted by her
movements, unfolded its arms and rolled forward,
bowing.

"May I serve you, lady domna?"

"Yes," Silence said. "Where would I find these shelf
listings?"

"I can bring them for you, Domna Jamilla, if you
wish," the homunculous responded.

"No, I want to look for myself," Silence said. "Where
would I find them?"

The homunculus gave an almost human sigh, shifting
its torso to point to the ramp's entrance. "The books are
shelved according to the Catalogue entries, first books at
the bottom, later books on the upper levels, and so on
to the top. These books—" The homunculus shifted its
body again with another sighing sound. "These books
are on the second level, halfway around."

Silence sighed herself—that meant climbing two and
a half stories—but said, "Thank you." She made her
way up the long ramp, very careful not to get too close
to the books. She could feel a sort of sound radiating
from them, from tiny disks buried somewhere in their
bindings, and she could feel her card vibrating with
that sound, ready to burst into dissonance at any moment. If she stretched out a hand, touched the source
of the almost-music, the vibrations would travel through
her bones, strike the card, and flower into an angry

noise. She could picture herself doing it, so vividly that she was tempted to touch the nearest book and get it over with, but fought the feeling under control, shuddering. She had felt something like that once before, looking down from the Nathra Tower on Cap Bel, seven stories from the open roof garden to the square below. She had imagined herself leaning forward, falling, a picture so horribly real that she had almost wished to fall just to stop the image.

Then at last she had reached the second level, and the buzzing above her heart faded away. The compulsion faded with it, and she drew a shaky breath. She moved slowly, scanning the bindings for the proper symbols, until she found the first of the volumes on her list. It was on the bottom shelf, perfect for her purposes. She knelt, glancing quickly through the railing to be sure the homunculus had returned to its corner, and laid her hand gently against the spine of the book. She felt the vibration swell under her fingers, travelling along the channel of her arm, setting bone and flesh singing to the same note. It reached the card, struck a sympathetic harmony from its receptor, and broadened into soundless song. Silence stayed frozen, letting the harmonies sound through her until she was sure she understood the system, then let the book slide back into place. I can change the card, she thought triumphantly. I can give myself the access I want.

Then her triumph faded slightly, and she sighed, reaching again for the book. She couldn't change the card here and now, and it was important that she have some solid work to show for her hours in the library. She settled herself in the nearest chair, half a turn down from the book's location, not far from the painted band that marked the beginning of the second level.

Before she could skim through more than a few pages, a gong sounded, seemingly in midair. Silence started, nearly dropping her book, and the homunculus sprang into motion, rolling toward the door. It opened at his approach, and the pilot caught a glimpse of the oddly foreshortened figure of Radiah's domna waiting just outside the door. The homunculus conferred briefly with her, then rolled back to the center of the library, gesturing for Silence to come down.

"Domna Jamilla, the Princess Royal has sent Domna Pilisi to fetch you."

For an instant, Silence was seized by utter panic, but then she caught sight of her own chronograph. She had been in the library longer than she had realized. It was already noon, and Pilisi was just arriving on schedule, not because the Princess Royal suspected anything. Still, there could be no harm in reinforcing the other domna's self-importance a little. Silence took a deep breath and leaned over the railing, calling, "Oh, please, Domna Pilisi, can't I stay just a little longer?"

Through the doorway, she could just see Pilisi swell like a puff-bird, gloating in her borrowed authority. "Of course not, Domna Jamilla. Her Serenity's orders were quite explicit. Come down at once."

Silence hid a smile and did as she was told, first returning the book to its place in the shelves. It had been a profitable day, she thought, as she followed Pilisi back through the corridors toward Aili's rooms. I know where the information I need is; now all I have to do is get at it. And once I change this card—she stroked it gently, very grateful that Isambard's teaching had emphasized harmonics—I shouldn't have any trouble at all.

Aili was waiting eagerly for her return. The shazadi had had their luncheon laid out on the protected balcony, Silence saw with approval. They would be able to talk in reasonable safety. While they ate, she explained what she had done that morning, and what she would have to do to get the information for their escape, tossing the user's card casually onto the table between them. Aili eyed it warily, touched it with a cautious finger, but did not pick it up.

"I don't feel anything," she said.

"Oh, it's there, all right," Silence said. Her skin still tingled lightly from its touch. "How soon do you think Marcinik can bring in my things?"

Aili shrugged. "Not for another three or four days, at least. It would take that long for a package to get here from Inarime."

"Too long." Silence bit thoughtfully at her thumbnail, a habit she thought she had conquered years before. Scowling, she went on, "We don't have a whole lot of time before your father's fleet lifts from Inarime."

"We still have three weeks," Aili objected softly.

Silence did not answer, staring out across the lake. The surface shivered a little under an unusually brisk breeze; otherwise, nothing had changed from all the other days. "The trouble is," she said, half to herself, "I need to make a tincture before I can work on the card. And I can't make a tincture without the materials in the kit. Well, I could, theoretically, but I doubt I could find the time or the privacy to make it work. . . ." She let her voice trail off, still staring at the lake.

"What sort of materials do you need?" Aili asked hesitantly.

Silence shrugged, her mind elsewhere. "*Nivi casi*, protean matter, *materia stellans*, things like that. Almost anything in which a magus has fixed power, actually. . . ." A lamp? she wondered suddenly. One of those fixed-fire globes? She discarded the idea almost as soon as it was formed, not without regret. But fire was probably the most dangerous elemental force, even diluted and adulterated as it must be in the lamps. There was too much chance of setting the entire Palace on fire—and besides, she thought, the homunculi would certainly spot a missing light-globe, and report it to the Princess Royal. The same held true for all the other nonmechanical objects she had seen in the Palace: if they weren't too dangerous to use, their absence would be noticed and reported.

The lake shivered again as the breeze struck its surface, but refused to break into whitecaps. Silence smiled slowly. The lake was held in place by an elaborate stasis web, the kind the magi used to keep unstable liquids from separating. Though this was on a much larger scale, surely the process could not be that different. And the first step in creating a stasis web involved infusing the liquid with a tincture of *materia stellans*. There would be enough of the stuff suspended in the liquid for her to distill and use.

"You've thought of something?" Aili asked.

Silence nodded, still smiling. "How close can we get to the lake?"

Aili shrugged, looking confused, but answered, "To the water, if we can get into the boathouse."

Silence grimaced. The boathouse was locked, and subject to frequent inspections and overflights from the giant jewelflies. The shazadi went on, "Or we could try the pleasance."

"Pleasance?" Silence asked. It was the first she'd heard of such a thing.

"One of the Hegemons built it for his mother," Aili answered, impatiently. "It's a bathing pool, let into the Palace walls. Nobody uses it because the Princess Royal doesn't approve of swimming, but she hasn't actually forbidden it. I didn't think of it before," she added, in answer to the pilot's unspoken criticism, "because it doesn't connect to the lake in any useful way. It's heavily screened. Nothing could get in or out."

"But the water comes directly from the lake?" Silence asked, and the shazadi nodded. Silence smiled. "Do you know how to swim?"

After some searching, Aili found bathing costumes for both of them, high-collared, sleeveless bodysuits and loose-fitting, hooded robes. Silence was enough taller than the shazadi to make the bodysuit uncomfortably tight, but Aili deftly slit and restitched the side and shoulder seams to make it wearable. It was harder than

Silence had expected to find something to carry the water in, but finally Aili sacrificed the contents of two bottles of scented oil, and the pilot tucked the carefully rinsed bottles into the pocket of her robe. Aili led the way onto the lower concourse, and from there to the lower perimeter walk, careful to stay out of sight of any of the Princess Royal's servants.

The bathing pool was little more than a sort of cage built into the angle of the outer walls where two of the four lobes met. A narrow tiled platform jutted into the water, and there were two smaller pools, each no more than fifteen centimeters deep.

"Wading pools," Aili explained, and laughed at the pilot's expression of disgust. "Not everyone can swim, Jamilla."

Silence did not answer, surveying the water beyond the platform. As Aili had said, the bathing area connected directly with the lake. The coppery bars of the cage, webbed with almost invisible mesh, swept out and down, to vanish below the surface some twelve meters from the end of the platform. Underwater, Silence knew, they would curve back to meet the Palace wall. She wondered how much depth the designers had left for swimming.

"We'd better get on with it," she said, and loosened the ties of her robe, letting the spongy cloth pool around her feet. The breeze was unexpectedly chill against her bare skin, much cooler than it had seemed inside the Palace. The pilot shivered. Aili hugged herself and reached quickly for her discarded robe. Silence dropped to her knees, fumbling for the first bottle. She was just about to pull it from the robe's pocket when a harsh voice froze her in her tracks.

"What is this, Aili?"

Silence let the bottle slide back into its hiding place, and turned slowly, still on her knees. The Princess Royal, flanked by two of her domnas and followed by a long-limbed household homunculus, stood just inside the doorway, frowning suspiciously at the two younger women.

Aili let her robe fall again, and heroically hid a shiver as she answered, "We wanted to swim, your Serenity. I hope I haven't offended. . . ."

The Princess Royal's eyes darted from Silence to the shazadi and back to Silence. "Domna Jamilla," Radiah began, disapproval heavy in her voice, "I might have expected such hoyden's behavior from the daughter of a mere admiral. I can hardly consider you fit company—"

"I beg your Serenity's clemency," Aili interrupted, managing to appear at once contrite and winsome. "It's all my fault. I persuaded Jamilla to come—it's been so long since I've been swimming, your Serenity, and I've missed it so much."

"Indeed."

Silence could see, in the hard, suspicious line of Radiah's mouth, that the Princess Royal did not believe Aili's story, and held her breath, waiting for the decision. Still, Radiah had no proof that they were lying. As long as the Princess Royal did not search the robes, they should be all right, Silence thought. And surely even Radiah needs some kind of excuse, if she's to treat a satrap's daughter like a criminal.

Slowly, the Princess Royal's mouth relaxed, curving into an unpleasant smile as she stared at Silence. "You should have informed me of your intentions, Aili," she said, with an attempt at cordiality. "But of course you can swim, if you like. Pilisi, stay with them as domna while they take their exercise."

For a moment, Aili seemed about to protest, and Silence tensed, willing her to keep quiet. Then the shazadi relaxed almost imperceptibly, and said, "Your Serenity is too gracious. Thank you—and thank you, Pilisi."

The Princess Royal's smile widened slightly. "Don't let me delay you, girls."

It might as well have been an order, Silence thought.

"Thank you, your Serenity," she said, through clenched teeth, and walked to the edge of the platform. Under the Princess Royal's watchful eye, there was no point in delay. Silence took a deep breath, not quite daring to dive, and jumped.

The water was icy. She sank deep, swearing to herself, and struck the floor of the cage about three meters down. She pushed off, hard, and broke the surface, gasping as much from the cold as from the lack of oxygen. Aili, standing on the edge of the platform, was watching dubiously. Silence could feel her teeth beginning to chatter as she beckoned for the shazadi to join her. Aili made an indescribable face and dove in, to surface neatly half a meter from Silence's outstretched hand.

She cursed feelingly, if softly, her lips already blued with cold, and said, "How long do we keep this up?"

"As long as we have to," Silence said, grimly. She could see the Princess Royal watching from the platform, the same unpleasant smile still playing on her lips. "Swim, and swim hard." The pilot followed her own advice, kicking strongly for the cage. *I should've known it would be this cold,* she berated herself. *Of course a stasis field would do this, especially when it's created on such a large scale.*

Her hand touched the fragile-looking mesh of the cage, and she clung there for a moment, gasping, until Aili caught up with her. The Princess Royal had vanished, but Pilisi was still standing on the platform, her dark robes conspicuous against the white stone of the Palace.

"Back again?" Aili asked, shivering, and Silence nodded, too cold to speak. "How are we going to get the bottles filled now?"

Silence shrugged, and started for the platform. The shazadi splashed after her, swearing.

Silence clung to the edge of the platform for a moment, gathering her strength, then hauled herself up onto the tiled surface. For a moment, it seemed warm out of the water, and then the breeze circled back, chilling her even further. In the pool, Aili ducked lower in the water, obviously preferring that to the touch of the air. Silence reached into the pocket of her robe and brought out the bottle. Checking to be sure the stopper was securely seated, she tossed it in Aili's direction, shouting, "Catch!"

The shazadi stared blankly at her for a moment, but dove obediently toward the floating bottle. Silence reached for the second one, and Pilisi called, "Stop."

The pilot froze, then forced herself to turn toward the other domna. "What's wrong?"

"It's time to come in," Pilisi said, querulously. Silence could see her hugging herself through the thick cloth of her overgown. It was cold on the platform, the pilot thought, hiding a grin, and Pilisi wasn't one to suffer for someone else's pleasure, or even the Princess Royal's revenge.

"But Domna Pilisi," Silence began, hoping Aili would use the diversion to fill her bottle. Pilisi shook her head.

"No more. My lady shazadi, you must come in at once."

Silence made a sort of half-bow, stooping to collect Aili's robe, and turned to help the shazadi onto the platform. Aili was already clinging to the tiled edge with one hand, the other out of sight below the surface. As Silence bent to help her up, the pilot let the robe spill out of her hands in concealing folds; in the same instant, Aili whipped the filled and stoppered bottle out of the water and tucked it deftly into the robe's pocket. The whole thing was over in an instant, as neatly, Silence thought, as if they'd rehearsed it a hundred times. She set the robe aside, mumbling something, and caught the shazadi's wrists, half pulling the other woman out of the water.

Aili was shivering painfully, and Silence was quick to

wrap the thick robe around the smaller woman's shoulders. "I'm quite all right," the shazadi said. "Get yourself warm, too."

Silence shrugged on her own robe, grateful for its warmth, and allowed Pilisi to herd them back inside the Palace, ignoring her grumbled complaints. At the crossroads, where a gently sloping ramp led up from the perimeter walks to the well-lit corridors of the main level, Aili turned abruptly, saying in a voice Silence had never heard her use before, "That will be all, Domna Pilisi. You may go."

Pilisi was obviously not prepared for that sudden assertion of authority either, Silence saw with delight. The older domna hesitated, and Aili said, with the same flat assumption of superiority, "Her Serenity was most gracious, but you may go now."

Routed, Pilisi bobbed a quick curtsy and edged away, glancing nervously over her shoulder as she went. When she was out of earshot, Aili said, tonelessly, "That bitch."

Silence shrugged, and said, driven by an obscure impulse, "It wasn't Pilisi's fault."

"I didn't mean her," Aili snapped. "I meant her damned Serenity. She knew how cold the water would be. She did that out of pure malice."

"I should've realized, too," Silence said. "I'm sorry, Aili."

"It's not your fault," Aili said, and shivered convulsively. "God, I don't think I'll ever be warm again."

"I know," Silence said, and the shazadi gave her a quick, rueful smile. "But at least we got the water."

Aili shivered again. "I think I'd rather have waited."

They followed the main arcade back toward Aili's quarters, no longer restricted to the back hallways. The sun streamed through the skylights, warming them. By the time they reached the triple arch that marked the boundary of the shazadi's quarters, Silence was feeling fully recovered, and thoroughly pleased with herself.

She was already planning the next part of her plan when an odd snuffling sound broke her concentration.

"What—?" she began, but Aili had already darted into the nearest alcove. Swearing to herself, Silence followed, to find the shazadi kneeling in front of a sobbing Ceiki, who obstinately refused to budge from her contorted position, pressed tight into the corner of the alcove. Aili gave Silence a meaningful glance, and awkwardly, the pilot held out her hands, saying, "Ceiki?"

Still sobbing, the girl launched herself into Silence's arms, and clung tight. Not knowing what else to do, Silence stroked her hair, saying, "Hush now, what's wrong?"

After a few moments, Ceiki's sobs eased a little, and Silence managed to get them both seated on the alcove's bench. Aili made herself as inconspicuous as possible in the archway. "What is it?" Silence said again.

Ceiki sniffled, cautiously wiping her face with the lining of her sleeve. "It's—I'm to be married," she managed at last.

"So soon?" Silence exclaimed, startled.

"It's for an alliance, they said," Ceiki answered. "To the satrap of Aja."

Aili gave a soft hiss, instantly cut off. Silence glanced up at her, and saw the shazadi's face set tight with anger. So it was not likely to be a good marriage, either, she thought.

Ceiki went on without noticing the exchange of glances. "He's old, and he's got three wives already. I don't want to marry him."

She seemed about to burst into tears again. Silence reached for her hand, saying foolishly, "Now, Ceiki. . . ."

"When is the betrothal?" Aili asked.

"Two weeks," Ceiki answered, and wiped her eyes again. "Twelve days exactly." She squeezed Silence's hand painfully tight. "Jamilla, what do I do?"

Silence shook her head, hating herself for not having a better answer. "I don't know, Ceiki. I'm so sorry. . . ."

"Ceiki." Aili straightened abruptly. "Your domna."

Ceiki gave a final choked sob, but straightened her back obediently as the large woman swept into view, almost filling the alcove.

"There you are, darling. I've been looking for you. Come along, we've a lot to do before you're betrothed." For the first time, she seemed to notice that the girl had been crying. "Now, now, no need for that, you're to be married. Think, Ceiki, and to a satrap, too. How marvelous, especially for a girl of your birth." Still talking, she led Ceiki away, the girl staring forlornly over her shoulder at Silence.

As soon as they were out of sight, Silence spat on the gilded tiles, furious with herself for being so ineffectual. "We couldn't bring her with us," she said, more than half to herself. "It just isn't possible. She sleeps in the Princess Royal's wing. . . ."

Aili was mumbling something under her breath, and the pilot looked sharply at her. "What?"

"I said, when my father wins. . . ." Aili broke off with a quick gasp of alarm. "What am I saying?"

Silence took a deep breath, calming herself with an effort. "There's nothing we can do now," she said, as much to convince herself as to convince Aili. "Later, this betrothal can be repudiated." She sighed and looked up at the shazadi. "But for now—Aili, doesn't a betrothal involve all sorts of festivities, feasting, fireworks, general merriment?"

Aili nodded, puzzled.

Silence managed a bitter smile. "And there's a betrothal twelve days from today. I think we have our diversion."

CHAPTER 8

Silence did her best to put Ceiki's misery out of her thoughts, concentrating instead on modifying the user's card for her own escape. That's the best help you can give the girl, she told herself firmly, and tried not to think about it any more. The first step was to distill from the lake water enough of the *materia stellans* to make a tincture strong enough to affect the user's card. That was a fairly simple process even without a magus's specialized equipment, and Silence set to work at once.

As Asterion's sun was setting, she took her place on the shielded balcony, the bottle of lake water balanced awkwardly between a flat silver dish and a dozen folded squares of Sareptan linen, all "borrowed" from the Palace storage cells. Silence set a work ring while the shadows deepened into evening, and as the first stars appeared, very pale against the darkening blue, poured the water out into the dish. It sparkled, very faintly, with a light that was not reflected starlight. It was a good thing Asterion had no natural moon, Silence thought, laying the first of the napkins across the dish. Lunar harmonies would only make the process more complicated.

When the last of the sunset had faded from the sky, Silence passed her hand gently over the dish, not quite

touching the draped napkin. She felt nothing, and
frowned, then composed herself and tried again. This
time, she felt a feather's touch in the palm of her hand:
the *materia* was reacting to the stellar harmonies, setting up the faintest of vibrations in the air around it.
Good, she thought. At least I know there's enough
materia to work with.

She had no monochord to set the proper harmonies,
but for this process, almost mechanical in its repetitive
simplicity, she hardly needed it. Murmuring the first
cantrip, she let herself slip into the waking trance. The
glimmering grew stronger beneath the napkin, silvery
at first, then tinged with flickers of other colors, no
sooner named than they were gone. The lake, too,
shone with the same cold fires. Silence smiled and
spoke the second cantrip, feeling the world shift and
broaden, then spoke the words that released the *materia*
from its temporary bond with the lake water. Very
slowly, it began to work itself free, rising only to be
stopped by the thin fabric of the napkin.

Silence waited while the *materia* gathered on the
underside of the napkin, caught up in the strange time-
lessness that was the magus's view of reality. Overhead,
the stars took on new depth and color, scattered against
the blue-black magnificence of the sky. Once, there was
a distant flash of red as a starship's keel touched
atmosphere; Silence watched it slide from near zenith
to the horizon, too far outside herself to wish she were
its pilot. The lake shivered and glowed, the bonded
materia in its heart writing strange patterns across its
still surface.

After a while, the napkin glowed strongly. Silence
passed her hand across its surface again, feeling the
materia still moving in the lake water, and reached for
another of the napkins. She spread it across the dish
above the first, then, very carefully, eased the first
napkin out from under the fresh one. She folded the
filled napkin with deliberate haste, making sure the

side that held the captured *materia* was turned to the inside, and finished by fastening the corners in an elaborate, significant knot. Despite her care, however, a little of the *materia* escaped, the glittering specks flashing up into the air as though they had a will of their own. Silence watched them rise faster and faster, the cloud dissipating as it rose. A distant part of her being hoped that the guards at the lakeshore post were not watching the Palace too closely tonight. Then she returned to her vigil.

Releasing the bonded *materia stellans* from the lake water took most of the night. Silence returned to her bed in time to snatch an hour's broken sleep before a household homunculus roused her for the Observances, and managed to doze for another three hours while pretending to read in the Palace library. She snatched another few hours' sleep that afternoon, pleading a mild, female complaint, and spent the evening preparing herself for another sleepless night.

This time, she had to reverse the process she had used the night before, returning the *materia* to water to make a tincture strong enough to allow her to change the coding of her user's card. This, too, was a long, quasi-mechanical process, and Silence was exhausted by the time she had finished. She dozed through the next morning's library session as well, waking up just in time for Pilisi to bring her back to the main section of the Palace. Aili was waiting with a message from the Princess Royal: Radiah had noted Jamilla's absence from the evening gathering with regret, and hoped the domna would be present today. There was no evading that veiled command, and Silence resigned herself to an evening of boredom, telling herself firmly that she would work the better for a good night's sleep.

It was not until the following afternoon that Silence was finally able to begin work on the user's card. She had spent her morning's session in the library ostensibly searching for a couple of oddly catalogued texts, but in actuality moving up and down the ramp in a last-minute check of her calculations. By the time she was able to return to the protected balcony, she was certain she knew what had to be done.

Aili had succeeded in borrowing a glassflute belonging to one of the other shazadis, and had left it on the balcony. The glassflute was a common instrument in both Hegemony and Rusadir; it was also close enough in form to stand in for a magus's pipe. On Solitudo, Silence had been forced to learn its simple fingerings. She glanced quickly at the crystal telltale, which still shone clear, set the user's card into the silver dish, and poured the tincture she had made the night before over it. Then she redrew her isolation ring, bringing flute and tincture inside it with her, and set to work.

The library's security system was based on a modified sequence of Mercury, with its five essential notes and almost infinite variations. The user's card was set to resonate to a limited number of those variations. Silence had to change its tuning, make it respond to the full range of the Mercurian sequence. Experimentally, she lifted the glassflute, fumbled through a trial scale. The notes were eerie, threaded with odd, semi-audible overtones, but the important ones sounded clear and true. Silence took a deep breath, set the flute aside, and bent over the dish that held the tincture and the user's card.

The tincture, which had stood motionless in the silver dish, indistinguishable from ordinary water except by the occasional mother-of-pearl shadow that crossed its surface, was releasing tiny bubbles, clustering around the edge of the bowl. So far, at least, things were going well. Silence closed her eyes, marshalling her strength— she was still not completely recovered from the effects of two nearly sleepless nights—and whispered the first cantrip. The water shivered lightly as she spoke—or was it just that she was able to perceive a shivering, she wondered. She had to drag herself back from that seductive line of contemplation. It was all right to lose herself in that sort of much-debated mystery when she had nothing to do but monitor an ongoing process; it was another thing entirely when she had an active role to perform.

She spoke the second cantrip, feeling the air tremble as the barriers between realities weakened and it met the submaterial reflection of itself, and quickly capped that with a third phrase, and a fourth. The user's card lay inert at the bottom of the dish. Silence frowned. She had been certain she knew the key words, had recognized the feel of the cantrips and invocations that had created the card. She hesitated, assessing what she had done, the tensions inherent in the air around her. Then, cautiously, she intoned a final phrase. The words, though spoken softly, rolled like thunder in the quiet of the ring. Silence winced slightly, but in the dish, the surface of the card seemed to move. The final phrase had hit the precise combination of Forms used to shape the card, unlocking it from its fixed state. It was ready to be reshaped to Silence's will.

The pilot took two slow, deep breaths and lifted the card from the dish of tincture. The liquid was so cold that she was mildly surprised to find it water rather than ice, and the card itself was cold enough to burn. Silence suppressed her curse and hung the cord on the air before her. It floated balanced on the conjunction of the three planes. The metal of the card looked odd, unfinished, as though only surface tension held it in its present shape. Strange shadows seemed to move beneath its polished surface.

Silence noted them without really appreciating their peculiar beauty, working her fingers to free them of the numbing cold. When she was certain they would not slip on the glassflute's keys, she lifted the flute and blew a single, experimental note. More shadows danced and twisted across the card. Silence watched these move-

ments with interest, mapping the pattern they formed.
She sounded a second note, and a third, and so on
through the Mercurian sequence, until she was certain
she had traced the card's tuning precisely. Then, very
carefully, she spoke a final word. The shadows in the
card writhed and pulsed, seeming almost ready to burst
through the deceptive tension that held it to its given
form. An edge bulged fractionally, fell back into place; a
corner shifted momentarily out of true, and snapped
back again. Silence lifted the glassflute and played the
Mercurian sequence a final time, watching the music
give new order to the card. Colors flared beneath the
golden surface, whirled through a rainbow-hued pin-
wheel like a miniature fireworks display, and settled
slowly. Silence spoke the phrase that sealed the new
form into material reality, and the tingling tension
vanished from the air. Deprived of its support, the card
fell clattering to the tiled floor.

Drained by her efforts, Silence stooped to pick it up,
already scanning its surface for any signs of her tampering. The card now felt very warm to her touch, but that
faded even as she noticed it. It seemed otherwise unchanged. Sighing her relief, she placed the card back
around her neck and took up the glassflute again. She
ran through the *Keplerian Variations* on the sequence
of Mercury and felt the card respond. Now, at last, she
was grateful for Isambard's insistence that she learn the
major sequential variations on a variety of different
instruments. The card trembled gently against her skin,
stinging into dissonance only when her fingers faltered
and she hit an out-of-sequence note. She had done all
that she could here; only using it would prove if she
had been completely successful. Stretching, she reached
to dissolve the ring.

By the next morning, however, some of her confidence had eroded. She found herself almost regretting
the moment when the Observances ended, and Pilisi
appeared to escort her to the Library. It was all she

could do not to lag behind, and despite her efforts, Pilisi gave her a curious look.

"Are you all right, Jamilla?"

Silence bit back a curse, and answered, "I'm fine— truth. I'm just tired." Pilisi's eyes narrowed, and the pilot added quickly, "Women's troubles." It was the perfect excuse. Pilisi's suspicion faded visibly, and there was even a touch of sympathy in her voice.

"A bad time of it? I'm sorry. Should you be working?"

"The best thing for me," Silence answered, and was proud of her rather martyred smile. Pilisi gave her another assessing look, and the pilot suppressed another curse. Surely I haven't overdone it? she thought.

Then they had reached the library door, and Pilisi gave a fractional shrug. "If you need help, tell the librarian to summon one of us," she said, and passed her hand across the sensor plate. The door opened, the librarian-homunculus creaking forward to greet them. Silence took a deep breath, hoping her modifications would work, and stepped across the threshold. The user's card thrummed against her heart. She flinched, waiting for it to burst into song or crashing dissonance, but after that one pulsing burst, it steadied to the normal gentle buzzing.

The homunculus brought her noteboard and stylus, then rolled back to its corner and seemed to become dormant. Silence settled herself in front of the Catalogue, selected a volume at random, and composed herself to look busy. She waited for seven minutes by the clock, then, stretching, slid from her high stool. The homunculus's eyes flickered open. Silence shook her head at it, smiling, and its eyes closed again. It had become used to her insistence on finding her own books.

Silence started up the ramp, and felt the card tremble against her skin as she came within range of the disks buried in the books. The trembling had a new feeling to it, a sense of harmony rather than of dissonance. She hid her smile of triumph: the retuning had

worked. The book she wanted—the *Custodiae*—was
well up in the tower, at the border of the fourth and
fifth levels. She took her time climbing the ramp, pausing once or twice to pretend to examine a book, and
tucked a pair of heavy naval volumes under her arm.
The homunculus did not stir from its somnolent state.

At the painted band that marked the division between the fourth and fifth levels, Silence paused, glancing back over the railing. Far below, the homunculus
drowsed in its corner, arms folded across its worn torso,
eyes closed. It should not move, she knew, unless the
security system alerted it. She took a deep breath, and
turned back to the shelves.

She found the book she wanted quickly enough. It
was the only one of its kind in the row, a massive,
metal-bound volume nearly twenty centimeters thick.
Bracing herself for disaster, Silence pulled it quickly
from its place. The card tingled, recognizing a sympathetic
harmony. The pilot glanced again over the railing: the
homunculus had not stirred. She allowed herself a quick,
triumphant smile, and settled on the floor of the ramp,
flipping quickly through the metal-edged pages.

Most of the book was taken up with particular schemae, the conventional notation of harmonic formulae.
Silence skimmed through them, barely acknowledging
the sting of regret that she did not have time to examine them more closely, until she found the section she
was looking for. This was an appendix intended for the
magi's employers: a layman's explanation of the processes, and, more important, of precisely what had
been done.

Some of it Silence had already discovered—the hovering giant jewelflies that kept a random watch on the
outdoor areas of the Palace; the guard-homunculi that
populated the lowest levels, where the service locks
were located; the watcher-nodes set in the boathouse
and the governors and recall/overrides set in the fantastically shaped boats themselves; the faces in the side

corridors' ceilings. It was good to have their presence confirmed, and to learn that the magi who installed them had not used any particularly esoteric techniques. There were other things that Silence had not even suspected: the corridor-spanning gates that could be closed in an emergency to seal off parts of the Palace, for one, and the elaborate auxiliary installations linked to the courtyard Seer. Worst of all, the magi had created the Palace and the lake together; buildings and lakebed were webbed with an elaborate sensor net that would report and track any unexplained movements. Silence swore softly to herself. If she and Aili were to escape, that net would have to be deactivated somehow. She reread the specifications, more carefully this time. The net was intended primarily to catch anyone trying to enter the Palace, not an inmate trying to escape; that was something in her favor.

Then a smaller notation caught her eye, directing her to the second volume of the *Custodiae*. She frowned, but searched the shelf in front of her until she found it. This was a much thinner book, bound in duplas rather than metal, and the publication date was considerably later: clearly there had been modifications to the system over the years. Silence sighed at the thought of having to take that into account as well. But as she skimmed through the second volume—less lavishly illustrated, and full of relatively clumsy schemae—she realized that all of the modifications had been intended to channel the original security system through a single control point. Silence muttered another curse, and flipped through the pages again to find the set of schemae that dealt with the control point itself. If the control point were located in the lakeside guard post, as was only logical, it would be almost impossible to put the system out of action, unless . . .

She found the schemae then, and set herself to read carefully. If the magi who made the changes had wanted to save time and effort—and they seemed to have been far less skillful than the magi who had created the first system—it was possible they had tied everything together in the Palace, and linked that primary control point to a secondary point on the shore. So far, the schemae pointed to that solution. Then she turned a page, and gasped at the drawing spread out before her. It was a sketch of the Palace—or no, she realized instantly, a sketch of the control point—which was itself an exact model of the Palace and its surrounding lake. Hieroglyphs along the margin indicated it was made of the most expensive materials the magi had been able to find—halcyon crystal, *shirai,* a bed of crushed gems for the waters of the lake. Halcyon crystal was an excellent harmonic conductor, too, Silence thought, though rarely used because of its cost. It would have been simple to set up a resonating copy in the guardpost, carved to sound to the same harmonies as the original; a small harmonium would provide any amplification that was needed. According to the notes, the copy, of less powerful material, remained inert until a special signal triggered it, presumably to conserve power. The question now was where the Palace's model was kept.

She turned the page, found that the section ended there, and turned back to the illustration, squinting at the square of tiny characters that filled one corner of the page. The words were not High Speech or coinë. Silence frowned at them for a moment before she realized that they were written in a drastically abbreviated magistical neo-latin. Sure now that she had found the information she needed—magi did not bother with neo-latin unless they had something to conceal from the uninitiated—she set to work, first guessing at the full word behind the abbreviation, then puzzling out the sense of the entire paragraph. "Word having been brought to us of the Hegemon's wishes, the installation will be placed in the quarters of the queen-mother." Silence swore briefly at that—the queen-mother's quarters were bound to be the rooms now occupied by the

Princess Royal—but there was a second sentence as well. And it was handwritten, Silence realized, though the magus had done his best to copy the neatly printed characters. She puzzled through it, and then, slowly, began to smile. "At his Most Serene Majesty's request," the crabbed characters read, "the installation has been removed to its present location in the library; appropriate modifications will be made to the serving homunculus."

Silence set both volumes carefully back in their places, and glanced again over the railing. The homunculus was still dormant, but the pilot's attention was focused instead on the dura-felt shrouded case that stood almost directly below her. It was easily big enough to hold the model described in the schemae. Certainly the homunculus's response to her innocent question about its contents would seem to indicate both the importance of whatever was in the case, and that the homunculus had been repatterned to protect it. The only thing is, she thought, how am I going to find out for certain?

She started down the ramp, trying to work out a way to get a look at the case's contents. Perhaps I could get the homunculus to leave the room? she thought. If I pretended to be ill, maybe. . . . But more likely it'd just send for one of the other women, and that wouldn't do at all. I wonder if it would bring me food or drink . . . ? Before she could think of anything better, chimes sounded loudly. Startled, she reached for her chronograph: Pilisi should not be arriving for another hour, at least. Silence tensed as the homunculus rolled toward the door.

From so high on the ramp, the pilot could not see who it was. She froze, listening hard, but could only distinguish that it was a woman's voice. Then the homunculus rolled back into the center of the room.

"Domna Jamilla," it called. "You are summoned to receive a visitor. Domna Pilisi will escort you."

A visitor? Silence thought blankly. Marcinik wasn't expected for another few days—and in any case, if it had been him, surely the homunculus would've said something about her duty? She started down the ramp, and Pilisi called from below, "Hurry, Jamilla, her Serenity doesn't want to be kept waiting."

Silence waved in answer and did as she was told. At the bottom of the ramp, she said breathlessly, "I thought you said there was a visitor."

Pilisi nodded, beckoning. "There is—and one come to see you, not her Highness. But it's her Serenity who has to supervise the veiling. Hurry, now."

Silence made a face behind the other woman's back, but quickened her pace until she was almost running. "Who is this visitor?"

Pilisi managed to turn and grin without slowing her rapid progress. "Oh, that's a surprise. Her Serenity made me promise. But I think you'll be pleased."

Wonderful, Silence thought, and braced herself to face almost anything.

The Princess Royal was waiting in the alcove usually used for the veiling ceremony. She was flanked by two more of her domnas, and several household homunculi hovered in the background. One held Silence's formal outer veil; another held the headdress and the underveil. Silence glanced around hastily, but there was no sign of Aili. Hiding her sudden unease, she made her best curtsy, saying, "Your Serenity requires?"

The Princess Royal regarded her with a distinct lack of favor. "You have a visitor, Jamilla. Not an ordinary occurrence, and one I doubt should be encouraged, but I cannot in good conscience turn him away."

Silence curtsied again, steeling herself against surprise.

"More such visits will not be tolerated," Radiah went on, "and I expect you to inform your brother Viljo of that fact."

"I will, your Serenity," Silence answered. Brother? she thought. Jamilla Sahen had a brother—two brothers, in fact—but Viljo, the eldest, was on duty with his father's fleets, commanding, by some irony, an antipirate patrol. Surely he can't be here—surely the admiral or the satrap would stop him. He must know of the plan anyway if he's part of the planetary fleet. . . . She forced her face to betray an excitement, an eagerness she did not feel. "Thank you, your Serenity, for letting me see him this time."

The Princess Royal's eyebrows rose slightly, the only visible guide to her emotions. "I accept your gratitude," she said. "Let's begin."

Silence submitted to the procedures, listening to the Princess Royal's droned strictures—how to behave in front of the guardsman who would escort Viljo, how to greet her sibling, and so on, all part of the ritual she had memorized on Inarime—while she allowed the other domnas to help her arrange her headdress and veils. At last the Princess Royal pronounced herself satisfied. A heavily built homunculus bowed twice, first to Radiah and then to Silence, and slid back the heavy door. Silence followed it down the long corridor, bracing herself again to meet whatever—whoever—would be waiting. The door opened at last, and she stepped out into the courtyard.

"Domna Jamilla Sahen," the homunculus announced, "I present Captain-lieutenant Marcinik and Captain Lord Viljo Sahen."

Viljo Sahen indeed, Silence thought, unable to stop a smile from spreading across her face. I know Denis Balthasar when I see him. She controlled herself with an effort, and managed to walk with decorum to the edge of the Seer. "Captain-lieutenant," she said, and nodded. "Brother." In spite of herself, her voice was not quite steady on the last word, trembling between laughter and tears.

Balthasar's face showed the same shadowy mix of emotions as he answered, "Sister."

He looked rather good in the uniform of Inarime's private navy, Silence thought, quite irrelevantly. The sober maroon tunic, badged only lightly with golden decorations of rank, flattered the Delian's grey hair and nondescript coloring. Suddenly, she wanted nothing so much as to embrace him, to hold him tightly enough to be reassured of his reality and of her own ultimate escape, but knew that it was impossible even to touch hands across the barrier of the Seer. She put the longing firmly aside, and took a tighter grip on the sensor egg in her pocket.

"What's happened?" she said, lowering her voice. "I didn't expect you for another couple of days, Marcinik."

It was Balthasar who answered. "Trouble, sort of."

"Sort of trouble?" Silence repeated incredulously, then shook herself, motioning for him to continue.

Balthasar gave her a rather humorless grin. "All the plans are the same. The time table's been moved up, that's all."

All? Silence thought. She said, "How much? And why?"

"The fleet will leave Inarime in eight days," Marcinik said, with a rather annoyed glanced at Balthasar.

"That's not long enough," Silence said. "I've hardly gotten started, and I wanted to wait for the betrothal—" She controlled herself with an effort, calculating. "Hell, on that schedule the fleet will arrive the day after the ceremony. We won't have time to clear the system."

"We might make it," Balthasar said. "A fleet like that, trying to make a two-stage trip? You remember what it was like at Arganthonios. Multiply that by ten, and you'll get the idea. They'll have to dress ranks after the first passage, and that'll add ten hours or so to their real time."

Silence nodded, watching Marcinik. The captain-lieutenant was perfectly expressionless, his eyes politely turned to Balthasar, but there was a subtle tension in the set of his shoulders, betraying anger and, beneath that, his own fears. Silence sighed, wondering just what the Delian had done. Balthasar was not always an easy man to like, and when he deliberately made himself intolerable. . . . He had memories of his own, from that nightmare journey in the conscript-transport, to spur him to make trouble. And am I expected to make a peace for them? Silence thought. No, that'd be impossible; better just to ignore the whole thing, and hope they work it out themselves. Aloud, she said, "If you say so, Denis, I believe you. You've more time in the long ships than I do."

"Can you make your escape before this betrothal?" Marcinik asked.

"I don't see how," Silence began. She paused, and finally shook her head. "I just can't finish everything that has to be done. And besides, we need the diversion."

Marcinik nodded thoughtfully. Balthasar said, "As to why the change. . . . We got word, yesterday, that a ship had gotten off Inarime without permission. A couple of long ships were chasing it, but didn't think they'd catch it. The satrap wants to move before word can reach Asterion."

Silence said, "Have you settled on a landing spot?"

"And a rendezvous," Balthasar answered. He glanced at Marcinik. "He's brought your stuff. The coordinates are taped to the outside, along with your whistle. But I wanted to tell you myself, just in case."

"Oh, for God's sake, Denis," Silence said, "we're in this together."

The Delian had the grace to look momentarily ashamed, but said, "Let me give them to you anyway."

Silence hesitated an instant longer, then nodded. After all, she told herself as Balthasar recited the map references, she should know them, just in case the written numbers were lost or confiscated.

"I told him there was no need for him to come here," Marcinik grumbled. "He's endangered everything."

Balthasar started to say something, and Silence said, "Stop it, both of you." She felt perversely maternal, glaring at them. Balthasar grinned slowly, guessing her thought, and reluctantly, the pilot returned his smile.

"This is the last time you'll have to see me, Marcinik," Silence said, "as long as you brought my kit."

Marcinik held out the sealed bundle he had held tucked under his arm. "He gave it to me," he said, jerking his head at Balthasar, and bit back the rest of his retort. Silence could guess what it would have been—*blame him if something's missing, not me*—and ruthlessly killed her own automatic answer. "I told them Viljo had a stopover in the system, and that the satrap wanted to make sure Aili—her Highness—was well," Marcinik went on, in a more normal tone.

"Good enough," the pilot said, and looked to Balthasar. "Obviously you made the landing all right?"

The Delian grinned. "No great problems. Having a magus on board helped."

Silence glanced involuntarily at Marcinik, and Balthasar said, "Yes, he told me about Isambard. But most people are too scared to question a magus."

"True enough," Silence said. Marcinik cleared his throat then, but Silence could already feel warmth spreading from the egg in her hand. She glanced hastily at her chronograph: her time was almost up.

"Julie—?" she said, and Balthasar answered, "Fine. We're both fine."

"Give my love—" Silence began, and heard the corridor door slide open behind her. "—to our father," she finished, like a dutiful daughter of the Ten Thousand, and wondered if Balthasar understood what she had been about to say. He gave no sign of it, bowing as he murmured a formal farewell.

"This is the package for her Highness, Domna Jamilla," Marcinik said, too loudly. He flushed, moderated his tone, and continued, "The doctors' instructions are inside."

"Thank you, captain-lieutenant," Silence said, stooping to retrieve the package Marcinik had laid carefully on the edge of the Seer. She felt something give under her fingers. A cylinder of paper—no, a slip of paper wrapped around her pitch pipe—was taped to one edge of the packet. She palmed the slick cylinder awkwardly, sliding it into her upturned cuff as she tucked the packet under her arm. "Until we meet again—until later, brother."

The two men murmured their own farewells. Silence turned sharply, forestalling the approaching homunculus, and followed it back through the doorway. It took all her strength not to betray herself by looking back.

The Princess Royal was waiting in the alcove at the end of the corridor. "So, Jamilla," she said, with a parody-smile of polite interest. "How is your brother?"

"Well, thank you, your Serenity," Silence answered warily. Four domnas were ranged behind the Princess Royal, and Aili was still nowhere to be seen. "He had a stopover in the system," the pilot went on, repeating what Marcinik had told her, "and the authorities were generous enough to grant his petition for a few hours' leave."

"So that he could check up on the shazadi, no doubt," Radiah said.

Silence arranged her face in what she hoped was the proper expression of uncertainty. "Your Serenity? I beg your pardon, I don't understand. . . ."

"I suppose not," the Princess Royal said, dubiously, and gestured to the hovering domnas. "Help Jamilla with her veil, if you please."

Silence started to protest, then realized that that would only make things worse. She allowed the other women to help her remove her veil, hiding her resentment as they prodded lightly at her gown in an unobtrusive, reasonably effective search. They did not touch her cuff, or the whistle inside it, held there by the same tape that had held it to the side of the packet. As she answered Radiah's formal questions, the pilot waited for someone to give an all-clear sign. She missed the gesture, but one of the women must have given it, as the Princess Royal nodded, dismissing the helping domnas. Pilisi stepped forward, bobbing her curtsy, and held out the packet Silence had gotten from Marcinik. The pilot did her best to stifle her apprehensive gasp, but Radiah saw, and smiled gently.

"You are concerned, Jamilla? Why, what does this contain?" She toyed with the wrappings, and Silence felt her heart sink. Telling herself that her best defense was to attack, she drew herself up to her full height.

"Of course I'm concerned," she said boldly. "This treatment is unexpected—and undeserved. Does your Serenity suspect me of something? Then I pray you, accuse me outright, but don't treat me like a common criminal."

Radiah said nothing for a long moment, clearly assessing her position. Silence held her breath. As a member of the Ten Thousand, Jamilla had some rights that protected her against even the Princess Royal's authority. Radiah had already come very close to crossing the boundary between legitimate exercise of her authority and actionable behavior by having Jamilla searched. Aili would be within her rights even now to complain to her father, and through him to the Hegemon. With luck, the Princess Royal would not press the issue.

"You will concede it's within my power to search this package," Radiah said at last, her tone more conciliatory than her words.

Silence bowed her head. The ritual of return did allow the welcoming matron to investigate anything brought into the Palace, though most omitted that section of the rite. She just hoped Balthasar had had the sense to disguise the kit's ingredients. "Of course, your

Serenity, I acknowledge that authority," she said aloud, imitating the Princess Royal's frosty dignity. Radiah gave her a sharp glance as she ripped loose the sealing tape, but said nothing.

The oiled paper folded back to reveal a dozen bottles and perhaps half as many squat, thick-walled jars, each labeled in magistical neo-latin and in coinë characters. Silence winced at the latter—the labels should probably have been written in the High Speech—but the Princess Royal did not seem to notice. She pulled a jar from its place, seemingly at random, and sounded out the tag glued to the rounded crystal stopper.

"*Oculi lacertarum,*" she read, "Essence of *amarans*." She looked sharply at Silence. "What is this used for?"

The pilot did her best to keep from smiling. The neo-latin and the coinë were widely different; whatever *amarans* were—some Inariman herb-flower, most likely—they were likely to bear no resemblance to the seedlike *oculi* in their oily suspension. She improvised hastily, "It's a bath infusion, your Serenity, to relax and soothe the troubled spirit."

The Princess Royal nodded, and picked up another bottle. "And heartsease?"

Silence took a deep breath. "Your Serenity, I confess I do not remember all the details of the prescription. Does your Serenity wish me to fetch it from her Highness's rooms?"

For an instant, it seemed as though the Princess Royal would say yes, but then, slowly, she shook her head. "That will not be necessary, Jamilla. You may go."

Trying to move without undue haste, Silence collected the bottle and jar, and did her best to reseal the opened package. She had it at last, though she had to use both hands to hold the contents together, and nodded for the nearest homunculus to take her veils and headdress. Before she could escape, however, the Princess Royal said, "Jamilla."

Silence turned, face carefully blank. "Your Serenity."

"I do not approve of your—attitude," the Princess Royal said. "I have my eye on you."

There was no answer to that. Silence managed a stiff curtsy and Radiah went on, "You may go. But remember what I said."

"I will, your Serenity," Silence answered, and knew the other woman heard the unspoken meaning. Battle was fairly joined.

CHAPTER 9

The next eight days were among the busiest and most frustrating of Silence's life. True to her promise, the Princess Royal did her best to keep a constant watch on the pilot. She revoked Silence's library privileges, saying that all the women of the Palace were needed to help plan Ceiki's betrothal party, and when Aili claimed some hours of Silence's time, conscripted the shazadi as well, pointing out that Aili's *tristitia* might be alleviated by the celebration.

Defeated, Silence and the shazadi did as they were told, running errands and recording notes for the older women who actually did most of the planning. In a few snatched planning sessions, mostly held at night after the other women were asleep, Silence managed to examine the coordinates Balthasar had given her and locate the landing site on one of her maps of the area. It was a clearing some six kilometers from the lake edge, well within the parkland that formed the Palace's official precinct. At first, Silence could not see why they had chosen that particular spot—there were other, closer, open areas—but then she realized that there Balthasar could mask his approach against a distant ridge. Silence nodded her approval at that, and turned her attention to the lakeside rendezvous Balthasar had selected. The lakeshore was not well endowed with coves, the pilot discovered at once, probably as a security measure, but at last they found the narrow indentation labeled "knobby cove." It was not directly opposite the Palace, requiring them to sail a diagonal course and spend more time on the water, but the most recent map showed that the fingers of woodland reached almost to the shoreline. It was better cover than anything else promised, but Silence found herself wondering just what "knobby cove" meant. Still, it was the best site available, and Aili signaled their acceptance of the coordinates during the next afternoon's chess game.

In the daytime they did their best to keep out of Radiah's sight, but Silence was only too aware, as she supervised the homunculi decorating the gardens or putting together elaborate new gowns and costumes for the fete, of the Princess Royal's hovering presence. Only when the queen-sister demanded their help composing the great farewell dinner were they briefly free of Radiah and her domnas, and then they were kept too busy making lists and consulting reference books to do anything else. Their work was made no easier by Ceiki's sad-eyed presence. The Hegemon's daughter refused to be cheered by the elaborate preparations and the promised parties. She submitted lifelessly to being measured for a new, adult wardrobe, but refused to take any part in the planning.

"The poor girl," Aili said quietly. She and Silence were sitting in the shazadi's bedroom, huddled inside a hastily drawn aphonic ring. It was well past midnight. Both women were tired, but still too keyed up to sleep. They had spent most of the afternoon and all of the evening with the rest of the Palace's inmates, arguing over the best fabrics for Ceiki's formal clothes.

"Poor us, too," Silence growled. She could almost feel the clock ticking, the hours passing, and she was no

nearer to managing their escape than she had been a
week ago. There was so much still to be done: the tools
that would let her take over one of the little pleasure
boats still had to be forged; the guard homunculi on the
lower levels had somehow to be neutralized; and she
still did not know for certain if the case in the library
really held the model of the Palace. Aili was still chat-
tering on, and Silence suppressed the sudden urge to
shake the younger woman. How dare she be so cheerful, when things were going so badly?

"—and I also swiped one of these," the shazadi was
saying, seeming quite blithely unaware of the pilot's
mood, "from the stuff for the bride-shivaree."

She held up an oval of thin black cloth, streaked and
splashed with flakes of glitter. There were lighter stains
here and there where some of the glitter had been
removed. Silence frowned at it for a moment before she
realized it was a mask.

"I haven't finished fixing it," Aili went on. "there's
still a lot of glitter I have to soak off, but—" She held the
mask up to her face, peering mischievously through the
eyeholes. "—it'll be a lot easier to manage than a
veil."

Silence felt a sudden pang of guilt, watching the
shazadi's eager movements. Aili's counting on you, she
told herself sternly. You can't let her down—not that
way, moping and feeling sorry for yourself. She shook
herself hard, watching the shazadi fasten the mask into
place. It covered all of Aili's face except for the eyes.
Concealing, Silence thought critically, but maybe not
good enough. And it looks extremely uncomfortable to
hike in.

"Can you breathe all right?" she asked.

"Oh, yes." Aili loosened the web of straps again, and
handed the mask to Silence. "Look, there's thinner
cloth at the mouth and nose. Plenty of air gets through."

Silence rubbed the material between her thumb and
forefinger, testing the thickness. Sure enough, there

were coarser, more loosely woven patches for the nose and mouth pieces, and when she experimentally fitted the mask over her own face, she found she could breathe in comfort. The straps, five of them, fitting across the back of the head and from the jawline around the nape of the neck, seemed very secure. Not much chance, she thought, of that working loose accidentally. That raised a new thought. She handed the mask back to Aili, saying, "Will the Thousand consider wearing this to be covered enough? You can sort of see the outline of the face through the material. After all the trouble we've gone to, I don't want to see you disqualified on a technicality."

Aili shook her head, picking busily at the remaining stripes of glitter. "It'll do."

"How can you be so sure?" Silence demanded.

The shazadi grinned. "I asked."

"You what?"

"I asked the queen-sister this morning," Aili elaborated, still grinning. "Or actually Ceiki did it for me. We were picking out the homunculi's costumes for the bride-shivaree. They're quite something—real springtide costumes. I picked up a mask and said I thought I'd wear it at the annual Presentation instead of a proper veil. Well, half of them screamed in horror, and the other half laughed, and then Ceiki asked if one of those masks would really count as a veil. The queen-sister thought about it for a while, I think just because that was the first time Ceiki'd asked a question all day, and finally said she thought it would."

Silence nodded, satisfied on two counts. The queen-sister, if she could do nothing else, could be relied on in matters of proper behavior. She could also be expected to forget that the question had ever been asked. And even if she didn't, Silence thought, it was Ceiki, not Aili, who had done the asking.

"You know, I really do feel sorry for the girl," Aili

went on, brushing a pile of glitter from her skirts. "The marriage is bad enough—you don't want to know what the satrap of Aja's like!—but it really doesn't seem fair that she should have such a small send-off. What sort of bride-shivaree can there be with only thirty-six of us to play, even if you bring in all the homunculi you can find?"

Bride-shivaree. Once again, the word stirred a half-memory in Silence's brain. She frowned, trying to track it down, then took a deep breath and summoned up the mnemonic chains she had so carefully constructed back on Inarime. She sorted out the proper strand and followed it, remembering first the great yearly holidays, then the specific feasts celebrated on Inarime, then the personal holidays of the Kibbe family and of families in general. But where the triggering image for the bride-shivaree should have been, there was only a vague image of bright colors and a sense that something had been lost. Silence made a face. These things happened, when one prepared a chain under pressure and then had no occasion to use it for a while. At least, this time, she had someone to ask. "Aili, tell me about bride-shivaree. Just what is it, exactly?"

The shazadi gave her a rather startled look. "What do you mean, what is it?"

"Exactly what I said. What is it? What do you do? All of that." Silence leaned against the cushion she had brought with her into the aphonic ring, wishing she had brought another. Outside the ring, she could see the pointer of an antique mechanical timepiece settle on the first hour of the new day. Tiny figures emerged from its base and scuttled about in preprogrammed patterns, but no sound penetrated the ring.

"It's—" Aili paused, seemingly still puzzled by the question. "Well, it's part of the traditional betrothal, especially when the bride-to-be is young. It's sort of a last chance for girlish tricks, a free-for-all hide-and-seek

game all over the Women's Quarter—or, in this case,
all over the Palace. Usually, the women are divided up
into teams on the basis of bride's-kin, groom's-kin, but
this time I guess the Princess Royal will divide us up
somehow. She's Ceiki's only blood-kin here."

"What do you mean by hide-and-seek?" Silence demanded, hardly daring to believe what she was hearing.

Aili spread her hands, wide-eyed. "Hide-and-seek.
Didn't you play it when you were a girl? You hide, and
try to catch members of the other team and spray them
with dye. That's why we've been having the homunculi
make those huge batches of dye-stuff, and that's why
the queen-sister's been so fussy about making sure it
will wash off."

"I haven't been working on those," Silence growled.
"I've been stuck with the damned dinners." She looked
wild-eyed at the shazadi. "That's it. That's the perfect
way to get us out of here."

Aili looked back at her. "I know," she said in a small
voice. "I thought that was what you meant when you
said the betrothal was the perfect diversion."

Silence stared at her for a long moment, then began
to laugh. After all her fretting and worrying, after her
near panic, the answer was handed to her on a platter—
and what was worse, Aili assumed she'd known it all
along. "No," she said at last, "I didn't know. I thought
it was just another of these boring rituals her Serenity
likes so much. I didn't pay much attention to marriages
on Inarime—I really didn't think the subject would
come up."

Aili was laughing, too. "I just assumed you knew,"
she said again. "I guess that proves you're not really of
the Ten Thousand."

"I'm not," Silence answered cheerfully. "My family
were merchants on Cap Bel." She sobered quickly.
"Spray people with dye, you said? What do you put the
dye in?"

"Big squirters." Aili held up her hands to demonstrate. "Usually they're shaped like toy heylins, or sonic rifles, things like that. The dye reservoir holds about a liter of liquid."

"Good." Silence leaned back against her pillow again, thinking fiercely. There were any number of compounds that would put a homunculus out of action; her problem had been one of delivering the compound efficiently. But with dye-squirters available, she could use any of the liquid compounds and not have to worry. "How long does the game last?"

Aili shrugged. "It depends. At least an hour or two, sometimes much longer. But I can't imagine it would last more than a couple of hours, especially when Ceiki's in no mood to play."

An hour was all they could count on, then, Silence thought. That wasn't much time to knock out the security system, steal a boat, and cross the lake, but it would have to be enough.

"Anyway," Aili said, as if she read the other woman's thoughts, "it'll take at least half an hour before they decide there's real trouble—that we aren't just hiding somewhere, or hurt, or something."

"Unless the Princess Royal calls an alert on general principles," Silence said. "No, an hour's really all we can count on." And if we only have an hour, she thought, I want some extra fire support when the alarm goes off. It's a good four kilometers to the clearing Denis picked to land in. "I want you to get word to Marcinik," she said slowly. "Have him warn Denis and Julie that time's going to be short and they should be ready for trouble. Bring heavy heylins."

Aili shook her head. "That would mean another meeting, and you didn't want to do that," she objected. "My code isn't set up to carry messages that complex."

"Damn." Silence rubbed at her chin, considering. The shazadi was right—they could not afford another meeting with Marcinik. But it was important to warn the others. "How is your chess game set up? What kind of a link is it?"

Aili shrugged. "An ordinary ghost-line, I think. Except it had to be specially shielded to make sure no one would see my hands."

"Then there may be a way," Silence said. "I have lime paper in my kit, and the treated ink. I'll give them to you. You write the message—keep it as short as you can—and then, when next you two play, put the paper on the board and make sure he passes one of his pieces over it. Both the paper and the ink are sensitive to the energies used to set up a ghost-line, so he'll see the message appear on his board. Oh, and tell him to have Julie bring us proper clothes, boys' clothes." She gave the shazadi a challenging glance. "Any objection to that?"

"No, I'll tell him," Aili said, and cocked her head to one side. "Should you be telling me all these magus's secrets?"

Silence hesitated, momentarily nonplussed. "No," she said, after a moment, "I probably oughtn't to be. But I want you to understand what you're doing."

"I wasn't objecting, mind you," Aili answered, "but I thought I ought to remind you. And speaking of that—" Her faced clouded slightly. "What are you going to do about this model Palace? If it's made of halcyon crystal, it's going to be virtually indestructible. . . ."

Silence shook her head, allowing herself a wolfish grin. "Halcyon crystal's a natural harmonic receptor, and the wrong tone can shatter it." She touched her bodice gently, feeling for the pitch pipe that rested between her breasts. "I know the sequence it's tuned to, so there should be no problem." I hope, she added to herself. As long as I don't hit the trigger sequence and open the link to the guardpost. . . . It was too late to worry about that. She sighed and reached to dissolve the aphonic ring.

The next three days were even busier than the previous ones. Aili managed to snatch time for the necessary chess game, and Silence had the satisfaction of seeing the slip of lime paper vanish in a curl of smoke as Marcinik's piece passed over it. The letters remained, fading slowly, and the captain-lieutenant signaled that the message had been received and understood.

Silence was able to spend very little time with the shazadi after that. The Princess Royal kept up her watch, making sure the pilot was fully involved in the betrothal preparations. Silence did her best to present herself as entirely engrossed in the planning, but the surveillance did not slacken. She was forced to work only at night, without the helping solar harmonies, but by the day of the betrothal she had managed to distill three full liters of *aqua intacta*. That, she thought, with a great deal of satisfaction, would be able to take care of any and all guard homunculi they were unfortunate enough to meet.

The betrothal was a day-long ceremony, beginning with the addition of three lines to the Observances, formally accepting Ceiki as part of the Hegemon's family for what was probably the first and last time in her life. The morning hours were spent in last-minute preparations, and it was only then that Silence was able to seize a quick word with Aili, catching her arm as she hurried past on some vital errand. After her first start of surprise, the shazadi let herself be drawn into the nearest garden, away from at least the most obvious watcher-nodes. Still, Silence kept her voice very low as she said, "It only just occurred to me that her Serenity will probably put us on opposite teams."

"I've been looking for you to tell you the same thing," Aili exclaimed. "We meet in the Nymph-garden?"

"As soon as we can get away from the hunt," Silence agreed.

"Your Highness!" That was the queen-sister's domna, a woman neither as placid nor as uncaring as her mistress. She stood, hands on hips, in the entrance to the garden. "They are waiting for the list."

Aili flashed the pilot the ghost of a grin, and was gone.

The noon meal was light, barely more than an informal of the sort Silence had studied on Inarime so many weeks before. Silence ate quickly and excused herself early, pleading a final errand for the queen-sister. The Princess Royal looked as though she would have liked to refuse permission, but the errand was quite real, and there was no one else she could legitimately send. Grudgingly, she allowed Silence to leave. The pilot made her way out of the terraced dining room as decorously as she could, but as soon as she was out of sight, she hiked up her skirts and ran for her own rooms. Hastily, she recovered the liter jars of *aqua intacta* and tucked a paper packet into her pocket. The jars hampered her—she did not dare move too quickly for fear of spilling their precious contents—but at last she slipped through the door to the Nymph-garden.

It was a lovely pleasance, open to the true sky rather than domed, like so many of the gardens. Native Asterionan plants were allowed to flourish in a semi-wilderness, clipped back only when they grew across a path or threatened to damage the building. A picturesque ruin stood at the center of the garden—Silence had never been able to decide precisely what it was intended to have been—and a number of suitably rustic statues of women and girls dotted the area, the nymphs for which the garden had been named. Silence worked her way rapidly toward the central ruin, to the hiding place she had spotted during her early reconnaissance of the Palace. She found it quickly enough, a massive dorta bush whose drooping, feathery leaves hid a sizable depression. She tucked the jars into that space and drew the leaves back over it. Then she hastened off to finish her errand.

Silence managed not to be too late returning to the small dining room, but nevertheless the Princess Royal regarded her with renewed suspicion. As Silence had feared, she and Aili were to be assigned to different teams for the bride-shivaree; neither she nor the shazadi protested, but Radiah was not appeased. She seemed positively to relish taking Aili off with the other women of the Thousand to supervise Ceiki's Robing.

Left to her own devices, like the other domnas, Silence dressed as slowly as she could, decking herself in the most elaborate and uncomfortable of the gowns she had brought from Inarime. Despite her efforts, it only took her two hours. She spent the rest of the afternoon playing cards with two other domnas, trying to submerge herself in the game. She was not very successful. Had the game been played for real money instead of imaginary fortunes, she thought sourly, she would owe the proceeds of two or three successful trading ventures.

At last, Pilisi appeared in the doorway, swathed from head to foot in glittering, gold-shot robes, and announced, "The Presentation."

Well briefed, the domnas rose without a hint of complaint, finding their proper places almost automatically, giving and taking precedence with a chilly grace. Silence let herself be shunted into her proper place, toward the middle of the pack, reading from the others' body language whether she was expected to give way or go ahead.

Pilisi led them down a long section of corridor, then turned into a second, wider hall that had a newly dusted appearance about it. The air had a musty smell, too, and Silence guessed the place had been opened specially for this occasion. Halfway up the hall, the homunculi had put down a richly purple carpet. As Pilisi stepped onto it, there was a distinct crunching, and an almost overpowering scent of flowers. Silence choked as she stepped

onto the carpet, and tried to hold her breath. There
was a noisy sighing as the domnas stepped off the
carpet to pass through a massive, arching doorway, and
Silence guessed they had all done the same.

The room beyond the arched door was the most
magnificent Silence had seen yet, a high-ceilinged,
mirror-lined hall. It culminated in a fantastically gilded
and jeweled object, a sculpture in high relief of clouds
rolling back to reveal a massive sunburst. Tiny starships
darted here and there among the roiling clouds. The
object was large enough to fill the entire wall. A two-
stage dais led up to it. Ceiki's party waited on the lower
of the two, the women arranged in a sort of semicircle
behind the Hegemon's daughter. There was a wind-silk
canopy over Ceiki's head, and her dress was stiff with
jewels. Despite the display, Silence could not help
thinking she made a rather forlorn figure.

At the Princess Royal's gesture, the domnas filed
forward one by one, to make their curtsies and murmur
some acknowledgement of Ceiki's new, adult status.
When Silence's turn came, she could think of nothing
worthwhile, so she muttered some conventional, inap-
propriate congratulations. Ceiki's eyes, almost drowned
by the streaks of makeup ringing them, followed her,
but the girl said nothing. Silence retreated quickly,
wishing she dared do something.

Dancing followed—the ring-dances considered appropriate for women alone—and then household homunculi
brought in the tables for the evening's first meal. Silence ate methodically, telling herself she would need
the calories before the night was over, but the exotic
dishes might as well have been made from sand for all
the pleasure she took in them. She drank sparingly,
doing her best not to seem conspicuous about it, and
saw that Aili was doing the same. The rest of the
domnas were drinking fairly deeply, enjoying their unexpected holiday. Ceiki sulked all through the meal,

barely saying two words to anyone, and Silence was
struck by the sudden, terrible thought that if the girl
did not cheer up, Radiah might well cancel the bride-
shivaree.

However, as concealed clocks chimed sunset, the
Princess Royal gave a discreet signal, and the homunculi
moved forward to roll the tables away again. The diners
hauled themselves to their feet, the older women moaning and complaining only half in jest that they were
entirely too old for such games, and came to stand in
the center of the hall. They made an insignificant group
in the middle of all that magnificent space, and Silence
found herself sharing the shazadi's regret that Ceiki's
betrothal could not have been more elaborate. If we're
successful, Silence reminded herself sternly, Aili can
stop this marriage. And that's the only way you can
help the poor kid.

"My ladies," the Princess Royal called, clapping her
hands loudly for their attention. Her voice echoed in
the empty hall, mocking her false joy. "We have a
betrothal to celebrate, as our mothers did before us.
Let the game begin!"

At her final words, brightly costumed humunculi
whirled into the hall, some bearing armloads of favors—
strips of cloth either purple or white for the two teams—
others carrying baskets of shiny dye-squirters. Still more
carried nothing, their pseudo-faces hidden behind the
glitter-banded masks. Half of the homunculi wore purple favors wound around their sexless bodies; the other
half wore white. Counting carefully, Silence guessed
that most of the household homunculi had been co-
opted for the bride-shivaree, and felt her heart lift.
The more that were playing, the fewer there would be
to interfere with her escape. Across the room, Aili smiled,
and Silence realized the shazadi had seen the same
thing.

The Princess Royal had assigned teams earlier in the
day; now she bustled about in unconvincing cheer,

urging the women to hurry as they accepted the favors and chose weapons from the homunculi's baskets. Silence, who had been assigned to Ceiki's team, took her purple sash and, after a moment's thought, wound it around her head, military style. As she took a squirter—a toy heylin with an immense dye reservoir—she saw Ceiki, after some thought, try to wrap her own scarf the same way. The girl could not quite manage the knot, however, and Silence, motivated by guilt, said, "Highness, may I show you?"

Ceiki looked up with worshipping eyes and said, "Yes, please."

Thoughtlessly, Silence started to loop the toy heylin's lanyard over her nonexistent belt hook, and stopped abruptly, flushing. That was a soldier's habit, not a woman's, she told herself angrily. Ceiki had not missed the gesture either, and her eyes widened. Cursing to herself, Silence rewound the girl's scarf, knotting it into an almost boyish headband.

"That's much better," Ceiki said. "Thank you, Jamilla."

"Partners, now," the Princess Royal called. "Time to choose partners." She fixed her cold gaze on Silence, adding, "Domna Jamilla, I trust you'll play with me?"

Silence had known she would be assigned a partner, and had half a dozen plans to get rid of an unwanted companion, but she had not expected the Princess Royal to choose such a drastic way of keeping track of her whereabouts. She opened her mouth, then closed it, unable to think of an effective protest.

At her side, Ceiki said, "Your Serenity!" There was a new note in the girl's voice, one that made the Princess Royal look almost humanly startled. "I want Jamilla for my partner," Ceiki went on. "It's my party, please, and I want her."

Radiah frowned. "I'm afraid it's not quite proper, Ceiki," she began, and the queen-sister interrupted her querulously.

"Oh, let the girl have what she wants, Radiah. The bride-shivaree only happens once. It's not that unsuitable."

The Princess Royal hesitated an instant longer, then surrendered grudgingly. "Oh, very well, Ceiki, if that's what you want. Now, the rest of you, choose partners!"

At last, the milling mass had sorted itself out into teams of two. Aili, Silence saw, had managed to get herself paired with a domna from Tharros, an older woman who complained constantly about her aching feet. The shazadi should have no trouble eluding her company.

A homunculus—the only one not wearing a favor—brought forward an immense silver bowl, holding it well above its own, and most of the women's, heads.

"Draw for places," the Princess Royal called, and the women pressed forward, laughing.

"Draw for us, please, Jamilla?" Ceiki said shyly.

Silence nodded, and elbowed her way up to the bowl, reaching overhead to scrabble among the five-centimeter-square tiles. She drew one out, glanced at the number, and barely suppressed a whoop of delight. They would be the third couple to leave the hall. That would give her ample time to get rid of Ceiki and get to the Nymph-garden to recover the jars of *aqua intacta*.

"Let me see," Ceiki begged, excited in spite of herself. Silence held out the token, and Ceiki gave a little crow of delight. The Princess Royal directed a single fulminating look their way, and Ceiki subsided instantly.

"Cheer up," Silence said, moved by some obscure instinct to offer what comfort she could. "Maybe you can catch her." She touched the butt of the toy heylin, and saw Ceiki's eyes brighten eagerly.

"Oh, wouldn't that be wonderful?" the girl said, too fervently.

It would at that, Silence thought, but it's not worth staying for.

The Princess Royal clapped her hands again, drawing their attention. "Ladies," she said again. "You'll leave the room in order, according to the lots you drew. You know the object of the game: to catch as many as possible of the other team and spray them well." She pantomimed turning her toy heylin on the nearest woman, and the others laughed dutifully. "In a moment, the lights will go off, and the doors will open. First couple, you leave then, and the lights will go on again. The lights will keep flashing, and each time one couple will leave. You can use the time to set up an ambush, or to hide, or however you choose to use it. Let's begin!" She clapped her hands again, the sound almost lost in the dutiful cheering, and the homunculi by the door began to swing back the heavy panels. The lights winked out before they were fully open. Silence counted fifteen seconds before they flashed on again, and caught a glimpse of a brightly colored skirt vanishing around the corner of the right-hand door. Ceiki bounced excitedly at her side.

"They went toward the fire-garden," she said. "Do we go after them?"

Silence shook her head. "Left, I think, for us. Be ready to run. They don't give us much time."

The lights flashed on and off again, and another couple vanished. Silence tensed, wanting to hike up her skirts and knowing she could not, and said, "Ready. . . ."

The lights winked out. The pilot seized Ceiki's hand and ran for the door. The girl stumbled for an instant, then caught up. They were well down the corridor before the lights came on in the hall, spilling a wedge of light into the corridor. Ceiki had her skirts knotted in one hand, lifting them almost to mid-calf. "This way," she said, pointing with her squirter down a side hall. There were stairs at the end of it, and she took them two at a time.

Silence shrugged, hiking up her own skirts, and followed, the toy heylin cradled easily in her right hand. "Where are we going?"

"I worked it all out," Ceiki said, a little breathlessly. She darted down another, still narrower corridor that bore unmistakable signs of cart traffic. "This runs to the kitchens—it's just a service passage. I figure, we cut through here, then through the little hall that backs on the storage cells, and up to the gallery that overlooks the royal promenade. With luck, we can catch a bunch of people there, and fall back on the fountain court without getting trapped."

"You sound like a soldier," Silence said, and meant it.

Ceiki hunched a shoulder at the other, clearly expecting a reprimand.

"What's more, I think it'll work," the pilot went on. And if the kid likes to think military, she added to herself, it'll make it that much easier for me to slip away "scouting," or something like that.

"I read a lot," Ceiki said, with a shy glance at Silence's face. "I didn't think *you'd* mind. If I'd been a boy, I'd 've been a soldier—and a good one, I think."

Silence nodded, trying to work out exactly where they were. Under the evening reception room, she thought. . . . "Probably," she said absently.

Ceiki gave her a delighted grin, then tugged at Silence's sleeve. "Hurry, we have to get there before someone else does. . . ."

Silence submitted to the girl's urging, letting herself be drawn through the unfamiliar corridors at whirlwind pace. At last, as Ceiki had promised, they climbed a narrow stairway and emerged, panting, at the entrance to the royal promenade. This is where I cut out, Silence thought, glancing over her shoulder to make sure they were unobserved. Most of the lights had been dimmed in this part of the Palace; only a few paper lanterns bobbed in the faint air currents, casting more shadow than light across the scene.

"Why don't I scout around," Silence began, hating herself as the forlorn expression reappeared on Ceiki's face. "I could make sure your retreat was all clear—" Something moved in the shadows to her left, coming quickly. A freakish breath of air swung one of the lanterns sluggishly in its direction, and light glinted from the barrel of a heylin. Before she thought, Silence swung, bringing her own heylin to bear, and fired. The homunculus—it was just a homunculus, Silence thought, disgusted with herself—squeaked slightly, almost as though it could be surprised, and fired its own toy before darting away again. The dye cloud fell short, but Silence felt a few drops spatter on her face. Ceiki was staring at her, open-mouthed, and the pilot fumbled hastily for a story the girl would believe.

"That was just like a soldier," Ceiki said, forestalling her. Her eyes widened even further. "Are you a man in disguise?"

Silence giggled, a little hysterically. "No, I'm a woman, just like you, Ceiki."

"But different." Ceiki studied her, the bride-shivaree and its game momentarily forgotten. "Her Serenity kept saying there was something funny about you. You really know how to use that, don't you? You've come for Aili," she added abruptly, cutting off the pilot's stammered explanation. "Take me with you?"

"Shh," Silence said. In the distance, she could hear footsteps moving along a corridor, coming closer. She grabbed Ceiki's shoulder and pulled the unresisting girl into the nearest alcove. Ceiki reached to close the curtain, but Silence jerked her hand back.

"No!" she added, her voice a mere thread of sound. "Too conspicuous," and saw Ceiki nod. They flattened themselves against the alcove wall as the footsteps came nearer, hiding behind the bulk of the open curtain. Two women—one of the other shazadis and a domna— appeared, giggling, and turned down the hall that led to the fountain court. Silence gave a slow sigh of relief.

Ceiki said again, whispering now, "Did you come for Aili?"

Silence hesitated, but the fierce appeal in Ceiki's face was too much for her. Anyway, she thought, the kid's already figured out most of it. "Yes," she said. "Her father sent me."

"Take me with you."

"I can't." Silence shook her head helplessly. "I'm sorry, I wish I could."

"Why can't you?" Ceiki demanded.

Silence wished she had a heylin, or any other weapon that could be set to stun, so that she could just put the kid to sleep for a few hours and get away. The realization shocked her. When she answered, she knew she sounded subdued. "Two reasons. First, you're not ready—"

"I don't need anything," Ceiki interjected. "I can come as I am."

"In those clothes?" Silence asked. "Through wooded country?" Ceiki's eyes fell, and the pilot pressed on. "Second reason. Both you and Aili have positions to protect. I've made arrangements for her, but not for you—and you don't want to throw away your position, not yet. When—" She caught herself abruptly, and Ceiki lifted her squirter.

"Take me with you, or I'll tell the Princess Royal."

Silence hesitated, cursing under her breath. There was no time for this. . . . She said, carefully, "Ceiki—"

The girl's face crumpled. "I can't," she whispered. "I won't, Jamilla, I promise. But I don't want to marry Aja."

"Ceiki," Silence said again, and tilted the tear-damp face up to look at her. "Listen. I believe you—I trust you. Listen to me, now. If all goes well, if we get away, you won't have to marry him. I promise."

Ceiki's face seemed to crumple again, but the girl fought back her tears. "I believe you," she managed. "You promised." She threw her arms around the older woman, and Silence, helplessly, found herself hugging Ceiki back. She disengaged herself as gently as she could.

"I have to go now," she said.

Ceiki gulped and nodded. "Promise you'll come back?"

"I promise," Silence said, though she knew she shouldn't. There were too many things that could still go wrong, and she might never be able to keep that promise. But I will, she told herself fiercely. I will. She set the girl gently aside and peered out into the hallway. No one was in sight. Silence took a deep breath, and started at last for the nymph garden. She glanced back only once. Ceiki was still standing framed in the arch of the alcove. Seeing the pilot turn, she waved bravely and started off toward the gallery, determined, Silence guessed, to take her best shot at the Princess Royal.

To her relief, Silence reached the Nymph-garden without further incident. Aili was already waiting, crouched in the shadow of the ruin. Her hands and sleeves were speckled with dye, light splotches in the dim light that filtered in from the distant corridors. Her face would be, too, Silence guessed, but the shazadi had already donned her homunculus's mask. She had also discarded her heavy overdress, the pilot saw with approval. It was crumpled in a ball on the ground beside her.

"What kept you?" Aili hissed, as the pilot dropped to her knees beside the dorta bush.

"I had some trouble getting away from Ceiki," Silence answered, rummaging under the trailing leaves. The oldest of them had grown coarse, toothlike ridges, and her wrists and hands were marked with scratches before she pulled the last of the jars from its hiding place. She rubbed impatiently at the sore places, staring around for a place to empty their squirters.

"Over here," Aili said. She pointed to a corner of the ruin, where two walls joined at a ninety-degree angle.

The resulting pocket of ground was well hidden from anyone standing at the edge of the garden. "I've already emptied mine."

"Take care of mine, then?" Silence asked, and tossed the toy heylin across without waiting for an answer. Aili caught it awkwardly and began to empty the dye reservoir, careful not to let too much of the liquid splatter on the stones of the ruin. Silence stripped off her own overdress and bundled it and Aili's gown back under the dorta bush. That left her in an ankle-length dress of dark blue velvet, wound incongruously with a sturdy leather belt. She hesitated, wanting to kilt up the skirts to free her legs, but decided against it for the moment as too conspicuous. She still had to face the librarian homunculus. Thinking that, she reached inside the bodice of the dress and drew out the user's card, letting it hang openly at her neck. She touched the pitch pipe on its chain, then reached into the dress's only pocket to reassure herself that the special packet was still there.

"I've emptied these," Aili announced softly.

Silence nodded and unstoppered the first jar. She poured the water very carefully into the dye reservoir; even so, a little spilled, smoking when it hit the grass. Aili eyed it warily, but said nothing.

The reservoirs each held a little more than a liter of the whole water. Silence kicked the two empty jars under the dorta bush with everything else, then restoppered the third jar and handed it to Aili.

"You carry this, in case we need to reload." The shazadi took it gingerly, clearly nervous, and Silence grinned. "Don't worry, it won't react unless it hits the earth-compounds they use growing homunculi. It won't hurt you."

"If you say so," Aili muttered, but jammed the jar into the purse she wore at her waist. It didn't fit particularly well, and she could not close the purse over it, but at least it left both hands free to handle the dye squirter. Silence nodded her approval.

"Where now?" the shazadi asked.

"First, the library," Silence answered. "If all goes well there, the boathouse."

They made their way cautiously through the darkened corridors. Once they heard laughing women, and ducked quickly into a side chamber, but the noises faded quickly. The bride-shivaree, though not officially restricted, seemed to be staying clear of the administration sections of the Palace.

The hallway outside the library was better lit than most of the Palace, all of its globes glowing at half-strength. Silence paused three meters from the door, then waved Aili back out of sight. "Wait here," she whispered. "And hold my heylin."

The shazadi nodded, apparently not put out by the peremptory order, and melted back against the curtains that obscured the single, distant window. Silence slid the folded paper from her pocket and carefully undid the taped seals, turning back each edge to expose the crimson powder that lay within. She was careful not to touch it or breathe on it as she approached the door, holding her breath as she passed her hand across the door signal.

It seemed to take forever for the homunculus to appear. Finally, the door slid back, and the librarian-homunculus rolled forward, an odd hesitation in its movements. "You desire, Domna Jamilla?" it asked.

"I left an earring here last time," Silence improvised, taking a quick step forward, "or at least I think it was here. It might have been somewhere else, of course, but I've looked everywhere else, and I haven't found it. Have you found it, or could you let me in to look?" She took another step forward, and the homunculus's eyes flared red.

"Stop!" it cried in a grating voice that seemed to fill the entire hallway. Silence took a deep breath, and blew the crimson powder into its face.

"Security—" the homunculus rasped, but the word trailed off into a sort of gasp. The creature froze in mid-gesture, and the red light vanished from its eyes.

I'll be damned, Silence thought. It worked. She folded the paper hastily around the remnants of the red powder and, shuddering, pushed the deactivated homunculus back into the library. She could feel the security fields pulsing in the air around her, but the modified user's card still protected her. Hastily, she pushed the homunculus back into its corner, then wasted a few precious seconds debating whether she should dust it again with the powder. No, she decided, the amount she had already given it would keep it from functioning for at least four or five hours; any more, and it might show outward signs of deterioration. If she could avoid that, she would. It might keep the guards from figuring out just what she had done to the security system.

She slid the crumpled packet under the nearest noteboard, and turned her attention to the cabinet. She could feel no special harmonies webbing it, but even so, she approached it cautiously, pausing often to sample the air around her. There was nothing, and she felt nothing extraordinary, even when she held her palms flat just above the surface of the case. She took a deep breath, and slid back the dura-felt cover.

The model Palace was breathtakingly beautiful. Silence stared at it for a long moment, unable to believe its delicate perfection, then shook herself and set the cover aside. The model seemed to float on a fox-fire sea, a sea of cold light, the gilt-green central island darkened by it and by the spectacular object that stood atop it. There had never been a single piece of halcyon crystal large enough to form that model, Silence thought, but she could see no join, no hairline imperfection where two blocks had been fitted together. It was perfect in every detail, down to the trees and wire-fine grass in each of the gardens; each tower was crowned with a tiny, carved crystal banner.

And she would have to destroy it. Silence almost
spoke her denial aloud, and bit her lip at her own
stupidity. This isn't just a pretty carving, she told herself sternly. It's the link, the receptor through which
everything is channeled to the guardpost. It has to be
destroyed. Still, it took every ounce of her will to draw
the pitch pipe from her bodice. She stood for a long
moment looking down on the model, fixing its heart-
breaking loveliness in her mind, then set the pipe to
her lips and blew a single soundless note.

For an instant, nothing happened. Then the air shivered around her, and with a sound like a bat's cry, just
at the edge of hearing, the model shattered. The sea
flickered and went dull. The crystal was suddenly criss-
crossed with cracks, and the internal resonance that
reflected and magnified the light so spectacularly fell
away. A single tower crumpled and fell. With a choked
curse, Silence reached for the dura-felt cover and dragged
it back over the case, hiding the ruin she had created.

She stood for an instant, recovering her composure.
At least she had not triggered the link with the guardpost.
Hastily, she checked the room for any sign of her
presence, her eyes avoiding the covered case, then let
herself out into the hallway. She fumbled for a moment
with the control panel before she found the code that
closed the door behind her. Aili was still waiting, pressed
up against the curtain. She beckoned urgently, and
Silence joined her, toy heylin ready. The whole-water
compound would not harm a human being, as she had
told the shazadi, but the surprise of being hit by something other than dye might give them a momentary
advantage.

"I heard something," Aili whispered, pointing her
chin down the hall. "Down there."

Silence listened, but heard nothing. Still, she thought,
there's no point in taking risks, and motioned for Aili
to follow her back toward the library, away from the

noise. The corridor would connect again with a smaller
cross-corridor, which in turn would join up with the
mirror-lined main passage. That would lead them back
to the staircase that would take them to the lower
levels.

They reached the staircase without incident, and Silence fiddled anxiously with the controls of the door.
Despite the restricted-access symbol painted on the
doorjamb, the door had never been locked before. It
was now, and the pilot reached again for her pitch pipe,
muttering a curse. She bent over the lock, one hand
pressed to its warm surface, assessing its internal harmonies, the other feeling for the proper stops on the
tiny pipe. Aili said, "Jamilla!"

The pilot looked up quickly, and Aili put a finger to
her own lips. Silence listened, and then she heard it,
too: footsteps moving lightly along the corridor. Silence
mouthed another curse, and looked quickly for a place
to hide. If she remembered correctly, there would be
another of the ubiquitous alcoves a few meters farther
on. When she started in that direction, Aili caught her
arm. The shazadi shook her head rapidly, and pulled
Silence in the other direction, back toward the distant
footsteps. When the pilot hesitated for an instant, Aili
tugged harder, mouthing, "Come on!"

Silence followed quickly as the shazadi led her diago-
nally across the corridor, counting mirrors as she went.
When she reached the ninth, she stopped, and tugged
frantically at one of the decorative cords festooning the
frame. The mirror groaned softly—both women winced
at the sound—and slid back, revealing a narrow slit in
the wall, barely a meter wide and rather less than two
meters deep. Something gleamed at the end of the
enclosed space. It was a window, Silence realized
abruptly, but an internal window, opening onto some
other part of the Palace. The footsteps were getting
closer.

"Quick," Aili whispered, "get inside."

Silence did as she was told, wedging herself into the opening until she fetched up hard against the glass at the far end of the space. There was barely room for both of them, and no room at all to turn around. Aili backed in, elbowing Silence painfully in the kidneys, and tugged frantically at a second cord. The mirror closed over them just in time.

Pressed up against the glass at the far end of the narrow space, Silence found herself staring down into a room she had not known existed. It seemed to be a bedroom, or at least there was a bed in it, but there was also an elaborate fountain and chairs and tables that looked more suited to a receiving room. Nothing had been cleaned for a very long time, however; even the single light burned dimly, obscured by the layers of dust.

"What the hell?" she said softly, intrigued in spite of her position.

Aili hissed for her to be quiet, adding in a barely audible voice, "It's her—Radiah."

The pilot tried to turn, to see over her shoulder, but the space was too narrow. "What's she doing?" she demanded instead, matching Aili's tone with an effort.

"Checking the lock, I think," the shazadi answered. She shifted position to see better, elbowing Silence painfully again.

Silence did her best to press even closer to the glass. She did not think she had had time to leave any signs of tampering on the lock mechanism, but she found herself holding her breath until Aili shifted again.

"She's moving off."

"Good," Silence whispered, still jammed against the glass. They waited for what seemed like hours, until finally the shazadi said, "I think she's gone."

"Let's go, then," Silence said. They had already wasted too much time, she added to herself, especially if the

Princess Royal had chosen to forego the celebration to check the security arrangements herself.

Aili tugged sharply at the lever controlling the hidden door. For a long moment, nothing happened, but then the mirror slid aside, groaning. Silence winced, and backed out into the corridor.

"She was still carrying her squirter," Aili said thoughtfully, as they hurried back to the stairwell door. "That should mean she's still playing. She was probably just passing along this corridor, and decided to check it on a whim."

"I hope so," Silence said, grimly. "What was that place, anyway?"

"One of the Hegemons kept a mad wife here, ages ago," Aili answered. "That was an observation point."

Silence nodded, and turned her attention to the lock, fumbling for her pitch pipe. This time she was able to find the proper combination almost at once. She set the end of the pipe against the lock and blew softly, playing an almost inaudible sequence of notes. The lock clicked, and the door sagged open. Tucking her pipe away, Silence led the way down the steep staircase.

The lower levels were brightly lit, in sharp contrast to the darkened corridors above. Silence blinked, rubbing her eyes, and glanced quickly around. The hall was quite empty as far as she could see, a spotless corridor covered with white floor tiles. Doors led off at intervals, but they were sealed up for the night. She hesitated for a moment, trying to get her bearings—one place was very like another on the lower levels—then turned to her left, where the corridor curved gently toward the outer edges of the Palace. As she walked, she hiked up her heavy skirt, using her belt to secure it just above her knees. She kept close count of the cross-corridors—white-tiled tunnels as featureless as the one through which they walked—and at the fifth fork took the left-hand passage. This was narrower, but as bright as the others. The quiet was almost deafening. She led the shazadi around yet another corner, and down a still narrower corridor. Finally, she saw a flash of color in the distance, marking the end of the corridor, and stopped dead, waving for Aili to stop, too.

"What is it?" the shazadi whispered.

"You see the red band ahead?" Silence asked in return. Aili nodded. "That's the perimeter marker, and there'll be guard-homunculi beyond it. Are you ready?"

The shazadi nodded again, lifting her toy heylin in answer. Silence forced a smile she did not feel, only too aware of Aili's inexperience, and started for the red-banded doorway. The trick, she knew, would be to deactivate any homunculi before they could raise a local alarm. In destroying the model Palace, she had shut down the system that would transmit news of the escape, but local alarms would bring more and more of the lower-level homunculi. She doubted she could hold off that kind of attack, even if she had an unlimited supply of *aqua intacta*.

Then they had reached the red band. Silence gestured for Aili to flatten herself against the corridor wall, then leaned forward, cautiously surveying the new corridor. Nothing was moving along the red-striped hallway. Beckoning for Aili to follow, she stepped across the red band.

Silence tensed as they moved down the corridor toward the boathouse, expecting any moment to feel the tingle of a breached alarm field, or to hear the dissonant shriek of a siren summoning the guard-homunculi. Nothing happened. The air remained still and soundless, and Silence relaxed a little as they turned into the little hall that led to the boathouse. The door was round and double sealed, like an airlock, and fastened with a massive, fist-sized freelock as well as the more usual palm lock. The pilot sighed and took out her pitch pipe again. She set her hand against the freelock, testing the harmonies.

"Jamilla!" The hiss of the shazadi's toy drowned the last syllable of her cry.

Silence whirled, dropping the pipe and bringing up her heylin in one smooth gesture. A guard-homunculus loomed in the mouth of the hall, eyes flashing erratically as it struggled forward. Aili's shot had been badly aimed, most of the *aqua intacta* splashing on the tiles beyond the creature. Silence fired. The cloud of spray struck the homunculus full in the chest, stopping it in its tracks. Steam rose in increasing clouds from its body, obscuring the flashing eyes. A moment later the eyes winked out, and it fell forward onto the tiles. A few pieces of pseudo-flesh, more affected than the rest by the *aqua intacta*, broke loose and skittered across the floor. Silence shuddered, kicking at the nearest piece, and made a noise of disgust as it crumbled into a grey powder.

"Do you think you can handle the next one?" she snapped, and knelt again beside the locks.

"I will," Aili answered affrontedly, then added, more calmly, "Did it send a warning?"

"Maybe," Silence snapped, still fiddling with the freelock. Then she found the harmony, and the lock fell open in her hands. More calmly, she said, "I don't know—I don't think so. But keep your eyes open."

"I will," Aili said again, and this time it was a fervent promise. Nevertheless, Silence listened for the sound of another homunculus, even as she fumbled for the proper code to unlock the door itself. Then, at last, she found the six-note sequence and played it through. The telltale above the lock flashed green, and Silence pushed open the door.

"Come on," she said, suppressing her own distaste as she reached for the homunculus's arm. "Help me get it out of sight."

Rather than lift the creature's legs, Aili seized the other arm, and together they dragged the heavy mass across the high threshold and into the boathouse. The job was far from perfect, Silence saw. The homunculus had left a smeared, grey-green trail on the white tiles. There was nothing to be done about that now, Silence told herself sharply, and closed the boathouse door behind them. Aili was already running ahead along the dimly lit docks, examining shell after shell. The pilot paused for a moment, studying the interior lock controls. She could lock the door from inside, all right, but as for keeping it locked against a powerful override. . . . She hooked the freelock through the inner hasp, and then, almost as an afterthought, brought up the toy heylin and sprayed the lock thoroughly. She didn't know precisely what effect that would have on the lock mechanism, but if there were any earth-compounds in it, the *aqua intacta* would dissolve them completely.

"Jamilla!" Aili was waving from midway down the left-hand dock, and Silence hurried to join her. "What about this one?"

The shazadi was standing beside a glossy, black-painted shell that had been molded in the form of some long-necked water fowl. Silence studied it curiously—she knew very little about such pleasure craft—then bent to examine the progressor at the stern, half hidden between the stiffly backswept tail feathers. It at least was a familiar model, from the Egria factories on Numluli. She bent to unlatch its cover with renewed confidence.

"What are you doing?" Aili asked nervously. She glanced up and down the docks again, eyes stabbing the shadowed corners. She was holding her heylin as though her life depended on it—which, Silence thought with a ghostly smile, it does.

"There's a governor and an automatic override on this," she answered. "I've got to get them off." She squinted into the progressor, wishing she had a better light. A moment later Aili was squatting beside her, a handflash taken from the shell's emergency kit tilted to illuminate the progressor's interior. Silence nodded her thanks, already busily separating wires. "We're damn lucky the governor's an afterthought," she said, more to calm herself than because it was really important. "Override, too." She braced herself against the dock, and yanked hard. The first set of wires popped loose, and she began reaching for the rest. "Or else—" She pulled again, hard, and the little box of the override flew free. "—we'd never get out of here," Silence finished triumphantly, and ground the override to powder underfoot.

"Are we ready?" Aili asked.

Silence nodded, gesturing for the other to climb into the shell. She started to follow, and Aili said, "Jamilla, have you ever sailed one of these before?"

Silence stared at her, momentarily taken aback. "Yeah, when I was a kid. Why?"

"Let me," Aili said firmly. "You open the lake door."

"How did you get so much experience with a shell, and you one of the Thousand?" Silence asked, not moving.

The shazadi gave her a rather strained smile. "I am the shazadi of Inarime, Jamilla—or whatever your name is. I have a lake all my own to practice on. These things can be a little tricky."

That was true enough, Silence thought, as she headed reluctantly down the dock. The shells, with their keelless treated hulls that rode on or just above the surface of the water, did require careful handling. And if she thinks she can do it, good enough, Silence decided. I can always take back control if she's not up to it. Hell, if she does know what she's doing, she'll be able to make better time than I could, and that's all that's really important.

The mechanism that controlled the water-gate was set in a pillar at the end of the dock, but Silence ignored it, looking instead for the emergency control. She found that after a moment's search, and stood

studying it for a brief moment. It seemed to be a simple
pulley and chain arrangement. Silence hesitated an instant longer, overcome by the sudden fear that this was
a booby trap, then shook herself hard. Even the Palace
had to provide this sort of elementary safety measure—
the inmates would have to have some chance of escape
in case of fire or a raid on Asterion. Swearing at her
own stupidity, she snapped off the brake and pulled
hard on the chain. The pulleys shrieked in protest—the
mechanism couldn't have been used for years—and Silence almost let go her hold. Cursing more freely, she
took another grip, and pulled again. This time, she felt
the chain give a little, and gave it another try. Slowly,
protesting loudly, the bars of the water-gate rose drip-
ping from their bed.

Breathing heavily, Silence secured the line, praying
that the ancient brake would hold long enough for them
to get out. Aili had already cranked the progressor to
life. Now she brought the shell scooting up to the end
of the dock and held it there, one hand on the
progressor's stick control, the other on the nearest pil-
ing, while Silence pulled herself aboard. The shell was
very light beneath her, lighter and edgier than she
remembered from her girlhood. She crouched uneasily
in the bow, trying to center her weight as she clung to
the bird's gracefully curved neck.

"All set?" Aili asked, lifting the control stick a fraction
without waiting for an answer.

Silence nodded as the shell slid forward across the
still water of the dock. They were too far inside still for
the shazadi to demonstrate any great skill, but so far
Aili seemed to be handling the shell quite neatly. The
progressor hummed very softly, hardly lifting it at all.
They were coming up on the gate itself now. Silence
found herself holding her breath as they approached
the portcullis's massive teeth. She looked away as the
shell slid under them, and caught a glimpse of a white

shelf, almost like a massive doorsill, a few inches below
the surface of the water.

Then they were through the gate and on the open
water. Aili increased the power slightly, keeping the
progressor's noise to a minimum, but the shell still
lifted powerfully, skimming more lightly along the surface of the lake. The water glimmered, radiating a light
that was literally chill, but Silence could hardly repress
her shout of delight. She glanced back at Aili, her face
set in a foolish, ecstatic smile, and saw the same expression on the shazadi's face. The Palace loomed behind
them, unaware of their escape.

CHAPTER 10

As they moved farther into the lake, Silence found the triple peak that was their landmark, and pointed it out to Aili. The shazadi nodded, and increased the speed until the shell was practically flying across the smooth surface, its flat hull barely skimming the water. Silence, still crouching in the bow, had to admit that this was faster than she would have dared to push the shell, and said as much, raising her voice to be heard over the wind.

Aili gave a sort of embarrassed half-shrug, but she was smiling. She said something in answer, but her voice was whipped away. Silence nodded and returned to staring out ahead of the shell.

It was very cold on the water, the air chilled by the *materia stellans* suspended in the lake. Silence was shivering violently, even though she had pulled her thick skirts back down over her legs. She glanced back, and saw that Aili was hunched over against the shell's molded tail, arms drawn tight across her body.

"Do you want me to take over for a while?" the pilot called, but Aili shook her head violently. Silence was just as glad to stay in the meager shelter of the bird's-neck prow, and turned back to her vigil.

They had covered maybe two-thirds of the distance already, she estimated, and she thought she could just make out the shadowy indentation of the cove. It was much too early, and the shell was much too far away, but she found herself scanning the shoreline for some sign of Chase Mago or Balthasar. Nothing was moving, of course, so she looked away, embarrassed at her own sudden desire.

The lake water looked odd, she realized suddenly. It was moving against the wind—or rather, cold blue lights were stirring in its depths. She frowned and sat up more fully, knowing it was likely to be only one thing. The sole of her foot was tingling strangely. She rubbed at it, only to feel the same tingling in her fingertips. It was the foot she had used to crush the override, she remembered abruptly. She must have gotten some of its active materials on her shoe. . . . And that means, she thought grimly, that they know we're gone, and are trying to use the override. She swung around again, mouth open to shout to Aili, as the entire Palace seemed to explode in a blaze of light. Fireworks shot from every tower, great spreading clouds of fixed fire that seemed to hang in the air, casting strange, flat shadows.

Aili jerked in her seat, nearly capsizing the fragile shell, and let their speed slack almost to nothing, recovering. "We're spotted," she said tragically.

"But not caught," Silence pointed out. A strange calm filled her: she had been expecting this for so long that its actual occurrence was something of a relief. She glanced toward the guardpost, and saw matching fireworks flaring from its location. The fireworks were followed by smaller globes of light: individual flyers, each one armed with a sonic rifle and a powerful searchlight. She glanced back at Aili, who still sat frozen. "How much faster can this thing go?"

"That was it," the shazadi answered, but made no move to bring the shell back up to speed.

"You better hope not," Silence said with a lopsided smile, but Aili still did not respond. "Damn it, Aili, either get us moving, or give me the stick!"

Aili gasped, and jerked up the control. The progressor whined but responded, sending the shell lurching across the water. The shazadi steadied it, tight-lipped, and shook away Silence's offer of help. "I'm all right," she said through clenched teeth. "You'd never do it."

She was right at that, Silence thought, clinging to the bird's neck as the shell skipped and bounced across the water. I could never control it at this speed. Still, she couldn't tell if it would be enough. She watched the smaller lights rise from the guardpost and fan out along the lakeshore, and held her breath.

Then, quite miraculously, they were sliding into the shallow cove, and Aili was twisting the control stick hard in reverse. The progressor shrieked again, trying to obey, but the shell slowed only a little before it slammed hard against the shore and skittered a good two meters up the rocky beach. The progressor cut out with a final angry buzz, and Silence sat up cautiously, rubbing the worst of her bruises. The shazadi did not move at once, and the pilot crawled hastily toward her.

"Aili? Are you all right?"

"I'm fine," the shazadi answered, a little breathlessly, and sat up. "Where're your friends?"

Silence looked around quickly and, as if in answer to Aili's question, a pinpoint of blue flickered twice from the tree line. "There," she said, unable to keep the relief out of her voice. "Come on."

Aili pulled herself out of the wrecked shell, moaning, and Silence moved quickly to support her. The shazadi leaned heavily on the other woman for the first few steps, and Silence said again, "Are you sure you're all right?"

"I will be," Aili answered.

She was already moving more easily as they reached

the edge of the trees, and Silence felt no qualms about releasing her hold. "Denis?" she called softly, moving a little into the woods. "Julie?"

"Here," Chase Mago said.

For all she had been expecting him, Silence started, then caught the big man in a close embrace. An instant later, Balthasar had wrapped his arms around them both. Silence held them tight, delighting in their warm presence, then, reluctantly, pushed herself away.

"Ah, I missed you both." It was not what she had intended to say. She shook herself, angry at such dangerous sentimentality, and said, "They know we're out."

"Us, too," Chase Mago said gently.

"Yeah, I know," Balthasar said. Dimly, Silence could see that he was grinning tightly. "But we've got local help."

"Oh?" Silence turned, to see a third figure standing in the shadows.

"That damned lieutenant," Balthasar went on, without particular malice. "Said he had to come with us—I just hope you really do know all the land around here, or we're all in trouble."

Aili gave a soft squeak of surprise, and Silence said hastily, "Marcinik?"

"How could I stay?" the captain-lieutenant asked, in his most reasonable voice.

He had a point, Silence thought. She looked around, squinting in the wan light of Chase Mago's battle torch. Balthasar said, "Talk later. Like you said, they're looking for you." He held out a military heylin, and the pilot took it gratefully, thumb going automatically to the touchplate. It was hot to the touch: full charge, a dozen shots. She started to ask for her clothes, but a light flashed in the woods to her left, and she stopped dead. The light veered away again an instant later, and she breathed more freely again.

"Shit," Chase Mago said, and dimmed his battle light

even further. He and Marcinik finished dragging the remains of the shell into the woods, and the engineer glanced nervously at Aili. She stood uneasily a little apart from the others, one hand to her mask, the other lifting her full skirts. "We're six kilometers from the ship."

"I know," Silence said, hearing the unspoken question. She tore at the clasps of her underdress and stepped out of the heavy material, to stand shivering in her knee-length shift. *Well, I won't be cold for long,* she thought, and beckoned to Aili. "Highness," she said, in the High Speech that was becoming as familiar to her as the coinë of the star lanes. "Highness, I present Captain Denis Balthasar—"

"Pith's sake, Silence," Balthasar hissed. "Save that, and come on."

"Shut up, Denis," Silence said in coinë, and continued in the High Speech. "—and Engineer Julian Chase Mago, both of the roundship *Recusante*. Captain-Lieutenant Marcinik you already know. If you'll come with us?"

Aili relaxed a little, though it was impossible to judge her expression behind the concealing mask. Hiking her skirt even higher, she moved to join them.

"Come on!" Balthasar said again. He was already a few meters along a narrow, overgrown trail, his own battle light flickering on and off as he picked out the way. Silence stooped, feeling across the heap of her dress for the belt she had discarded with it, and tossed that to Aili. The shazadi accepted it gratefully, using it to fasten her skirts at about knee-length. She did it on the move, but could not help lagging behind a little. Silence glanced back, worried, but saw only the distant fireworks display still rising from the Palace. Then Aili had her clothes adjusted, and picked up the pace again. Chase Mago and Marcinik exchanged a quick, grim smile and followed. They were a more than adequate rear guard, Silence thought, and hurried after Balthasar.

The Delian had marked the trail military fashion, with unobtrusive smears of oil that flashed bright blue as the light hit them, and vanished an instant later. Seeing that, Silence called softly to the shazadi, "Stay close, Aili. The trail marks aren't lasting."

The shazadi nodded, not wasting her breath on speech. She was breathing heavily already, Silence saw with dismay, her mouth gaping wide beneath the mask.

"How's it look, Julie?" Balthasar called.

It was Marcinik who answered, his voice oddly formal. "No sign of pursuit." He hesitated, then added, "Procedure is to search the lake first, then the shore."

To Silence's surprise, Balthasar did not comment on this usurpation of authority, concentrating instead on seeking out the next trail marker, the dim blue beam of his battle light weaving back and forth across the path half a meter ahead of his feet. Instead he said, not looking at her, "What was all that about? Formal introductions required?"

"Yes," Silence answered, a little irritably. "I told you on Inarime, we have to follow all the traditions or she loses face, and all this is wasted. Trust me."

"I do," Balthasar muttered. Up ahead, the trail forked. He cast about quickly until he found the splotch of oil that indicated the right-hand branch, and held it in the beam until it vanished. He glanced over his shoulder and scowled. "Come on, Julie, pick it up."

Chase Mago waved in answer, then pointed unobtrusively at the shazadi. Aili was struggling, unused to the exertion. The mask and the gown would be hampering her badly, Silence thought, not to mention the bruises from that crash landing we made. Shifting her heylin to her right hand, she let herself drop back, and offered the shazadi her arm. Aili clutched it wordlessly and struggled on. Silence suppressed a yelp as the clinging fingers touched bruises she had not known she had. Silence could feel the younger woman limping, and uttered a soundless curse. That was the sort of injury that would only get worse, and they still had at least five kilometers to go. After a moment, she shifted her hold again, putting her arm around the shazadi's waist. Aili made a soft noise of relief, a startling admission of weakness, and let Silence support her.

Despite the pilot's efforts, Aili continued to lag, making occasional soft sounds of pain. Silence found herself stumbling more and more frequently as she tried to ease the shazadi over the rough ground. "Rest?" she called, and saw Balthasar shake his head.

"Three kilometers more," he answered. "You can do it."

I can do it, Silence thought angrily, but I'm not sure Aili can—and I'm not sure after all that I can support her that far. The shazadi chose that moment to trip, falling sideways unexpectedly so that Silence was knocked off balance, too. Both women stumbled and fell, landing hard against a rotting log, Aili half across the pilot's lap. Silence swore at the damp muck coating her legs and arms. Grimly aware of a fresh crop of bruises, she pushed herself to a sitting position. The shazadi gave a choked half-sob, but did not move.

Frightened, Silence leaned forward to touch the other woman's shoulder. "Are you all right?"

Then Balthasar and Chase Mago had turned their lights on the scene, the Delian's angry expression turning slowly to one of concern. Aili sat up slowly, holding her ankle. Silence scrambled to her knees and knelt beside the shazadi. Aili's mask looked damp across the cheeks, the lower portion stretched as though the mouth beneath was set in a grimace of agony.

"Aili?" Silence said again.

"It's my ankle," the shazadi said through clenched teeth. "I hurt it when we landed, and now . . ."

"Can you walk?" Marcinik asked.

Aili looked away. "I'll try."

Silence pulled herself upright, then she and the captain-lieutenant bent to help the shazadi to her feet. Aili rose without a cry, but she could barely put her foot to the ground, much less put any weight on it. Even with Silence's support she could do little more than hobble, and each wrong move forced a soft cry of pain from her lips. The others exchanged glances. It was obvious she could not walk ten meters, much less three kilometers.

"I'll carry her," Chase Mago said abruptly.

"But—" Marcinik began, then shook himself.

"Damn it, Marcinik," Balthasar said angrily, and Silence cut in.

"She's injured, and this is an emergency. It falls within the acceptable cases."

Chase Mago had already freed himself of his battle light and backpack, handing both to Marcinik. Silence accepted the engineer's heavier heylin and handed him her own. He tucked it into his belt, and then, with surprising ease, swung Aili up into his arms. The shazadi made no protest as he settled her weight more evenly across his body.

"Let's go," Balthasar muttered.

Hurriedly, Silence adjusted the sling of Chase Mago's heylin so that it fit more comfortably around her forearm, then took back pack and battle light from Marcinik. The captain-lieutenant was burdened by an unfamiliar weapon harness and powerpack, the pilot noticed for the first time, but there was no time to ask about it. She concentrated on keeping the battle light squarely on the trail, and hurried after the others.

They covered another kilometer and a half before Chase Mago began to slow a little under his unaccustomed burden. Balthasar glanced back, uncannily aware of his partner's movements, and managed a smile of his own.

"Courage, Julie," he began, and then the smile faded

from his lips. "Shit," he said, and pointed back along the trail.

Silence whirled, bringing up her heavy heylin, and saw ghostly lights bobbing in the distance—three or four of the armed flyers. At her side, Marcinik squinted at them, lips moving as he counted, then said aloud, "They're still back at the cove, I think."

Chase Mago said, panting, "They can't miss the shell, once they start looking."

"Double-time," Balthasar announced, and surprisingly, grinned at Marcinik. "You may get some use out of that thing after all."

Even more surprisingly, Marcinik grinned back, but did not answer, saving his breath. Silence did her best to keep up with the pace the Delian set, but she found herself looking back every few minutes to check the positions of the lights. For what seemed a long time, they stayed more or less steady, circling the cove where the shell had landed. Then, as she scrambled to the top of a low shelf of rock and glanced quickly back, she saw the lights make a final circle, then peel off one by one and start down the trail.

"Denis!" Silence called, pointing.

The Delian turned, scowling, measuring the distance with a practiced eye. "Going to be close," he said, quietly. "Hurry."

They did their best to obey Balthasar's order, but Chase Mago, struggling now under Aili's weight, was unable to move any faster. Silence, looking over her shoulder every few steps, could see the lights drawing steadily closer. Marcinik was watching nervously, too. Seeing the pilot's glance, he said, "Standard procedure is to check ten meters on either side of a trail. But it won't slow them much."

Silence nodded, and opened her mouth to ask if Balthasar had heard. Before she could speak, however, the Delian said, "It looks like they'll overtake us just before we reach the ship. I don't want—"

He broke off with a curse, pointing. Silence swung, bringing up her heylin. One of the lights had detached itself from the others, and was coming directly down the trail, moving at speed. The other five flyers milled aimlessly for a moment, as though undecided, then followed more slowly. Muttering an oath of her own, Silence ran the power wheel from safety to maximum, and steadied the heylin against her body. The touchplate was reassuringly warm under her thumb.

"Get going, Julie," she said.

The engineer obeyed, not wasting strength on words. Aili made a sound of protest, but was ignored. In that instant, the flyer came blazing over the ledge of stone. Silence fired on instinct, half-blinded by the light. Her first shot went wide, then she and Balthasar fired together. The light shattered, but the shadowy flyer merely fell off to one side, unbalanced but unhurt. Then Marcinik finished adjusting his strange weapon, and fired once. A bolt of lightning seemed to sear the air, momentarily lighting up the forest. Silence caught a brief glimpse of the flyer, a crimson-coated trooper astride an object that seemed to be little more than a sounding keel equipped with a padded saddle and steering bars, and then the keel exploded, spraying chunks of keelmetal across the trail. Silence ducked behind the nearest tree while metal splattered around her, emerging only when the last rattling had died away. Balthasar rose cautiously from behind a fallen log, a bemused expression on his face.

"What the hell is that?" Silence asked.

Marcinik grinned at her. He was still standing in the middle of the trail, untouched except for a dark smear across one cheek where a flying splinter had caught him. "Beam rifle," he said, patting the power pack proudly. "It's especially effective against those things."

It would be, too, Silence thought, rather dazedly. The unstable fire compound mixed by the power pack would react violently with the complex tuning of the flyers' keels. She shook herself, annoyed that she had wasted even that much thought on such a trivial matter, and adjusted her heylin again, lowering the output fractionally to save shots. The touchplate was growing warmer again as the pack regenerated itself. The rest of the flyers were coming closer, so she glanced around for an effective ambush point.

"Silence!" Balthasar crouched behind his log, but instead of beckoning, he waved the pilot away. "Go with Julie, we'll take care of them. Get the ship ready for liftoff."

Silence hesitated an instant longer, but recognized the logic of the order. Chase Mago would need a pilot's help to get *Recusante* tuned up, and Balthasar had plenty of experience in ground fighting from his time with Wrath-of-God. Flicking the wheel back to safety, Silence turned and ran up the path after Chase Mago. Light flared behind her, followed by the pop of Balthasar's heylin and the eerie hiss of Marcinik's strange weapon. The explosion jarred the ground beneath her feet, but she did not turn.

She overtook Chase Mago two hundred meters farther along the trail, and slowed her pace to match his. The trail behind them was raucous with lights and the popping of heylins, but neither spared it a glance, concentrating on reaching the ship. Then Silence felt a peculiar tingling, like the tingling she had felt when the override was activated, and the scene before her seemed to swim drunkenly. A refraction field, she realized, and closed her eyes against the distortions. Then she was through the invisible barrier, and emerged into a clearing. *Recusante* sat in its center, keel shrouded in a crude baffle. The main hatch was open but dark, ramp extended almost to the ground.

Chase Mago set the shazadi down at the end of the ramp, saying, "Can you make it inside?"

Aili nodded, and the engineer gave her an encouraging smile as he turned to Silence. "I've got to get the baffles off. Don't start the preflight 'til I give you a green."

"Right," the pilot answered, and turned to help Aili up the ramp. The rest seemed to have helped the shazadi's injured ankle; she made her way up the ramp with only a little help from Silence. Chase Mago had set the ship's systems on a trip lock. As they passed through the hatch, lights flared on around them, and Silence could hear a distant hum as the harmonium woke to life in the stern compartment.

"Silence?" Isambard's familiar voice asked from the entrance to the common room. "Well done."

Silence looked up, startled at praise from such an unexpected source, and felt Aili beginning to sag again. "Where did Denis decide to put her?" she demanded.

"This way," Isambard began, but Silence shook her head. She could hear Chase Mago's feet on the ramp, and knew the engineer had already pulled away the baffles.

"Aili, I present Doctor Isambard, my—teacher—and a magus in your illustrious father's employ. He will help you to your cabin."

Isambard raised an eyebrow at that, and Silence continued roughly, "I've got preflight to run, Isambard. We've been spotted—Denis and the lieutenant are holding them off, but we're going to have to leave in a hurry."

The magus nodded gravely and held out an arm to Aili, who accepted it with as much grace as she could muster. "Very well. And when her Highness is settled?"

"Go to your own cabin and strap down," Silence called over her shoulder, already heading for the control room. "This is going to be rough."

She practically collided with Chase Mago at the entrance to the common room, and managed to gasp out the information that the magus and the shazadi were

taken care of. The engineer gave her an abstracted nod
and headed on toward the engine room.

Silence continued forward toward the ladder that led
to the lower bridge. A familiar bag dangled from the
middle rungs. She pulled it down and snapped back the
clasp to run her eyes caressingly across the starbooks
inside. Controlling her excitement, she slung the bag
over her shoulder and scrambled up the ladder to the
lower bridge.

The standby lights were already glowing orange, the
systems triggered by the trip lock at the hatch. Silence
swung herself into the captain's couch, pulling her headphones into place, and leaned forward to switch on the
triple viewscreen. All three faded on, showing the same
featureless shots of forest topped by a cloudless night
sky. Then the portside camera caught a sudden movement, a flash of light at the edge of the screen. Holding her breath, Silence rotated the camera until she had
a clear view. For a long moment nothing moved, and
then she saw a second flash. It was unmistakably the
track of Marcinik's beam rifle. The brighter flash of the
explosion came a moment later, followed by a thunder-
ous rumbling and a sound like a tree falling.

Silence grinned nervously, hoping the others would
be all right, and turned her attention to the controls. A
glance at the engineering repeater showed that Chase
Mago had not yet adjusted the harmonium. Silence
turned to other tasks. The rough-reckoning console was
fully lit, numbers showing in all five windows. This was
the equipment used to land and lift a starship without
the aid of a port and the preset harmonies of the landing beam. Silence studied its readings carefully. Core
and atmospheric readings showed stable, the lunar reading was at zero. The etheric reading showed a steady
flux, the numbers rising and falling in a definite but
unfamiliar pattern. Silence watched it for a few moments
longer until she was certain it was indeed steady, then

applied the conversion factors to obtain the median note.

At that moment, the lights on the engineering repeater flashed from red to orange, and the keyboard chimed, announcing itself unlocked. Silence gave a sigh of relief, and leaned across the second pilot's couch to punch in the proper notes. The coplanetary reading seemed a little odd, however. She studied it dubiously—it did not seem to match precisely the numbers she remembered from her starbooks—but then shrugged. It was possible that the books listed a composite factor. In any case, there was no time to worry about it. She keyed in the vectors, and waited while Chase Mago's tuners digested the numbers. A few moments later, the keyboard chimed again, and the green preset light went on. Silence allowed herself a momentary smile, and turned her attention to the other systems.

"All set below," Chase Mago's voice announced in her earphones. "You can start power-on anytime you want."

"Beginning power-on now," Silence answered, watching the last row of engineering indicators flick from red to orange. Lifting from an established starport was much easier than this, with the shielded table to dampen the core notes and the more sophisticated astrological equipment in the tower to choose the optimum lift path. Even at its best, lifting from bare ground was difficult and usually unpleasant. This time, with pursuit almost certain, it was going to be very hard indeed. In spite of herself, Silence's eyes strayed to the left-hand viewscreen, empty now except for the trees.

With that thought, she leaned across the second pilot's couch again, and flipped a set of switches on a new console. Three lights came on, first flashing red, then steadying to a brilliant red that brightened slowly toward orange and held there. Silence bent even more awkwardly to examine the numbers beneath the three lights. All were comfortably within the operating range: *Recusante*'s four cannon were fully powered.

Not that they would do a whole lot of good against a real warship, Silence thought, as she turned to switch on the rest of the systems. *Recusante*'s popguns might pierce an armored hull at close range, but she would be destroyed long before she could get that close. The guns could be more useful turned against an enemy keel, where an explosion could disrupt the tuning. Silence winced at the memory of *Ostinato,* keel shocked and dead, plunging into the ice on Arganthonios. She shut out that thought, and flipped on a final bank of switches.

A new light flared orange on the internal monitor board. Silence jumped, and reached for the heylin lying on top of the bag of starbooks. Then the hatch status light went from flashing red to steady green, and an instant later Balthasar's voice sounded in her ears.

"We're aboard. Marcinik and I will man the guns. Now get us out of here, there's more flyers coming."

Silence flipped on the astrogation console and the Ficinan display, saying, "Did you hear, Julie?" To her surprise, her voice was almost calm.

"I heard," Chase Mago answered. "Ready with the first sequence."

Silence nodded, scanning her readouts. Everything showed orange or green, ready to go. In the left-hand viewscreen, she could see a swarm of bobbing lights converging on the ship, followed by a larger, less well lit shape. The Ficinan model was useless this close to the planetary core, but the musonar showed a fuzzy image. It looked like one of the armored vehicles she had seen when she first arrived at the Palace. She swore softly—the double cannons could crack *Recusante*'s hull like an egg—and opened the all-ship's channel.

"Stand by for liftoff," she said, and heard her voice

echoing dully through the corridors. "Stand by for lift-off. Everybody, be sure you're securely strapped in." She touched the toggle that switched her back to the engine room, and said, "First sequence, Julie."

"First sequence." The harmonium roared, swallowing Chase Mago's words. Silence winced, feeling the biting dissonance as the lifting harmony struggled against the music of the planet's core. The ship trembled, shuddering through its entire length, then lifted about a meter from the forest floor and refused to rise any farther. In the viewscreen she could see the flyers coming closer; even as she watched, one spat a sizzling ball of energy. It struck low on the port side, and Silence could feel the sudden quaver as the keel adjusted to the stress.

"Guns," she called, and reached across to touch a correcting key. The harmonium steadied. She touched another key, feeling her way, and felt the ship shudder again, more violently this time. The port cannon fired, knocking the ship sideways. Silence swore, scrambling to correct that, and out of the corner of her eye saw the flyers dodge sideways, out of the way of the falling trees.

"Come on, Julie, more power," she called over the shriek of the harmonium. She did not hear any answer, but an instant later the music surged strongly, a wave of pulsing, glorious sound that lifted *Recusante* from her place. There was a moment of painful pressure, and then the harmonium's envelope was fully established. The ship rose faster and faster, cutting through the atmosphere as though it did not exist. The Ficinan model flashed to life, displaying the planets' positions relative to each other and the flaring rings of the *musica mundana*. Silence glanced at it, but the musonar shrilled a warning. Instinctively, Silence put *Recusante*'s nose down, skimming the edge of the atmosphere in a blaze of interference. The lighter passed just overhead, the reflection from its keel momentarily filling the bridge.

Silence cried out as the keelsong passed over and through
her, the sound racking body and bone, and clung for a
moment to her bucking controls before she could recover herself.

Then Chase Mago had stopped down the harmonium
a little. Silence hauled back the controls and pulled
Recusante around again, up out of the soup of Asterion's
atmosphere. The controls moved more easily this time,
without the interference of another ship's keelsong to
blunt the response. The musonar clamored for her attention, but she ignored it long enough to find her course
in the Ficinan display. The safest—most harmonious—
path ran from Asterion in an almost straight line that
just skirted the edge of the influence of the outermost
world, Niminx. Niminx also possessed the most elaborate
of the system's fortified moons. Silence instantly discarded that path, and chose the second—a long curve
that skimmed between the music of the two intermedi-
ate worlds, Falathar and Mim Seras. The light surrounding the pinpoint of Mim Seras pulsed slowly in
the Ficinan display, striking sparks of interference from
the *musica mundana* of Falathar. It was a risk, Silence
knew, but less of one than facing the installations on
Niminx's moon.

The musonar shrilled again, more insistently. Silence
glanced up at it and swore. Two more ships, their
keelsong marking them as light military craft, were
coming up over the planetary horizon; a third, heavier
ship was sliding down the harmonic line from distant
Falathar. *Recusante* would not have to worry about the
latter, Silence realized instantly. They would be well
into the interference zone, where the military ship
could not follow, before its captain could correct course.
The other two ships were another matter, and Silence
hoped they were only lightly armed.

"Guns," she called. "Two ships—fifties or small
threes—coming eight by seven."

"On our scopes," Balthasar answered with reassuring promptness, and a moment later the ship shuddered to his first shot.

Watching the musonar with one eye, Silence saw the shot fall short, but one of the pursuing ships changed course anyway, falling back a little. It turned its keel toward *Recusante*'s sensors as it did so, and the musonar shifted to display new information: a fifty, lightly armed and incapable of true interstellar flight. She repeated that information to the men sitting back to back in the gunners' pod in the center of the hold, her eyes still roving across her instruments. A light flashed on a sensor panel: the fifties were returning fire.

On nothing better than a hunch, she rolled the ship to her left and put the nose down again. The harmonium shrilled in protest, but the fixed fire of the cannon shot exploded far to the right. Silence brought *Recusante* back to her original course, eyes roving as she calculated distances. The harmonium roared as Chase Mago opened the stops, and *Recusante* seemed to leap forward. The fifties fired again, and the gunners in *Recusante*'s hold returned the fire, but none of the shots seemed to have much effect. Then *Recusante* was in the narrow channel between the two spheres of planetary music, and Silence's perception narrowed to that tiny corridor of interference-free space.

The musonar hazed almost to uselessness, its sensors overridden by the planetary harmonies surrounding the ship. Silence could feel that same deep music echoing in her bones, could hear the keel laboring against it. In the Ficinan model, she could see thin wisps of interference crossing her projected course, and lifted one hand from her controls to trip the harmonic filter on the forward camera. The central viewscreen, empty of everything but starscape until now, dimmed a little. The stars, though paled, showed larger disks, the reflection of their essential music. To either side of the screen, a mist seemed to obscure them slightly, like ragged curtains of fog. Slowly, vast reddish prominences faded into sight where the two curtains met, their colors barely brighter than the blackness around them. Silence bit her lip, not wanting to lose the perfect line, but afraid to risk too close contact with those spikes of dissonance. She eased her helm a little, letting *Recusante* fall off, dropping "below" the flaring interference. The harmonium whined sharply, a note awry in the heart of its song. Silence heard, but could not spare a hand to correct it. After a moment, Chase Mago made some adjustment, and the whining faded.

Then *Recusante* was through the convergence, and the extraneous notes vanished from the keelsong as the harmonium fixed firmly on the proper harmony. Silence relaxed a little, and lifted her hands from the controls. The musonar showed mostly fuzz astern. She extended its range, and caught a glimpse of the fifties, left far behind at the edge of Asterion's influence. Below, the three had pulled free of Falathar's sticky harmony, but was having trouble retuning to the inner system's notes. *Recusante* would reach the twelfth of heaven long before the three could overtake it. Ahead and to the sides, space was startlingly empty.

Rather shocked by the ease of their escape, Silence keyed the intercom. "I show clear skies," she announced. "Nice shooting, Denis, captain-lieutenant."

"Thanks," Marcinik answered, his voice hoarse with fatigue.

"Yeah," Balthasar said. "This is too easy." There was a noise of muted snapping, and then the Delian announced, "I'm coming forward, Silence."

"Fine," the pilot answered. There was no response, and she assumed Balthasar was on his way. Sighing, Silence scanned her readouts, able to check the lesser systems for the first time. Most had survived the transition reasonably well, requiring little or no adjustment from their preset positions. She made the few minor corrections, then opened the intercom to Aili's quarters.

"Aili? Are you all right?"

There was a long pause. The intercom was not easy to reach from the bunks, Silence remembered. Then the shazadi answered shakily, "Fine. Let's do it again?"

Silence laughed and, hearing footsteps on the bridge ladder, answered, "Maybe later." She flipped a second switch, and said, "Isambard?"

"Well, thank you," the magus answered promptly.

"Good." Silence cut the connection and turned to face the ladder as Balthasar pulled himself onto the bridge. The Delian was sweating heavily, face and clothes still smudged from the trek through the woods.

"Spell you?" he asked, and Silence shook her head. "Not just yet."

Balthasar nodded, and dropped heavily into the second pilot's couch. "Nothing on musonar?" he asked, reaching for the controls himself. Silence raised an eyebrow as Balthasar once again ran the sensors to full pickup range, and sat staring at the empty screen.

"Good enough," the Delian muttered, half to himself, but his tone was less pleased than his words. "I guess the diversions worked."

Silence nodded, agreeing with Balthasar's unvoiced doubts. Even if the close-orbit patrol was fully occupied by the satrap's planned distractions, the ground commander could still call on the double-strength pursuit squadrons based on Falathar and Mim Seras, or the threes and fours based on Niminx's moon. They had never expected the diversions to do more than buy them enough time to pull free of Asterion itself. "I suppose we should be grateful," she said aloud.

"I suppose," Balthasar said, but he didn't sound convinced. "I left Marcinik to mind the guns," he said, more briskly. "I gather the passengers came through all right?"

"They seem to have," Silence answered.

"Let me take over now," Balthasar said again, and, when Silence would have protested, gave her a rather taut smile. "You still have to learn the voidmarks. I marked the road in your *Topoi.*"

"The *Topoi*?" Silence asked, as she unfastened the safety webbing. "Do you think that's wise?" The *Topoi* was the official text of the Hegemonic Navy; to use it seemed to invite pursuit.

"They had the best marks," Balthasar said. He had already slid out of the second couch, and stood ready to take over. Silence gave her controls a final glance and slid from the couch. Almost before she had cleared its cushions, Balthasar had taken her place, drawing the safety net comfortably around himself. Silence picked up her bag of starbooks and settled herself into the second pilot's place, putting aside her doubts.

As promised, Balthasar had left a marker tucked into the *Topoi* at the proper pages. Even so, Silence quickly rechecked the table at the back, making sure this was a proper road between Asterion and Inarime. It was, of course. She turned back to the illustration, hoping Balthasar had not noticed.

The image—very crudely drawn, like all the *Topoi*'s illustrations—was an unfamiliar one. The central focus was a tree, one side of which was in full leaf, the other blasted and dead. A skeleton sat on a heap of gold beneath the dead branches, playing with a handful of gemstones. Coins and more stones spilled between the dry bones, but the skeleton did not seem to notice its losses. A figure in a magus's robes and a fool's belled cap sat beneath the living branches, one hand resting on an open book, the other holding an elaborate orrery. His eyes were fixed on the orrery, but the expression on his face was not the conventionally contemplative gravity of a magus, but the vacuous grin of a fool. He sat on the very edge of the cliff, and the ground seemed about to crumble away beneath him. A narrow path ran between the two figures, and seemed to continue up the side of the tree, to vanish in the leaves. The commentary was no more than usually terse: "Great knowledge may lead to folly, and great wealth to Death. Only by moderation is the goal achieved."

Silence made a face—she hated the *Topoi*'s habit of cloaking specific piloting instructions in general moral homilies—but murmured the cantrip that put her into the learning trance. The multiple meanings of the various component images seemed to explode into her consciousness like fireworks. Patiently, she disciplined herself to exclude everything but the specific pilot's knowledge, and slowly the sense of the road came clear.

It was not a particularly tricky road, but it was narrow, threading its way between two extremes. Other systems would probably have used Scylla and Charybdis to mark the road, Silence thought, rather than strained for this moral. The wise fool would mean a sink of some kind, the skeleton a dead zone, where the reflection of various mundane harmonies canceled each other's influence in purgatory. *Recusante*'s course lay along the narrow path, then "up" the trunk of the tree and out through the leaves of the living left-hand branch.

Sighing, she let herself slip from the learning trance, and glanced quickly at the control boards. The musonar still showed no signs of pursuit. Frowning, she extended the range astern, upping the power to punch through the interference of the congruent zone, but even the three seemed to have turned back to Asterion.

"I don't like it," she said aloud.

Balthasar glanced quickly at her, then at the musonar, and grunted agreement. "We shouldn't complain, I suppose," he said again, but dubiously, and Silence managed a wry smile.

"I suppose not," she said. "But it makes me nervous."

The musonar chimed, a rippling run of notes that

drew a curse from Balthasar. Silence reached hastily to readjust the main horn until it pointed forward again. The picture swam dizzily, then cleared. Ahead, just outside the ghostly line that marked the orbit of Niminx, a cloud of lights swarmed and circled. The readout at the bottom of the screen chittered, its numbers shifting wildly: there were too many ships, in too close contact, for the musonar to make an accurate count. The satrap's fleet had reached Asterion ahead of schedule.

CHAPTER 11

Balthasar swore softly and flicked the intercom switch. "Julie! Stop down, we're aborting the run-up."

Silence looked up quickly. "You can't do that," she began, and Balthasar cut in angrily.

"We can't reach purgatory if we have to pass through that lot. If one of them didn't blast us, we'd still have to fight their interference. You really want to try it?"

"No," Silence admitted, still staring at the cloud of lights. The Delian had piloted warships for Wrath-of-God, she reminded herself, and knew what conditions would be like. Besides, she could see the interference clouding the musonar, fuzzing the images and making it impossible to get an accurate count. "What do we do?"

Balthasar was frowning at his readouts. "I don't know," he said. "Find a dead spot, I guess, and wait it out."

"Could we correct to the other departure line?" Silence asked, already adjusting the musonar to display the space around Niminx and its fortified moon. It seemed empty of traffic, and Silence allowed herself a moment's hope. Then three more flecks of light—threes, almost certainly, dispatched to harass the satrap's fleet rather than with any hope of doing serious damage—

293

detached themselves from the disk of the moon, and flashed off toward the fighting. "Damn it."

Balthasar looked up from the Ficinan display. "It wouldn't have worked anyway. We'd have been fighting a cross harmony the whole way, unless we went back practically to Asterion. That congruence is setting up a minor flux all through the area."

"Damn," Silence said again. "So we just wait to see what happens—and hope nobody notices us first?"

"We find a dead zone, if we can," Balthasar corrected. "But, hell, even if there isn't one—"

"There isn't," Silence interjected. "At least not on this side of the system."

"—they should be too busy to look," the Delian finished. Despite the cheerful words, his tone was grim.

"What's the decision up there?" Chase Mago asked from the engine room.

"We drift," Balthasar answered, "and hope for the best. Can you adjust the tuning so we look like we belong to the system?"

"I can try," the engineer said. "It'll mean cutting power, though."

Balthasar hesitated for a moment, then answered, "Go ahead." He gave Silence a flickering smile. "We tried this once before," he said. "It's a question of adjusting the keelsong so that it gives much the same resonance as a naturally occurring body. Of course, the power's different, so we'll look much larger on their screens—about the size of a small moon."

He was talking more to distract himself than to inform her, Silence realized, and said, "Won't they notice a new body?"

"There's a certain amount of debris in any system," Balthasar said with new confidence. "They can't keep track of all of it. And Julie'll fade it in—he's good at that." The confidence faded a little, and he leaned to the intercom again. "Make sure our drift takes us away from that mess, huh, Julie?"

"I will if I can," Chase Mago answered, rather impatiently. "Trust me, Denis."

"I do," Balthasar said, unhappily, and cut the connection. "I do."

Silence sighed, understanding both of them. She trusted the engineer implicitly and with good reason, but at the same time, it was very hard to leave the ship's fate entirely in his hands. She glanced sidelong at Balthasar, and saw the Delian's eyes roving from musonar to Ficinan displays to the viewscreens and back to the musonar. Then she remembered precisely what Balthasar had said, and sat up straight in her couch. "Denis? You said you *tried* this before?"

"Yeah." The Delian did not look at her, his attention still focused on the screens.

"Did it work?"

"Yeah," Balthasar said again, and managed a rather strained smile. "For long enough, anyway."

And what do you mean, long enough? Silence thought, but before she could say anything, the intercom sounded.

"Captain Balthasar," Isambard said. "I have some experience with this sort of thing. Perhaps I can be of assistance to your engineer?"

Balthasar grimaced, looking at Silence for guidance. The pilot shrugged—she had no idea whether the magus would be of any use—and the Delian reached for the private channel to the engine room. "Did you hear, Julie?"

"I heard," Chase Mago answered. "Hell, tell him to come back. He couldn't do any harm."

Balthasar relayed the invitation—suitably edited—to the magus, then began fiddling with the musonar, trying to get a better look at the battle. Silence leaned back in her couch and tried to relax, listening to the sounds of the ship. Chase Mago had slaved control of most of the systems through his own keyboards. As Silence watched, lights on her own panels faded from green to orange as the engineer turned nonessential systems back to standby levels. Column indicators fell to the minimum marks, and a bank of lights winked out completely as Chase Mago cut power to the loading mechanisms in the hold. At the same time, the keelsong changed. The bass notes seemed to swell, a new note sounding at the bottom of the scale, a grating growl that was felt as much as heard. Silence could feel its slow pulsing in every bone. At the same time, the higher notes faded, almost but not quite vanishing entirely. The pilot glanced at the astrogation readouts: the readings for the ship and for the systemic harmonies were uncannily close. It isn't natural, she thought, and looked away uneasily. The numbers should be different, the ship tuned to the celestial notes, or at least to purgatory, and the system matching its own peculiar notes. . . .

"Got it," Balthasar exclaimed. He was pointing at the musonar, and Silence looked up obediently. With the keelsong muted and tuned to a less discordant note, it was easier to adjust the musonar. The screen now showed distinct dots, slowly circling each other in a predictable pattern. Half the dots now showed green, the others red.

"Green's for the satrap," Balthasar said, "and the red ones are the navy ships."

"How do you know?" Silence asked, scanning the screen. From here, it looked as though the green ships were getting the worst of it. Even as she watched, a green light vanished from the screen. She hoped Balthasar was wrong.

"The navy tunes to the Asteriona scale, the satrap to the Castagi," the Delian answered. "I set the unit to distinguish by keelsong."

"It looks bad," Silence said softly, and hoped the other would contradict her. After all, Balthasar knew more about warships and fleet actions than she did, had been through a few himself. Maybe she was misinterpreting things.

Balthasar shook his head. "Yeah."

"If the satrap loses," Silence began. She didn't have the heart to finish the sentence. If he lost, they were all in serious trouble. They'd have Aili to deal with, as well as their own problems. None of their plans had really taken that possibility into account.

Marcinik said, "His Highness is losing?" It was the first time he had spoken since they had passed the congruence, and Silence jumped.

"At the moment," Balthasar answered.

"We have to do something to help," the captain-lieutenant said.

Balthasar grimaced. "Just what do you have in mind? I don't think our cannon would do a whole lot of good against a couple of navy sevens."

"I'm coming up," Marcinik answered.

"No, wait," Silence said. "We need someone on the guns."

The scuffling noise stopped abruptly, and when the captain-lieutenant spoke again, he sounded utterly beaten. "But we have to do something."

"Committing suicide isn't it," Balthasar growled, but Silence saw he had his hand over his microphone. She looked back at the musonar, watching the red and green specks weaving in and out of the fight. It would be hellish in the sphere of combat, she knew from Balthasar's stories, the keels shrieking in protest as they were pushed to the limits of their tuning, that very protest only adding to the interference. At that point, it would not take much to disrupt a keel. A near-miss, barely enough to disturb the tuning under normal circumstance, could utterly blank a keel or even shatter the tinctured metal itself. *Recusante*'s light cannon could be effective—but its keel was hardly built to stand that kind of stress, Silence reminded herself bleakly. If only they carried sonic mines. Even one would make a considerable difference if it opened inside the battle.

But if *Recusante* carried no mines, she possessed something potentially as useful. Silence leaned across

Balthasar's couch to press the intercom button. "Isambard. It's theoretically possible to use a sounding keel
as a kind of projector isn't it? Could we retune to a scale
that would disrupt the Hegemon's ships without dam-
aging the satrap's fleet?"

"Wait a minute," Balthasar said. "It's been tried before, Silence, and it doesn't work. You'll tear the ship
apart."

"Not by a pilot who's also a magus," Silence said
grimly. "Do you have a better idea?"

Isambard answered slowly, "I believe you said the
Hegemon's ships tune to the Asteriona scale, Captain
Balthasar? And the Inarimans are tuned to the Castagi
and this ship to the Numluli scale." He paused, considering. "Yes, it is theoretically possible."

"It'll destroy the ship," Balthasar protested again.

The magus ignored him. "Silence, I will need your
assistance, please."

Silence began unfastening the safety webbing, but
Balthasar put a hand on her arm. "If we lose this
ship—" he began, and Silence shook herself free.

"Denis, we have to try. If the satrap loses, we're as
good as dead anyway."

" 'As good as' isn't dead yet," Balthasar said, but
released his hold. "Damn it, be careful."

"I will," Silence promised, and fought free of the
webbing at last. She dropped down the bridge ladder
and hurried past the closed cabin doors toward the
engine room. As she stepped through the orange safety-
light that ringed the doorway, Isambard said irritably,
"You took your time about it."

Silence lifted an eyebrow, but said nothing. Chase
Mago, on his knees beside the open panel that gave
onto the inner workings of the harmonium, made a
choked noise that might have indicated either amusement or outrage. Behind him, the pipes and clear columns of the harmonium pulsed gently, brighter colors

occasionally strobing from the upper end of one hexagonal column.

"To work," the magus continued briskly. "I have calculated the sequence that will negate the Asteriona tuning, and set it there." He gestured to the massive double keyboard that controlled the music of the harmonium. Several keys—perhaps as many as a dozen, Silence thought—flashed on and off, waiting for the command that would release their music.

"We can use the steering board for ship's power," Chase Mago interrupted from the deckplates. "There's no problem getting to the fight."

Isambard, standing at the intercom, cleared his throat impatiently. Chase Mago groaned and hauled himself off the deckplates.

"All finished, Isambard," he said, and crossed the engine room to take up his position by the secondary keyboard that controlled the steering harmonium. It was a smaller and much more limited engine than the main harmonium, generally used to power the ship's systems or to run in tandem with the main harmonium. Silence eyed it with some misgivings. Now it would have to provide enough power to move the ship, and she was not sure they could trust it. Chase Mago gave her a reassuring smile, then flipped switches on the panel above the board, watching the test lights race across his indicators. He nodded. "Control transferred and secured. Tell Denis we can move."

"Captain Balthasar," Isambard began, and the Delian cut in angrily. "I heard. Give me first sequence, Julie."

"First sequence," Chase Mago answered, and touched a single key. The secondary harmonium sounded, its note thinner, almost painfully attenuated compared to the sound of the main harmonium, but Silence could feel the keel respond to its urging.

"I have about half-response," Balthasar's voice reported, "but good enough. The satrap's people seem to be holding their own, so we should get there in time."

"Holding their own?" That was Marcinik again. Silence spared an instant's pity for him, the satrap's loyal agent, trapped on this ship so far from the battle that would decide his fate.

"Yeah. They've pulled into a Castagi ring," Balthasar answered. "And his Most Serene Majesty's failed to find the break-point."

"Good," Marcinik answered, and cut the connection.

"How close do we come, Isambard?" the captain continued.

Isambard's eyes closed, and his lips moved briefly as he calculated something. "Tell me when your vox indicators show strength seven," he said at last.

"Vox seven," Balthasar answered. "I'd estimate you have about fifteen minutes."

"Thank you, captain," Isambard said. He turned to face the pilot. "Now, Silence. It is true, as Captain Balthasar said, that no one has succeeded at this before, but it is theoretically quite possible. What you must do is find the music of the Hegemon's fleet, then find the correct antithetical sequence that will destroy that music utterly, and project it through your keelsong. The approximate sequence is already set, but you will have to control and adjust it according to conditions—"

"*I* have to?" Silence asked.

"Yes," Isambard answered impatiently. "Now—"

"Why me?" the pilot asked. Somehow, she kept her voice calm, as though she had all the time in the world to get the answer to a question that was merely academic anyway. "You're the magus, you've got a lot more experience than I do."

Isambard was shaking his head. "You have an affinity for harmonics, and more important, you're a pilot. You have the pilot's intimate knowledge of the starships as well as a magus's talent. That should be enough."

Wonderful, Silence thought. It all falls back on me again. She shivered, feeling the sudden chill that came with fear, and knotted her hands together to quell their shaking. You're no magus, a voice was screaming inside her. You can't possibly do it. You'll just destroy the ship and everything in it, everything you've worked so hard for. . . . She shook herself hard, and said, with only the slightest tremor in her voice, "What do I have to do?"

Isambard gave her an approving nod. "Come here," he said, and led her across the engine room to the open panel below the harmonium. Chase Mago moved to join them.

"What I've done," he said gently, "is put the harmonium into free drift. It's passive now, no power going in, but the link's still there. You'll have to work through it to shape the keelsong, though. There's no way I can change that."

Silence nodded, staring into the main harmonium's warm interior. The long columns—some metal, some crystal, some of a substance in between the two—glowed softly, the multicolored lights momentarily at rest. Those open pipes, the actual source of the harmonium's uncanny music, were not meant to be controlled directly, but through the sympathetic linkages of the keyboard. To bypass that linkage, and the keyboard's preset limiting harmonies, was to risk letting the music flare out of control, under- and overtones building until the keel itself shattered under the pressure. A pilot doesn't have much to do with those kinds of harmonic adjustments, Silence thought. That's really the engineer's responsibility. I don't know if I can hear that clearly.

Chase Mago touched her shoulder, and Silence jumped. "Good luck," the engineer said, and returned to his place by the steering board.

"Now," Isambard began, bending stiffly to peer into the open panel. His voice deepened, its timbre compelling both attention and instant obedience. "Put yourself into a listening state, as deeply aware as you can be."

"I understand," Silence whispered. Beneath the momentary calm produced by Isambard's voice, she was terrified. But she knew, too, that to allow herself time to feel that fear would be to feed it, let it grow until it overwhelmed her. She shook herself hard and forced herself to relax, muscle by muscle. The tension eased, and she felt the fear retreat.

"Vox reads seven," Balthasar reported. "Let her drift, Isambard?"

The magus closed his eyes, testing the air. Silence could feel the distant music, too, the jarring dissonance of the battle. "Yes," Isambard said at last, glancing at Silence. "You must begin now."

Silence took a deep breath, seating herself on the deck beside the harmonium's open panel, and murmured the first cantrip. She slipped easily into the first stage of awareness, and hung there for a long moment, fighting for the deep calm that would let her take the next step. She pictured herself wrapping up a black amorphous mass that was her terror, wrapping it in layers and layers of paper, then shoving it into a lockbox and turning an imaginary key that would hold it prisoner for as long as she needed. The last sensations faded; she floated serenely in the center of her body, detached and comfortable.

She could hear the dissonances of the battle much more clearly now, two uncomplementary scales made painfully dissonant by stress and proximity. She filtered out the one that was familiar, that woke a soft echo in her bones. That was the Castagi scale, the one to which the Inariman ships were tuned, and close counterpart to the Numluli scale to which *Recusante* and *Sun-Treader* before her responded. She studied the other scale for a long time, listening until she was certain she knew its every variation. Then she lifted her hand and pointed to the main harmonium. It seemed to take forever for her hand to shape the gesture, and even longer for Isambard to respond. Then the magus's hand came down on a central key, and the harmonium spoke, a great tolling like the voice of a hundred bells.

Silence thought she cried out, jolted to the core by the impact of that sound, but her voice was swallowed up in the surging music. Then her control reasserted itself, and she withdrew a little, to a place where she could hear both the discord of the Hegemon's ships and the keelsong that was the negation of that sound. Already, the keelsong was having some effect, amplified and sounding through the entire length of *Recusante's* keel. She felt a ship die, its keel shattered, and knew it as clearly and certainly as if she had seen it happen. Another of the Hegemon's ships pulled abruptly out of range and out of the battle, stressed beyond endurance. Then the music of the Hegemon's ships began to shift as their engineers responded to this new threat. Silence frowned at the open harmonium, barely seeing the streaming flux of light that was a reflection of the music within it. The song changed in response to her will, assuming a new shape under her guidance, but too slowly. The Hegemonic ships reeled under the new attack, but were able to counter. This was too slow, Silence thought, too drawn out to be of any use. She needed direct control of the harmonium. Before she could think about what might happen, she thrust her hands into the open panel, laying them flat against the nearest column.

There was an instant's searing agony, and then the stern music seized her completely, or perhaps she took possession of it. It filled her, became an extension of herself, became herself though she was something more. Its sound faded to a faint thrumming, no louder than the sound of her blood moving in her veins. With almost contemptuous ease, she reached through the silence, sought out each of the Hegemon's ships, and overrode their keelsong with her own demanding music. The last faint notes of the Asteriona scale faded, then vanished completely.

She relaxed, letting the keelsong swell again to almost painful volume before she reasserted her control.

Then Chase Mago was at the main keyboard, touching the switches that brought the harmonium back under the board's dominion. Instinctively, Silence took her hands from the pipes, newly aware of the pain in her palms and fingers. Wincing in anticipation—she could see already that her hands were red and blistered—Silence allowed herself to fall from the height of awareness. Her hands ached and stung, but she had expected much worse. After a moment she mastered the pain, and looked around. Chase Mago snapped a final switch on the steering board, and came to kneel beside her.

"Are you all right? My God, your hands. . . ." Without waiting for her answer, the engineer crossed to a cabinet welded into the bulkhead, and brought out an aid kit. Silence gave Chase Mago a grateful smile as he popped open a jar and smeared a compound like thick jelly over her burned skin. A tingling cool seemed to follow his touch, killing the worst of the pain. Silence sighed, and rested her head against the engineer's shoulder as he wound meters of bandage around each hand.

"Well?" she asked, rather sleepily. The jelly was taking effect, she thought, then realized how much the attack had taken out of her.

"That should hold you 'til we can get you to a real doctor," Chase Mago muttered, half to himself. He started a little at Silence's question, then smiled widely. "Listen for yourself."

For the first time, Silence became aware of the voices sounding from the intercom. She recognized Balthasar's, raised in indignant protest, and then Marcinik's, seconding the complaint. Then Aili spoke, the cool authority in her voice enough to intimidate any mere captain. Silence grinned. If their rescue of the entire fleet was not sufficient proof of their good intentions, the presence of the satrap's own daughter certainly should be.

"Yo, Silence," Balthasar said. "Listen to this."

Static crackled momentarily, and then the intercom was adjusted to the main channel. "—order all my ships to provide any assistance necessary to the ship that saved us, on my authority as Hegemon, won this day." The voice was unmistakably that of the satrap of Inarime. Silence heard Aili give a choked sob, and fight to recover her composure.

"I extend my gratitude to that ship, and to her crew," the satrap—the new Hegemon, Silence corrected herself muzzily—went on, "and will condemn out of hand anyone who offers the least insult to any of her people."

"Nice work, Silence," Balthasar said. "Damn nice work."

"Thanks," Silence whispered. She doubted that her voice could reach the intercom pickup, but she was too tired to care. She roused herself enough to ask, "*Recusante*?"

"We'll be all right," Chase Mago answered promptly. "The keel's dead, tuning's blasted, but we'll get a tow to Asterion and a d/w beam down to the sheds. Then we'll call in a little of that gratitude he's so free with to pay for the repairs."

Silence laughed softly at the thought, but could not rouse herself to make a more appropriate answer. As her eyes closed, she caught a glimpse of Isambard standing by the engine room hatch. In the glow of the safety light, Silence was sure she could see him smiling in satisfaction. And then she slept.

Silence was never able to remember the events of the next few weeks clearly. As Chase Mago had promised, ships of Inarime's fleet took turns towing *Recusante* back to Asterion. The satrap's men, Balthasar reported with malicious satisfaction, were practically fighting for the privilege. And then crew and passengers were transferred to the satrap's massive flagship while a d/w beam was set up to draw *Recusante* down into the repair cradle. At some point, Aili was restored to her father, but Silence had already been taken into the flagship's sickbay, where half a dozen doctors clucked disapprovingly over her burned hands and vied with each other in suggesting treatments. Silence slept a great deal, but insisted on joining her husbands as soon as they were established in quarters on Asterion. After the initial battles, Adeben met with surprisingly little resistance. His allies had chosen their targets well, knocking out the major garrisons on the crossroads worlds of Ariassus and Hal'n Tek, and seizing control of the Grand Arsenal on the Malath Dag after fierce fighting. Adeben's ally among the True Thousand had brought his supporters— perhaps a third of the entire force—over to the satrap's side as soon as the Inariman ships appeared off Asterion, and with the old Hegemon dead, his fellow officers were glad to negotiate an honorable surrender. By the time Silence was allowed to leave the flagship's sickbay, only Tricca, held by a distant cousin of the late Hegemon, still offered active resistance. A sizable minority among the noble Thousand had had family members imprisoned or held hostage on Asterion or other worlds, and gave Adeben their support immediately; the rest of the Thousand and Ten Thousand were shocked into acquiescence by the speed and thoroughness of the takeover. Within a month, the satrap had established himself on Asterion, and assumed the title of Hegemon pending his coronation, scheduled for three weeks after the approaching New Year.

The doctors told Silence to keep the bandages on for three weeks after her release from their care. By the time the clumsy, mitten-like wrappings came off, work on *Recusante* was well advanced. Silence insisted on being taken to the dock, and was startled by the reception they received. Instead of showing shock or leering speculation, the new Hegemon's men treated them with almost exaggerated deference. It was somewhat unnerving, after everything they had been through. Silence inspected the beautifully rejuvenated keel and the new harmonium and keyboards, and politely refused a dozen other modifications and new pieces of equipment offered by the dockyard workers. She was almost glad when a bowing equerry brought their visit to an end by bringing up their brightly painted gever.

Despite all the unofficial signs of gratitude, however, there was no message of any kind from the new Hegemon. Aili had rejoined her father's household, and Marcinik—now promoted to full captain—had joined the reconstituted Thousand as the Hegemon's special investigator, responsible for finding any remaining loyalists. It was a job he hated, but did well. The four members of *Recusante*'s crew remained in the luxurious villa provided for them by the new Hegemon, and wondered. Isambard spent most of his days either in the villa's library or in the magi's hostel in Anshar' Asteriona; the other three lounged about the villa, read dockyard updates on *Recusante*'s repairs, did their best to consume the exotic meals prepared by a skilled human cook, and waited. It was not until three days before the Hegemonic New Year that Adeben finally sent for them.

The vizier n'Halian himself brought the summons, and chivvied them into the waiting gever before anyone could think of changing into more formal clothes. He gave no clues to the Hegemon's wishes on the short ride from the villa to the Palace, and ushered them directly into a private pavilion almost before the gever had stopped moving. He stopped abruptly outside the audience chamber, frowning. A small, veiled figure was waiting by the door, a domna hovering unhappily at her shoulder.

"My lady," n'Halian began, and the small figure took a step forward.

"Jamilla? I mean, Silence?"

"Ceiki?" Silence took a step forward herself, then paused, uncertain of her reception.

With a cry of delight, Ceiki flung herself at the other woman. Silence caught her in a quick embrace, and set her down again.

"I'm so glad you made it," Ceiki said. "I'm to be one

of Aili's domnas. She's taking me into her household. But what you did—I wish I could be part of your household."

"You would be if I had one," Silence said, smiling. "I'm glad for you."

"And I don't have to marry Aja's satrap." Ceiki glanced at n'Halian, and pulled herself up short. "But I'm keeping you from his Majesty. I beg your pardon, my lord vizier."

"Of course, my lady," n'Halian said frostily, but his eyes were smiling. "If you will follow me, sieuri?" Without waiting for an answer, he swung open the door of the audience chamber. Silence gave Ceiki's shoulder a quick squeeze, and followed him.

The satrap—the Hegemon, Silence corrected herself—sat on a high-pillowed chair of state, the scarlet turban of his new rank the only note of color in his jet-black robes. Aili was there, too, two massive necklaces visible beneath her translucent outer veil. All of her face except her eyes was hidden beneath the inner veil; nevertheless, Silence could have sworn she winked as they entered. A more heavily veiled domna waited with her. Marcinik was present, too, and the pilot wondered with an inner smile if anyone had told the captain he was Aili's prospective husband.

At her shoulder, n'Halian coughed discreetly, and Silence moved forward hastily to make her obeisance. She felt suddenly very drab, dressed as she was in man's trousers and an oversized shirt borrowed from Chase Mago, and chose the most severe bow in her repertory in compensation. Both Balthasar and Chase Mago copied her, the Delian with less grace than the well-born engineer, and then Isambard bowed gravely, his hands folded in his sleeves.

"I submit, your Majesty," the magus said, "that we have kept our part of the bargain."

Someone—the domna, Silence thought—gasped in

shock. One did not speak to the Hegemon until spoken
to. But Adeben did not seem to be offended.

"Indeed," he said, gravely, "and more. I stand in
your debt, Isambard."

The magus bowed again, but before he could answer,
Adeben pointed to the hovering vizier.

"First, the agreed-upon payment."

N'Halian stepped forward with a short bow, and drew
from beneath his coat an ancient book, its covers cracked
and stained with age. Isambard took it cautiously, running a covetous hand across its battered surface. Silence
could see a compass rose, the symbol she remembered
from the magi's library on Solitudo, etched in gold
across the cover.

"The portolan?" Balthasar hissed.

Silence nodded, a lump in her throat. They had
worked very hard for that battered text, and a part of
her wanted to snatch it out of Isambard's hand, to claim
it for herself. She controlled herself with an effort,
clasping her hands behind her back. Chase Mago gave
her a look of amused sympathy, but said nothing.

"I am still in your debt, Isambard," the Hegemon
went on, "and I wish to make that payment publicly. I
know you intend to find Earth. I know also that to give
you public aid would hamper rather than help you. I
pledge now to aid you privately, but I ask you also to
name a reward that I may grant you publicly, for per-
sonally destroying the enemy fleet."

But *I* did that, Silence thought, startled. Out of the
corner of her eye, she could see Balthasar scowling, and
she heard Chase Mago's sigh of resignation. Well, the
pilot told herself, it was only to be expected. After all,
Isambard is the experienced magus; of course anyone
would assume he did it.

Isambard grimaced as though he had bitten into something sour, but when he spoke, his voice was as urbane
as ever. "Your Majesty is laboring under a misappre-

hension. It was not I who destroyed the fleet; Doctor Leigh did that."

Doctor? Silence thought. That was a magus's title. . . . She glanced sharply at Isambard, and the magus nodded, not without regret. It was an unexpected honesty, and one Silence had to respect.

The Hegemon frowned. "Perhaps in execution, Isambard, but surely the idea was your own."

"I regret to say it was not, your Majesty," Isambard answered firmly. "Both concept and execution were Doctor Leigh's work. It should be her reward."

He said it again, Silence thought. Then I am a magus, or at least he thinks I am.

The Hegemon was still frowning. "Isambard—Doctor Leigh," he began. "I. . . . This places me in a most awkward situation, sieuri. I am not yet secure on the throne—what new monarch is? I cannot publicly admit that I owe that throne to a woman, no matter how talented or exceptional, without giving my surviving enemies a weapon to use against me. And a very strong weapon, at that. I will, of course, offer help in reaching Earth, but privately, and without any mention of the debt. I cannot acknowledge it. I ask you, sieura—forgive me, Doctor—Leigh to accept that private help in lieu of my larger debt."

He looks genuinely unhappy, Silence thought, with some surprise. I can see that his political situation won't let him do that—the Hegemony's never liked the idea of women with power. I don't need the public praise, as long as he keeps his private word. And I think he will. She opened her mouth to agree, but Aili said, "Father."

The domna made fluttering gestures of distress, and the Hegemon glanced curiously at his daughter.

"Will you go back on your word?" Aili went on. Her voice was neutral, neither accusing nor angry, but Silence was sure the other woman was furious behind her calm facade.

"Daughter, I have no choice," Adeben said. "Do you

want me to lose all this, and my life as well, most likely?"

"No." Aili bent her head slightly. It was hardly a gesture of submission. "I suggest that there is another alternative."

"Name it," Adeben said instantly, with genuine relief.

Aili's head lifted slightly, and Silence thought she saw a smile behind the veil. "Defer this favor. Oh, it need not be recorded in the Public Archives. We have familial records enough, not to mention the records at the Great Seclusion—that ought to be private enough for anything. But record that debt we owe Doctor Leigh, so that when the time comes, and you are secure enough, Father, you may pay her as she deserves."

"Child, I may never be that secure," Adeben murmured, a wistful smile on his lips. He straightened abruptly. "Do you hear me, Doctor Leigh? I may never be secure enough to admit I owe you, a woman, my throne. Do you still want this deferred favor?"

"You will be," Aili said strongly, her eyes fixed on Silence. The pilot saw the other woman nod slightly, urging her to accept this offer.

Silence hesitated. She had nothing to lose—most of the repairs were complete, and in any case, the Hegemon had promised his help in their search for Earth as a separate favor. It would only help them to have the Hegemon's debt written down somewhere—and besides, she thought fiercely, I did save him. I earned this reward. I want it—and I'll have it, no matter how long I have to wait. "I understand your position," she said slowly. "I accept the shazadi's—forgive me, Serenity, the Princess Royal's—suggestion that the public favor be deferred." She hesitated, then could not resist adding maliciously, "Until a more convenient moment."

The Hegemon frowned sharply, and even n'Halian looked a little taken aback. Adeben said curtly, "Very well. Lord Vizier, prepare the record."

"At once, your Majesty." N'Halian bowed twice and

crossed to a wall cabinet. He rummaged in it until he
found a slab of the thick, shiny paper used for hegemonic grants, then searched further until he unearthed
a scribe's wand. He seated himself at a low table,
flourishing the wand, and said, "I am ready, your
Majesty."

"Begin." The Hegemon leaned back in the chair of
state. "I, Adeben Kibbe, satrap of Inarime, Hegemon
of the worlds subject to Asterion, hereby acknowledge
that I am truly and deeply indebted to the sieura Silence Leigh, star pilot and maga."

He would have stopped there, Silence thought, but
Aili turned her veiled head sharply. Adeben sighed and
added, "For her services both in rescuing my daughter
and in destroying the enemy fleet at the fourth Battle of
Niminx. This debt cannot presently be paid, and it is
heavy." He waited while n'Halian finished inscribing
that conventional phrase, and went on more normally,
"Given this day under my hand, and so on, Halian."

"Yes, your Majesty," the vizier murmured, sketching
busily. At last he was done, and the Hegemon rose
from his chair to examine the neat characters. He nodded his approval at last, and n'Halian handed him the
wand. The Hegemon signed his name, then drew a
metal oval from his waist sash and passed it across the
signature. Light flashed briefly from beneath the oval,
and the Hegemon returned the seal to its place.

"It is done," he said formally.

N'Halian lifted the first sheet deftly away, bowed and
handed it to the Hegemon, who folded it and put it into
his waist sash. The vizier made an adjustment to the
wand and passed it rapidly back and forth over the next
sheet of paper. Words—the precise copy of the Hegemon's original—sprang into existence. N'Halian tore it
loose and handed it to Silence. The pilot accepted it
with some amazement, running her fingers across the
still-warm characters. Balthasar and Chase Mago leaned
close to see.

"Very nice," Balthasar whispered. "Let's just hope he remembers to file the original."

"He will," Silence murmured. "Aili will see to it."

"Sieura Leigh." The Hegemon had resumed his place in the chair of state, staring down at them all. "I—. My gratitude is real, if deferred." He nodded stiffly to the vizier, and stood. "The audience is ended." He was gone before the others could remember to bow. Aili and Marcinik followed, leaving them alone with n'Halian.

"I will summon your gever," the vizier said smoothly, "to take you back to the villa."

"That'll be fine," Chase Mago murmured.

"God," Balthasar said abruptly, "did you hear that? We've got the run of the yard, and at someone else's expense."

"We still have to get to Earth," Chase Mago said. He nodded toward the magus, who seemed already engrossed in the portolan. "We've got a debt of our own to pay off."

Silence said nothing, smoothing the thick paper between her fingers. This is it, she thought. Everything I've done from the time we left Solitudo Hermae, all boiled down into a promise that could mean everything, or nothing at all. But I can—I will—make it mean something. She smiled abruptly, and tucked it securely into her pocket, closing the security strap across it. "You're right, Julie," she said aloud. "Let's keep our own bargain first."

WE'RE LOOKING FOR
TROUBLE